BROKEN CHANCES

EVE KOGUCE

CONTENTS

CHAPTER 1   1

CHAPTER 2   15

CHAPTER 3   23

CHAPTER 4   31

CHAPTER 5   40

CHAPTER 6   52

CHAPTER 7   68

CHAPTER 8   79

CHAPTER 9   90

CHAPTER 10   103

CHAPTER 11   115

CHAPTER 12   129

CHAPTER 13   140

CHAPTER 14   148

CHAPTER 15   159

CHAPTER 16	167
CHAPTER 17	180
CHAPTER 18	190
CHAPTER 19	205
CHAPTER 20	214
CHAPTER 21	233
CHAPTER 22	239
CHAPTER 23	249
CHAPTER 24	268
CHAPTER 25	275
Epilogue	290
Acknowledgements	301
About the Author	303

CHAPTER 1

Isle of Southbay
Dorset, Southwest England
May 2005

My perfect life ended on my wedding day. The day that is supposed to be the happiest in any girl's life.

It's not that at the time I realised I was happy. My mom wasn't rich or even what you'd call well-off, and I never knew my father. Truth be told, I didn't know who he was. Mom never told me, and I never bothered to ask.

We lived in a small apartment in a five-storey building, like everyone else. If someone had asked me then, I'd have said we lacked many things. Now I'd tell you we had everything we needed.

I had a crappy job. Try a waitress's role in a busy cafe in Riga Old Town, and the word crappy gains a whole new meaning. Imagine tourists from wealthier countries feeling free from the morality norms limiting them back home, behaving like pigs. Drunk from the moment they've had breakfast at their hotels and heading into the bars right after wolfing down pastry and eggs, not caring about the taste. It's a shame, mind you. Everything that's served in cafes in Riga is delicious.

So, the guys I used to serve beers to – it was always at least a few too many – are the type that don't bother to think before shouting 'Hey, beauty!' They don't wait for you to approach their table. Where is the fun in waiting, right? And let me tell you, after the first few months on the job, my ability to ignore the meaning of their words and do what I was paid for was honed to perfection. Even though 'beauty' was the nicest word they used.

I didn't hate the scene. It's just that, after waiting tables for two years while trying to evade grabbing hands and tune out insulting remarks, I was somewhat disillusioned. Riga Old Town restaurant and bar scene was the pretty picture flipped upside down to me. It overshadowed the good things in my life. All I could see was the downside.

I met my husband when I was having a particularly bad day.

The café I worked in opened at ten to beat the competition. Posher places opened at noon. From the business perspective, it was a wise move. We got to have all the early birds who couldn't wait until lunchtime to remove the hangover consequences. On the day I met my husband, I had to fight those consequences too. The first client who stumbled into the café at ten a.m. sharp puked all over the table, and his vomit dripped down on the chairs I'd neatly arranged around it before leaving the previous night.

The café owner believed in multitasking, so we waitresses had to do cleaner's work during opening hours. He also had a strong faith in effective resource distribution, so in the mornings, there was only one waitress to serve customers – and to clean whatever mess they created.

I hated cleaning clients' vomit. I don't think anyone on

this planet can see the task as rewarding in any way. I won't lie: such things didn't happen often. Although these guys did consume ridiculous amounts of alcohol during their visits to Riga, I must admit they had strong stomachs. Still, it did happen from time to time, and when it did, I thought my job was even crappier than I did on a regular day.

I'd rubbed the disgusting mass from all the surfaces it had come into contact with, covered everything with antibacterial spray – its smell made me gag almost like the vomit had – and wiped everything first with a wet and then with a dry cloth. I'd straightened my back, cursing silently. I suspect that all the unkind words running through my head were written clearly on my flushed face. At that moment, my husband walked into the café.

"I apologise for the early intrusion. I just wanted to let you know that I'll take a seat outside." He took in my appearance – certainly dishevelled after an impromptu deep cleaning – and added: "Please don't be in a hurry because of me. I'll be grateful for a coffee when you have time to make one."

This is my prince, I thought. What else could a girl of twenty, with the rubber gloves still smelling of vomit, think?

Shaking off the memories, I turn from the main road that leads slightly uphill to the business area of the village and continue across the field to the coastal path. I always take this detour, although it prolongs the time to reach my destination. I do it even when the path gets slippery and muddy after the rain. The views are absolutely worth it.

I reach the stone with 'Coast Path' written on it, and as usual, marvel at how authentic it looks. *Isn't it lovely?* I think. It makes me laugh inwardly. Since I arrived in England a year and a half ago, I started using local expressions even when talking to myself. No 'cool' or 'fantastic' for me anymore. *Lovely*, I repeat, glancing at the stone with footprints painted in yellow below the words.

The waters of the English Channel are calm today. I still call it La Manche in my head. It's a name I remember from the geography classes at school. God forbid I let this blunder slip in my husband's presence, though.

I slowly walk down the path along the cliff edge. The scenery is breathtaking. Our village boasts an especially dramatic stretch of the Jurassic Coast's rugged coastline. Cliffs rise high from the water. Grass-covered natural terraces roll down right to the abrupt edge.

A woman with two shaggy dogs walks past me. She nods, "Hiya!" and I smile back, "Hiya!" I would reply with a 'hi' a year ago, but just like 'cool' has gradually transformed into 'lovely,' I now feel comfortable using the local 'hiya'.

The path snakes along the cliffs' top, wide and flat in this coast segment. The road would have been more challenging if I had gone in the opposite direction. I'd have to do more climbing up and down. Some places have stairs carved into the rock with stone walls bulging out and making the path narrower.

I stop before the coastal walkway makes a sharp bend. It is a perfect spot to admire the majestic South Rock, one of the Isle of Southbay's prominent landmarks. I always pause here to let nature's magnificence sink in. Around four hundred feet high, South Rock's walls are absolutely vertical. I love how the stone colours change depending on the time of the day. Now, under the direct blazing sun at noon, the rock is a warm beige, while at sunset, it turns almost orange.

I follow the path and cross the South Rock plateau. Then, I turn inland. My destination – Groveland Business Park – is already in view.

The Isle of Southbay is a small place. Its ten thousand inhabitants are scattered around three villages and cliffside cottages. A business park is a too-loud name for the collection of one-story grey-stone buildings. Once a part of the military infrastructure, they have been converted to fit the needs of local businesses. Groveland Business Park houses a café, a fish restaurant with a view over the English Channel, a print shop where locals order business cards and flyers, and other small companies. Even a crab trap maker rents a small workshop space with a separate entrance here. He used to make these traps in a shack on his property. "Times have changed. Clients want to do business in a real office now, not in your backyard," I once heard him saying to a guy who looked like his drinking buddy.

I make my way through the main entrance of the business park. Having passed the print shop on the left and an architect's office on the right, I arrive at the closed door of the Groveland Bakery.

I stand dumbfounded for a few minutes, eyeing the sign *Closed*. My chest starts swelling with an irrational wish for the sign to disappear so I'd see the familiar door ajar, welcoming customers.

I can't return home without those bloody muffins. The thought makes my heart in the swelled ribcage thump erratically. I swallow the painful lump in my throat. I imagine my husband's thin face frozen in a silent reproach and his pale blue eyes looking at me in disgust. *I married you, took you away from that miserable place, brought you here into the civilized paradise, and you can't even buy muffins.* He wouldn't say these words; still, I know he would think them. And he wouldn't talk to me for the whole evening.

I sigh. *Bloody muffins. They aren't even that tasty!*

"Do you think...? Could it be...? No way..."

I hear muffled voices from somewhere down the corridor. Hope makes me hurry in the direction of the sounds. Suzie, the Groveland Bakery's owner, might be there. My day might not turn into a disaster after all. I almost run to the room where the voices are coming from. Having caught some movement from the corner of my eye, I take a few steps backwards.

I stand in the wide doorway panting, and three pairs of eyes with polite incredulity stare back at me.

I blush and clear my throat. I know these women. It is enough to know they disapprove of me because of my marriage. It would be terrible if they thought I didn't know how to behave.

"Margo, love, you've probably come after your muffins!" Suzie Fortuneswell, a tiny brunette in her fifties, takes a few steps toward me. "I am so sorry you've arrived at the closed door. It's unpardonable. Come, love, I've saved two blueberry muffins for you."

The Groveland Bakery's owner walks over to me when another woman calls after her: "Will you come back after you served your customers, Suzie? We have an emergency here."

Maureen Easton, short and plump, a few years older than Suzie, looks almost comical with concern written all over her face. Her cheeks are red, and her lips tremble. I've never seen the South Rock B&B's owner distressed. Maureen Easton is the epitome of hospitality. Always with a smile on her lips and with a cheerful twinkle in her grey eyes, she runs her flourishing business, with guests returning to her cosy bed and breakfast every summer for decades.

"What kind of an emergency?" I blurt out without thinking. "Maybe I can help?"

The three pairs of eyes stare at me with disbelief again.

"I'm sorry," I say helplessly. It would have been better if I'd bought the muffins and left.

"No, no, love, you have nothing to apologise for. You are such a kind soul." Suzie comes to my rescue again. I am grateful to her for that. She took me under her wing from the moment I appeared on her bakery's doorstep, confused and unsure if I understood what my husband wanted from me. Suzie seemed to understand everything at once. She knew what pastry Michael loved and made me feel welcome by saying she'd keep a standing order for me so I never had to come home empty-handed. I've come to value her mindfulness. Especially after that time when blueberries were unavailable for some reason – and Suzie sold only freshly baked products – so I bought vanilla muffins instead. Michael threw them into the bin, refused to eat dinner, and slept on the couch that night.

"Betty Burton was found dead this morning." Maureen's lips tremble stronger when she speaks. "I am surprised you haven't heard. You are neighbours."

The news makes me blush again. Betty Burton, indeed, lives – lived – next door. It isn't that we live virtually door-to-door, at the same staircase, as it would be back at home in Latvia. Still, Mrs Burton's cottage is the closest to ours, even though both houses are separated by two rather spacious lawns and a low stone wall.

In her seventies, Betty Burton was the kindest person I've met on this island. A bit airy-fairy, but in the most adorable way, she had a halo of white hair that existed as if of its own will. Her shy smile made you want to rush to help her cross the street. I thought Mrs Burton was amazing. And here I am, having missed the news about her demise.

"I... I didn't notice anything unusual when I passed Mrs Burton's cottage today..." My excuse sounds lame even to me.

"The police came, and also the ambulance..." Maureen's voice trails off as she purses her lips and dabs her eyes with a handkerchief.

"As if it would wake even the lightest of sleepers." Suzie is determined to discard all accusations Maureen seems eager to throw at me. "They don't arrive with their sirens screaming to fetch a body of an old biddy. I would have slept all through the police roaming around your house, Maureen, if you had the misfortune to be found dead in the wee hours of the morning."

English humour still shocks me. Mrs Easton doesn't look offended by Suzie's words. On the contrary, they have had a calming effect on her.

"I apologize, *Margarita*." Mrs Easton always calls me by my full name. She does it with an effort as if to stress that I am a foreigner who's brought difficulties to them, islanders, with my arrival. "I hope you understand it's been such a huge shock for all of us. Poor Betty. And we don't have the slightest idea what has happened to her..."

"Stop talking nonsense, Maureen." A loud voice interrupts the distressed Mrs Easton before its owner appears in the doorway.

Barbara Southwell strolls into the room with her usual air of ultimate self-confidence. Tall and stately, like the other ladies, she is in her fifties. Her greying hair is arranged in a neat bun at the nape of her neck. I can't get rid of the feeling even the woman's hair is terrified by her, so unnaturally immaculate it is.

"We have a very clear idea of what happened to Betty," Barbara announces with assurance, making anyone who thinks to argue with her look irrational. "She was seventy-five, for goodness' sake. A perfectly acceptable age to meet our maker, by any standards." Barbara stops where we all stand and looks at us pointedly. "Betty Burton died peacefully in her sleep, sitting in her favourite chair and watching the sunset over the channel. I've already talked to the police and the medics. There is nothing mysterious about it."

Although displaying an appropriate level of intimidation, Maureen still finds the courage to ask: "Who found her, Barbara? Who found our poor Betty?"

I am impressed.

"She isn't – wasn't – poor. She died with dignity, having lived a dignified life." Barbara pins Maureen with her small grey eyes. "The postman saw her through the window when he brought her the knitting catalogues. He knocked to say good morning, and when she didn't come to the door but kept sitting in the chair, he called the ambulance and the police." Barbara sighs as if to show that she's reached her patience limit. "The arrangements for the funeral have been made. I'll let you know the details when I have them. And I'll need your help with the tea after the funeral. There won't be a big reception since Betty's sorry excuse of a *family* doesn't care about anything except selling her cottage."

Maureen, Suzie, and the third woman, who hasn't

spoken a word so far, nod vigorously. Barbara Southwell has a talent for making everyone not only listen to what she is saying, but also promptly start doing what she wants them to do.

"Now," Mrs Southwell continues in her authoritarian voice, "it is highly unproductive to waste our time chewing over something we can't add anything useful to. So, what is really important at the moment is that we have no one to accompany our choir rehearsals on the piano."

During the formidable woman's speech, I try to look anywhere but at her. Still, I hadn't realised until now that it's the piano tucked into the corner I've been looking at whilst Barbara was speaking.

"I could do it!" I speak before thinking it through. "I mean, I can play the piano. I'm not a professional. I didn't go to a music school or anything. But my grandmother wanted me to play, so she bought me the instrument and paid her friend to give me lessons…" I stumble upon words under the scrutiny of four pairs of eyes.

The women keep silent for a while. What I've learned about English character so far is that no one sees it as necessary to make anything easier for you.

"Is that so? You can play the piano?" Barbara Southwell looks doubtful.

"Yes. And I can prove it to you. I can play something right now." I am used to being looked at like this. It has taken the Southbay inhabitants a while to accept that I speak decent English rather than mumble incoherently with a strong Eastern European accent.

"No, no, that isn't necessary." Mrs Southwell dismisses me with a wave of her hand. "We meet here every Thursday at three. Be here next week, and we will see if we can make it work."

"I could…" I want to ask if I could take the sheet music they have so that I can practice before the rehearsal.

Barbara Southwell doesn't let me finish. I've already understood about her that she is the woman who knows what you want to say before you open your mouth. "It's obvious that today's rehearsal must be cancelled." It is clear that the need to explain something obvious repulses her. "Today, we have other priorities."

I almost blurt out what priorities she is discussing since she's just declared everything about seeing Betty Burton to her final journey has been taken care of. Still, I manage to hold my tongue.

"Well, every cloud has a silver lining, as they say." The peacemaker Suzie steps in to save me from embarrassment one more time. "I have to open the café. My customers will go elsewhere next time if the closed door greets them. Come, love," she turns to me, "we have to get you your muffins."

"Come over for tea tomorrow, Suzie." Mrs Southwell issues an order rather than an invitation. "We have to go over what we must do before the funeral."

"You can count on me, Barbara." Suzie nods at the formidable woman, whom she doesn't seem afraid of. "I'll bring what won't get eaten from the café. Don't bake or buy anything."

I say my jumbled goodbyes to the three women and hurry after Suzie to the Groveland Bakery.

Suzie opens the door and quickly flips over the *Closed* sign. "Come on in, love," she speaks over her shoulder, heading to the counter. "I feel I need a cup of tea now. It would be lovely if you joined me. If you don't have other plans, of course."

I often stay for a cup of tea or coffee when I come after the muffins for Michael. Suzie has made me feel she likes my company. I don't have anyone else who makes me feel this way here in Southbay, so I appreciate her friendliness.

"Tea would be nice, thank you."

Groveland Bakery is a spacious rectangular room with about ten tables covered in red and white checked tablecloths. The view over the English Channel, the Groveland Lighthouse, and the pasture dotted with white sheep make up for the basic furniture and nondescript design. Suzie once shared her plans for renovations with me. She wants to install new floor-to-ceiling windows and add a wooden terrace where people can enjoy drinks and her pastry in summer. Since my husband Michael is in the construction business, I know it can't be easily done. Although I don't think strict regulations are bad – and in construction they save lives – I still find English laws ridiculously draconic. It could take years before Suzie obtains all the permissions to start her renovation project. And knowing the speed at which anything gets done here, it would take a few years more to actually get it done. Like any small business owner, Suzie can't afford to keep her café at a standstill for so long.

A few people from the business park's offices come in to have their lunch. It doesn't cease to amaze me how locals sustain from a sandwich for breakfast and a piece of pie for lunch. The main meal here is dinner people have after work. Back in Latvia, people eat a proper meal around noon. There are cafes specialising in lunches for office workers. They offer soups, hot second dishes, and desserts at a reasonable price. Since Michael would stop talking to me altogether if I refused to keep the schedule he was accustomed to, I eat hot food at noon or a little later only when he isn't at home. Luckily, it happens more often once his new business has begun to take off.

Having served the clients, Suzie joins me at our favourite table by the window next to the counter. She's brought a box with two blueberry muffins, a teapot, and chocolate cookies.

"So, love, does Michael return today?" Suzie asks, sipping her tea.

"Yes, he had another big job in Abbotsbury. A full conservatory renovation. He said he'll have to get back there next week." I take a bite of a crunchy cookie. I haven't acquired a taste for these as I haven't for the muffins. They are sweet, and that is all to recommend them. I make a mental note to take a bus into Eastpoole, a bigger town across the bay. The sweet treat I have acquired not even a taste for, but rather a mild obsession over, is a *Tesco's Finest* Strawberry cheesecake. There isn't a Tesco on our island, so once a week, I take a bus to the mainland to do some shopping and get a feel of a busier lifestyle.

"Abbotsbury?" Suzie rolls her eyes dreamily. "Have you been there?"

I shake my head, my mouth full of tea and cookies.

"It's where our legendary swannery is located. Actually, it's the only managed colony of swans in the whole world. More than five hundred swans live there. Can you imagine how beautiful the place is?"

I shake my head again. "No. I've never seen more than two swans in one place."

"Ask Michael to take you with him next week. You can wander around the swannery while he works."

I take another bite of the cookie to hide my embarrassment. I can't tell Suzie the truth. What will she think of me if she learns I prefer to spend as little time with my husband as possible?

"I don't want to distract him. And there's no place for the two of us in the trailer." I opt for a safer version. "Michael's business is new, you know. He doesn't stay in B&Bs when he travels for work. It's too expensive."

"Oh, you don't have to tell me, love." Suzie nods sympathetically. "Running this place hasn't made me rich yet too."

Two men dressed in overalls walk into the café and head to the counter. Suzie takes the last sip from her cup and nods at me: "Okay, love, the busiest time of the day starts soon, so I'd better get back to work. Please don't hesitate to pop in if you need anything before the rehearsal next week."

"Thank you, Suzie. I'll come over on Monday after Michael leaves." The hope not to appear unprepared under Mrs Southwell's piercing stare – and get the sheet music before the rehearsal – makes me smile.

BROKEN CHANCES

I sit in the café for a while, finishing the tea that is left in a huge teapot. I don't want to go home. Still, I know it is in my best interests to show up well in advance before Michael returns from Abbotsbury. I must heat up dinner so the pork stew has time to cool down enough to be warm rather than scalding hot. I also have to prepare fresh salad so the leaves are pleasantly crunchy rather than soggy. My husband has taught me well.

I decide to take a slightly different route on my way back. Instead of walking straight to the coastal path, I take the narrow walkway that leads to the Groveland Lighthouse. Low thorny bushes grow on both sides of the path.

The walkway is short, and soon, I see the white and red cone of the lighthouse cutting through the blue sky. I think it looks romantic, like something from nineteenth-century novels. It's such a pity that it loses some of its appeal during the touristy season peak when buses full of lighthouse visitors arrive every hour and the entire area gets filled with crowds.

I see a sleek black Mercedes parked in front of the Lighthouse Keeper's Cottage. It is an unusual car to see in our village. I don't stop, but I can't help staring at it. The vehicle looks extravagant and out of place.

The white cottage door opens, and two people emerge. The woman stops at the doorway while the man turns to speak to her before leaving.

I know that the woman's name is Jacqueline Fisher. She moved to Southbay around the same time as I arrived here. Rumour has it she used to be some high-flyer at the BBC before she left London's hustle after divorcing her unfaithful husband. I never spoke to her, but I sometimes see her on the coastal path, walking a golden retriever. I think she looks classy, even though she never wears any make-up and dresses in jeans and sweaters like everyone on the island.

"Thank you for coming, Lionel." I hear Jacqueline speak to her guest.

"You have my number, darling. I shall not stop expecting to receive your call one day."

The man gives Jacqueline a polite peck on her cheek and climbs down the stairs, heading to his posh car. I am already too far off to see him clearly; still, I manage to notice that he is older, in his sixties, dressed in a well-cut, expensive suit, with soft white hair tousled by the ever-present breeze blowing from the channel.

I quicken my step. Could this man be the infamous husband of Jacqueline Fisher? *No*, I think, *they look more like father and daughter*. I chuckle humourlessly at the paradox. That is exactly how Michael and I look to those who don't know we are married.

CHAPTER 2

I take a peek through the sooty glass to check the roast sizzling in the oven. It doesn't help to determine if the meat is ready. Still, I wouldn't risk opening the oven door. The only time I did it, Michael walked into the kitchen and made me feel like the most worthless cook in the world. I am a quick learner, so I make sure not to repeat the same mistake.

I love cooking. My grandmother allowed me first to watch and then help her cook whenever I came to spend school breaks or weekends with her. I was fascinated by the old-fashioned tiled stove with a spacious oven and metal rings on top.

Cooking for Michael is challenging. He has an extremely specific taste in food. He lets me cook solely British cuisine dishes and is never satisfied with the results of my culinary endeavours.

I fill a small pot with water and put it on the stove to boil carrots and Brussels sprouts. Together with green peas, these are Michael's preferred vegetables to go with the

Sunday roast. If I had the right to choose, I'd go for a boiled beetroot salad with sour cream, garlic, and pickles. It isn't only Michael's fault that I can't. There isn't any sour cream in local supermarkets. To get it, you must go to a bigger town like Bournemouth, which has so-called Polish stores.

When the water bubbles, I put Brussels sprouts into the pot and wait until they are ready. Michael is specific about how he eats his vegetables, too. If I overcook them, they'll end up in the garbage bin.

Having washed the pot to get rid of the Brussels sprouts' smell, I repeat the process, this time boiling carrots.

I leave vegetables in a big white bowl – they'll lose their crispy texture if I leave them in the hot pot – and turn to make gravy.

I like the roasted meat: pork, lamb, or beef. I also like the carrots and peas combination. It reminds me of a similar dish we often ate back home in Latvia. Its original recipe requires the vegetables to be simmered with sour cream, but I like the taste without it anyway. Yorkshire pudding is okay, although nothing special. My biggest issue with the Sunday roast is gravy.

Michael doesn't demand that I make it myself. Not out of kindness, though. "You would never make it even half as good as my mother made it," he said, issuing the instructions about how he expected his Sunday roast to be cooked and served. He then placed a handful of small packets on the counter. *Original Gravy Powder* saves me from adding yet another thing I can't do the right way to my already long portfolio. Michael even allows me to prepare gravy in the microwave rather than on the stove. "Everything will turn cold whilst you're messing with sauteing it."

I take the roasted beef out of the oven and place it on the metal rack to cool. Michael doesn't like the food to be tongue-burning. I quickly place a tray with Yorkshire puddings I've baked in the morning in its place to heat them up.

I go into the dining room – a narrow walk-through space between the kitchen and the living room – and light the candles in heavy holders. I've already laid the table earlier today.

I look around. Everything looks just as Michael likes it. I sigh. With my husband, you can never be certain, though.

At least he'll be gone tomorrow, and I won't see him until Thursday. My heart makes a little leap of joy at the thought. I immediately feel guilty. No one forced me to marry a man twenty-six years my senior. My mom was always too tired from working extra hours to teach me about love and men. My beloved grandmother died when I was sixteen. For someone from her generation, it meant I was at least a couple of years too young to discuss marriage and sex. As for my friends, all of them believed I'd drawn a winning ticket by marrying a foreigner and moving to England.

I walk back to the kitchen and put the food in the serving dishes. Washing my hands, I look out of the window above the sink. The view over the coastal path is beautiful. Whenever I feel down, it never fails to cheer me up. My marriage might have not turned out the way I'd imagined, but the Isle of Southbay has surpassed all my expectations.

It's breezy today, and the green grass undulates as if repeating the dance the waves below steep rocks perform. I can't see the cliffs from this point. The green fades into blue and white, blending the land and the channel together.

I don't have to call Michael to let him know the dinner is ready. He has set up the times meals must be ready, and he expects me to follow this schedule.

My husband arrives on time, and we sit down to dinner.

Tomorrow, I'll eat in peace, alone, I think, chewing the meat and not feeling its taste.

"How is this project in Abbotsbury going?" I ask. It's not that I am truly curious. I want to know whether my first rehearsal with Groveland's ladies isn't at risk. There is no way I'll be able to attend it if Michael returns home before Thursday evening.

"The house owner is a stubborn fool." My husband takes a big gulp from his glass of lemon water. "He keeps showing up on site and bothering me with new ingenious ideas. He'll end up paying more for extending the time I have to spend on his conservatory."

I smile what I hope looks like a sympathetic smile – rather than triumphant, the way it really is. "These troubles are in your favour, then. You'll earn more. It's a good thing."

He gives me a look from under his eyebrows.

I pray he doesn't turn my words against me. When we had just got married and I arrived in Southbay, he said he'd start renovating his old cottage once his business takes off. Then, for a while, he repeated he'd begin doing something on weekends. The only reference to the renovations in the last six months was the frustrated: *Don't you see how tired I am?*

"It's not enough to have one client no matter how much he pays," Michael speaks with annoyance, but at least he doesn't get into accusing me of greed.

"Of course," I agree hastily and move a plate with Yorkshire pudding closer to him. This is one of the rare things I've learned to do the way he likes. He has never praised my Yorkshire puddings. Still, I know he approves of them since he has never complained about them.

Michael takes the pastry, and I leave him to his Sunday dinner. I know better than to push too hard.

"I've got a new job in Bournemouth starting the week after next," Michael informs me after he finishes eating. "Some guy with the old money. Inherited one of those estates the size of a village. The house is huge but needs a heavy refurbishment. He has already hired a construction crew to change everything from floors to windows. Their manager told me he agreed to pay a fortune without arguing about a single contract point. The conservatory there is more like an orangery section in a museum. I'll have to order everything custom-made. I'll be able to charge them extra for that."

"That's fantastic!" I am genuinely pleased. I haven't abandoned the hope that my husband might change once his financial situation improves. After all, he was a different man when we met. It's not that I agreed to marry someone who treated me like I was the most annoying creature in the world. He was polite and attentive when we first met. He didn't change immediately after the wedding either. He even went to considerable expense to bring my old piano from Latvia. "That client might recommend you to his friends and neighbours."

Michael smiles. He rarely does these days, so I smile back. "Yes, I count on that. It's incredibly tricky to get access to these rich guys. But when they notice you, and you do your job well, you are in. You don't have to knock at closed doors anymore. They offer you work themselves."

"That's great. I'm really glad for you. I know how hard you work." I speak the words mechanically. I can't help but think that I'd love to spend some time in Bournemouth. It is the biggest town on our coast. Only Poole is larger. Still, I don't suggest Michael books a B&B rather than staying in his old trailer during the assignment. *There'll be other jobs like this,* I reason with myself. *It's not worth making him angry over.*

I bring up the topic of Betty Burton's death only after I've served the dessert. Today, it's a carrot cake – not my favourite, but Michael loves it.

"Mrs Burton, our neighbour, was found dead today," I tell my husband, never sure if he wants more details or otherwise.

"Really?" Michael puts down the spoon he was stirring the sugar in his coffee with. "Blimey! That's terrible."

"It is, isn't it?" I feel encouraged by his emotional reaction. "She was such a nice old lady. The kindest I've met here so far."

Michael waves his hand, still holding the spoon in it. "She was an old bat." My hope crushes. "She just sat there, pretending she was already out of her mind, so she didn't have to deal with the land border issue."

"Land border issue?"

Michael puts a hearty piece of carrot cake into his mouth and chews quickly. Aggression emanates from him in waves.

"Yes, this property has direct access to the coastal path, but due to her husband's vicious plotting back in the sixties, they built a stone wall just where our exit to the path was supposed to be."

My husband always refers to 'the cottage we live in' as if it doesn't belong to him. I find it strange since he spent his childhood in this house.

"Why didn't your parents object to him doing it?"

"My parents," he scoffs, "were too well-bred to argue with neighbours. They believed that good relationship with neighbours was more important than increasing their property value."

I don't say it aloud that I agree with them. Instead, I ask: "Did you plan to talk to Mrs Burton about it? You think she'd agree to move the wall?"

My husband shrugs. In this movement, I see that I'd better stop asking questions. "I have no idea what was going on in her head. She was probably so far out of the real world already that she forgot we had territory planning issues. Anyway," he puts more carrot cake in his mouth and chews methodically, "I didn't have time to deal with crazy neighbours. I'm building a business." He gives me a pointed stare as if he suspects I could ever forget the thing that has become central to both of our lives.

"Maybe her heirs will agree to make changes. Especially if they want to sell Mrs Burton's cottage. They can't do that without dealing with all the legal issues first."

Michael looks at me but says nothing. When I am right, he prefers not to acknowledge it. It's when I'm wrong that I get a thorough account of my transgressions.

"We'll see," he says. "It's never easy with heirs and inheritance."

I nod and concentrate on my coffee. He knows the difficulties imposed by inheriting property first-hand. He had inherited this cottage together with his brother. It took them a few years to come to an agreement on what to do with the property. In the end, it also took a huge chunk of Michael's money from selling his own family's property as per the divorce settlement.

I'd never asked, but it surprised me that he'd gone to such trouble to get this cottage. Even I seem to have warmer feelings for the small stone house facing the English Channel's ever-changing waters.

After we finish the dessert, Michael goes up to rest before the next busy week, and I clear the table and fuss about the kitchen. I put the dishes into the dishwasher. It is ancient, but I'm grateful it still works. Then, I wipe all the surfaces. I'll vacuum-clean and wash the floors on Monday after Michael leaves.

When I'm finished with the chores, I look longingly outside. I'd love to go for a walk, but Michael likes to have me around in case he needs a cup of tea or help with packing. It's a sunny day today, and I can see that the sunset will be magnificent. I remind myself that I'll have three days of freedom to wander around our picturesque island until my feet hurt.

I settle in the living room with a book. I hadn't been an avid reader before my marriage. There always seemed to be more interesting things to spend my time on after school. Besides, almost all the domestic chores were on me since my mom worked a lot.

After I arrived in England, I felt there was a void I needed to fill, not to be drawn into self-pity. I could play the piano, and I did play while Michael wasn't at home. Still, music seemed to deepen my melancholy rather than dissipate it.

Not long ago, I came across a bookstore in Eastpoole that had a huge shelf with a 'buy three paperbacks for five pounds' offer. I couldn't believe my luck. Michael doesn't give me any pocket money, only a small amount for things like milk and bread. However, I am good at handling limited finances. I manage to save a fiver and buy a stack of three paperbacks every two weeks.

My current read is about a woman who discovers that her husband is having an affair. As the story unfolds and the main character's life crumbles more into pieces, I find myself wondering if it isn't a blessing that I don't love my husband.

CHAPTER 3

I walk down the coastal path. It's a beautiful, clear day. In May, it is almost summer here in Southbay. I've noticed that here it gets warmer earlier than back at home, and I like it. A cold May is the last thing you want, especially after a long winter. We'll get our portion of rain – this is England, after all – still, showery days will mix with glorious ones like today when you have to squint in the sun, unable to look away from the piercing azure of the sky.

I have things Michael expects me to do this week. But it's only Monday, and the weather calls me outside after two days spent within four walls. I have almost four days of freedom to plan my time as I wish. I might wake up to an overcast sky and a drizzle tomorrow. Then, I'll get all the chores done with a calm heart.

Today, I've taken a more challenging route. Between the villages of Groveland and Clifflodge, the coastal path doesn't lead through a flat plateau on the top of the cliffs as it does around the South Rock. Instead, it descends to the ledge level and snakes between the rock walls and steep drop-offs.

I climb the narrow stone stairs carved in stone, holding on to the wall to keep my balance. The rock formation protrudes ominously over the path as if unwilling to yield ground to humans. I imagine how it stood for thousands of years before people came here and started adjusting nature to their recreational whims.

Having ascended the stairs, I stop to catch my breath. As usual, I take a look around, and the scenery makes my heart jump in admiration.

The Isle of Southbay is a feast to the eye for nature lovers. It is so picturesque that it looks like a scene from a movie or a location for a National Geographic Channel show. I could've never imagined that I'd live in a place like this. My home country, Latvia, is beautiful, and the Old Town of its capital is included in the UNESCO World Heritage List. But I wasn't born in the capital or one of the former Hanseatic towns with medieval castle ruins and historic architecture.

The town where I'd lived with my mother was built to serve the needs of the factory located there. I don't think I'm biased when I say that functional dwellings for factory labourers weren't built with beauty in mind. My hometown was dull and grey, with many inhabitants working in the capital Riga and the nearby bigger town Jelgava.

I could start enjoying the beauty of the capital after school graduation. But when I joined the commuter crowds travelling by train to the capital, my head was full of more practical worries than admiring the charm of cobbled streets and old churches.

I make my way through a short, flat segment of the coastal path. Then I climb down more stairs, weaving around the rock ledge and find myself in a secluded cove. I love this spot with a crescent-shaped beach that neither locals nor tourists seem to favour. I discovered it last September when the summer was almost over. Since then,

I've been thinking about exploring it. Autumns and winters are mild here in Southbay. Still, it gets too windy to wander along the rugged coastline, and after the rain, the rocks and stairs become slippery and dangerous.

I walk along the water's edge, pebbles crunching musically under my feet. It still surprises me that there are only two places with direct access to the water in Southbay. It is an island, after all. I bend and pick up a handful of pebbles. I decide that I'll bring a bag next time to fill it with pretty stones. Some are so pristinely white that they seem artificial. Others are obsidian black and asphalt grey with contrasting freckles of burgundy. They would look nice in a glass vase.

The waves lick the shore, leaving white froth in their wake and making pebbles tinkle gently. I stop to listen to the melody of the sea. It is soothing and invigorating at the same time.

The sun is right above the cove. It has become hot, and I sit down on a bigger boulder, having draped my jacket over it. I look at the horizon. This spot must be perfect for watching sunsets. I imagine coming here before the orange disk dives into the water. It would be so romantic to eat grapes and cheese sitting on a spread blanket while the sun descends majestically, spilling the last sparkles of glow.

I sigh. Michael would think it a stupid idea. Nowadays, we never go anywhere. He wouldn't stir from his favourite place on our bed to climb up and down rough stone stairs only to watch a sunset.

I wonder if it is my fault and if I should have seen what kind of person he is before I married him. My twenty-first birthday comes to my mind. Michael hired a boat that took us and my two best friends to watch the sunset over the Gulf of Riga. It wasn't a yacht as it was said in the advertisement, but we had a great time. We laughed and drank champagne, gliding through the Daugava River. I remember how fascinating it was to watch the cruise ships docked at the Riga Passenger Terminal and the tall lift cranes in the industrial harbour. I'd never been on a boat trip before that day. And when the boat went through the river mouth and out into the open sea, I felt like I was Rose standing on the bow of the Titanic. I felt free and happy.

The sound of pebbles clattering behind my back startles me.

I turn just in time to prepare myself for not falling when a huge Leonberger dog leaps at me.

The animal is so big that our heads are on the same level when it stands on its hind legs. I hug the giant as I would hug a person while it enthusiastically licks my face.

"Berlin!" I hear a voice shouting, but the dog's massive head obscures its owner. "Berlin, stop! Get off her! Come here!"

After a few more furious licks – I think even my hair got a portion of the dog's love and saliva – the dog reluctantly obeys. It trots away, happily wagging its fluffy tail.

I can see the dog's owner now. My heart sinks. One of the downsides of living in a small community is that even if you aren't the most sociable person in the world, you still know everyone, and everyone knows you.

"Hi," the Leonberger's owner waves, walking toward me, the huge dog by his side already on the leash. "I'm sorry, Margo," he says when he reaches me. "I have no idea what came over this big boy." He pats the dog's head, and the long pink tongue promptly comes out to lick the owner's hand.

"Hi, Finley." I take out a tissue and wipe my face. I don't want to make a small talk. Still, I can't make up a plausible excuse for a quick retreat. "It's okay, I'm used to Berlin's tricks. We are friends, aren't we, Berlin?" I say, looking at the dog. Berlin wags his tail vigorously and whines. He shifts from one paw to another, and his body twitches.

"Berlin, sit," Finley says, and the dog obeys.

"You are such a good boy, Berlin." I keep focusing on the dog. In my defence, with his leonine mane, pronounced black mask, and thick but not long reddish-brown fur,

Berlin is an extremely handsome dog. "I often meet your mom walking Berlin on the coastal path." I reluctantly switch my attention to Finley.

Finley Hammond is as impressive in the looks department as his dog. I blush at the inappropriate comparison. Only a year younger than I, Finley is tall. At five foot eight, I usually tower above people. With Finley, I have to raise my chin to look at him, just like with my husband. I notice that Finley has cut his black hair. Last year, when I saw him, he wore it longish and slightly unkempt. Now, he has a neat short crop.

Lean and muscular, he looks great in faded denim shorts and a black T-shirt with some logo.

"You can let him go," I nod at Berlin. "He's calmed down."

"Thanks." Finley bends down and unclips the leash from the collar.

With his tongue rolling out, the leonine dog trots happily to the water's edge. There, he sniffs the bubbling froth, splutters when it gets into his nostrils and barks indignantly at the wet enemy.

"He does it every time." Finley shakes his head.

"He is an optimist. He believes that it can be different next time."

"I don't blame him."

We stand watching Berlin playing with waves. I feel awkward. I haven't seen Finley since last summer when his parents invited Michael and I over for dinner a couple of times. We didn't get on well with each other. It isn't surprising. We have nothing in common. He is a spoilt son of privileged parents. And if that doesn't make the gulf between us impassable, the fact that his father and my husband went to school together certainly does.

Berlin trudges over to us with his muzzle and front paws wet. Pebbles make running difficult for him.

"You need to take him to South Rock or somewhere where he can take a proper run." I put my hands into my jeans pockets and turn.

"Are you in a hurry?" Finley asks, and I stop, surprised.

"I don't think it's a good idea to make Berlin climb all those stairs." I wave at the cliffs where the coastal path starts.

"You could come with us through the village." Finley kicks the pebbles with his trainers. "Berlin seems to love you." The dog sits, demonstrating his best behaviour, and lets out a whine, his tongue rolling out as if he is smiling. I am about to agree. "Come on, Margo. You can't spend all your time scrubbing the floors and cooking."

I spin around and walk away. Finley calls after me, but I refuse to stop.

Beautiful pebbles suddenly turn into frustrating, slippery obstacles under my feet. I stumble and almost twist my ankle. Still, I stubbornly keep walking, with my cheeks blazing and my heart thumping in my chest. Only after having climbed the stone stairs, marched through the short flat stretch, and climbed down more stairs do I stop to catch my breath. I am sure Finley hasn't followed me. The coastal path here is dangerous for Berlin.

My eyes sting, and I brush away the tears.

You can't spend all your time scrubbing the floors and cooking. Finley's words ring in my ears like a church's bell. They make me feel bad about myself.

Is this what his parents think about me? Is this what they say about me while eating dinner? I want to cry, but I grit my teeth, pushing back tears.

The thing is, I like Finley's parents. Rowan and Melissa Hammond are a perfect couple. Confident and refined, they aren't arrogant like Barbara Southwell. It's not written anywhere, but they are the wealthiest inhabitants of the island. Mr Hammond is a urologist with a well-established practice in Bournemouth, while Mrs Hammond is rumoured to come from the *old aristocracy*.

I felt welcome in their home. More than that, I felt the Hammonds were interested in listening to my stories about my life back in Latvia. They didn't have that polite but dismissive expression that said: "Yes, this is exciting, but we already know everything we need to know about you and your country."

Was their interest only a well-masked pretence? The Hammonds clearly belonged to a higher class than other people I've met in England.

Until now, I hadn't realised that I'd been waiting for Michael to sort out the issues with his new business, so he'd become more sociable again. When I arrived in Southbay, he took me to meet his friends. We went out every weekend, visiting local pubs and restaurants in quaint little countryside hotels. I didn't notice when all of it ended. I shared Michael's enthusiasm about his conservatory renovation company. I saw it as my wife's duty to support him. I knew how important it was for him to prove to himself and others that he could regain what he'd lost because of the divorce.

When has my husband become obsessed with his business?

We never invited the Hammonds back. Michael kept talking about renovating the cottage at the time, so it didn't cross my mind that we might appear rude for not doing so. Later, when these talks ceased, all I could think about was doing everything the way he wanted. If I slipped, he stopped talking to me. At first, it was only for an hour, but gradually, the punishment extended to days. I couldn't stand it. In addition to the general isolation, living in a foreign country, far away from my mother and friends, the silence was too heavy a burden. So, all my thoughts have focused on making my husband satisfied.

I walk down the coastal path and don't notice the breathtaking scenery. The sun generously pours the light and the warmth on everything it can reach. Its shimmering rays slide into the dark crevices in grey rocks, illuminating what usually stays hidden. Reflecting the golden glow, the cliffs don't appear dangerous.

For once, I don't care about the beauty that surrounds

me. A pretty picture is not enough. Inside, I am hurting.

I want to break free. I almost mistake the song for my own thoughts. I stop, trying to locate the source of the music. I am alone on the coastal path. My only companions are rocks, but they always keep quiet.

Finally, I see a boat fighting the feisty waters by the cliffs. The small fishing vessel bobs up and down, cutting through the froth. For a moment, I feel scared the reckless fishermen get smashed, hitting the underwater rocks. Still, the boat keeps moving forward.

I want to break free. Freddie Mercury's inimitable voice reaches me, the words partly swallowed by the roaring waves.

I listen to the song while watching the brave little ship disappear around the cliff ledge. I haven't paid attention to the lyrics before, but now, every word pierces me through. I want to be free from my husband's oppressive demands. I want to have a choice. But I don't want to be alone. I'm afraid to be alone again.

I don't want to be like this boat: always fighting against the currents with no one but yourself to count on.

CHAPTER 4

I put down the pen and stretch, clasping my fingers behind my back. I've read that it helps to relax the spine. I'm not sure the effect will be long-lasting if I continue sitting bent over the papers.

I help Michael with his company's accounts. Math was my favourite subject at school. I was among the few students who got state-funded places in the Accounting and Audit programme at the University of Latvia. And one of even fewer of those who managed to keep it until graduation.

The accounting systems in Latvia and England are different. Still, it helps that the one we have back at home is more complicated. Michael pays a local accountant to prepare financial reports for submission to tax authorities. But everything else is my responsibility.

Figures and calculations calm me. They are straightforward and can't be misinterpreted. You don't have to vex your head over multiple options. The answer is always only one.

I collect the papers that are scattered on the table and put them neatly into a folder. I decide it's a good idea to pop over to the accountant's office to drop them off. I was planning to go to the Groveland Business Park today anyway. I hope Suzie will give me sheet music for their rehearsals. I can't disgrace myself in front of formidable Barbara Southwell.

Clouds hang low, having sneaked up the sky overnight. They are so dense, it's hard to believe that only yesterday, the sky was a glorious riot of blue.

I ensure all the windows are closed before I leave the house. Life on an island makes you a quick learner. The weather might not be done with surprises for today. The moderate wind can turn into a storm within an hour.

This time, I don't plan to take a detour via the coastal path. I walk up the street lined mainly with one-storey detached stone cottages. Here in Groveland, we don't have terraced houses like in Fortunescove, another village on the island. In Fortunescove, rows of terraced houses are painted in light blue, eggshell yellow and even terracotta. They snake down the hillside to the harbour. While on the other side of the island, the tiny Clifflodge is full of practical cottages for rent perched high on the cliffs.

I pass by Betty Burton's cottage. It looks exactly like it did when its owner was alive. Rose bushes on both sides of the door prepare for an early bloom. Last year, I noticed how beautifully the orange and red roses contrasted with grey stone walls.

This year, Mrs Burton won't see her pretty roses. The thought makes me sad.

The funeral will be held on Saturday. Michael rolled his eyes when he informed me about it. I'll have to ask Suzie what's wrong with that. I was surprised he wanted to attend the service at all, so I asked if he really wished to go. He said it was a chance to meet Betty's children who'll inherit her cottage and try to find out their plans for it. "Before they make some huge plans about selling it for a million, I'll put a damper on their parade," he explained his sudden neighbourly zeal. "They must take down that bloody wall first. And I'll make it absolutely clear that it's them who have to pay for it. I won't spend a pound on it."

I walk at a brisk pace. It can start drizzling at any moment. Local drizzles are something else. I mean, it's not as though I come from a place where rain is an unusual occurrence. Still, back home, if it rains, it either pours down ferociously for half an hour or rains steadily all day. Before I came to Southbay, I didn't know the air could get saturated with fine drops that fill every pore and make you feel like with every breath, you inhale moisture.

I enter the Business Park, and a delicious smell of fresh pastry hits my nostrils. I almost walk straight to the Groveland Bakery but remind myself that I need to pop into the accountant's office first.

Raymond Billings. Accounting Services. A laconic door plaque fits Mr Billings perfectly. New clients find Mr Billings through word of mouth. His impeccable reputation as a thorough and trustworthy professional doesn't require pompous slogans and catchy banners.

I knock and enter. Raymond Billings looks up and puts down the pen. His desk isn't cluttered with papers like mine usually is. The documents he's working with are organised in neat stacks.

"What a nice surprise." Mr Billings stands from his chair and rushes to meet me. "What can I do for you, Margo? Please sit." He leads me to the visitors' corner: a low table with two armchairs. There aren't any chairs for clients at his desk. I think the idea of other people intruding on his workspace makes him uncomfortable.

"I've brought you some invoices, Mr Billings," I take the documents out of a waterproof folder. I'm sure he would never say anything, but I prefer not to check if his meticulous personality can endure the sight of financial documents touched by water. "I know it's too early to start on the reports," I add while he opens a metal file cabinet and fingers through the folders. I wonder if this file cabinet is fireproof. Having found Michael's company's folder and placed the documents in it, Mr Billings returns.

"It is never too early to start preparing for a financial report. The more thorough the preparations, the better the result." The accountant smiles and sits in an armchair facing me. In his fifties, slight and with a receding hairline, he is an amiable man. Although I can't be sure, I think he genuinely likes me. Besides, he doesn't mind explaining work-related things to me when I ask him questions. I'm always glad for an opportunity to talk to him since I'm eager to learn.

This time, I have a question for Mr Billings regarding the relevance of some invoices to be included in the company's expenditure report. Michael insisted that I should add them, and yet, I'm unsure. I know better than to argue with my husband, but I can count on Mr Billings's professional consultation.

We have an animated discussion about the subjective nature of expenditure relevance that leaves me armoured with some useful knowledge.

"Please don't hesitate to bring me the documents as you get them." The accountant offers me a tin with digestive biscuits.

I shake my head. "Thank you, Mr Billings. I eat too many sweets. And thank you for the explanation about those invoices. Now I understand better the logic behind what expenses are relevant."

Mr Billings gives me a quick look before returning the tin to the table. "You don't have to worry about an irrelevant invoice getting into the final report. I look through every document before including it. But I admire your determination to get to the core of things."

I blush. "Thank you. Have a nice day, Mr Billings."

"And the same to you, Margo." The accountant walks me to the door. "I hope that the weather has a pleasant surprise in store for us today for a change."

"It was a beautiful day yesterday. So, there is hope."
"Indeed."

We stop at the doorway to say our goodbyes when I hear familiar non-English speech. A young, dark-haired woman walks down the corridor, talking on her mobile. Dressed in a two-piece sand-coloured set with a knee-length mermaid hem skirt, she stands out in the grey and basic hallway of the Groveland Business Park like an exotic bird. Even the clicking sound of her steps is odd.

I used to be a high-heels enthusiast back at home, always wearing – okay, not exactly stilettos – but at least wedges. Even the dangers the cobbled streets in the Old Town of Riga presented to local fashionistas didn't deter me from marching around in style. Michael would laugh every time he saw me sashaying in footwear incompatible with smooth cobbles polished by time and thousands of feet. Still, he would say I looked fantastic and hold me gently by the elbow.

The woman smiles and nods, passing us by. Her smile is charming and sincere. She is the kind of person you immediately get drawn to. I fight back the ridiculous impulse to run after her.

"Who is she?" I ask Mr Billings, following the woman with my eyes. I can't help sounding awe-struck. She has an hourglass figure you see only in the old Italian movies.

"Oh, I believe this is the young lady who wants to rent an office for her recruitment business." Together, Mr Billings and I watch the woman leave the business park. "Phil from the main office told me about it the other day. It's an extraordinary occurrence. Such a young woman and already in charge of setting up an international venture."

Sometimes, solid gossiping traditions of the tightly knit society are a blessing. I'm hungry to hear more.

"She is from Latvia, right?" I steer kind Mr Billings to giving me the information I crave the most.

"Oh, I apologise, Margo. It hadn't occurred to me that you might be interested in finding out about it." The accountant looks genuinely upset. "Yes, I believe Phil told me that she is from Latvia, or maybe it was Lithuania."

"Do you know if she rented that office?"

Mr Billings shakes his head apologetically. "No, sadly, I don't. I guess we'll soon see if new lessees move in."

Unsatisfied, I head to the Groveland Bakery. What are the chances of a Latvian company setting up an office in a remote place like Southbay? Still, I have no doubts the dark-haired woman is from Latvia. It feels strangely comforting that I might have someone from my home country close by. It would be a blessing to talk to someone who understands the things locals can't sympathise with.

The café is packed with people. No one chooses to have their lunch sandwich outside on the lawn when it rains.

I offer to come by later, but Suzie asks me to wait. She sits me down at our usual table with a big pot of tea. Not to stare at the bakery's customers, I gaze at the scenery outside the window. The usual view has changed completely. The lush green and the cobalt blue are all obscured by a misty veil.

"What a fog," I say to Suzie after she joins me.

A smile disappears from Suzie's face. She looks as if I kicked her cat. "It's not a *fog*," she almost whispers the last word.

"What is it then?" I instinctively lower my voice too.

"A low cloud, of course," Suzie announces with a stern schoolteacher's expression.

I open my mouth to apologise when she bursts out laughing. "I'm sorry, Margo," she says, having caught her breath, "it was rude. You couldn't have known about it. Besides, it's an old stupid joke almost no one here remembers anyway."

I admit I did have a moment of fright. The last thing I need is to offend locals. Not everyone here is as understanding as Suzie.

"What's wrong with fog?" I ask.

Suzie shrugs. She waves to the last customer, flashing a

smile at the grey-haired man from the Groveland Business Park administration. "I don't know. It's one of those things you hear from childhood and never think to ask what it's all about."

"Okay." I take a big gulp of tea. "I'd better not use this word anyway. Low cloud?"

Suzie nods apologetically. "I guess you can't go wrong with avoiding the f-word."

"I'll keep that in mind. It seems it's often the case with f-words."

A smile illuminates Suzie's pleasant face with fine lines around her dark eyes. "Indeed. I haven't thought about it from such a perspective. You're doing a great job getting accustomed to our strange ways."

After having at least three cups of tea each, Suzie and I go to the rehearsal room.

"Take whatever you need," Suzie tells me, pointing at the piano where sheet music lies in a neat pile. "Neither of us can play, so no one will need it. Betty always left everything here. She said she didn't want to be reminded of her age should she forget to bring the sheet music to a rehearsal."

Suzie smiles sadly. I also feel downhearted thinking about Betty Burton.

We keep silent while I put the sheets into my bag.

Suzie gently sweeps her hand across the closed keyboard cover. "Have you heard that not everything is as clear about Betty's death as we thought?"

This is the first time I'm hearing about it. "Really? But Mrs Southwell said that she talked to the police?"

"Barbara likes to make everyone think she knows best." I think I catch a shadow of triumphant malice on Suzie's face, but it passes quickly. "Matilda Peckham told the police that Betty had a visitor that morning when she died."

"How could she see anything? She is, like, a hundred years old!" I blurt out, shocked.

Matilda Peckham lives in a cottage across the road. I've

never seen her go out further than her front porch. Even then, she doesn't linger a second longer than needed to fetch a package or let in a social worker. I remember thinking that it's good the lady isn't curious about the outside world. Were she interested in spying over her neighbours, Mrs Peckham's living-room was an excellent vantage point to keep track of our comings and goings. Without the luxury of the island's trademark views over the World Heritage coastline, the old lady's cottage has an uninterrupted perspective of at least three cottages.

Suzie smiles. "Yes, Matilda is old. But it doesn't mean she is blind."

"I didn't mean…" I feel that even my ears turn beetroot red.

Suzie waves her hand as she continues: "She *is* old. To be honest, I sometimes forget she is still alive. I haven't seen her around the village since I was still a marrying material. And *that* was a couple of decades ago." She giggles. "Anyway, the police came to talk to her, you know, following the procedure even though the case was clear, and Matilda told them she saw that someone had come to Betty. The visitor came really early, before the postman. That person arrived by car, but, of course, she didn't pay attention to the registration plate. Such a pity, isn't it? It's only in the crime shows everyone who happens to witness something important for the investigation has a photographic memory."

"Did she recognise the person? The visitor?" I can't help it: it does sound rather exciting.

Suzie shakes her head, puckering her lips. "She couldn't even say if it was a man or a woman. She said her eyes aren't as before." She chuckles. "I can imagine how many neighbours' secrets she'll take to her grave. Well, now the police have to determine if there is a connection between this visit and Betty's death."

"Wow," I chew on my lip, the uncomfortable feeling crawling in, "and everyone thought she died peacefully in her sleep." I wonder why the police haven't come to us yet. With these new developments, they will definitely come to talk to Michael and I. And once they find out that Michael isn't at home for most of the week, they'll focus on me. It's not that I have anything to hide from authorities. Still, it is unsettling to have to deal with the police in a foreign country.

"Well, that's what happens when you are forced to rushed conclusions."

Suzie doesn't say it's Barbara Southwell's fault, but it's clearly implied. The two women seem to have fallen out over something in the past. Still, they put a good face on the conflict between them.

"And what now? Will they postpone the funeral?" As curious as I am about islanders' secrets, the current issues are too unsettling to dwell on the historic clashes.

"No, thankfully, it hasn't come to that. There aren't any doubts about the cause of death. It's unmistakably been a heart failure. There's nothing poor Betty can help them with."

As I walk back home through the drizzle, I think about the mysterious visitor who was the last person to see Betty Burton alive. Was it a coincidence that someone had shown up on the old lady's doorstep just before she joined the maker?

CHAPTER 5

People believe they know what will make them happy. The problem is they usually want things that they have never had.

I had no idea what might bring me happiness. Nowadays, I've come to the conclusion it was because I'd already been content with my life.

The flat where I lived was small. Still, it was cosy since my mother and I filled it with pretty things. It was also warm during harsh Latvian winters, with central heating working at full blast on the third floor of our five-storey *khrushchyovka*[1].

Here, in England, our cottage has more rooms but not more space. The stairs are so narrow that when I take the

---

[1] *Khrushchyovka* is an unofficial name for a type of low-cost, concrete-paneled or brick three- to five-storied apartment building which was developed in the Soviet Union during the early 1960s, during the time its namesake Nikita Khrushchev directed the Soviet government (Wikipedia)

vacuum cleaner up, I clutch it in front of me rather than simply holding it in my hand. The house is incredibly damp. Old-fashioned carpeted floors on the second floor are supposed to make it warmer, while in reality, they only add to the time and effort needed to clean them, as well as a faint mouldy odour. Michael doesn't switch on the heating for long enough in colder months to let the house warm up thoroughly, so it is bone-chilling inside.

Back home in Latvia, I was a young professional with a Bachelor's Degree and a prospective career ahead of me. My mom always told me it wouldn't be difficult for me to find a job as an accountant. True, it would not be well-paid enough to afford to rent a flat and move to the capital right away. But my chances to eventually make a career that would let me do those things had been high.

Here, I am a housewife who does her husband's accounts for free in between *scrubbing the floors and cooking*. Finley Hammond's words have hurt me deeply. It still stings when I remember them.

To be honest, none of these things would matter if only my husband loved me.

I didn't grow up in a perfect family from a washing powder ad. My mom has always worked from dusk till dawn, her boss ignoring such trifles as working hours' norms stipulated in Labour Law. Mom had neither time nor strength for the mother-and-daughter quality time. We didn't go shopping together or giggle on the couch watching Hallmark movies. Nevertheless, I knew she loved me. My well-being was her priority, and she supported me in everything that could help me build a better future.

Michael doesn't care about my future. Frankly, he doesn't care about me at all. I feel like I am one of the many tools he uses to make his life the way he wants it to be.

I feel guilty every time these thoughts crawl into my head like uninvited guests.

I quicken my step. It is Thursday, and I am on my way to my first rehearsal with the Groveland ladies' choir.

The weather has made yet another flip; today it's all blue skies and dazzling sun again. I skipped my usual morning walk, though. Michael will be back right after I return from the rehearsal, so I've made sure everything is ready for dinner and that the house is spotlessly clean.

When I arrive, the ladies are already assembled in the music room. I take a look at the clock on the wall. I'm not late.

"Good day, Mrs Birkett."

I almost turn around at Barbara Southwell's greeting to check if Mrs Birkett has tiptoed noiselessly and stands behind me. I realise that it's me she's addressed just in time not to make a nuisance of myself.

"Thank you for joining us today." With her trademark stern expression, Mrs Southwell makes me feel anything but welcome. "I hope you are acquainted with everyone." She purses her colourless lips.

I nod quickly. "Thank you for this opportunity." I look at the assembled ladies, hoping to see some friendlier faces and to my relief, I do see many. Suzie waves from the corner where she's talking to the woman who was here last week, when I volunteered to take Betty Burton's place in the choir. Maureen Easton also greets me. Today, she doesn't look like a terrified hare under the wolf's stare. For some reason, it gives me the confidence to face Barbara. "You have a beautiful repertoire." I smile at the formidable woman. "It's an honour to accompany your choir. I know I can't replace Mrs Burton, but I promise to do my best to help your voices shine."

All the women in the room smile, nodding appreciatively. Suzie gives me a thumb-up from across the room, but Maureen squeezes my arm gently on her way to take what I think is her usual place.

"Very well, Mrs Birkett." Barbara Southwell hasn't earned her place as a pillar of Southbay's society for being easy to move. Her lips remain pursed, and I can't get rid of the feeling that it must be her impossibly tight hair bun that stops her facial muscles from moving. "Ladies, let us begin."

Barbara walks regally to a compact dais fitted into a corner. Next to it, the piano stands by the window, its polished brown wood surfaces sparkling amber under the sunlight streaming through the window. In their leader's wake, other ladies take their places.

"We understand you might have difficulties with the new repertoire," Barbara announces. To my relief, she doesn't sound condescending. "Is there a song it would be more comfortable for you to start with?"

"*Memory* from *Cats*," I answer without hesitation. Albums with Andrew Lloyd Weber's musicals have been in my collection since I was twelve.

"Very well." Barbara turns to the choir. "Lilly, you'll be the solo."

A petite woman, her short hair as white as the fresh snow, takes a step out of the group.

Mrs Southwell gestures for me to begin.

My fingers strike the first chords, and I am not in a room full of virtual strangers. I'm in my happy place where playing the piano never fails to take me. I feel like I'm becoming taller and stronger with every stroke of the keyboard. A hot energy wave rises inside me, and the colours grow brighter. When I play, hope blossoms out in my heart like a lush exotic flower.

Still, Lilly's voice pulls me out of my inspirational cocoon. I almost stop playing, so strong is the urge to turn around and make sure the magical sounds are indeed coming from the tiny woman. Competing with the canonical legendary song performances by Barbara Streisand or Elaine Paige, Lilly pulls at the strings in my soul, making me feel I'm able to fly. Her voice rises and falls, gentle one moment before it gradually builds up strength again.

My fingers fly over the keys. I lose the connection with the present moment, and my ties with reality break. I am on the top of South Rock, the piano glistening under the beams of sparkling glow. I see myself as if the camera circles around me from above. It moves further, and I see the froth bursting up when waves hit the rocks. Then the camera moves closer, and I see my face with my eyes closed. My hands move, and the music fills the expanse of the rugged coastline.

The harmony of Lilly's voice and the sounds of piano envelop me and swirl me up.

I am a bird sailing in the sky above the island. It isn't Isle of Southbay where I'm trapped in an unhappy marriage. Still, it is the same place. Quaint stone cottages dot the green stretch atop the cliffs. The red and white cone of the Groveland Lighthouse slices through the azure sky. Grey rectangles of the Groveland Business Park sprawl across the plateau. The sheep are only speckles on the grassy blanket.

The music has wiped out all the pain and troubles, leaving only the stunning scenery and joy.

The rest of the choir joins, and Lilly's solo sounds even richer, set off by other voices.

For the minutes while the choir sings and I play, I feel complete and happy.

The feeling of loss hits me when I strike the final chords, but a round of applause doesn't let it linger.

I look at the ladies, clapping and smiling, and it's like a veil has fallen from a bride's face. It is that moment when you realise that a girl is truly pretty where you could only guess before, while her features were still partly hidden under the thin fabric. I hoped the Southbay ladies were nice, with emotions hidden under the façade of English reserve. Now I know it for sure.

"That was amazing." Suzie smiles at me from her place in the choir. "It felt like we've always been doing it together. Have you felt it too, ladies?"

Women nod enthusiastically.

"You play beautifully," Maureen Easton's plump face is flushed, and her eyes twinkle. "We are lucky to have you join us."

"Thank you. Thank you very much for inviting me." My cheeks begin to burn too.

"Indeed, it was a very adequate performance, Mrs Birkett." From Barbara Southwell, it sounds like the highest praise.

"Thank you, Mrs Southwell. I'm glad I could be of help." I give the Southbay's choir leader a direct look. "And please, call me Margo."

"But of course," Barbara dismisses me as if what I ask for goes without saying. "If you are comfortable with us having a proper rehearsal today, we can proceed with performing a few more songs. There are some you are familiar with, aren't there?"

"It would be my pleasure." I take a stack of sheet music from the piano and give it to Mrs Southwell. "You can choose from these. And I'll take home the ones I'm unfamiliar with to practice so that we can perform them next time."

"Very well." She gives me back some sheet music for *My Bonnie Lies Over the Ocean*. She turns and resumes her place in the choir. "Let's begin."

I still feel the warmth and exhilaration from the rehearsal when Suzie and I walk to the Groveland Bakery. The business park corridor is empty and quiet. I can't help but feel amazed at how, here in Britain, business owners don't overexert themselves with longer working hours to accommodate customers' needs. On Friday, offices close at three so that employees can enjoy quality time with their families – or in their local pubs.

One of the choir members comes over while Suzie fumbles with the key, opening the café's door. "It was so good. Thank you, Margo." *Thornton*. I can't remember her first name. She is petite and slim, with a shortly cropped dyed black hair. "Betty was an absolute darling," she continues, "but age isn't merciful to anyone, you know. Her fingers weren't what they used to be."

"Thank you. I'm sure Mrs Burton had way more

experience in performing than I do."

Suzie opens the door. "Shall you come in, Camille?" she asks.

Camille Thornton. I try to commit the name to my memory.

"No, thank you, Suzie. We have an early dinner on Fridays." Camille looks at her wristwatch.

"What do you usually cook for dinner?" I ask automatically.

Camille gives me an incredulous stare. "*I don't cook,*" she punctuates every word. "My partner cooks."

After Camille leaves, Suzie pats me on the shoulder. "You've touched her on a sore spot. But don't worry, she won't hold it against you. She is just touchy about these things."

"But I didn't know…" The feeling I was finally getting closer to being accepted by the locals has evaporated as swiftly as it unexpectedly appeared at the rehearsal.

"You couldn't know. Come, let's have a cup of tea. Do you have time, or you have to rush home?"

I look at the clock hanging above the counter. I have plenty of things that I ought to do before Michael's arrival. For some reason, I feel ashamed to confess that I do.

"Tea would be nice." I make my way to my regular table while Suzie busies herself with putting the kettle on.

"It's never a bad idea to have a cuppa," she says, taking out the plate for cookies.

"That's true," I reply, although I feel like a shot of vodka would do better work to calm my nerves right now.

I know it would be wiser to drop the subject but ask anyway: "Is Camille a feminist?"

Suzie laughs. She pours hot water into a white teapot with peacocks painted on its fat sides. "She most definitely is not. But that's if you ask me. If you ask her – and I strongly advise you not to ever attempt to do this – she'll probably say that feminism is the only fair form of existence in this unfair world designed by and for men."

Suzie fetches the tray laden with tea things with a practised move.

"Did someone hurt her?" I ask when she places everything on the table between us and sits down.

Suzie looks at me, her kind dark eyes surrounded by crow's feet. "Isn't it always the reason why a woman turns resentful? You are very perceptive, Margo."

"Not enough, it seems." I pour tea for both of us. "It's not that all the women in Latvia cook and clean all day long while men lie in front of a tv drinking beer. We have women who are big bosses in business and also in the government. But I never thought a question about cooking could offend anyone."

Suzie laughs heartily. "Since you mentioned it, there are plenty lying and beer-drinking types here in Britain. And wives of such treasures rarely complain, let alone divorce these losers."

"Was Camille's husband like that?" She made it clear by saying *my partner* so pointedly that she wasn't married.

Suzie takes a sip of her tea and pushes the cookie plate closer to me. I take one crunchy disc covered with coconut flakes. "Worse. Noah Thornton was a great guy. Every woman's dream. He was good-looking, hard-working, and successful. He is, actually. I haven't seen him for years, but people like that don't change. They are like cognac: years make them only better."

"What happened?"

Suzie takes a bite of the cookie. She looks out of the window at the lush green field rolling down to the cliffs. "They were a perfect family. You know, the kind you see in tv shows. They lived in a beautiful house. Camille loved to gather her friends for birthdays and other occasions to show off. I still miss those parties. Camille was an amazing host. Some of the dishes she served I haven't tasted anywhere, not before and not after. She was always busy with some improvements that would make her already perfect house even better. She watched all those fancy cooking shows where they teach ordinary people to cook dishes to be served in Buckingham Palace. She also ordered cooking magazines and cookbooks by tv chefs." Suzie pauses and sips her tea. "They had a pretty little princess of a daughter. Camille dressed her like a doll, and Gemma loved it."

I try to imagine the younger version of Camille Thornton and her beautiful daughter. It is clear that the fairy tale hadn't lasted until the day death did part Camille and her handsome husband.

"Noah loved to pamper his little family," Suzie continues, "but the problem was that he wanted it to be bigger. He wanted more children. Camille didn't say anything about it, of course. But in those times, if a woman had only one child, it wasn't because the birth control method she used worked perfectly. It meant only one thing. We all knew Camille had female health issues. And, Margo, I'm not proud of it, but we all thought it was a kind of higher justice."

Suzie sighs and gives me a sad look. I nod. "I understand."

"It was such a shock when they divorced. Noah never looked at other women, let alone cheated on Camille. Southbay is a small place, we'd know. Camille was forty-one. For her, it was a disaster. Her whole life revolved around her marriage. I think in a month or so, Noah married a girl from some islands, maybe the Philippines, but I'm not sure. They moved to Tenerife and had three children. One boy and two girls."

"Poor Camille. I can't imagine what it's been like for her to overcome this. At least she wasn't alone. She had her daughter."

Suzie shakes her head. "Gemma chose to live with her father."

"That's awful."

We sit in silence. The sun slowly creeps away from the spacious room of the café. The white of the tablecloths turns grey.

"Poor Camille," I say again.

"Well," Suzie speaks in a brighter tone, "life is a bitch, and then you die."

As I walk back home, already too late to do everything as Michael likes, I wonder if it's worth the trouble at all. If a perfect family like the Thorntons couldn't make it, what chances a crippled one like ours has?

I should have chosen the most direct route home, but instead, I head to the coastal path. I walk past the Groveland Lighthouse, and the view of the cliffs calms me. The waves dance far below, caressing the rocks with white froth.

A tennis ball rolls past me and bounces down the slope to the grassy ledge. I jump after it, having spotted a cream, fluffy silhouette darting in the same direction. I pick up the ball before it reaches the cliff's edge and falls into the waves.

When I straighten up, a golden retriever stands on the coastal path over the ledge, wagging its tale.

"Stop! Stay there!" I tell the dog, hurrying up the slope. "Here is your toy. I have it."

I reach the top in time with the dog's owner. It's Jacqueline Fisher, the mysterious woman who lives in the Lighthouse Keeper's Cottage.

"Oh, hi," she says breathlessly. "I was afraid he'd dive headfirst down the cliff. I shouldn't have allowed him to take that ball on the walk." She bends down to pet the dog's big head. "Winston, you've scared the daylights out of me. Don't do that again." The dog wags its fluffy tail enthusiastically and licks Jacqueline's hand. "Good boy," the woman adds affectionately before turning back to me. "Thank you. Thank you so much. I'm Jacqueline. Jacqueline Fisher."

Shaking the offered hand, I can't find the right words to reply to the introduction. I'm absolutely captivated by the woman.

Dressed in jeans and a white T-shirt – the most popular choice of clothes on the island – she looks like she is from another planet. She wears no make-up, and her shoulder-length hair isn't styled. However, the way she speaks and holds herself sets her off from everyone I've met in Southbay. She is confident but, at the same time, reserved somehow. It seems it would be equally acceptable to her if you talked to her or ignored her. In both cases, she wouldn't give you a second thought after you parted ways.

"Hi, it's nice to meet you." The only words I find are from the English phrase book. "I'm Margo. Margo Birkett." My married name still sounds alien to me, but it does help me regain balance. "I don't think Winston would have jumped. He was just excited to catch his ball. But I'm sure he would have stopped in time."

The golden retriever sits down by his owner's feet as if to confirm my words.

"Yes, he is usually very obedient." Jacqueline pets Winston between his ears, which move in response to her praise. "It's my fault that I didn't insist he leave that ball at home. Thank you again. It's a pleasure to meet you, too. We are neighbours, aren't we?"

Of course, she has seen me passing by her cottage many times just like I've seen her in the village. "Yes, I live down the road to Clifflodge. I moved here last year."

Jacqueline nods. "I'm also new here. I haven't been very sociable…" Her voice trails off, and her gaze wanders for a brief moment focusing on the horizon. She quickly collects herself. "I'll take Winston's running away today as a sign that I should pay more attention." She smiles. I watch in fascination how the smile softens her chiselled features.

"It's a good idea to pay attention to the signs. My grandmother used to say that everything happens for a reason. It's just we usually don't care to try to understand what these reasons are." I hope I don't sound like a complete fool.

Jacqueline nods again. "Your grandmother was a wise woman. We aren't as wise as our grandparents. I think it's where most of our problems come from." It seems that she struggles to stay focused on the present moment. Her eyes wander off again, but she makes an effort and smiles again. "I would like to invite you over to tea to thank you for helping me with Winston today. If that's okay with you, of course."

"Of course!" I blurt out too quickly. "I mean, thank you, Jacqueline. It would be lovely."

"That's settled then." Her enigmatic smile touches her eyes this time. "I don't have my mobile on me now. Simply drop by the cottage anytime, and I'll give you my number."

We say our goodbyes.

I run all the way home, but it's not the fear of provoking Michael's cold wrath that makes my legs move faster. It is the hope that the day will come when I'll be able to call this beautiful island home.

CHAPTER 6

Everybody in Southbay loved Betty Burton.

I find it sad that often, such things only become evident at funerals.

The church during the service was packed. People filled all the pews and stood in the aisles. After the traditional sermon, the priest shared his personal memories about Betty since he'd known her for many years. His words about her being the light of the community touched my heart, and I cried.

I liked the fact that the crowd wasn't supposed to linger by the grave for too long. It is the most painful part of an already dispiriting event. The reality of my beloved grandmother being truly gone crushed me when I saw her face disappear under the closing coffin lid. I couldn't stop tears from falling and only vaguely remember what happened after that. People kept talking after the coffin was lowered into the grave. Still, all I wanted was to run away from the cemetery.

At Betty Burton's funeral, everyone present seemed to share my sentiments. The men from the undertaker's office efficiently lowered the casket into the ground, and the crowd dispersed without further delay.

Mrs Burton's cottage is even more packed than the church was earlier. The house is small, so only friends and family have been invited to the wake. All the same, it feels like a beehive with those who came to pay their last respects to the deceased crawling past each other in compact rooms and a tiny corridor.

I hide in the kitchen. Since everyone wants to talk about their grief and not replenish the snack platters, this is the calmest place in the house at the moment. It's not that I'm alone. People occupy every free space, including the kitchen's open doorway, a few steps from the counter where I stand distributing the cookies topped with egg salad on the platters.

Even so, it's a good enough hideout, for I know my husband is not going to pop in here.

During the funeral service in the church, Michael made sure he identified Betty's children. To talk to them about the property's legal issues is the sole reason he attended the funeral in the first place. In my turn, I made myself scarce before Michael found them. It is incredibly rude to attack people with such things at the time of grief, but I wouldn't be the one to risk sharing such thoughts with my husband.

"This might be the only chance I get to talk to them," Michael told me in the morning while we dressed. He was in a bad mood, annoyed by the necessity to go somewhere on Saturday. Since his business picked up last autumn, he preferred to spend weekends at home, moving as little as possible. "And I'm not going to chase after them all around the country or pay lawyers to do that. There is nothing to discuss here. I'll tell them to remove the wall. It's an easy thing to do. After that, they can build whatever they want to stockade themselves off. I don't care if they build a ten-foot-high fence, provided that it doesn't violate my property owner's rights."

I am sure Michael wouldn't talk to Betty's children in such a manner. His grumpy boldness is reserved solely for communication with me. Sometimes, I even admire my husband's ability to mask his true nature. He can be charming when he wants to.

"Here you are!" Suzie squeezes past two people who stand talking in the doorway. "Indeed, it's a strange world we now live in," she says, taking two platters I've just replenished with egg salad canapes. "The old are enjoying themselves while the young slave away in the kitchen."

I raise my eyebrows, unable to resist Suzie's dry sense of humour. "They say the Cinderella-type is back in fashion."

"Is that so?" Suzie fetches the plates. Her cheeks are blazing after mingling with too many people in a too compact space. "As I said, I'm completely out of date. Don't go anywhere. I'll be right back."

"No hurry. I'll be here all day."

Suzie chuckles and squeezes back into the living room chaos, holding two snack platters above her head.

I don't manage to fill a new platter with food when Suzie returns. "What madness out there." She puffs out her cheeks. "That's it. My duty is done. I'll stay here until someone else remembers there aren't hired caterers here and someone has to distribute the food if they want to keep on chewing. Why would anyone want to do that anyway? We are at a wake, for goodness' sake! It's not a party."

She plops down on a low stool by the oven. My guess is Betty used it to get things from the upper cupboards.

"How are you, Margo?" After her cheeks regain their normal colour, Suzie turns her attention to me. "Where is Michael? You've come together, right? I think I've seen him in the church."

Since we've started to see each other more often, Suzie treats me with even more warmth. I'd already noticed when I first met her that she was naturally more open than most locals. Now, I feel a genuine personal interest in me has been added to her usual friendliness.

"I have no idea." I shrug. I am not ready to share too much about my marriage. "He wanted to talk to Betty's children about some legal property issues."

"There they are." She stretches her neck, looking out of the window. "Either they are in a huge hurry, or your husband is so unbearable he can scare people away from the funeral of their own mother."

For a moment, I stare out of the kitchen window in shock. But the scene I see helps Suzie's dry sense of humour sink in.

Michael is standing outside, talking with a man and a woman in their forties. My husband leans against the low stone wall, clearly the subject of their conversation, and smiles.

I look longingly at the man whose last name I've adopted. These days, only seeing him in the company of other people, do I catch a glimpse of the Michael Birkett I married. Tiptoeing around the man, concentrated on doing everything in the way he prefers, I'd forgotten that a different version of him exists. Under the constant threat of being the cause of his displeasure, the feelings I had for him have faded. Love isn't a part of our marriage equation anymore. I'd still be over the moon if a quiet satisfaction on both sides had replaced it. Alas, it is my fear that it has not. I push away the thoughts about the real reasons behind it. It's not his game of silence that scares me. At the back of my mind, I feel that this is only the first step an abuser takes to probe the resilience of their victim.

Michael laughs, throwing his head back. I watch him as if he is a stranger. He isn't a good-looking man. He is tall with a lean, unremarkable face. His thin frame hasn't changed since he started to do manual labour last year. His dark hair is streaked with grey on the temples. It isn't obvious yet, but his hairline slowly starts to recede.

"I wonder why they came without their better halves." Suzie watches intently the interaction between my husband

and Betty's children. I'm glad it prevented her from noticing my faraway look.

"I thought it was Betty's daughter or a son with a spouse," I say to fill the silence.

"No." Suzie shakes her head, not averting her gaze from the trio. "It's…" she chews on her lips, raking her brain, "Maddy. Yes, Madeline. And Robert. I remember them as kids and then as lanky teenagers. Maddy never seemed to put a single pound, even at the time of a hormone rebellion. She always wore her skirt a bit too short, pushing it higher and tightening her belt. But she was such a good girl that no one, even teachers, ever scolded her for it."

I switch my attention from my husband and look closer at the woman he is talking to. In her early forties, Betty's daughter has kept her girlish figure. She is slim, almost waifish, with dark shoulder-length hair styled into a smart bob. The simple-cut black sleeveless dress shows off her elegant arms and slender ankles.

"Robert was a treasure too. Never took part in boys' brawls. Graduated school with the best marks," Suzie continued. "Both took off the moment they got accepted into the universities. Manchester or Liverpool." Suzie pauses, trying to remember. "Or maybe it was Birmingham. I don't remember. Didn't pay attention to it back then. Anyway, both of them left Southbay, and we never saw them again."

"Haven't they kept in touch with their parents?" I watch my husband follow Madeline and Robert to the gate. Robert looks tired, with his shoulders slumped in his black suit. Or maybe he simply feels hot in his mourning attire.

"I'm sure they have." Suzie stands up from the stool and stretches, pressing her hand to the small of her back. "But knowing Betty and Harry, it was enough for them to get a call or a letter from time to time to know their kids are alive. The two were totally wrapped up in each other."

I'm intrigued and want to know more, but my husband stalks into the kitchen. "Here you are," he says, rubbing his hands. "I've been looking for you for ages. I thought you'd snuck away without telling me. Let's go. There's nothing left to do here."

My cheeks turn crimson at his disrespect for Betty's memory. Still, I know better than to say anything. I mumble a goodbye to Suzie and leave, quickly following my husband.

We are home in a few minutes, our cottage the next one up the road from Betty's.

"Don't start cooking," Michael tells me, heading to the second floor. "George King invited us for a few drinks later. He'll pick us up on his way home."

I swallow a sigh. This is so typical of him, not to ask my opinion before accepting an invitation. However, in this particular case, I don't mind. The prospect of spending yet another dull Saturday in my husband's company – just cooking, cleaning, and not talking – isn't exciting.

George King and my husband went to school together. After graduation, Michael moved to London to continue studies, but George stayed in Dorset. He took over his father's limestone quarry firm and added the cottage building business line to it. He is rich, and my husband envies him. I am surprised he didn't decline the invitation. We haven't done any social visits for the last ten months.

I follow Michael upstairs. When I enter our bedroom, he is already taking off his black suit. "Bloody choker," he pulls off a tie. "Twenty-five years in this bloody uniform." He takes off his dark blue suit, a reminder left in his wardrobe of the times he had a posh job in London. "But enough is enough. No more parading in a monkey suit in front of those arrogant pricks who consider themselves kings of the world."

When we met two years ago in Riga, Michael held the position of Senior Business Advisor in a huge international corporation. Although he loves to repeat that the job was a rat race, I secretly believe it did him a lot of good. I wonder if my husband would have turned into a different person had he remained a high-flyer from the City. He says leaving the fast-paced corporate environment has made him free. Still, from what I see, that radical move has made him nervous and unhappy. After reading dozens of contemporary books focused on people's relationships and their work and family life patterns, I am not so naïve as to believe grumpiness wasn't a part of his character before. But I've come to think those sharpest edges were smoothed by the high salary, substantial bonuses, and the standing in society Michael's previous role brought him.

During our meetings before we got married, even the look in his grey eyes was different. He looked at me with warmth and treated everyone, including waiters in the restaurants he took me to, with a fatherly kindness. Benevolence and content emanated from him. Now I know that the things that drew me to him weren't his natural traits. They came in a package with the *king of the world* role. After he lost it, I found myself married to the man who Michael Birkett actually was underneath those layers of gloss. A man whom I wouldn't have married, or followed thousands of miles from everything I knew and loved, if I'd seen the truth of him before I'd said yes.

I stare at Michael as he's changing into his casual clothes. It is difficult to gather the courage to ask him even the simplest question. I've learned what usually triggers him into snapping at me. Still, I'm not sure I've discovered all the ways to displease him.

"Should I change into jeans then?" I finally ask, touching my dress. I stopped wearing dresses after Suzie asked me if it was my birthday when I came to her café dressed in a jeans skirt. The dress I put on for the funeral today is a simple black sheath midi affair that I bought on sale in Topshop in Eastpoole. It cost ten pounds but looks like it belongs on a catwalk. It's not too form-fitting, and I feel confident in it.

My husband gives me a fleeting glance. I haven't heard a compliment from him since our wedding. "No, leave it on. George is used to the women around him looking like

Moulin Rouge dancers."

I almost dash to the wardrobe, but then we hear the car horn. "Let's go." Michael leaves the room, having not cast a look my way.

******

George King's house in Clifflodge is impressive. It's not like other houses I've been to in Southbay. The owner of one of the oldest businesses on the island lives with all the style of a Hollywood star. The cottage itself is not large. I've already learned that even those who could pay extreme utility bills here were too practical to waste money if that could be avoided.

Even so, George King hasn't sacrificed his obvious urge to show off in full. An open-plan kitchen and living room form one airy space that merges into a terrace overlooking the channel. Fully open now, floor-to-ceiling windows transform the indoors, making it feel like you are outside.

Our host ushers us to the sofas placed right by the open windows. Before we sit down, a man stalks from under the stairs that lead to the second floor. He is in his late twenties with longish blond hair. Its greasy strands are pulled back into a ponytail. He is short and thin, but his wiry limbs betray strength. "Hey, boss, I fixed the toilet, but you'll still need a new one soon anyway."

"Sure, thanks, Marek." Barely looking his way, George waves his hand.

"See you tomorrow, boss." Marek nods at Michael and I and leaves.

"Polish guy. I hired a few of them once they allowed them to work here last year." Our host doesn't bother waiting until the man in question is out of the door. "This one even speaks bloody English." George roars with laughter. "Can you imagine? When I heard him speak, I hired him on the spot. Others don't speak a word."

The front door clicks.

"Sit, sit, I'll get us drinks." George saunters to the kitchen island. "What can I get you? Michael, you'll have whiskey with me, right? Do you drink whiskey, Marta?"

George King has already called me Marta a few times since Michael introduced us.

"Margo." I correct him automatically, knowing he'll probably not pay attention to it. "I'll have still water if you have it, please."

George turns his head slightly to look at me. "Sure," he rummages in the cupboard of the kitchen island full of bottles and glasses.

After we settle on the sofas by the open windows, I tune out the men's conversation. Instead, I look out, taking in the amazing view. The breeze is picking up, and soon it will become chilly. As for now, I enjoy the salty waft of the breeze touching my face.

I vaguely remember Michael boasting that our house is one of the few with unobscured views over the water. He went on lamenting the *stupid* rules restricting building closer to the cliff edge and prohibiting construction on ledges. I wonder how George King has managed to perch his house right on the rock terrace. All other houses in Clifflodge, while enjoying breathtaking views over the English Channel, sit on top of the ridge and a little further from the precipice.

"So, have you talked to the Burtons about the cottage? I'm thinking about buying it if I can get permission to build two more on that land plot. The ones I'm building by the business park are already sold out. You should strike an iron while it's hot. Have you heard that London and Paris are two favourites in the next Olympics race? If they choose London for the 2012 games, Eastpoole and Southbay Sailing Academy will be where they'll hold all sailing events. If it happens, real estate prices will rocket right up."

George King obviously doesn't need a reaction from the audience to continue talking. He is a loud man with a self-important presence about him. Thick around the stomach, he is only a little shorter than Michael, the difference muffled by his sturdy frame. He has a shock of wiry, greying hair and a booming voice.

"Don't hold your breath," Michael speaks calmer but with edginess in his voice. "They say Paris is the judges' favourite."

"Aye, the French always get the choice cuts." George takes a hearty gulp of his whiskey and brushes off sweat from his forehead with the back of his palm. "But it doesn't matter. The business is steady. People are elbowing their way through the crowd to live on our little island. Who could have thought it'd end up like this thirty years ago?" He chuckles smugly, the confidence that he indeed has been a prophet written all over his face.

"I've talked to the Burtons, and they agreed to settle the issue with the wall promptly. They want to sell and are interested in putting the property on the market as soon as possible."

I'm surprised Michael has changed the conversation back to its initial subject. I expected him to fume over his friend's bravado.

"Give me a shout when the matter is settled. I don't want to miss that offer." George keeps on sipping his whiskey. The bottle on the low table between the sofas is half empty, George having drunk most of it. "And what about you? Haven't you thought about selling your parents' shack?"

Michael laughs. I notice unnatural notes in his voice. "Even if I did, you wouldn't be able to afford it. Only if you sell your little flat in London."

George puts down his tumbler on the table. "We'll see about that." His small eyes glisten from the copious alcohol intake and the rush of a challenge. "If they announce the Olympic games will be held here in Southbay, I'll find a way to buy every single available land plot on the island. And every house that has at least some commercial value. I'll do it even if I have to pawn this house and my London flat."

Michael takes a small sip of his drink and sits back on the sofa. "I haven't thought about selling the house."

The chill runs down my spine. I can see it when my

husband is lying. Does he plan to move from Southbay? My strong reaction to the thought startles me.

I stand up, unable to sit still. "I think I'll go out on the terrace before it gets too chilly."

"Dad! Are you there?" George's son, Mark, bursts into the room with Finley Hammond in his wake. "Oh hey, here you are. Sorry, I didn't know you had guests."

"We are paying our last respects to the old Mrs Burton, son." George raises his glass and takes a generous sip. "You should have been at the funeral." He turns to Michael. "But, of course, youngsters nowadays always have more important things to do than what their parents tell them."

"Hi, Mr King." Finley steps forward with that assured, easy air about him. "I asked Mark to show me the quarries that aren't in use. You see, I'm thinking about making a project for my studies. I can get some cool footage at the quarries. Maybe the BBC will even use it for commercials about Dorset."

"That's good. That's good." George nods, concentration obviously already a burden for him. "See, son, you should follow Finley's example and do something with your life. Entering a college would be a good start."

I suspect that George King doesn't care a bit about whether his son gets a formal education or not. The way he delivers his lecture speaks volumes of his non-existent intentions to persuade his son to do anything.

"Yeah, Dad." Mark runs his hand over his blond hair. "You know I don't have time for this."

"Sure, sure." All Mark's father wants is to be left in peace, without the pressing need to teach his offspring life wisdom. "You already know about business much more than I did when I was your age. Have fun, kids."

"We're off upstairs. Have to check the footage we made. Bye, Mr Birkett," Mark nods at me, not addressing me directly, and turns to the stairs. "It was good to see you."

"You too, Mark." Michael raises his hand in a quick gesture of goodbye. My husband is even less interested in his friend's son than the guy's father.

"Mr Birkett," Finley says before following Mark, "my mom says hi. I think she plans to invite you for dinner."

"Thank you, Finley. Tell Melissa I said thanks. I'll give your father a call when I finish the big project in Bournemouth."

"Mrs Birkett." Finley turns to me. "It was nice to see you."

Is it an apology for the insulting words he said at our last meeting? The thought draws my attention from the piercing green eyes looking at me as if trying to say more than their owner can express in words. I don't have time to blush and embarrass myself as Finley leaves, right after the shout of 'Are you coming, Fin?' echoes from the second floor.

"I'll go get some air." I walk outside, grabbing my glass from the table.

The view is stunning. I can't believe I'm standing here, on the terrace of the house that belongs to someone I know, and around me is the scene from a James Bond movie.

The terrace doesn't sit directly on the verge of the cliff. More wide ledges cascade down the rocky slope to the water, where ferocious waves attack the stone. To the right, I can see the rugged shoreline. I think I can even discern the silhouettes of the Groveland Lighthouse and South Rock. To the left, a mountain wall rises tall, obscuring the view of the coast and protecting the house from the wind.

I move closer to the balustrade and lean on the smooth marble. The white railing encircles the porch. It tucks right into the rock to the left while making a full half-circle to the right, where it is attached to the house wall. George King is certainly eccentric in his choice of exterior design. The terrace resembles an Italian villa rather than an English home. Still, I have to admit that I like it.

The evening chill descends gradually. I don't want to go back inside to fetch my jacket. It'll be another hour until the temperature gets uncomfortable, so I remain on the terrace. Watching the relentless waves attacking the rocky shore is therapeutic. When I look at nature following its unchanging and, at the same time, versatile circles, I can detach myself from my problems. The waves will hit the rocks whether I am happy or not. The white foam will hiss and dissipate, giving way to the next wave.

"I can't believe Birkett married that Barbie bimbo."

The words sound from somewhere above. My first reaction is to hide inside the house, but I stay rooted in place.

"He isn't even a millionaire or anything," Mark continues, oblivious to being overheard. "But he brought her from Eastern Europe. They are all so desperate there that they'd marry a council street sweeper. I heard all the women are hookers there. Ready to fuck you if you show them money."

I press my hand to my mouth not to throw up.

"And I heard that Riga and Vilnius are very beautiful cities with old architecture." Finley doesn't sound like he wants to argue. He simply states the fact.

"Old Towns in those counties are tiny." Mark's voice is dismissive. "And there's nothing to see there if you stay for more than a day. Those places are full of ugly soviet blocks of flats and abandoned factories."

It's not that what Mark is saying is entirely untrue. Still, hearing such a harsh account of beautiful Riga hurts. I deeply regret not taking the time to explore the capital of my home country. I was always in a hurry, never thinking I was missing something I'd lose a chance to see or experience later.

"Have you seen the factory workers' terraces in Manchester? I bet they look as ugly."

I am grateful to Finley for standing up for something he doesn't have to care about one bit. It is my job to defend my home, and I'm ashamed to admit I haven't thought I'd ever have a need to do so. The truth is, all the locals I've met so far were too polite to criticise my home country to my face. I even suspect that they simply aren't interested enough to learn about some small ex-Soviet republic that joined the European Union five minutes ago. Only now do I realise that people here might have an opinion about Latvia. And chances are high that they project this unflattering and degrading opinion upon its people.

"There are many ugly places in the world." Mark roars with laughter. "It's good we don't live in one. Do you plan to move to London or come back here after you get your degree?"

It's news to me that Finley studies at the university. Last year, when we had dinner with the Hammonds, I snapped at him. I said he was lucky he could afford to waste his time fooling around and not bothering to get an education.

I don't hear Finley's answer. The pair seem to have moved back into the room from the balcony.

"Margo, we're leaving." Michael pokes his head outside. "Let's go."

"I have to use the bathroom," I say reluctantly. "I know it's a short drive, but…"

My husband rolls his eyes as if I'm the source of the most pressing inconvenience. "Be quick. George is ready to pass out any minute."

I walk into the living room to find our host slumped in his chair, the tumbler in his hand filled by one-third with amber liquid.

"Where is the bathroom?" I ask, knowing my question would provoke more eye-rolling in Michael.

"Go upstairs, sweetie." George indicates the direction with a wave of the glass of whiskey. He slurs, so I can barely make out the words. "Trust me, with three men in the house, you don't want to use the downstairs loo."

I stalk to the second floor, hoping Finley and Mark are too busy to notice me. After using the bathroom, I tiptoe back and almost make it to the top of the stairs when Finley walks out.

"Oh hey, Margo," he stops, then takes a few steps toward me.

"Hi, Finley." I'm not in the mood for small talk today. All I want is to be out of this house and, preferably, out of this weekend, so it's Monday already and I can be alone. "If I understand correctly, you decided to study after all. I hope you like it at the university."

Finley's face lights up. "I wanted to tell you when I see you. But the last time I met you, with Berlin... Look, I'm sorry. I didn't mean it that way. I mean, I didn't mean to offend you." He runs his hand through his cropped black hair in a manner that makes it clear he is used to wearing it long. "I'm not good at it, all right. I just wanted to say I'm sorry. I don't think it's bad to be a housewife or anything. And I'd like you to come to South Rock with me and Berlin. My mom asks about you. But I understand he is busy with his business and everything."

He looks so unlike his usual laid-back self that I can't hold a grudge against him any longer. He is also intimidatingly handsome, with his green eyes looking almost translucent on his deeply tanned face.

"What did you choose to study?" I smile, letting him know there aren't hard feelings on my side.

"Television Production." The enthusiasm on Finley's face shows before words are uttered that he's made the right choice. "It's so cool. I'll probably get a work placement at the BBC." He grins as a little boy allowed to sit at the wheel of his father's car for the first time.

"Where is your university? In London?"

"Bournemouth. The Television programme is great there."

I nod. "And it's convenient not to be too far from your family."

"Yeah. I didn't think I was going to miss Mom and Dad." He laughs to mask the embarrassment. "I was a fool not to pull up my marks before graduation. I had to do a foundation year. I could have used the fourth year for a full thirty-week placement, not for repeating the school programme. But I can't do anything about it now, so..." He shrugs, not looking upset.

I don't follow his explanation about marks and the foundation year since I'm unfamiliar with England's education systems. I simply nod and smile. "That sounds great. We can't always make the best choice. At least you are there now and you like your studies. That's the most important thing."

Mark walks out of his room. "You are still here?" He looks like he's just woken up. I wouldn't be surprised to learn he took a nap while his friend downloaded the footage into a computer.

"Already leaving." Finley doesn't give Mark a look, his gaze still fixed on me as if I'm about to utter the next prediction that will change his life. "How are you going to get back home?"

I hadn't thought about it. Now, that he's mentioned it, I start to panic. George drove us up to Clifflodge, but at the moment he is in a state unsuitable for driving. The walk down to Groveland wouldn't be a pleasant experience due to the absence of sidewalks. Besides, it wouldn't be safe to trot the winding, narrow road at night. It isn't an option to go along the coast either, since the Clifflodge's section of the coastal path is too rugged for leisurely strolls.

"I bet by now, Dad is totally wasted." Mark's remark isn't helpful.

"I'll take you home." Finley finally turns to Mark. "I'll take your car, okay? I'll bring it back in the morning before you need it."

"Sure." Mark waves his hand carelessly. "I'll sleep till noon anyway."

On the way home, the three of us keep silent. Even when Finley drops us off at the cottage, we don't say anything except formal goodbyes. I want to ask him if he's going back to the university on Monday and what time he's likely to take Berlin for a walk. Instead, I only thank him for the lift and follow Michael into the house.

CHAPTER 7

June 2005

Summer has brought the holiday spirit to Eastpoole. The main street is crowded with locals and tourists wandering in and out of shops and cafes. It has been hot since the beginning of June, with the heat reaching its peak way before noon.

I was putting off the visit to the mainland because of the blissful weather for as long as I had books to read. But yesterday I finished the last paperback I'd bought during my previous shopping visit. Besides, I would do with a new pair of shorts to add to the two I'd brought from home.

Today, it is too hot and crowded for me to enjoy the bustle of the bigger city. I like Eastpoole more during the off-season when it's quiet and sleepy. Now, all its numerous hotels and B&Bs are swarming with guests. It makes me feel like tourists are pushing me aside, determined to take it all from their vacation in Dorset. In truth, I don't mind. I understand their frenzy. They have a week or maybe two to bask in the cheerful resort atmosphere while I live here and don't have to hurry.

Happy with my finds both in the bookstore and at Matalan, I decide to walk down to the beach rather than head back home right away. It is Wednesday, and Michael will be home tomorrow. The next week is the last one he'll spend in Bournemouth, working on his big project. I haven't asked what his work plans are after that.

Having manoeuvred out of the shopping street, I walk past a statue of some king and turn right to cross the road to the beach. It still confuses me that the beach lies next to the road with busy traffic. A wide promenade doesn't do anything to mute the sounds of car engines. I prefer the coastal path in Southbay. It doesn't have an abundance of places to relax by the water. But I like the feeling of being alone with nature more than swimming with my back to the traffic and the row of hotel fronts.

I walk along the promenade, looking for a vacant bench. All benches are packed with people eating ice creams or fish and chips. The pebbled seashore line allocated to recreation is full of people as well. There is a narrow sandy stretch right by the water that doesn't run the whole length of the Eastpoole beach. Someone told me the sand gets brought here for the convenience of holidaymakers, for the natural big-pebbled coast wouldn't attract families with smaller children. That would reduce the city's profits from tourism.

I reach the end of the beach, where the rocks take over the pebbles. Stony slopes rise here, marking the border of the Eastpoole tourist area. A little further, the coastline curves, revealing yet another cove with a white hotel perched midway up the cliff.

Here, serving as a makeshift lawn for the holiday condominiums, is a beautiful garden with several paths and well-tended flower beds. Since all the benches on the lower level are occupied, I climb up the slope until I find a free one. A few metres away, on another bench, sits an elderly couple. They hold boxes with fish and chips.

They smile at me, and I smile back.

I take in the lush blossoming of flowers in the garden. I was here a month ago, and the vivid blooms have completely transformed the scene. The neatly manicured green now overflows with colours. Red, yellow, orange, and white flowers spill out of flower beds' limits as if trying to fill the whole slope and cover the paths.

Still, even though the blossoms are gorgeous, I can't resist sneaking a look at the elderly couple. Both into their seventies, white-haired and frail, with their hands touched by arthritis, they movingly take care of each other.

I watch as he gently removes a piece of food from the corner of her mouth, and she giggles like a girl on her first date. She wipes her lips with a handkerchief, giving him a coquettish glance from under her eyelashes. Then, she pours tea from the thermos into one of the paper cups and wraps it into a protective cardboard sleeve before giving the drink to him. His hands tremble slightly when he accepts the cup, but the deepest feeling of love in his eyes makes up for the physical weakness and gives him an aura of incredible strength.

Involuntarily, I sigh. I pull my eyes away from the adorable couple. I'd like nothing better than to sit down next to them and ask them to share their life and love stories. What the two of them have is something Michael and I will never have.

Only silly little girls believe that age doesn't matter. It matters a great deal, especially when it comes to relationships. When I am seventy, my husband will be dead. Who will take care of me when I need it most?

I take a glance at the couple again. They'd be almost helpless if they weren't together. As it is, they share their age challenges as if they are one whole. Where one has already lost the grip, the other one picks up. This way, the two continue living their lives as fully as it is possible.

It strikes me how much I've lost by marrying a man almost three decades my senior. After all the romantic notions about the endless power of love are put aside, I'm left with the realisation Michael and I don't have an age gap between us. I am twenty-two, and my husband is forty-eight. It is an abyss rather than a mere gap.

The sun is too generous, and after a while, I feel like I'm being baked under its afternoon rays. I set out back to the main street. I still need to pop into Tesco to buy my favourite strawberry cheesecake before catching a bus to Southbay. I also have to buy something to bring Jacqueline Fisher. We met on the coastal path last week, and she reminded me about her invitation to have tea together sometime.

I was indecisive before, but now I've made up my mind to buy Jacqueline some flowers. She doesn't look like someone who indulges in cheesecakes. Bringing flowers for the host is an acceptable gesture of appreciation for their time and effort.

Michael will be home tomorrow, but I refuse to get into a gloomy mood just yet. I'm looking forward to getting to know the mysterious lady of the Lighthouse Keeper's Cottage a little better. And tomorrow is the choir's rehearsal.

My husband isn't the only one with a right to build his life in a way that suits his preferences.

******

I take a short walk along the coastal path to the Groveland Lighthouse. In my hands, I hold a pot with pink sweet peas wrapped in floral-patterned paper. The fragrant, bi-coloured flowers remind me of my childhood. My grandmother loved sweet peas and always shook her head disapprovingly when my friends complained about its strong smell causing them a headache. "This is a gift from nature we are supposed to receive with gratitude," she used to say. "If your head aches from flowers, the most natural thing in the world, there is something wrong with you, not with the plants."

With its whitewashed walls and fuchsia and magenta phlox in full blossom under its windows, the Lighthouse

Keeper's Cottage looks like a movie set. I knock at the door, and Jacqueline opens it instantly as if she's been waiting for me.

"Margo, I'm so glad you could make it." Jacqueline smiles. Although her smile doesn't reach her eyes, I feel warmth behind it.

"Thank you for the invitation. These are for you." I give her the flowers. She takes the pot with sweet peas and immediately puts her head down to inhale their scent. "I hope you aren't allergic to them," I add hastily.

She smiles again. "What nonsense. If I were allergic to such a beauty, I'd take pills only to be able to enjoy them." She places the pot on a table that's standing under the window and readjusts the wrapping paper so it is folded back evenly. "But thank you for your concern. I appreciate it."

She leads me through the corridor and the living room to the conservatory. I've never seen one with one wall that can be removed to transform the space into a kind of terrace. Tall plants in massive pots stand closer to the main building wall, obviously intended to make opening and closing of the movable glass wall easier. Rattan chairs with cream cushions have a designer furniture look, and there is even a rattan sofa with a neatly folded ivory throw blanket in the corner.

"Please, take a seat." Jacqueline shows at the chairs. "I hope this new roof will protect us from the sun."

I look up. I've heard from many people that conservatories turn into ovens in summer. One of the reasons Michael has chosen a conservatory renovation specialisation for his construction business is that it is in high demand. I vaguely remember his words about roof replacement being one of the most popular things people ordered.

"If it's the solar control glass, then we'll be fine." I smile at my childish willingness to impress my host.

"Yes, builders said it offers the best protection from the

sun. Let's hope it's true."

I sit in the chair facing the South Rock. "I could look at it all day." I nod at the majestic formation, now almost eggshell coloured under the whitening June afternoon sun.

"Yes, it's beautiful here." Jacqueline barely glances at the stunning landscape. "I'll bring us tea and join you in a moment."

She returns with a silver tray laden with a set of bone china and small strawberry pavlovas.

"So, Margo." Jacqueline pours me a cup of camomile tea. The aroma is rich, and again, childhood memories hit me. "How come you have chosen Southbay as a place to live?"

Her choice of words startles me at first. I wouldn't think about the place where I lived or live from such a perspective. How could I if someone else always chose it for me? Then I realise that this is what it must be like for her. Despite her veiled vulnerability, Jacqueline looks like someone who doesn't let anyone make choices in her place. "I got married," I reply after a moment of hesitation. "And my husband is from here. Why have you moved here? I guess it's a huge contrast with London?"

She raises her eyebrows. They are immaculate, and I decide they are a part of what makes her look classy. "It's not a secret that I've moved here from London, is it?"

I blush but shrug. "It's a small community. Everyone knows everything about everyone."

"You are right. It is inevitable on the island this small." She pours herself more tea and sips it slowly. "Yes, I moved here from London, that's true. But I'm a country girl. I grew up in Surrey, in Virginia Water." She pauses and looks at me. I know nothing about Surrey except that only the wealthiest people live there. Jacqueline continues: "I've never truly grown to appreciate the hectic London life. I loved my job and enjoyed everything the capital had to offer. But it never made my heart beat faster. Except when I was late for a meeting and had to run up the stairs because the lift got stuck." She smiles, and I smile back. "And even though life in London has never been my dream, I don't think I'd have ever gathered enough courage to leave it. Or maybe it's not about courage but inertia. Anyway, life sometimes makes decisions for us we wouldn't have made ourselves."

Jacqueline sips her tea. I like the way she doesn't expect anything from the person she speaks to. I've noticed that people tend to label you depending on whether the views you express coincide with their own.

"Why didn't you return to your hometown when you had to move from London?" I ask because I'm genuinely interested, but also because I want her to continue talking.

She puts down the cup and sits back in her chair. Her gaze wanders to the cliffs and the water. She is a beautiful woman. Her beauty is the kind that pulls you in gradually. First, you notice the harmony of her features, then the smoothness of her skin. There is nothing about her that screams 'I'm hot!'. She has an air of royal subtlety about her.

She turns back to me. "I didn't want to be anywhere familiar. I needed a place I had no memories of. No emotional connection with."

"And no people who know you?"

The warmth creeps into her impassive eyes. My heart leaps as if this is the moment I've been waiting for. "You are a very perceptive young woman, Margo. I am sure you've been told that many times. Yes, I didn't want to be close to my family and friends. It wouldn't be the retreat I was seeking if I were surrounded by familiar faces." She pours me more tea, and a tiny yellow disc plops out of the teapot's gooseneck into my cup. "Sorry," she gives me a glass with teaspoons. "You can fish it out. So, your husband is born and bred here in Southbay. I admire his determination not to leave the island for the big city temptations."

"Oh, Michael left Southbay after he finished school. He only recently returned here." I take a bigger-than-necessary gulp of tea. "He worked in London for almost thirty years."

Jacqueline doesn't open her eyes wide or let an exclamation of surprise slip. Only the corners of her mouth twitch a little as she watches me, waiting for me to go on.

"After the divorce, he didn't want to stay in Essex. Besides, they sold their house there."

Jacqueline nods. "I can relate to that."

"Michael was thinking about a career change for a while. After college, he worked for big companies, and it can be stressful. He was a Business Advisor and said he felt it was time for him to use what he knew to start his own business." I remember my husband sharing his plans about being his own master and not having to comply with endless rules. Back then, I thought there was logic in his words. "He was very successful at his job. I think it's difficult for anyone to quit if everything is going well. It's different when you've tried and haven't achieved anything. When you have, it's hard to throw it all away. Maybe the divorce was, as you say, a decision life has made for him."

"What does he do for a living now? I suppose he has followed his vision and started a firm?" Jacqueline asks with genuine interest.

"Yes, Michael runs a conservatory renovation company. He started last year, so the business is still small. But he gets more clients now. He's now working on a really big project in Bournemouth. He hopes the client will recommend him to others." The word *vision* has stirred me. I can't shake off the uneasy feeling that I have no idea what my husband thinks about following his dream, or I should probably call it an idea. Michael isn't a dreamer. I'm too afraid to do or say something that would trigger his contempt and lead to the game of silence, so we never talk anymore. We exchange the necessary phrases but nothing more.

Why am I so terrified by him not talking to me? This isn't the first time I have asked myself this question. I wonder if I subconsciously choose not to deal with the answer. If I admit that I'm afraid of my husband hitting me, it will say as much about him as about me.

"Bournemouth?" Jacqueline raises her immaculate eyebrows. "It's a long drive to make every day."

"He stays at the project site and comes home on Thursdays."

"I see." She moves in the chair, changing her pose. Dressed in light blue jeans and a simple white shirt, she looks like a celebrity who is being photographed in her home. Still, I know there is a significant difference. Celebrities usually put huge effort into making everything about them look effortless, while for Jacqueline, it comes naturally.

I wait for the question if I don't feel lonely without Michael, but it doesn't follow. "Please, taste my pavlovas," Jacqueline says instead. "I've already had three while I cooked them."

I obediently take a white cake crowned with strawberries and put it in my mouth. The meringue melts, leaving slightly sour berries in a cocoon of sweetness. I close my eyes. "So delicious."

"Please, take more. I love them so much that I sometimes forget others can be absolutely indifferent to them. I'll put the kettle on." She stands and stretches. "Age doesn't add agility to our bodies, but it definitely stimulates the appreciation of things like tea."

"I've always loved tea."

She smiles and leaves for the kitchen. I wonder how old she is. I'd be surprised if she were older than forty, although she looks even younger.

I cast a glance around the modern conservatory. I was so absorbed by Jacqueline that I hadn't taken a proper look.

Winston trots in from outside. Upon seeing me, he begins to wag his tail enthusiastically.

"Winston, hello, boy! Come here!" I'm glad to see Jacqueline's golden retriever.

Winston doesn't need to be asked twice. He comes over to me and puts his head on my knees. "You are so amazing.

Such a good boy." I stroke him as he shifts from one leg to another, trembling with excitement. His kind eyes seem to search for approval. I'm mesmerised by the deep intelligence shining from their warm brown depth.

"Be careful with this heartbreaker. He'll be sitting on your lap before you know it." Jacqueline returns with a freshly filled teapot.

"I don't mind." I can't stop stroking the silky cream fur. "I'd love to have a dog. They are incredible creatures."

"They are, aren't they?" Jacqueline pours us both tea and sits down in her chair. "There is enough space for them to run around here. They can enjoy life in the countryside. I didn't have a dog in London. Of course, there are parks there, but I was busy all day."

"I understand." I think about my life in the five-story block house back in Latvia. I always felt uneasy watching our neighbours walking their massive Rottweilers, German shepherds, and even huge St. Bernards in the morning before work. It bothered me that these dogs were held in small flats instead of being treated to outdoor space adequate for their physiques.

"I grew up in a house full of dogs, so it was the first thing I did when I moved to the country. You should think about taking a dog from the shelter."

I sigh. "I'd love to. I think dogs taken from shelters are the most loyal and loving."

Jacqueline nods. "Yes, you are right. Sometimes they are deeply traumatised by their owners abandoning them. But if they feel they are loved again, they become your best friends."

Michael's face seething with contempt prevents me from falling into fantasies about saving a beautiful dog from a shelter. I imagine it so vividly that I involuntarily shudder.

"It is a rather complicated process." As if feeling my distress, Jacqueline closes the subject. "It's almost like adopting a child. Everyone in the family should take an informed decision to go through this before getting themselves into it."

Her intuitiveness embarrasses me. Although I'd love to talk openly to someone about Michael and how I feel in our marriage, I'm not ready to open up yet. I don't have any solutions to the situation, and simply talking it through wouldn't make me feel any better.

We spend a few more hours discussing less complicated things, drinking camomile tea, and watching Winston's antics. On my way home, I feel the hope rising that when I'm ready to talk and ask for advice, I seem to have found someone I can trust.

CHAPTER 8

I lie on a warm, flat stone, basking in the sun. Today is a glorious summer day.

As June continues to pamper the Isle of Southbay with more July-like weather, I use every opportunity to enjoy it. Michael doesn't care about spending time outside or visiting neighbours, so I do both when he is away. Sometimes, I even forget that we are married and treat him like someone I have an obligation to take care of but nothing more. It is easy to do since we don't have sex.

My husband hasn't touched me for months.

I can't say for sure, but I think the last time we had sex was last summer, after my mother had stayed with us a week. I remember how Michael and I giggled, snuggling between the sheets. "Finally, we don't have to worry about this old bed groaning too loudly," he joked, and I laughed, rolling on top of him.

The next day, he got his first order for conservatory renovation in Lyme Regis. I looked up the town online and was excited it was a place with history, also featured in one of Jane Austen's novels. My enthusiasm – both for seeing more of Dorset and reading Austen's books – faded after Michael told me he wouldn't be taking me to any renovation sites with him.

I turn onto my stomach and press my forehead to my folded hands.

I've only recently discovered these flat stone beds hidden under the cliffs. Before that, when I needed to rest during my walks, I spread my blanket on grassy ledges to stay out of the way of coastal path hikers, dog walkers, and horse riders. One day, in search of a place closer to the water, I climbed down a rather steep slope and found a secluded spot. From here, you could walk down the shore all the way to the famous Pearl Herring Beach, a miles-long shingle strip connecting Southbay to the mainland. The most expensive properties in the village of Fortunescove boast a spectacular view over Pearl Herring Beach, stretching along the rugged Dorset coast. It is a unique natural formation that looks as if it was made by the hands of some almighty creatures.

The sun is hot on my skin. I'm not wearing a bikini but denim shorts and a spaghetti-strap tank top. I'm still not sure about the sunbathing culture here on the island. Back home, I wouldn't hesitate to strip down to a bikini, even in a green area in a remote part of a city park. And I definitely wouldn't question the propriety of doing so on the seaside. Here, it is different. There are so many things I was unfamiliar with. Although locals are friendly, if not smiling a thirty-two-teeth smile all the time, they do display a degree of shock whenever I make a blunder. It makes me feel uncomfortable, so I do everything to avoid such situations.

The heat makes my head swim. It's a pleasant sensation. I'm between consciousness and sleep, with visions rather than dreams floating lazily through my head. The blanket I've thrown on the stone bed protects me from its rough surface but doesn't prevent the warmth from seeping through the thin fabric.

Then I see Finley Hammond. He walks toward me across the vast green field dotted with flowers. The emerald grass canvas is interspersed with red, white, yellow, and purple blooms. The breeze makes the vegetation move in unison, making the field look like a multicoloured sea.

Finley comes nearer, and I see a smile on his tanned face. He runs a hand through his now short hair. He extends a hand, and I take it. His skin is so warm and soft that I can't resist caressing his palm in circular motions. Finley, in turn, cups my cheek and brushes his fingers over it. His face is close to mine, and I can feel his breath. I fling my arms round his neck. The skin there is hot and silky. My lips part as if inviting him, and his mouth is on mine.

I slowly open my eyes, turn on my back, and sit up. The waves nudge the shore, making the shingle clink gently. The water sparkles under the afternoon sun. Rainbow circles float in front of my eyes, and I blink to restore my vision. The heat seems to pierce through my skin.

Out of the corner of my eye, I see a dark figure raising from the water. Startled, with my vision still blurred and my head spinning, I rub my eyes.

Pulling down his full-body wetsuit, the real Finley Hammond is walking out of the water.

With the upper part of the wetsuit stripped from his torso, he looks like a movie star on a film set. He moves slowly, and I watch him advance to the shore, completely mesmerised. He is lean and muscular, more in a natural way, although it is clear that he is familiar with a gym routine or two. He lifts his hands to run them through his wet hair, and toned biceps roll under his tanned skin.

I am grateful to the slippery and rocky sea bottom for giving me time to collect myself. When Finley notices me, I'm already on my feet with my blanket crumpled in my hands. I'll fold it later, after I am far enough from Finley Hammond to be safe from his magnetic green eyes.

Climbing the slope back to the coastal path is a

challenge. I'm only halfway up when I have to stop to catch my breath. I don't look back, afraid that Finley might be following me. For all I know, if I see his handsome face and athletic figure, I will run to him rather than from him, unable to think about anything else than to find myself in his arms.

I take a few hurried breaths and continue my way up the slope. I'd give anything for something to push my reluctant body so that it starts moving faster.

I don't stop when I reach the coastal path. Instead, I almost run along the wide, flat segment until I come to the steps that lead up and around the rock protruding over the road. Here, I halt and, putting my hands on my legs, lower my head and bend slightly forward. When my equilibrium is more or less restored, I carefully walk up the stone stairs. This is the only truly dangerous place on the whole coastal path in Southbay. No matter how flustered I am, my head remains clear. I'm glad that my emotions haven't gotten full control over me.

I almost run all the way to the cottage, for once completely oblivious to the charms of the World Heritage site.

At home, I rush upstairs and take a long, cold shower. I stand under the weak jets until it is no longer comfortable. Shivering, I get out of the cubicle and rub myself with a towel until my skin turns red in places.

Switching on the kettle, I stand by the kitchen window and stare at the blue and green stripes of grass and water, a beautiful scenery only a blur of colours for my troubled eyes.

Under no circumstances can I be unfaithful to my husband. I would never be able to live with myself if I cheated on him. And it has nothing to do with my fear of him turning violent.

Still, it's not this thought that makes my eyes sting. It's the realisation of what can never be because of it.

I want to feel loved. I want to seek and find shelter in loving arms. And this can never happen if I remain married to Michael. With him – I feel it in my heart more than I could ever explain it with logic – I will never experience the feeling of being treasured.

Tears spill, and I brush them angrily away.

"What a sentimental fool!" I say aloud into the empty house. "Life isn't a walk in the park," I repeat the phrase that I heard from Suzie.

The kettle clicks off. I take a deep breath before pouring boiling water.

I feel better after a cup of hot Earl Grey.

Having put on clean denim shorts and a short-sleeved shirt, I head outside. I am determined not to think about sentimental things. I know that no good will come out of these futile deliberations. I am alone most of the time, and one's mind can play nasty tricks if you let it wander freely.

******

Maureen Easton is the woman everyone declares to be the kindest soul in the community, at the same time, not daring to cross paths with.

With the look of motherly concern on her ruddy-cheeked face, the owner of the most thriving bed and breakfast on the Isle of Southbay is probably the keeper of all islanders' secrets. And this is what makes her a force to be reckoned with.

South Rock B&B is ideally located between Groveland and Fortunescove, just before the rows of terraced houses start cascading down the latter's steep slope. Behind it, stand the Southbay Museum and a monument to those lost at sea. Maureen Easton's bed and breakfast is famous among those who prefer to spend their vacation locally. You don't need to take a bus to get to the Pearl Herring Beach. You can simply walk there, take in as much fresh air and dramatic views as you can bear, and then enjoy a meal in one of the many cafes and pubs.

I walk up the path to the South Rock B&B. The trademark of Southbay tourism – the view over the Dorset coast – is awe-inspiring here. Added to the regular cliffs, waves, grass-covered slopes, and menacing rocky ledges, the golden stretch of Pearl Herring Beach makes the scenery not simply stunning but also unique. You'll see the rugged coastline for miles and miles in Dorset and Devon, continuing further in Cornwall and up the English shore. There'll be coves, and tiny pebbled beaches tucked under the vertical rocky walls, even patches of sand the inhabitants of local villages will tell you about with a special pride. Still, nowhere along the almost hundred miles long Jurassic Coast can you see another shingle beach running along the coast detached from the mainland by water.

I stop at the side of the neat cottage with whitewashed walls to admire the view for a moment.

Maureen sees me through the window and waves at me.

"*Margarita*, you look so lovely today," she says when I enter the hall. It is narrow, with the stairs starting a few steps from the front door and a corridor leading to the dining area for guests and the kitchen.

"Thank you, Mrs Easton." I smile. I can't get rid of the feeling that when locals pronounce my full name and don't get it quite right, they expect praise for their efforts. Whereas when I mispronounce something, it's often met with condescending stares. "It is such a nice day today. I think it does something to the skin colour."

Maureen smiles back. "Indeed. What can I do for you today?"

"My mom comes over for a visit next week. I'd like to take her for a traditional English breakfast again. She says last year she enjoyed herself here at your bed and breakfast more than at any other place we took her."

Maureen's grey eyes twinkle with pleasure. "Oh, that is so incredibly kind of her. I do love my little place dearly and do my best to provide my guests with the best possible experience."

"Your place is special, Mrs Easton," I assure her. "Anyone who comes here immediately falls in love with it."

"Thank you, *Margarita*." Maureen's rosy cheeks become

a shade darker. "Let me have a look at my booking schedule. Can I offer you tea or coffee?"

She leads me to the dining room. Located at the back of the house, it boasts huge windows and an additional space from what used to be a traditional conservatory. South Rock B&B's guests enjoy not only Maureen's delicious cooking but also the stunning views over Pearl Herring Beach.

Maureen shows me the table by the window. "Please, have a seat. I'll be right back with your coffee and my notebook."

I look out of the window, and the feeling of rapture washes over me. I am in love with this island. Southbay is the most beautiful place I have seen in my whole life. It's true that I haven't been to many places, and still, I doubt anyone would argue that this quaint corner of Dorset is worth the deepest admiration.

"Right, tell me what day you have in mind, and I'll see what I can offer." Maureen places the tray with coffee things on the table. The delicate china cup is pure white with sculptured birds on its sides. The glass pitcher and the sugar bowl are similarly elegant.

"Any day from Monday to Thursday is good for us." I know I'm giving food for thought and gossip to one of the best information keepers in Southbay. I have no doubt that Maureen won't miss the chance to drop something into her conversation with other local ladies, perhaps along the lines of: *Our Margarita tiptoes around her husband, afraid to plan even a breakfast with her mother when he is at home.*

Mrs Easton thumbs through the pages of her cute notebook with roses on the cover. "Let me see…How about Wednesday? Your mother will have gotten tired of cheese on toast by then."

I don't react to what isn't, after all, an insult. Maureen Easton sincerely believes that *ordinary* people never cook a proper breakfast and grab what they can find on the go. Besides, nothing good would come out of sharing the details about my cooking skills with the person known as the best cook on the island. I do make a fluffy omelette that stays fluffy after being served. And this is only one of the things declared to be almost impossible that I am really good at.

"Wednesday is perfect. Thank you. I know it's a short notice for your business." I take a sip of my coffee.

"So," Maureen makes a note, "will it be a full English breakfast for two then?"

I smile sweetly. *Yes, my husband doesn't give a damn about the English breakfast. He even calls it a trap for tourists.* "Yes, that's right. Michael will be away until Thursday." Michael told me his mother never cooked English breakfast. In his view, this is the best argument against the traditional morning meal.

"All right. Wonderful." Maureen scribbles something in her notebook and puts it away. "I'll leave one of the tables by the windows available for you and your mother."

"Thank you so much. I want Mom to have a great vacation."

"Does she still work?"

I wonder if Maureen remembers how my mother looks. She should since she saw her last year, after all. Mom is forty-five, and she doesn't look her age. "Yes, she is a dressmaker. She sews wedding dresses."

Maureen raises her eyebrows. "It is a hard work. Doesn't she want to quit so she could move closer to you?"

I shake my head. It's impossible to imagine my mother idle for longer than a couple of weeks. Always tired, with needle marks all over her fingers and palms, her usual reserve shows cracks only when she talks about a dress she is working on. "No, she loves her job too much."

"It's a shame. She could sell her house and buy Betty's cottage. There might not be a chance like this again."

I smile and don't voice my thoughts again. It isn't wise to try to explain the differences between real estate markets in England and the small Latvian town I am from. "By the way, is there any news about the investigation?" I change the subject. There is no need to say which investigation I am asking about.

"Have you heard that the police talked to Betty's doctor?" Maureen's eyes gleam. I've chosen the right topic to divert her interest from my mother and her dwelling arrangements.

"No." I open my eyes wide to demonstrate an adequately strong reaction to Maureen's knowledge. "I haven't spoken to anyone really since the last choir rehearsal."

"Well, the police talked to Betty's doctor." The South Rock B&B's owner puffs her cheeks, energised by the feeling of self-importance. "Charles Huxley had been her family's doctor before all the NHS reforms started. And even after that, Betty still preferred to consult with him on more serious issues. It was expensive, of course, a physician with a private practice and all, but Arthur – Betty's husband – didn't care about expenses when his dearly beloved wife was concerned."

It is the second time that I've heard the reference to the Burtons' devotion to each other. I wonder if both Suzie, who mentioned the couple's pragmatic attitude toward their children, and now Maureen Easton, with her remark about Mr Burton's generosity, are admiring or jealous. Suzie is single. As far as I know, she and her husband divorced a long time ago. And everyone in Southbay calls the South Rock B&B's owner's spouse Mr Maureen Easton.

"So, Charles knew her health better than those youngsters from NHS – a new one every time you come over for a check-up," Maureen continues. "And he told the police that despite her age, Betty had excellent health." She pauses for a dramatic effect.

I almost giggle, so comical is she, with that knowing look on her plump face and her rosy cheeks. "Does that mean that the person who came to her cottage that day actually *killed* her?" I can't refrain from mimicking Maureen's conspiratorial tone.

"Well, the police didn't put it like this exactly." I feel guilty for treating the serious matter easily when I see Maureen's cheeks turn crimson. "They said it might indicate an accidental killing. They believe that whoever visited Betty on the day of her death didn't have an intention to kill her."

"But it's possible that she wouldn't have died if that person hadn't shown up. It is still punishable, right?"

Maureen nods, looking genuinely sad. "Yes, that's why they're continuing the investigation. And I sincerely hope they will find that person. Betty could have been still among us if he or she hadn't come and upset her. Poor soul." She pulls out a handkerchief – a real one, trimmed with lace – and dabs at the corners of her eyes. "Betty was a wonderful woman. Wonderful."

I can't get rid of the suspicion that for Maureen, if not for a good portion of the island's female population, Betty Burton became even more wonderful after her devoted husband had died.

"I didn't know her for long, but I miss her too." Tears start swelling in my eyes. Both from embarrassment and grief. I hadn't realised I could be so cynical. *Maybe it's the effect of living among cynical old matrons.* The thought only makes me feel more guilty. It is not the Southbay ladies' fault that I hadn't properly thought through the idea of marrying Michael and relocating to a small place in Dorset.

"She was wonderful," Maureen repeats, fumbling with her notebook's tie-string. She casts a glance at the scenery outside the window. "Anyway," she puts the notebook on the table, "life goes on. I'm sure the police will find that person, and they will receive a suitable punishment for what they did. Voluntarily or not. I am looking forward to seeing your mother again. I hope she will have a pleasant stay in Southbay." She rose. "Please, don't be in a hurry. Do you want more coffee? Or a scone? I have fresh ones in the kitchen."

"No, no, thank you. You are very kind." I rise too. "I have to run back home. So many things to do before Mom's visit."

"Of course. You are a very good daughter, *Margarita*. I'm sure your mother is very proud of you."

BROKEN CHANCES

My face burns when I walk out of the cosy B&B with the best views on the Isle of Southbay.

I'm turning into a middle-aged woman, I think, *and it's no wonder, since I have to live the life of one.*

CHAPTER 9

I run down the corridor of the Groveland Business Park with a bag of blueberry muffins, not yet late for meeting my husband with everything immaculately prepared for his arrival. As usual, I stayed to talk to Suzie after the choir's rehearsal. I almost bump into the woman from Latvia I met leaving Mr Billings's office last month.

"I'm so sorry," I blurt out in English. "Let me help you."

The woman is carrying an office plastic box filled with papers. "Oh, I'm fine. But thanks a lot for offering." She smiles her enchanting smile that beckons me to follow her. She has a deep, strong voice without a girly shrill.

"You are from Latvia, right?" I switch to my native language, hoping I haven't made a mistake.

"Yes, actually I am." The woman smiles again. I haven't spent five minutes with her, but I seem to know her smile is an integral part of her. "Are you too? Isn't it amazing to meet someone from home here? Who could have thought? I am Laura. Nice to meet you." She speaks in the confident manner of a professional who is used to talking to strangers.

"Do you rent an office here, in the business park?" I can't refrain from asking what I want to be true. "Raymond Billings, my... well, my husband's accountant told me."

"Yes," she shifts the box under another arm. "We've just opened a small recruitment office here, a place of business, really. It's a branch of a Latvian company. By the way, Mr Billings is our accountant too."

I am torn between helping her with that box so I could talk to her a bit more and running home to spare myself from Michael's cold wrath.

"Are you staying here in Southbay?" My eyes involuntarily dart down the road as if I could see Michael's trailer pulling at the cottage from here.

"Yes. We've rented a flat right here in the business park. They have converted one of the buildings into studio flats. It's very convenient. When I'm here, I'll be staying there."

"Don't you plan to live in England permanently?" The thought that someone who came here from home could do that hasn't even occurred to me.

"No. I'll be travelling back and forth until the office is all set." Laura shifts the box again, and I feel obliged to let her go.

"Oh, I'm Margo, Margarita." I catch myself on not having introduced myself. "Maybe when you are all settled, we could have a coffee in the local café somewhere?"

"Of course. It's a great idea. I'd give you my card, but it's dug somewhere too deep in there." She takes the box in both hands. "I can leave it with Mr Billings next week – I don't think he is at the office on Fridays – and you'll pick it up when you have time."

"Fantastic!" I know I'm overly enthusiastic, but I can't help it. "I'll call or text you next week then."

"Perfect." Laura smiles. "I don't plan to go home before July." She tries to get a grasp of the door handle holding the box.

"Let me help you." I hasten to open the door. "You'll

like it here. The coastal path is beautiful."

"Thanks." She walks in while I hold the door. "See you next week."

She smiles at me as if she isn't tired of the box's edges sticking into her body.

I run all the way home, not caring about the muffins dangling in the bag. I make it just in time to heat up the shepherd's pie so that Michael is satisfied with his wife's performance.

******

My mother arrives on Sunday, and for a week, I forget about everything except making her visit pleasant and memorable.

The three of us spend a nice enough Sunday with a traditional roast and chocolate muffins Suzie baked especially for my mom's welcome dinner. I feel bad I didn't gather the courage to ask Michael to drive to Heathrow to meet her. Still, Mom made it by train from the airport to the Waterloo station and, from there, to Eastpoole. My husband was gracious enough to drive to the Eastpoole train station to take his mother-in-law to our island.

I can hardly wait until Michael leaves for Bournemouth, thanking providence that he got another assignment there. When he does, I'm able to relax.

On Monday, I take Mom around Southbay. I wasn't familiar enough with the island when she was here last year to show her its attractions. Now, I know every path, hidden cove, and the spots on the cliffs with the best view. I feel excited I can show all of it to Mom.

After a three-hour walk, we sit by the window in Groveland Bakery, sipping tea. Mom insists on treating me to lunch so I don't have to start cooking right away after we return to the cottage. I would have done it with pleasure; besides, I feel energised from her being here. Even so, it feels incredibly nice to know you are loved.

Suzie brings us plates with sausages, bacon, mashed potatoes, and green peas, and we tuck in.

"Fresh air makes everything tasty," Mom says, rolling a strip of bacon on her fork like spaghetti.

"You don't like the food?"

"I do. As I said, it is tasty. It's just I haven't eaten sausages with mashed potatoes in years. All these modern diets make us forget about plain food." Mom puts bacon into her mouth and chews with pleasure. "Very tasty. I've never cooked bacon in my life. My mother never did, so I guess it's a matter of traditions."

"I got used to local food," I say, taking a sip of tea. "At first, everything seemed so strange. Either too fried or salty or sweet. But I've found the things I like. We'll have a strawberry cheesecake for dessert one day. It's so delicious."

"It is a matter of traditions," Mom repeats. "If you were used to this food from childhood, you wouldn't find it strange. British people probably find many of our dishes uneatable."

An image of Michael tasting dressed herring – 'herring in a fur coat' as we call it in Latvia – in a restaurant in Riga two years ago pops into my mind, and I giggle. "Yes. And you know, our dishes are harder to get used to if you haven't eaten them since you were a child."

My mother smiles, the corners of her lips lifting up slightly.

Mom isn't a demonstrative person. She wasn't overly emotional even when I was little. I don't remember her cooing over me or calling me 'princess' or 'sunshine' like other mothers did. Still, I always knew I was the centre of her life. Not in a suffocating way that forces an uneasy feeling of obligation for the parents' sacrifice on the children. Without saying it, my mother made me feel she loved me. She is the wall I can lean on whenever I step on a shaky foundation.

Before returning home, I thank Suzie and pass on Mom's words about the exceptionally tasty lunch. "It's a pity Mom doesn't speak English," I feel I have to say it, "otherwise, she'd thank you herself." The women exchange smiles, and I feel even more acute regret about Mom's language skills' deficiency. They would have gotten along so well.

"I'm glad I could feed you, girls." Suzie smiles and nods at Mom. "Enjoy your time together. You need it, love."

"That woman, the café's owner, she likes you," Mom tells me while we trudge from the business park to the coastal path. "I'm glad. There is someone here who can look after you."

I'm looking after myself just fine. I refrain from saying it aloud. Although I believe it is true, I know it isn't my line. It is a line of all those *strong contemporary female characters* from the paperbacks I have read. In fact, I wouldn't mind having someone take care of me. That's why I don't think about divorcing Michael and returning to Latvia. My mother would take better care of me than my husband. But that's exactly why I can't burden her by coming back.

"Suzie is wonderful," I say instead. "She's been kind to me since my first day here."

"And what about others? Do you have other friends? You told me about the choir. But as far as I understand, all the ladies there are Suzie's age or even older. You communicate only with people who are older than me. It's not good at your age."

I don't say anything for a while. Mom is right. I do live surrounded by older people.

"There's a girl from Latvia." I come up with a satisfying remark. "She's just opened an office here. She is in her twenties. We agreed to meet up when she's less busy."

"That's good." My mother nods and drops the subject. It's enough for her to know I've heard her. She isn't the one to pry into other people's lives. Even into her daughter's. "Do you plan to start looking for a job? Your husband's business seems to be going well. It's a good time for you to think about your career."

My mom motivated me to do well at school. She didn't give me sermons about the advantages of education.

Neither did she threaten to leave me without pocket money. Her methods were more subtle.

I remember we sat once in my grandmother's kitchen in her small house. I was about to finish the ninth grade, and the first exams loomed on the horizon. The results of those exams decided whether I would get accepted into the tenth grade or not. If I wasn't accepted, my chances of getting to the university would become slimmer.

My mother came to take me home after spring break, and the three of us drank tea before taking a train back home. Mom told my grandmother about the exams I had to pass and how difficult the school programme was.

"Poor kids," my grandmother shook her head, replenishing the empty bowl with cookies from the oven, "so many tests, such pressure. Back when I went to school, it wasn't like that. Not like that at all." She flicked a match and switched on the gas range under the kettle. "But we had no idea what to do after school. That wasn't a good thing. I applied to our local *kolkhoz*. Everyone went to work there. After the first day, I came home doubled up, with my palms in blisters. The next morning, I was the first in the queue to submit the application to the nurse training school in Riga."

It didn't work as a magical life-changing revelation they show in movies. I don't think I even registered the connection between Granny's life and my own future prospects at the time. Still, the fact remains: not for a moment did I think about skipping university and joining the labour market right after school graduation.

I wonder when I stopped listening to common sense.

"It's complicated, Mom." I don't want this conversation to spoil our time together. "Southbay is a small place. There aren't that many workplaces here. I need more experience in local accounting systems before applying, even for a junior position. Without practical experience, they won't even invite me to the interview."

"You could start with something simpler. It is a tourist area. I'm sure they always have open vacancies for receptionists."

"These jobs are mainly temporary. For the summer season. Most of the hotels close for the winter."

Mom purses her lips and says nothing. I know what it means. She disagrees with me but doesn't want to argue.

"I'm learning a lot from Mr Billings, our accountant." I hasten to say anything that will please my mother. After all, she isn't angry at me but worried about my well-being. "It's really more difficult at home. You can break your brain trying to figure out our double-entry system. Here, it's much simpler."

"You aren't officially employed," Mom points out. "It's good that you learn how it's done here. But you won't have any official record of your work experience."

She doesn't say it; still, it's clear that she disapproves of Michael using my help without any legal basis.

"I'll ask Mr Billings to give me a reference. And if it doesn't work out, I'll apply for a receptionist position in every hotel here in Southbay and down in Eastpoole." I smile, hoping to disarm my mother. "Look!" I notice a cream-coloured fluffy silhouette darting between the Lighthouse Keeper's Cottage and the parked car. "It's Winston. Jacqueline's dog."

When we come closer, the cottage door opens, and a man in pale grey suit-trousers, and a white shirt walks out. He stops and turns with one foot on the ground but another still on the porch steps. "Jackie, please," his pleading voice contrasts with his imposing appearance. The man is tall, with wide shoulders emphasised by the thin shirt fabric. "You've made your point. I said I am sorry. What else do you need to end this charade?"

"It's not a charade!" I've never heard Jacqueline speaking in a shrill voice. "Maybe it is for you. For me, it's the choice I have made. And it is final. Winston!" Jacqueline cries out as her dog runs after something he's seen behind the house. She notices me and Mom. I raise my hand in a greeting.

Jacqueline's face is red and puffy. She's been crying. I have already guessed the man is her husband.

Winston, who, upon seeing me, has stopped short, stands by the porch, frantically wagging his tail.

"Let's go," I say to Mom, feeling uncomfortable about intruding into other people's private scenes. "I'll call you," I mouth to Jacqueline, making a lame gesture with my hand as if putting a phone to my ear. She nods and turns back to her husband. "I won't change my mind, John. You better accept it and let us both move on with our lives." With that, she shuts the door with a bang.

The man turns and walks to his car. I can't refrain from stealing a glance at him. His jet-black hair is brushed from his forehead in a seemingly natural manner. The sleeves of his white shirt are rolled up, revealing tanned, muscled arms.

Jacqueline's husband looks like a movie star. *Maybe he is an actor.* I remember rumours about her leaving her work for the BBC. It wouldn't be surprising that I didn't recognise a British star. I don't watch television.

The man climbs into a dark burgundy Jaguar and drives off, leaving a wall of dust behind.

"Men never believe when a woman tells them it's over," Mom says when we reach the stone with a 'coast path' sign. "Your friend will have to repeat it to her husband for quite a few more times. He will come back."

I don't ask my mother how she's guessed the nature of the relationship between two people she has never met before. Not because I am not surprised. Her words evoke the questions I'm not brave enough to ask.

Did my father refuse to accept it was over between you and him? Or did you want him to, and he let you go without a fight?

We walk along the coastal path in silence. The breeze gently dilutes the afternoon heat. The water far down is almost azure, the way it is only in the middle of the summer. The froth flies up with the usual drama. Still, today, even the cliffs defying the force of the waves look peaceful.

"Do you like it here?" Mom asks. She shades her eyes

with her hand to look at the horizon. She is wearing sunglasses, but on days like this, they don't save anyone from the bright light.

"Yes, a lot," I answer truthfully. If Michael had brought me to some other place in Britain, I might not have stayed. "I feel at home here."

Mom shoots me a quick glance. "Good. That's good."

Having crossed the wide plateau on top of the South Rock, we start on the narrower coastal path segment. It is also grassy and comfortable for walking, but you have to walk closer to the cliff edge.

I see two riders on horseback approaching us. They must have just turned around since this is where the path suitable for horses ends and rocky slopes begin.

Both horses are beautiful. One is bay with a white mark on its forehead, the other one is black, and they both have long, shiny manes and tails. The animals move at a leisurely pace while their riders talk to each other, obviously at ease in the saddle.

Mom and I step a little from the trail to give the riders space to pass by. With the riding helmet obscuring her face, I don't recognise Melissa Hammond until she turns her head to thank us.

Dressed in beige tight-fit riding breeches and a dark blue T-shirt, Finley's mother could have passed for a girl half her age. She is slim and petite, with shoulder-length blonde hair in a ponytail.

"It is so nice to see you, Margo." Melissa takes the reins in one hand, putting it on the saddle. "I hope Michael and you will find time to dine with us this summer."

My cheeks turn crimson. I can do nothing to make my husband stop neglecting invitations from the Hammonds. "We'd love to, Mrs Hammond. It's just Michael is so busy with that big project in Bournemouth. When he gets home, he is so tired, he says he isn't a good company for anybody." I want to pinch myself for lying. If I've learned anything about my husband over the last year, it's the fact that he doesn't care about hurting other people's feelings.

Melissa nods sympathetically. "I understand. No worries. I am glad his business is flourishing. It is important to work hard when establishing a reputation."

"Thank you, Mrs Hammond. I'll tell Michael about your kind invitation."

"Please, do." She takes the reins in both hands. "We had a wonderful time together last summer. It would be lovely to repeat it. And Finley will be home for a few weeks from the university."

I blush deeper. "Thank you." I don't want Mrs Hammond to think I am rude or stupid. "Oh, this is my mom. Linda."

My mother nods politely.

"It is a pleasure to meet you." Melissa inclines her head in acknowledgement and then turns to me. "Please tell your mom that she has raised a wonderful daughter she can be proud of."

"I... Thank you, Mrs Hammond." I give up on trying to suppress my embarrassment. "You are very kind."

"The invitation is open. Tell Michael he can call anytime, and we'll set up the date."

Melissa and her companion ride off, their beautiful horses walking gracefully, unperturbed by the interruption.

"It's Melissa Hammond. Her husband and Michael went to school together," I explain to my mother.

We resume walking.

"Are they still friends?" Mom asks, and the unpleasant realisation hits me. My husband has no friends. I wonder if he lost them because of the divorce or if he has never had any.

I shrug. "Yes, they keep inviting us to dinner."

"This woman seems to like you."

"I hope so. I like her and her husband too. They are very nice people."

"And well-off."

"It's not why I like them, Mom."

"Oh, I know. Usually, people with money aren't nice. I've seen enough spoilt rich brides to know it for sure."

Her words make me remember Maureen Easton's question about my mother's retirement plans.

"Don't you want to quit that job, Mom? Aren't you tired of those spoilt rich clients?"

My mother smiles widely. I've seldom seen her smiling like this. "And what would I do if I quit? Look for another job? Where? At the *Bisoks* factory, making tights and socks?"

"You could start your own business. This way, you would have all the profits and not Victoria."

Victoria is the owner of the wedding boutique that Mom has been working in for over a decade. She started her business in the nineties using her husband's money and protection. Competitors killed the man a few years later, as often happened to members of criminal gangs. But Victoria's bridal venture was already striving by then. According to some bandits' code, as a mourning widow, she was treated respectfully and didn't have to pay a *protection fee* to one of the gangs. By the time the racketeers' era ended, Victoria was a respected businesswoman, driving around in her new Porsche Cayenne and giving interviews to local fashion magazines.

Mom laughs. I'm torn between joy and frustration. I'm glad to see her laugh. She looks so young and carefree, not the image I'm used to. But I'm determined to make her see her true worth. In my opinion, her employer underappreciates her. "It's not funny, Mom," I press my idea further. "You'd earn more if you had your own studio and shop. And you wouldn't have to listen to Victoria's…," I almost utter 'crap' but catch myself, "…endless demands," I say instead.

"And who would pay the studio rent, the accountant's and sales assistants' salaries? Who would search for clients? Who would call their friends from the local *beau monde* when the business gets low and needs a spur?" Mom smiles at me kindly, and I feel ashamed. I know nothing about life. It's not surprising I made a mistake when choosing a husband. "I understand that it all seems so exciting. When you are young, it's normal to dream big. It's only when you get older that you become more practical."

"You are not old, Mom," I blurt out off the mark.

"I didn't say I am." She keeps smiling. "What I wanted to say is that although Victoria can, at times, be a handful, there is more to the business than sewing. And I'm happy that my only responsibility is that the bride gets her dress on time."

"But business owners earn more." Michael's complaints about the tycoons, who want their employees' flesh and bones while paying them peanuts, ring in my head.

"I have already earned enough." Mom purses her lips as if we've touched the topic she doesn't want to discuss.

"Don't you want to travel more and buy things?"

"I'm here, right?" Mom makes a gesture, indicating our beautiful surroundings. "I can afford to visit my daughter. And to leave her something after I'm gone."

"Mom! Don't talk about such things!"

My mother smiles reassuringly. "It won't happen tomorrow."

"Mom!" My chest tightens with fear. "You have to start learning English. You'll fit in with the locals and their black humour. I still haven't gotten used to it!"

"I can see why you like it here. It's a good way to treat life – with humour."

I relax. "You wouldn't say that if you heard some of the things they say." Until this moment, I haven't realised how nervous I am.

"Then don't repeat them."

"I wasn't going to."

We walk in silence. Gradually, the breeze and the noise of the waves crashing against the rock far below calm my nerves. By the time we reach the cottage, I forget about the existential issues and, with enthusiasm, start sharing the plans I have made for us for the next few days.

CHAPTER 10

Time flies, and that's not an exaggeration. My thoughts are gloomy as I follow Michael and Mom along the narrow sidewalk past the long row of terraced houses. It is Saturday, and tomorrow, Mom will be on a plane home to Riga.

We have come to Eastpoole to have dinner in an Indian restaurant. It's Michael's treat, and I am grateful. I prefer not to dwell on the reasons for his thoughtfulness. Besides, my gratitude is mixed with irritation at his habit of parking far away from the centre. "I'm not going to pay the prices designed to rip off crazed tourists." His words make me cringe when I replay them in my head. *We never go to Eastpoole, so it wouldn't hurt our budget to park in the centre just this once.* I know I'd never have enough courage to talk to my husband like this, and that makes me feel even worse.

It is a warm early evening. The residential street is empty except for an occasional car driving by. I am wearing a dress and ballet flats. When I chose the outfit for today's dinner, I did take down boxes with the wedge sandals I'd brought from home. I even tried them on, and it shocked me how tall and slim the heels made me look. The effect was lost once I put on my usual ballet flats. Still, the yellow summer dress looked pretty. Despite his raised eyebrows, I marched past Michael, not giving him a chance to comment on my choice.

Strolling along the street, with at least a twenty-minute walk to the restaurant, I'm glad I haven't pushed it too far with my outfit rebellion. Although far less dangerous than Old Riga's cobbled walkways, Eastpoole's residential alleys also don't resemble an even catwalk's surface.

The row of terraced houses ends, and we cross the small square where the terminus of the Eastpoole-Southbay bus line is located. It's not clearly marked, and there isn't even a ticket office here. I wouldn't have noticed the bus stop if not for the post with a schedule attached to it. People don't stand there waiting, but once the bus appears from behind the corner, a small crowd gathers as if out of the blue. As we make our way past the passengers, I notice a familiar face. "Laura!" I stop. "I was planning to call you later this week. My mom is visiting."

People start piling onto the bus.

Laura smiles. "Hello, Margo. It's so nice to see you. It's okay. It's been a hectic week anyway. They've finally sent me help from the Riga office."

I notice a young man standing next to her only now. "Oh, hi," I say hastily. I am torn between the wish to keep talking to Laura and the ever-present fear of annoying my husband.

"Hello." The young man transfers his luggage bag from one hand to another.

"I'm sorry. I'd love to chat, but we have to get on this bus." Laura nods at the open door. "You never know if the next one arrives on time or ever." She smiles again. "I haven't been here for too long, but this I've already learned. If you see the bus, you get on it."

I imagine the easy chat Laura and her colleague will have

during the ride to our island, and I want to hop on the bus with them.

We walk down the main street and then along the seaside promenade. The Indian restaurant Michael favours is located off the main tourist area. It is moderately priced, with a basic and a little outdated interior. But the food is superb. Michael took me here when I'd just arrived in England.

The owner greets us personally and offers us welcome drinks and naan bread on the house. We sit at the best table for six by the window. It is still early, and we are the only visitors. Locals and tourists will start to arrive in a couple of hours, around seven.

Mom's mobile phone beeps. She pulls out her new silver flip model Samsung. "It's Anna," she explains. "She asks about my flight tomorrow. She wants to pick me up from the airport. Sor-ry," Mom says to Michael, pointing at her phone.

"I'll order for you, okay?" I take the menu. "Not too spicy, right?"

Mom nods, already tapping at the small buttons.

I make the choice quickly and, putting away the menu, stare out the window. Michael doesn't look up. He is always meticulous in selecting what he's going to pay for. Although he'll probably end up ordering the same thing he did when we were here the last time, he still takes his time scanning the thick menu.

I am not happy. The thought isn't new, but I don't push it away this time as I always do. I watch a woman walking a French bulldog on the opposite side of the street. The woman is in her forties. She is wearing beige chino pants with a white polo shirt and elegant loafers. I follow her with my eyes. Her look starkly contrasts the more relaxed baggy style of the locals and tourists.

Who said a person should be happy? It's not a law. It's people's wishful thinking.

My wishful thinking got me into the situation I am now.

I don't try to sweeten the pill. No one forced me to marry Michael. I made that decision myself.

I frown as the memories from two years ago flood in.

The summer when I met Michael was hot. There were enough sunny days to satisfy even the grumpiest people who kept complaining about 'those wet and chilly Baltic summers'. After our first meeting in the café in Riga Old Town, more followed. Michael came to Latvia once a month and stayed for a week. As a top executive, he stayed in the best hotels and dined in the best restaurants. He took me everywhere with him, and I got to see places I hadn't thought I'd ever visit. Our relationship was easy and carefree, centred around having a good time. During the first six months, I didn't give a single thought to where it all was going. I considered myself a progressive modern woman who could enjoy a relationship without vows and obligations, just as any man could.

Was it because I wasn't in love with Michael? I tear my eyes from the now-empty street and look at my husband. He is still studying the menu. I feel the familiar frustration rising in my chest.

What did I see in him that I agreed to marry him?

I try to remember when we had started talking about marriage. People usually don't believe it if a girl declares that she doesn't care about getting a ring on her finger. Still, I know that for me, it was true. Long gone were the times when twenty was the age at which a woman was supposed to get married. I had a few girlfriends from school who got married right after graduation. With all the emancipation, birth control pills weren't something teenagers could get hold of easily. But those were exceptions rather than a rule. In the new millennium, girls dreamt about a career, buying their own flat and a new car. Marriage has slid down the list of priorities.

I watch my husband scan the menu, page after page. He squints, having not taken his reading glasses with him. Crow's feet and laugh lines show distinctly, adding years to his thin face. On his forehead, cheeks, and hands, there are liver spots I haven't noticed before.

Michael proposed in a posh restaurant on the last floor of a five-star hotel. The red and yellow lights of the traffic twinkled below. It was January, and people rushed through the park, trying to get home as quickly as possible. Walkways were covered in a layer of snow. Its pure whiteness was turning into a muddy slosh quickly.

From the restaurant's sumptuous warmth, the city hustle seemed distant, almost unreal. Background music played softly, and I slowly sipped the martini I'd ordered before the meal. I felt relaxed, confident, and happy.

The memory feels like a punch in the gut.

I sigh and then hold my breath.

I do remember how Michael had proposed and how my girlfriends giggled when I told them about it afterwards. What had preceded the proposal, I completely forgot.

I sit up straighter in the chair with a rigid back. My spine feels as stiff.

I've never considered why Michael suddenly asked me to be his wife after a six-month no-strings-attached relationship. At the time, it seemed natural. I was excited to tell my friends and my mom about it. It felt good to be someone who was going to get married.

Now, I feel like a complete idiot.

I look at my engagement ring. A thin gold band with a cubic zirconia stone. It is pretty and can be bought in any mall's jewellery store.

Michael's visit in January two years ago had started like any other of his previous visits. I met him at the airport. I always found it sophisticated and exciting to run into his arms when he exited the arrivals area. After speeding through the city in a white Mercedes taxi, we dropped his luggage at the hotel and went to our favourite Irish pub in the Old Town. Later, we went shopping. Michael liked shopping in Riga. Obviously, the things he bought there were more expensive in England. We had dinner in an

Italian restaurant. We chatted about his weekly business meeting schedule and made plans for what we would do in the evenings. I spent the night with him at the hotel.

Not once during the day we had spent together did Michael mention marriage.

In the morning, over the copious buffet-style breakfast, I told him that in six months, I was going to graduate with a Bachelor's degree in Accounting and Audit from the University of Latvia.

In the evening, Michael took me to one of the oldest and most luxurious restaurants in the city and asked me to become his wife.

Nothing about his proposal or its timing had bothered me at the time. I felt elated and a real adult woman. Like many other girls, I thought I was a feminist. It didn't occur to me that Michael could at least have asked the waiter to place the ring on top of a dessert cake. Instead, he just put the small black box on the table between the starter and the main course.

"Are you ready to order?" The smiling restaurant owner comes over.

I tell him what I've chosen for Mom and myself. Michael looks up from the menu. Just like I thought, his order is the same as it was the last time we were here.

"All sorted." Mom announces, putting her mobile into the bag. "Anna will meet me at the airport tomorrow. I'm so glad. The bus ride to the centre always drags with all that traffic. And then I have to wait for the train."

"Tell her I said hi," I say automatically. The idea of being left alone here suddenly feels unbearable.

"I will. Anna says they might come next year to England by car. Do you remember Guntis's son? He's moved here as well. He works at the packing factory in Bristol with his friends."

Anna and Mom have been best friends for as long as I can remember. Anna's first marriage was a disaster. She'd stayed alone for ten years, declaring that she'd never get herself trapped again. "Men are like buses," she used to say. "No need to run after the one that has departed. The next one will arrive, and you can exit it at any stop." When she met Guntis, her narrative had changed. After confirming that decent men existed, she tried to find a husband for her best friend. Mom didn't refuse to go on yet another date with *a great guy*. "You are perfect for each other!" Anna exclaimed every time she managed to fix a date for Mom with one of Guntis's friends. It never worked the way Anna hoped, and after a few years, she dropped her plans to make a happy married woman out of her best friend.

I always thought Anna was lucky to have met Guntis. He was a quiet and kind man. He was never the type to take women's breath away with his masculinity. He owned a small car repair shop in our town. While not earning much, he still earned enough for a decent life. He raised his son alone, and until he met Anna, there wasn't a single rumour about his amorous adventures.

Anna used to bring her stepson with her when she came to have a chat over tea with my mother. We were the same age and got along fine, but we didn't become friends.

"If he settles here, they'll visit him next summer," Mom continues. "They'll take me with them. They want to drive around a bit to see more of England. You could come with us. Your island is beautiful, but I'm sure there is much more to see."

I flinch. I recover quickly and smile. Still, I'm sure Mom has noticed. "What a wonderful idea." I make sure I sound enthusiastic. "We'll see, okay? A lot can change before next summer." I blush, and this time, I know that Mom has misinterpreted my reaction.

"Oh," she says with a warm smile that I rarely see. "But of course. Anyway, travelling can wait. Newlyweds have other issues on their minds."

While we walk back to the car from the restaurant, I can't get rid of unsettling thoughts. I can't believe how blind I have been. I don't even try to look for another explanation after I've seen it all so clearly for the first time. I am pretty sure that my husband didn't have any thoughts about starting a family when he proposed to me. It wasn't kids that were on his mind when he bought a cheap ring and thrust it at me as if giving a tip to a waiter. All Michael wanted was a free accounting assistant who would double as a cook and a housekeeper.

******

As I stand on a train platform beside my mother, I'm close to bursting out crying. It is so different from what I felt last year when we stood on this very spot, waiting for the train to take Mom to Waterloo Station in London. I was full of excitement and hope. I couldn't stop giggling, impatient to return to an empty house that would belong to only Michael and me again.

Today, all I want is to board the train with Mom and let it take me to the place where I'm loved rather than used.

Michael dropped us off at the station entrance and drove away to find free parking. For once, his money-saving habits don't frustrate me. I don't want my husband to hover over us while we say our goodbyes.

"I'm sorry we couldn't drive you to Heathrow," I say for the umpteenth time. "Michael drives around all week…" I have no idea what my husband's plans are for tomorrow. I know that he has completed his last assignment in Bournemouth. He hasn't found it necessary to inform me whether he has a new client or not.

"It's okay, sweetheart. I enjoy your English trains. They have comfortable seats and toilets. Do you remember our ancient trains back home?"

My eyes mist with tears. Mom seldom calls me 'sweetheart'. "Oh yes, wooden benches and no toilets for you in those ones!" I smile, and my voice is too loud. I don't want my mother to become worried about me.

Of course, it doesn't work. "You can return home anytime." Mom sees through my pathetic attempts to mask my feelings. She looks at me attentively as if reading my thoughts. "If you stop liking this place, you can always come home. You know that, don't you?"

I nod. My throat is too constricted to speak. "I know, Mom. But you don't have to worry about me. I still like our little island. I feel like it has become my home too."

Mom gives me her tiny trademark smile. "I'm glad that you feel this way."

We both look in the direction from where the train should arrive. Mom's unrelenting but silent support has always been enough while I was growing up. As a kid, I didn't know things could be different between mothers and daughters. I wasn't used to hugs, kisses, and baby talk. To be honest, I don't think it would have made a huge difference if I'd had all that. Regardless of the expression form, I felt loved and protected. As a teenager, I was proud that my mother wasn't treating me like a child. My friends suffered from such an attitude, and I believed that I had the coolest Mom.

It catches me unprepared that at twenty-two, I want to spill my guts and cry on Mom's shoulder.

I hear a familiar voice and turn. "Laura!" I am so glad to see her that I don't keep my tone in check. "What are you doing here? Are you going to London?"

Laura and her colleague come over to us. Both are dressed in jeans, T-shirts, and sport-style shoes. They resemble tourists who are heading to the capital for the whole day of walking.

"Hi, Margo." Laura's smile, which lights up not only her face but everything around her, makes me feel better. "Yes, we're going to London to pick up a car. Don't ask why we have to go so far to get one." She rolls her eyes. "Our business is new, and money does matter. It's a pity that our investors aren't some gas and oil oligarchs." She smiles again. "Anyway, we'll have a car, and if you need a ride to Eastpoole, just ask."

"Thanks. It would be great not to rely on the bus."

"Oh yes, I've already gotten back pain from those hilly

streets of Southbay. The car will be a revenge to that rock of an island."

"I haven't introduced you when we met last time," I remember about politeness in time. The train has just appeared as a small dot in the distance. "This is my mom. She's been visiting me this week. Mom, this is Laura and…" I'm embarrassed about not having asked Laura's colleague's name.

"Max." The young man doesn't look offended by my negligence. "Nice to meet you," he says to my mom.

"Nice to meet you, young people. I'm Linda." The three of them shake hands. "I'm glad my daughter has someone to turn to here, so far away from home."

Instead of protesting, I smile and nod, feeling less lost and unhappy than I did only moments before.

"We'll keep an eye on her, don't worry." I admire the ease with which Laura talks to someone she's just met. I can see that the troubled look has left Mom's eyes.

The train arrives, and passengers pile out of the carriages.

"Everything will be okay, Mom." I turn hastily to my mother. "Please take some time to learn how to use the email and that chat I gave you the link to. We'll be able to talk more if you do."

"I will, sweetheart, I promise. Take care of yourself, and think about finding a job. It'll do you good to meet new people."

"I will. You can count on it."

Tears blur my vision again when we hug. Mom kisses me on the cheek and clears the lipstick's mark with her finger. "You've always been a good girl. I'll send you a text when I land in Riga."

Michael joins us just at the last moment of boarding. He hugs Mom quickly, and they exchange stiff goodbyes.

"Pop into our office next week," Laura tells me before getting on the train. "If we get back in one piece, that is. Max has never driven with the wheel on the wrong side."

"I've read the traffic rules manual," Max says, taking Mom's luggage bag.

"Be careful. But drivers are generally polite here. Everything will be alright." I walk them to the carriage door. "I know you have your own plans in London, but maybe you could help Mom find her train to the airport."

"I'm perfectly capable of finding the train myself." Mom rolls her eyes and smiles good-naturedly. "I am the mother here, remember?"

"Of course, we will see Linda safely on her way to Heathrow," Laura assures me, already in the doorway. "The guys we're going to buy that car from don't have a good sense of time. I'm sure we'll have to wander around for a while before they appear. We can put this time to good use."

"Thank you so much. I'll pop in next week." I feel relieved that Mom will have companions during her journey.

I watch the three of them disappear in the train carriage. I want to wait until the departure so I can wave them goodbye. But Michael takes me by the arm and starts pulling me away. "Let's go," he says impatiently. "We'll be eating late as it is."

I fight back the urge to yank my arm free. *I hate Sunday roast*, I want to say. *If you want it, cook it yourself.* Instead, I follow my husband without saying a word.

I hear the train begin moving after we have exited the station.

"Mom says her friends are planning a car trip here next year. She might come with them." I try to switch my thoughts to something more pleasant.

"That's great." Michael walks briskly, not giving me a glance. "Just warn them so they don't expect free accommodation from you."

Suppressed anger burns my chest. "They aren't coming to *me*." My voice trembles. "They are coming to see their son in Bristol."

"Fantastic." Michael turns to cross the street, pulling me

after him. "Nowadays, everyone expects everything to be given to them for free. I am not a charity organisation."

I don't reply to his remark. We walk along the residential street in silence.

We reach our car, and I get in, not looking at my husband. I go through the ingredients for today's dinner in my head like an insomnia sufferer counts sheep. I too seek oblivion.

"And Margo?" Michael turns to me from the driver's seat. "I don't think it's a good idea for you to hang around those Latvians. You'll never blend in if you pretend you haven't left home."

I stare straight ahead all the way until we arrive home. Once there, I go to the kitchen and get to work.

CHAPTER 11

On Monday, I leave the cottage the moment Michael pulls away from the driveway. I need fresh air to clear my head and get rid of the heaviness in my chest.

Only after we'd had our Sunday roast did Michael inform me about his plans for the week. He had a three-day assignment down in Poole, and instead of Thursday, he planned to be back on Wednesday evening.

I walk along the road, trying to put a lid on my frustration. It has become too much. The pressure of my husband's demands and the overall uncertainty of my life have taken their toll. I feel worn out. I know I have to do something to get out of this slump. But none of the immediate options seem to be the right solution.

I don't want to return home to Latvia. There is a chance that I might find a good job in some international company in Riga and make a career, but the path is too long. I'd have to spend years proving my worth to the employer before I earned enough to afford to rent a flat in the capital. I love my mother, but I don't want to go back to living with her.

I don't want to live with my husband either.

I've made a mistake, I mutter to myself. *It doesn't mean I have to spend my whole life paying for it.*

I turn from the road to the coastal path. The day is grey, but the low cloud hasn't yet descended upon the island. Still, the air is somewhat milky. I can see the path, the rocks, and the water down below as if through a transparent film.

I walk on, still absorbed in my thoughts, when I hear a dog barking.

Jacqueline Fisher stands on the path while Winston frantically runs around her in circles.

When I reach her, I notice at once the difference in her appearance. Her eyes are almost slits under the puffy eyelids, and her nose is red.

"Hi, Jacqueline," I greet her, bending down to pat Winston, who has rushed up to me.

"Good morning, Margo." Jacqueline sneezes loudly. She hastily puts a paper handkerchief to her face. "I apologise for this. I'm not in the best shape today, I'm afraid."

"Are you sick? What are you doing outside, then? You should be in bed, resting."

Jacqueline points at the golden retriever that snakes between us, his body shaking from restrained energy. She sneezes again before replying. "The yard is too small for him to have a proper walk."

"I can walk with Winston until you feel better." I pat the dog's silky head again, and his pink tongue sneaks out to give my hand a quick lick. "Go home and rest. I'll bring him in... Is an hour enough for his morning walk?"

A mix of relief and embarrassment shows on Jacqueline's face. "I can't ask that from you. My dog is my responsibility."

"You haven't asked. I offered myself. It isn't any trouble

at all. I love dogs, and I'd love to see what it's like to have one." Winston sits down beside me, playing along smoothly. "See, the guy himself doesn't mind."

Jacqueline blows her nose. "I'm sorry. I'm a complete mess. Thank you, Margo. It's very generous of you to offer help."

"It's my pleasure. No trouble at all. I'll bring him to your house in an hour. And I'll come over in the evening to let Winston take his run before bedtime."

"You are too kind, Margo. I really appreciate it." She looks at me through watering eyes, and her face, usually set into an aloof expression, is softer. "I'll make it up to you when I'm better. We could go to Eastpoole and have a girls' night in one of the restaurants with a sea view. How does it sound?"

"Perfect!" I show her a thumbs-up. "That sounds absolutely perfect. Now, go home, make yourself some tea, and get to bed. That's what my mom would tell me to do."

Jacqueline smiles and nods. "Thanks again, Margo. I'm going to do exactly that. Moms don't give wrong advice. It's a pity that often we realise it after we'd made the mistakes we could have avoided if only we'd listened to their wisdom. Sorry, it's the fever talking."

Jacqueline hands Winston's leash to me. "Bring him back in ten minutes if he's naughty or doesn't listen to you."

I attach the leash to the leather collar on Winston's neck. "He'll be on his best behaviour," I say confidently. "Won't you, Winston?"

The golden retriever issues a high-pitched whine and then a bark.

After Jacqueline disappears around the path's bend, I start walking back to the South Rock plateau. I think it's the best place in the area for walking a dog. It is flat and grassy, and there is no danger of tripping and falling into the roaring waves under the cliffs.

In the next hour, I run around with Winston, who seems to have a perpetual motion device installed in him. I've found a stick to throw so he could bring it back to me, and we have a blast of a time before he breaks it with his jaws. When he falls to the ground with his tongue rolling out and all four legs dangling comically in the air, I know that it's time to take him home.

At a leisurely pace, we walk to the Lighthouse Keeper's cottage, and it dawns on me that all gloomy thoughts have dissipated during the time I spent with Winston, just like the thin film that blurred the transparent summer air earlier in the morning.

******

On Tuesday evening, Jacqueline looks considerably better when I arrive to pick Winston up for a walk. She tells me she is feeling strong enough to get back to her dog owner's duties. I talk her into having one more relaxing evening so I can enjoy one last walk with Winston.

I've always loved animals and thought having a pet was a blessing. I didn't ask Mom to take a cat or a dog, for she had enough on her plate without another mouth to feed. I dragged along after my friends when they took their dogs for walks. I also was the one who volunteered to check on neighbours' cats, dogs, fish, and hamsters when they went away to the countryside for a weekend.

After spending time with Winston, I realised that there is more to pets than their undeniable cuteness. They were better than therapy, yoga, or meditation. Winston didn't have to do anything special to completely take my mind off my problems. I would have sulked for days on my solitary walks, and the beauty of the Dorset shore wouldn't have been enough to divert my thoughts. Running and playing with the golden retriever has lightened my mood and focused my mind.

Walking with Winston to the South Rock plateau, I decide to make the most from our last walk. We stay there for longer, playing with the ball I took to guarantee that the active dog has a great time. I make sure we keep a safe distance from the cliffs.

When I take Winston back home, he drinks greedily from his bowl in the kitchen and then trudges to the conservatory. He plops down on his dog bed and immediately begins to snore softly.

I walk from Jacqueline's cottage to the Groveland Business Park, and from its parking lot, I turn to the road that leads home. It is almost nine in the evening, and the area looks a little sinister without cars and people.

I quicken my step. Walking through the residential area rather than taking a coastal path on my way back doesn't seem such a good idea anymore. It isn't dark yet. In summer, it's only completely dark for a few hours after midnight. Even so, bright colours lose their radiance after the sun sets.

I feel vulnerable, and the feeling of loneliness weighs me down. *Why am I walking here alone? Shouldn't my husband be taking an evening walk with me?* Michael never does. Although I don't believe that things stay the same forever, deep inside, I know that my husband will never change. His present behaviour isn't induced by temporary circumstances. It's how it will be for as long as we stay married.

The thought of not wanting to stay married returns to me. It makes me restless since I have no idea what to do. Besides, I realise that my helplessness is my fault. It didn't occur to me to learn about any practical things like flat rent prices or average wages in the area. I came to England as a wife, not an immigrant. I had other things on my mind to adjust to.

Now, my optimism seems foolish.

I've learned my lesson, I think bitterly. *From now on, I'll always have a plan B.*

Walking as fast as I can, I run through the things I have to find information about. I discarded Mom's advice about getting a job instead of focusing on it. I decide to make it my number one priority. Finding a job shouldn't be a problem. People from my home country are coming to England in large numbers, and it doesn't look like there'll be a shortage of vacancies anytime soon.

I'm lost in my thoughts, and a sudden screech of tyres startles me. It is so unusual to hear loud sounds in the pastoral idyll of the island that I stop and turn to look at what caused the disturbance of peace and quiet.

Mark King is already getting out of his dark blue BMW. I remember the car from the time when Finley Hammond gave us a lift home.

"Hey, Marta!" Mark shouts. "How come you are wandering wild streets alone? Get in. I'll take you home safely." He roars with laughter, obviously pleased with himself and his joke.

"Hi, Mark. Thank you. It's very kind of you. But I'm almost home. It's around the corner." I wave with my hand in the direction of my cottage.

"Come on, let a gentleman help you. Don't be like local stuck-up chicks. They'll sue you if you as much as call them beautiful. I know you aren't like that." Mark's voice turns pleading. He even pouts his lips childishly. I can see that he's been drinking. Despite climbing out of his car, he still stands, leaning on its door. I consider it good luck he isn't fully mobile. I have no intention of making our conversation any longer than it's absolutely necessary.

"Thank you," I repeat. "I like to take a walk before bedtime. Say hi to your father." I turn and start walking.

"Why are you like this?"

I hear the car door bang. The pang of fear flashes through me. *Have I underestimated Mark's inebriation level?* I stop and turn reluctantly. Mark has staggered from the car and is hovering over me. I take a step back and trip over the stone that indicates the way to the coastal path through a small forest. Mark catches me. He doesn't let me go; his hands grip my forearms painfully.

"I didn't mean to offend you." I try to stay calm, but my voice quivers. "It is very kind of you to offer help. I really appreciate it. It's just I need to take a walk before sleep. You see, I have insomnia, and some fresh air helps…" I continue mumbling, trying unsuccessfully to get out of Mark's grip.

He is surprisingly strong considering how drunk he is. The smell of his breath is so strong that I feel nauseated.

"I know a better way to help you get rid of insomnia." Mark leans closer, and the alcohol odour becomes unbearable. I avert my face to take a breath. It makes Mark angry. "Why are you playing hard to get?" He slurs the words. "Do you think I don't know who you are? You all come here from that pit of nowhere, flash your butts and boobs in front of men, and what do you expect? To be treated with *respect*?" He spits the last word. Drops of saliva land on my face. I wriggle to break away.

I'm terrified. My stomach is in knots, and I feel the urge to double over. The pain is intense. I'd once worked in a busy bar. The sight of drunk people is as familiar to me as the leaves turning yellow in October. I know exactly how drastic and quick the change between 'before' and 'after' in a person consuming alcohol is. After a few shots of something strong, usually following a couple of beers, decent men turn into pigs. I'd witnessed this transformation more times than I care to remember. Bar visitors did become loud and brave, behaving as if they owned the place. They puked all over the tables and in toilets, broke glasses, stole toilet paper, sugar bowls, and even candle holders. They never left bigger tips to compensate for the inconvenience and damage. Many of them made chauvinistic comments when talking to waitresses and never apologised for their rude remarks. They also got into shouting matches with other visitors – only foreigners and never with locals.

Still, they never turned aggressive. During several years of working in the bar, where after six o'clock, two waitresses and a barman were the only sober people in the crowd, I didn't feel threatened once.

Now, I feel I am in danger.

"Mark, let me go," I manage to utter. My throat is sore, and my heart beats quickly. I take short breaths that do nothing to help my lungs get enough oxygen.

"Why? Aren't you tired of your old husband? I bet old Mike can't get it up most of the time."

Mark keeps trying to kiss me. His wet lips touching my cheek make me wriggle more actively. My eyes burn, and my head pulsates as if it's going to burst.

"Let me go." I want to scream, but the words come out muffled. In his urge to put his mouth on mine, I doubt that Mark has heard me.

I'm trapped. Mark is stronger than me. He stands so close that I can't even raise my knee to thrust it into his groin. Black dots and bright flashes obscure my vision, and the paralysing fear of going blind stiffens my limbs.

"Come on, I know you want this." Mark's slobbery lips brush over my ear. I feel like I've been electrocuted. I strain my neck to turn as far from him as I can, and it starts aching. My eyes regain the focus for a brief moment. I catch a glimpse of a narrow track that leads down to the coastal path. I almost dart for it, led by an impulse.

"Stop it. You are drunk." I make another attempt to reason with him.

Mark laughs. "It makes life brighter. You need a drink too. Let's go." Suddenly, he lets go of my forearms. Grabbing my wrist instead, he pulls me to his car.

My legs are wobbly, and all I can do not to fall is to stumble after him. *Maybe his father is at home,* I think. *He won't let him do anything stupid.* My work in the bar has taught me that it's useless to argue with drunk people. Buying time, if possible, usually leads to better results.

The sound of an approaching car makes me stop abruptly. Mark slams into his BMW door, scraping the window with the remote-control key. "Fuck!" he shouts. "You bitch!" He turns, ready to hit me.

"Margo!" I hear before the car door opens, and then I see Laura getting out of a compact dark burgundy vehicle. "Look what we've got." She raps on the car roof. "Do you need a lift?"

With her long hair not tied in a ponytail and without

lipstick, Laura only looks about eighteen.

"She's fine," Mark grumbles. He has opened the front door and pushes me to it. "Let's go."

"Laura, hi!" I finally find my voice. I don't care that now it sounds high-pitched. "You've got that car after all. That's great!"

Mark tries to push me into the BMW. "Let me go!" I am sure he has heard me this time. He looks confused. Still, he grabs my hand.

Laura gets out of the car and walks toward us. "The first drive from London – that was something else." She speaks as if nothing is wrong, although I see that she has noticed the pressure between Mark and me. "I have to tell you all about it. We have to go to London again tomorrow. Are you free now? The café at the business park is closed, but we have tea and biscuits in our office."

"She is *busy*," Mark snaps, still holding my hand. "You'll talk tomorrow."

Laura gives him an appraising look. The cold expression in her eyes transforms her girlish face. I shiver, even though her anger isn't directed at me. "I said," she speaks slowly, "that tomorrow we are going to London. I *need* to talk to Margo *today*. And you need to go home and get a proper sleep."

Mark's eyes bulge, and his face turns blotchy red. "Don't tell me what to do. You…"

Laura raises her hand. I stare in amazement that it works as a magical stop sign. "I think that's a bad idea," she says calmly. "My colleague Max," she waves at Max, who has climbed out of the car and is standing by the open door, "you see, he was in the army before he switched to a career in the private sector. Certain things we find common are still challenging for him." Laura pauses, letting her words sink in. As clouded by alcohol as Mark's brain is at the moment, he understands when it's more sensible to back off. "Are you able to drive yourself home safely?" Laura asks pleasantly. "If not, Max can give you a lift."

Mark nods dully, then frantically shakes his head. He releases my hand and stalks to the driver's door of his BMW.

"Great. Fantastic," Laura says to his retreating back. "Have a nice evening. Sleep it off, and tomorrow you'll be like new."

The BMW roars like a wounded boar, tyres screech, and the flashy car speeds away at a break-neck speed.

"What was that about?" Laura turns to me, not waiting for Mark's car to disappear from view. "Margo, are you alright? My back is wet after talking to that creep."

I smile weakly, make a few unsteady steps, and collapse into her arms. I sob loudly, and I can't care less about how my face looks right now. Laura rubs my back, holding me. "It's okay. Everything is fine. You are safe."

I can't stop crying. My breath comes out in short pants until I start gulping for air. My face feels swollen, and my vision is blurry. Laura keeps comforting me during the ugly display of emotions. She says nothing except short, soothing phrases.

Finally, I am more tired from sobbing than from the shock of what has almost happened to me. I don't say a word. My head is empty. I simply look at Laura, waiting for her to make a decision for me.

"Come, we'll take you home." Laura puts her hand around me, having gently untangled herself from my clinging embrace. She leads me to the car, and I follow. I hadn't noticed that Max had parked closer to the curb so as not to disturb the traffic.

We drive for a few minutes in silence. I tell them where to stop when we reach the cottage. Max parks by Michael's trailer.

"Will you be okay?" Laura turns to me from the front seat. I almost start crying again.

"I... I don't know," I stammer. I don't want to admit that I don't want to be alone. It's not that I'm afraid that Mark might return and try to break into the house. It's just I feel I can't take it anymore, and it would be unbearable to be in the empty house by myself.

"When will your husband be home?" Laura asks.

"To...tomorrow."

"Do you want to come to our office to have a cup of tea?"

I take a deep breath, trying to steady my nerves. "It'd be more convenient to have tea at my place." I nod at the entrance.

Laura and Max exchange glances. "Call me when you're finished, and I'll come to pick you up," Max offers, and Laura nods.

I am so relieved that he spared me the awkwardness of asking Laura to come alone. Laura's colleague has such a calming presence. It seems that nothing can put him off his stride. At the same time, I feel that there is strength underneath his well-balanced façade.

Before we go in, Laura rakes around the boot and produces a pack of cakes. "I have no idea if these are tasty, but I can't come empty-handed."

If I weren't feeling shaken, I'd protest and say I have plenty of sweets for tea. As it is, I only nod.

Max doesn't leave until he sees we have entered the house safely. I hear him drive away when I lock the door.

"Did you know Max before he came to work for your company here?" I ask Laura, taking off my shoes.

"No," she laughs, following my suit, "we met a few weeks ago. It's just the way he is. I feel like with his arrival, I got not only an assistant but a bodyguard. In the best possible sense."

"You are lucky." I show her to the kitchen.

Out of the corner of my eye, I see her shrug. "It's about time I got some luck too." Her tone is easy, but I feel there is more to her words.

I put on the kettle and rummage through the cupboards. Because of Michael's fussiness about food, I have a whole arsenal of salty and sweet snacks at the ready.

"Let me help you." Laura's simple words tug at my

heartstrings. I give her a tray laden with bowls with cookies and a plate with the cakes she's brought.

"I think it would be better to sit in the living room," I offer. The dining room has started feeling suffocating lately.

We settle on the couch with steaming cups of Earl Grey. I take a small sip of the hot liquid, and suddenly, I can't contain myself. Not waiting for Laura's questions, I pour out everything that's been troubling me for months, along with the culmination of my disappointment.

"And the worst thing is that all of it is my fault," I finish my revelations with a sigh. "No one forced me to marry Michael. And no one forced me to agree to marry him so quickly."

Laura has finished her cup whilst I've been talking. Now she put it on the table and sat back. "There is no use in blaming yourself." She looks kindly at me when she speaks, and I relax under her gaze. "No matter what they say, people change. They change under all kinds of circumstances, and these changes can't be predicted. You met your husband when he was a different person. He earned good money – had been earning it for years. He could afford everything he wanted. He naturally got used to it and started taking it for granted. At some point, people with money stop being able to imagine how it is not to have it. Your husband wanted to get rid of the frustration that often comes with such high-end positions. Again, no matter what those who haven't been there think, well-paid jobs always come with tremendous stress. Your husband wanted to get rid of that stress. He simply didn't think that he'd have to say goodbye to the money as well."

I munch on a cherry Bakewell, and the delicious pastry distracts me from heavy thoughts. "They are so tasty." I raise my hand with a half-eaten cake. "Thank you. I don't know why I haven't bought to try them before." As soon as the words are out, I know the answer. Michael doesn't like Bakewells, so I haven't thought about buying them. The frustration returns. "You are right." I nod and put the cake down. "I understand. It was a huge change in his life and career. But I had to think about its effects *before* I agreed to marry him. I could tell him that I needed time to make such an important decision about marriage and moving to another country. Instead of jumping in headfirst."

Laura shakes her head but says nothing, so I continue. "If only I'd waited, I'd have seen that he isn't the person I thought he was."

"It's also possible that you wouldn't have seen him again if you had refused to marry him. In this case, you'd spend years playing different scenarios in your head of what could have been. And you'd never get any answers. Unanswered questions, like unfinished business, are at the top of the things that make life miserable."

I chew on Laura's words. There's a lot of sense in them. "You are right," I say slowly, thoughts running in parallel with speech. "But what should I do? What *can* I do? I can't just leave." I know it's childish to expect someone else to solve my problems. Besides, Laura is almost a stranger. "Sorry," I add quickly. "It's my mess, and I have to fix it. It's just such a relief to finally talk about it with someone. Thank you."

Laura smiles. "It's okay. You don't have to apologise. I'd help you with more than talking if I could. But the business is new. We have only a couple of assignments. And they aren't the right fit for you. One is for a railway maintenance team, and another one is for welders and fabricators. But I'll let you know if someone asks to find them office staff."

I am finally able to offer a smile too. "Thank you. I won't make you blush. But I have to be more active in my job search. People from home wouldn't be coming here if there weren't available vacancies, right?"

Laura nods. "And you have an advantage. More than one, actually. You already live here, and you speak English. Many of those who want to come and work here depend on someone to help them. Both with relocating and communicating with their employers and colleagues."

Cheered up, I make us more tea, and we talk until it gets dark. I feel so comfortable with Laura that I almost offer her to stay the night. I am glad I now have someone I can talk to.

"We're going to London tomorrow," Laura says while we wait for Max to pick her up. The night is quiet and warm. Cottages stand dark where their inhabitants have already gone to bed. "It's a short one-day trip. And we have to set out really early. I have a meeting in the City. Would you like to come with us?"

I told Laura earlier that I've never been to its capital despite living in England for a year and a half. I jump at the opportunity to see the legendary city. "Wow, thanks! I'd love it! I won't be a bother, I promise."

Max arrives, and they drive away. I stay on the porch until the car lights disappear around the bend.

It is going to be an exciting day tomorrow. I am determined not to let thoughts about Michael's disapproval spoil it for me.

CHAPTER 12

Laura and Max arrive just after six, and we set out to London. It's almost one hundred and fifty miles to the capital from Southbay. The sky is a gentle hay of azure, promising a beautiful sunny day.

We leave Eastpoole and turn inland, away from the Jurassic Coast. For over an hour we drive along dual carriageways. At this hour, the roads aren't busy. A car speeds past us from time to time, but Max calmly keeps within the allowed speed limit.

We don't talk much, the need to rise so early having tied our tongues. But I am so absorbed in watching the landscape around me that I am glad I can give it my undivided attention. I like everything I see. Cute names of unfamiliar towns and villages fascinate me. I let my imagination wander, figuring out what these places look like, hidden behind the hills and forests. If I had a car, I'd regularly go exploring the area. Everything looks so different from home, and I feel that my heart opens up with every pretty view of the English countryside.

On the motorway, the traffic becomes denser, and the picture outside the window duller. I turn my attention to my companions. Although we don't know each other well, I feel comfortable in their presence. I feel safe and looked after. I have no idea where this peculiar feeling comes from, but I enjoy it. Only now have I noticed that I was tense and alert before.

I watch Laura and Max with interest. There is a synergy between them that glues my eyes to them. I know that they are colleagues, and Laura told me they met only recently. Still, looking at them, I can't shake off the impression that there is more to their relationship. They don't touch each other or demonstrate sexual tension in any way. I can't say if they are lovers or even if it is the attraction that I see between them. They are attuned to each other. That's the closest I can put my impressions into words. I have never seen anything like it.

"We'll be on M25 soon, and then, we are almost there." Laura turns to me from the front seat. She smiles in a way that always makes me want to smile back. "We'll leave the car at our friends' place and take the underground from there to the centre. I'm sorry about that, but driving in the centre of London is a nightmare."

"It's fine by me." I raise my palms to stress my words. "I've never been on a metro before. It's going to be an adventure."

"If you aren't claustrophobic," Max makes a remark, not turning away from the wheel. It's impossible to understand if he is joking or serious.

Laura bursts with laughter. "We could take a bus, of course. But I'm afraid we'll end up in an opposite part of the city from where I need to be," she looks at the watch on the panel, "in an hour and a half. I've never even tried to figure out their ground transport system."

"I'll be fine," I giggle. "But just in case... do you have a paper bag?"

Laura laughs again and wipes her eyes with a paper tissue. Even Max gives a reserved smile.

"Everything will be fine," Laura says, taking a look at the map on her lap. "There'll be a monstrosity of a roundabout in a few kilometres. Drive straight through. But the next octopus is where we have to take the first exit to the right," she gives Max the instructions.

He nods.

After driving for about thirty minutes, we arrive at the quiet residential street lined with red-brick two-storey houses. Max parks the car in the driveway just as Laura indicates. A man of about twenty-five comes out from the house. It looks like Laura and he are acquainted, while Max watches him with suspicion.

"I don't know when we'll pick up the car, so if you aren't at home at that time, it's no bother. I'll send you a message when we've left," Laura says to the man.

"No problem. You can stay for the night if you want. It's cramped in there," he waves at the house, "but for you and your friends, we'll always find room."

"Thanks." Laura smiles warmly. "Next time, maybe. It seems that I'll have to come to London often. Nothing gets done in a heartbeat here."

"Yeah." The man smiles back. There is an unsettling roughness about him, but he seems kind. "If I or Alex are home when you get back, come in for tea."

Laura smiles again. "Absolutely. And you promised you'd come over to Southbay sometime. I'll show you where I've settled. It has some spectacular views you won't find in London."

"I will. It's just, you know, there is always something that has to be looked into."

"Sure. But the invitation is open."

We all say our goodbyes and walk to the tube station.

At barely after ten in the morning, it is already hot. The sun blazes down at our heads. I put on my sunglasses. I'm curious about what business Laura has with the rather shady-looking man. Despite being absolutely different, they seem comfortable in the company of each other. But I decide not to pester her with questions.

We walk into a tube station, which I'd have easily walked past, so nondescript is the entrance to it. Laura says she has tickets for all of us from her previous visit to London, and we walk straight to the platform. The train arrives soon. I forget about strange men and any questions I have about them. I'm excited to see the capital of Great Britain, an iconic place from books and movies.

******

London is magnificent. With crowds hurrying down the streets, impressive buildings, and the endless flow of cars, it is grand and intimidating. I didn't have any specific expectations of how the city would look like. Maybe that is the reason I am so deeply impressed by it.

Laura had to change lines to go to her meeting, and we said goodbye to her at the Green Park station. I saw that Max would have preferred to go with her rather than on an excursion around London with me. His concern about his boss's well-being seems touching and thoughtful rather than overbearing. I feel envious. My husband doesn't even care how I am doing while he spends weeks away from home.

We walk to Buckingham Palace and stand admiring it through the fence together with dozens of other tourists. I've never dreamt about visiting London and seeing where the queen lives. Still, actually being here seems huge. My chest bursts with emotions.

"Wow," I say, looking at the famous façade behind which the royal family members lead their mysterious lives, "who would have thought we'd see it with our own eyes?"

Max doesn't smile. It isn't his style. He nods, though, in agreement. "Yes. It was hard to imagine walking the streets of Dickens and Doyle from the little town in the middle of Latvian countryside."

I nod too, embarrassed to admit I haven't read the books

by either. At least, I know they were writers.

"Let's go and look at the famous Big Ben?" Max asks, and I nod again. I feel so overwhelmed that it is difficult to speak.

St. James Park is full of activity. People hurry along the park alleys while others sit on benches feeding squirrels. I try not to squeal with delight like a little girl when I see a grey squirrel perched atop the back of a bench. It holds something in its tiny paws. In a moment, the squirrel is gone, having gotten what it wanted from the humans.

"Are these pelicans?" I exclaim, stopping and pointing at the birds on the small island.

Max stops too. I like that he never looks irritated. With him, I feel safe. "Yes, there is a whole colony of them living here, on the Duck Island," he explains.

We watch the birds for a while. *A few hours are not enough to spend here.* I try to suppress the rising annoyance.

We leave the park behind, and on our way to Big Ben, I have to fight back the wish to stop and stare at every impressive building. The disappointment I felt when we arrived in London and I saw residential streets lined with similar-looking two-storey houses dissipated. The centre of the city is absolutely spectacular. I shiver, imagining that I walk the old streets that have witnessed the events we now read about in history books.

"It is so small!" Among the general grandeur, Big Ben fails to make an impression on me. But the Palace of Westminster quickly makes up for it. The enormous building is mesmerising. To me, it looks like a gigantic sandcastle that someone has built on the river bank.

We follow the promenade, which runs along the Thames.

I'm still trying to get used to the crowds and the diversity of faces around me. Both in Southbay and back home in Latvia, it isn't like this, and I feel fascinated. I have to remind myself that it isn't polite to stare at people when my gaze involuntarily lingers on a family eating lunch on a bench or a man looking at the water. Their exotic looks and clothes hypnotise me. More than anything, I'd like to just stand and observe them doing what they are doing. It's a pity it would be considered stalking.

"That's impressive." I point at the London Eye observation wheel. "I've never seen anything like it."

"Do you want to take a ride?" Max surprises me with his question.

"Of course!" I can't contain my enthusiasm. "That would be such an adventure!"

We cross the Thames by the footbridge that runs along the railway bridge. The queue for tickets is long, but it moves quickly. Once I enter the passenger capsule, which looks like a compact spaceship, I can't tear my eyes away from the view. We spend the thirty-minute ride in silence, the great city sprawling underneath having grabbed my undivided attention. The day is clear, and I can see as far as my eyes let me. I am in awe of London, and having gotten a bird's-eye view of it makes me wish to explore its every corner.

Once the London Eye ride is over, we cross the river again and continue walking along the Thames. I feel like I am on a different planet, rather than in an unfamiliar city, so different the routines and habits of its inhabitants and guests are. I wonder what it'd be like to spend a week or longer here, walking these streets every day, absorbing the atmosphere, getting acquainted with what Londoners do.

I'm used to long walks, so I don't notice the time as we stroll and chat about insignificant things.

"St. Paul's Cathedral should be somewhere nearby," Max says after taking a look at the map. "We can go and have a look." The mobile buzzes in his pocket before I can reply. "Is everything okay?" he asks after initial 'hello'. "We are almost by the St. Paul's Cathedral. Is there a tube stop nearby? Okay. We'll be waiting for you there."

I guess that it was Laura. "She's finished with her meeting?" I ask, afraid that it means we should drive back to Southbay right away.

"Yes. We agreed to meet at the cathedral."

"That's great." I follow Max through the maze of unfamiliar streets. He seems to have a built-in navigator, for he doesn't look at the map after he checked the route.

St. Paul's Cathedral is majestic, but since it is tucked between other imposing buildings and streets with traffic, I fail to admire it in full measure.

We walk around yet another London landmark I've seen today for the first time until Laura appears from around the corner. She is her smiling and relaxed self, and my worries about immediate departure fade.

"Have you signed the contract?" Max asks after we exchange brief stories about what we managed to accomplish in the last few hours.

Laura shakes her head and shrugs. "No, they are slow like everyone else here. You'll get used to it. But they didn't say no. That is what matters. We'll be in touch."

Max nods. The news obviously hasn't upset him.

"So," Laura turns to me, "what would you like to do next? You don't want to be heading straight home to the island, do you?"

I blush. "No, I don't. I'd love to see more of London."

"Perfect." Laura claps her hands. "Despite coming here for what seems like a hundredth time in the last months, I haven't seen many of the famous sights myself. Let alone visited a museum. Do you think you'll be up to that formidable drive back after all the sightseeing?" she asks Max.

"Sure," he replies in his unperturbed manner. It is impossible to understand if he says what she wants to hear or what he really thinks.

"That's settled then. He is the driver. He has the last word." Laura and Max exchange one of those glances that puzzle me. It speaks volumes but doesn't reveal anything about their connection. "So, it's your day today, Margo. Where would you like to go?"

I want to see a dozen other places I read about yesterday before going to bed to divert my attention from Mark's attack. I was still feeling nervous after Laura left and wouldn't have been able to sleep anyway. I know it's impossible to do in one day, so I choose the most iconic place. "I'd really like to see the Tower of London."

"Perfect. Do you know how we get there from here?" Laura asks Max. It is obvious that she expects nothing but a positive answer.

"Yes, we have to go back to the river, and then it's about a twenty-minute walk from there to the Tower."

"Is that okay?" Laura asks me. "We could go by tube, but I don't think it'll save us any time."

"No, let's walk. We'll see more this way." I look at both of them, and I'm relieved to see they don't seem to have anything against my plan.

"I like your attitude," Laura announces. "I've had enough of underground experience for today. And that Northern line is something else. It looks like the city officials keep it looking like trains and stations have come straight from a horror movie. Maybe they use them as filming locations and earn millions from American filmmakers."

Max gives her a concerned look.

"I think we should grab something to eat first." Food is the last thing on my mind now, but that's everything I could come up with to ease the tension.

We set out in the direction of the Tower of London. Luckily, we find a small supermarket, buy packed sandwiches, snacks, and water, and have an improvised lunch on the go.

The feeling of elation doesn't leave me all the time while we wander around one of the most popular landmarks of London. Max is extraordinarily knowledgeable about history and architecture, and I listen to him in wonderment. I even ask him if he really was in the army, since he sounds more like a teacher or a librarian.

"I was in the army," he explains, a hint of a smile

touching his serious face. "But I was a lawyer. I did have a military rank. They couldn't employ a civilian for my position. So, I graduated from the Academy of Defence and participated in all kinds of drills. But I worked with papers and contracts."

The respect I feel for this young man rises. I'd never met such controversial people in my life.

After spending four hours exploring the iconic castle's exhibitions, Laura offers for us to go to Covent Garden. "If we are on a grand tour around London anyway, we might see as much as we can." We walk back to St. Paul's Cathedral, and from there, we take a tube ride.

I like the atmosphere in Covent Garden. It is artistic and laid-back, with stylish people shopping and sitting in numerous cafes and pubs.

Laura spots the Body Shop and declares she definitely needs to go in there. Max waits for us outside while we roam between the shelves of bright-coloured jars, bottles, and tubes. Laura buys a handful of body creams and scrubs. I make a mental note to look for a Body Shop in Eastpoole.

I've been feeling so elated all day that not once did I think about Michael and what his reaction to my sudden day trip might be. Only when already in the car, watching the London outskirts rushing past me in a kaleidoscope of changing images, the uneasiness envelops me. I check my mobile to see that Michael hasn't turned his phone on: his usual habit when he drives somewhere on business. It means that until he arrives home and finds a note I left for him on the kitchen table, he won't have a clue that I've gone to London. He also wouldn't know that today he would have to heat up his dinner himself. He hates the microwave and always repeats that after being heated up there, the food tastes like paper.

Has it been worth it? I brush away the unwelcome thought that threatens to spoil such a perfect day. *It will be okay,* I say to myself firmly. *Michael will understand.*

******

The first thing I notice when I enter the house is a murderous look on my husband's face.

I stop short at the kitchen entrance. "I've left you a note and also sent a message," I blurt out, skipping the greeting.

"Where the hell have you been?" Michael stands by the kitchen cabinets with his fists on the counter.

"I've been in London. I told you that in the note."

The moment Michael turns and starts walking toward me, I realise that logic isn't going to help me. He hasn't unclenched his fists.

I involuntarily take a few steps backwards.

He reaches me midway in the hall.

"Bloody hell, Margo!" Michael shouts, towering over me. His thin and usually pale face is covered in red blotches. His bloodshot eyes pierce me with rage. "I won't let you treat me like an idiot!" He continues shouting, and I almost dart to the front door and run away. "I haven't married you to be treated like a fool!"

I keep silent. I sense that trying to offer any excuses would only make things worse.

"I will not tolerate disrespect!" he spits. "Do you understand me?" I don't reply, and he goes on. "If you ever do anything like this again – if I return to an empty house ever again…." He doesn't finish, his already blotched skin turning even redder.

My stomach churns with fear and indignation. My face burns, and my eyes sting. I take a deep breath to prevent either screaming or puking. My hands start to shake, and rainbow circles float in front of my eyes. "I'm not your slave," I utter in a strangled voice. I don't sound like a strong, independent woman defending herself. I sound like a pathetic victim.

I don't see Michael's hand before it connects with my face.

A slap comes as a shock, and I freeze for a moment. *It's not that painful,* I think in bewilderment when my brain finally registers what has just happened. I don't feel pain, only coldness that spreads over my cheek, making the ear on the same side tickle.

"You are my *wife*!" His lips curve in disgust at the last word. "You'd better act like one."

He starts climbing the stairs. He stops before reaching the second floor's landing. I almost faint when he turns and fixes his bloodshot gaze on me. "I have an assignment in Cornwall. I'll need both the trailer and the jeep for it. You are coming with me. We leave tomorrow."

I stare at him, too dumbfounded to reply.

"And get the supper ready," he adds. "I'm not going to starve because you decided to spend your day prancing about the country."

I walk to the kitchen on autopilot, with my head empty and my cheek tingling from the slap.

CHAPTER 13

Thoughts erupt in my head like a volcano the moment I wake up. I lie quietly, not getting out of bed. I hear Michael shuffling downstairs.

The clock by the bed shows me that it's five in the morning. Too early for my husband's usual routine.

An uneasy feeling pulls my stomach in a knot. *Does he expect me to go down and make his breakfast? What will he do if I don't read his thoughts and do what he wants?*

Despite feeling scared, I stay under the covers. Today, I don't have enough mental strength to play my usual game of making Michael's life perfect. Besides, it doesn't feel like a game anymore. If I make a mistake, the consequences are more serious now than skipping a move.

In a few minutes, I hear the front door click. *At least he didn't slam it,* I think.

I climb out of bed and walk out of the room. I stop at the top of the stairs, listening to the sounds downstairs. I want to be sure Michael is really gone.

All seems quiet.

I trod downstairs. The delicious coffee aroma still lingers in the kitchen. I put my favourite cup in the slot and press the button. While the machine churns and gurgles, I look out of the window.

It is dull and grey outside. The low cloud is so dense that I can't see the grass properly.

A beep lets me know my coffee is ready.

I take the cup, add some milk, and go to the living room. I sit down in my favourite spot on the couch and take a sip. *Why does the first sip always feel absolutely heavenly?* My mind distracts me from the important issues, and I let my thoughts drift for a while.

I hear a noise by the front door. I know it is a postman.

Opening the door, I find a stack of building and construction catalogues. When I pick them up, they slide out of my hands. From one of the glossy covers, a little white dog stares at me, with its rosy tongue lolling out. A tiny knitted hat adorns the head of the cute lap dog. *Knitting for the Soul,* I read the title. *Why on Earth would Michael order this?* My brain doesn't work quickly today, so I just look at the dog on the cover for a few moments. Finally, my gaze falls on the printed address tag attached to the magazine. The tint is smudged where the house number is. *Matilda Peckham,* it reads where the letters are intact.

I raise my head and look at the cottage on the opposite side of the street. I am not in the mood for communication with neighbours at the moment – even less so when neighbours with dementia are concerned – but a good girl in me wins. She always does. And my latest guess is that it's exactly what has gotten me into the biggest trouble.

I sigh and cross the road. It's predictably empty at half past five in the morning.

The door swinging open startles me, for I intended simply to leave the magazine on the neighbour's porch. When I straighten up, having picked the magazine back up, the look of Mrs Peckham shocks me even more. An elderly lady is dressed in a hot pink dressing gown dotted with hearts in a slightly darker shade of the same colour. White strands of grey fluffy hair stick out from the pale violet crocheted nightcap.

The way Mrs Peckham watches me through her watery blue eyes makes me think she fully realises the effect she makes on people with her attire. A faint smile lurks in the corners of her colourless lips, and her surprisingly young eyes twinkle with suppressed mischief.

I give her the magazine. I am still unable to speak.

"Thank you, love," Mrs Peckham chirps in that cracking voice of elderly people. "It always happens when Mr Pritchard is on vacation. Young people these days are too distracted with more exciting things to pay attention to details."

Her sensible manner of speaking, without any trace of senility, pulls me out of my trance.

"You are welcome, Mrs Peckham." I self-consciously run both hands over my hair. I hadn't even thought about brushing it or washing my face before stalking out of the house.

"The young man." Mrs Peckham cocks her head to one side. It makes her look like a bird. "The one that passed by right before you returned home the other day with those foreigners." She looks at me expectantly.

"Mark King?" I am surprised by my mental agility.

"Yes, yes, young George's son." Mrs Peckham coquettishly pats her white hair under the cap. I can't help but wonder what the local businessman could have in common with Matilda. He is some forty years younger than she. "I know you'll say he isn't that young," she giggles, "but for me, he is still a boy in that cute sailor's hat…" Her voice trails off.

I don't know what to say. Luckily, Mrs Peckham doesn't need encouragement to share what she believes the world needs to hear. "Well, what was I saying?" She puts her hands in the pockets of her hot pink dressing gown. "The car George's son drives." She pauses and narrows her eyes before continuing. "That is the same car I saw in Betty Burton's driveway on the day when she was murdered."

If, at that very moment, I were drinking something, I'd have spat it out. *Was it Mark who'd caused Betty Burton's heart attack?*

Mrs Peckham chews on her lips. "But it wasn't George's boy who was in that car," she continues as if talking to herself. "My eyes aren't like they were before, but this much I am perfectly capable of seeing."

"But it was a man?" I gather myself enough to ask. I remember Suzie telling me that the only thing Mrs Peckham could tell the police was that Betty Burton had a visitor without any description.

Matilda glances at me as if I have just said the most nonsensical thing one can imagine. Her face scrunches. Suddenly, she looks like an almost one-hundred-year-old frail woman again rather than an alert citizen always on the watch for her neighbours' safety.

"Do you also think that I have lost my mind?" Mrs Peckham's lips start trembling. "Everyone thinks that I've gone completely gaga. But you know what?" She squints, watching me intently. "I'm very much in my right mind. More than many of those youngsters…" She pauses as if she has lost the trail of her thoughts.

"Of course not," I hasten to reassure her. I hope she hasn't retreated into her happy place, the one so many elderly people seem to prefer to the real world. "I just think this would be extremely valuable information for the police to know. Have you told them about Mark King's car?"

For a moment, a completely vacant look lingers over Matilda's watery blue eyes.

"You told the police that you saw someone visiting Mrs Burton… that day." I try to stimulate her thinking process.

"Y…yes, I did." She looks uncertain.

"And you also told them you can't say anything specific

about that person."

Matilda nods slowly.

"But have you mentioned the car? Have you told them that it was Mark King's car that you saw?"

Mrs Peckham clasps her hands. They are touched by arthritis, with blue veins bulging out. "No, I haven't told them about the car! Do you think they'll arrest me for not giving them all the information?" She looks like a scared child.

"No, no, of course they won't!" I hope she won't have a heart attack like her previous neighbour. I am so not up to explaining to paramedics why Matilda Peckham lies dead on her porch dressed in a hot pink dressing gown. "But you have to tell them about it."

She looks doubtful, like a toddler torn between keeping some innocent crime secret from her parents and spilling out the truth.

"They won't punish you." I try to find some sensible arguments. "They'll be grateful for your help. Imagine, you'll help them solve the most important case they've had in Southbay in the last... last decade!"

Matilda's eyes start twinkling with subdued mischief again. "I'll be like Miss Marple!" she exclaims. Her cheeks turn slightly pink.

I have a vague memory of a TV series with 'Miss Marple' in its title. My knowledge ends there, so I have no idea if the association is good or bad. Still, I take a risk. "Yes, exactly!" I nod enthusiastically. "Everyone will admire that you've solved the case even professionals couldn't solve."

A dreamy smile plays on Mrs Peckham's lips. She casts a glance at Betty Burton's cottage across the street. "I'll go and call them now," she announces and turns to get back into her cottage.

"That's a great idea. It was nice to meet you this morning, Mrs Peckham." I also turn to leave.

"Thank you for popping in, love." Mrs Peckham gives me an absent-minded smile, fiddling with the doorknob.

I am already halfway down the gravel path when Mrs Peckham calls out: "Love?"

I turn. "Yes, Mrs Peckham?"

"Compact powder will help to hide it." She taps her cheek with her hand lightly. "At least, that's what we used to do in my day to avoid nosy questions."

She turns abruptly and walks inside, closing the door behind her.

I raise my hand and touch my cheek. It doesn't hurt, but it is hot.

New developments in Betty Burton's case have made me forget that my husband has hit me for the first time.

******

Back at the cottage, I rummage through drawers, looking for my make-up bag.

Even for special occasions, I don't bother with anything more substantial than a few mascara and lip gloss strokes. Since we haven't gone out anywhere for a while, I've simply forgotten where I've put my make-up.

When I finally locate the cosmetic pouch, I take out a Chanel compact powder. My two best friends gave it to me as a farewell gift before I left for England. I don't think I have even opened it.

Indeed, the transparent sticker is still in place. I tear it off. Opening the elegant black box, I catch my own gaze in a small mirror. My grey eyes are wary. I move my hand further from my face. The mark that Michael's slap has left looks uglier in the mirror of the expensive Chanel compact powder.

My reflection stares at me, and I don't like what I see. My face is drawn, and my complexion is ashen. *I am twenty-two years old*, a voice, as if it's not my own, screams inside my head. I wince. *And whose fault is that?* Another voice adds unhelpfully. *I'm going mad.*

I start dabbing with a sponge on my cheek, then stop abruptly. "Bloody hell!" I say aloud. Frustrated, I march to the bathroom. I need a proper mirror to apply the make-up.

A big mirror over the vanity is even more merciless than the small one in the Chanel box.

I grit my teeth to prevent tears from spilling. Puffy eyes are the last thing I need right now. It is enough with a hideous red blotch on my cheek.

I pat my face with the sponge furiously. The exclusive French cosmetics obviously haven't been designed with helping women hide the signs of abuse in mind. Fragrant powder with a delicate texture feels luxuriant on the skin. Still, it does nothing to conceal what I want others not to see.

I put the compact powder down.

I have to do something. I know it. I also know that no one can take the first steps in my place. I have to find a job, rent an apartment, and tell my husband that I want a divorce.

Tears begin swelling again when thoughts that have been disjointed so far have finally taken shape. I realise with a frightening clarity that I can't put off making serious decisions any longer. I might be only twenty-two and awfully inexperienced about life, but one thing I know for certain: it is useless to hope that Michael will ever change.

I want to leave, and not only because my husband has hit me. Although the slap definitely was the last straw, it was clear that my marriage didn't work before it happened.

The decision to leave hasn't been taken on a whim. No one can accuse me of not having worked on the relationship. I have put all my heart into our marriage. I believed in the importance of my husband's dreams and did my best to support him in achieving them. The thing is that Michael doesn't consider my dreams equally important.

I rub my hands. I hadn't noticed that my knuckles had turned white, so hard I was clutching the vanity counter. I raise my chin and meet my own gaze in the mirror. My lips are still pressed into a thin line, and there is still a worried look in my eyes. But as if by magic, my skin tone has evened, and red spots on my cheek are barely visible.

I take the compact powder and read the product description on the back of the black box. *Light-reflecting and colour-correcting pigments create a luminous complexion and correct the appearance of imperfections*, it reads.

It is not only the appearance of imperfections that I want to correct. I want to get rid of the cause, so that these imperfections don't ever appear again.

CHAPTER 14

Morning hours tick away as I busy myself with things that bring me joy and calm me down.

Michael hasn't returned yet, and his mobile is switched off. I have no idea what he expects me to do since he hasn't left any instructions. I have no idea how long we are going to Cornwall for, which means I can't pack our bags. I don't know when my husband will be back, so I can't start cooking.

I check the fridge contents and put everything that can be reheated later into a freezer. I go around the house and water the plants. Having checked laundry baskets and closed the shutters on the windows in the second-floor rooms, for a moment, I am at a loss what to do next.

I feel restless and loiter about before my eyes fall on the piano. I sit down at the instrument and play, letting my mind switch off from my troubles. The music is immersive and relaxing. After playing for an hour, I tear my hands away from the keyboard with a smile playing on my lips.

I check the time. It's already eleven. There is still no sign of Michael.

I look at a desk calendar standing on the windowsill. Something clicks in my head, and I jump from the stool. Today is Thursday. The day of the Groveland ladies' choir rehearsal. The last days' turbulence made me forget about my commitments outside of marriage.

I look at the watch again. What time will Michael be back? I have no clue, and there is no way I can find it out. My palms start to itch, and I scratch them nervously. My head tingles unpleasantly, and I feel the urge to brush my hair hard with a metal brush. My face begins to itch too. I raise my hand to rub off the annoying sensation and stop.

Anger overrules fear. I run upstairs, put on my capri jeans and a white T-shirt, and, grabbing my small handbag, I storm out of the house.

Let him hit me again, I mutter, hurrying down the street. *What else can he do? Kill me? He won't get away with it. Two murders with barely two months between them are two murders too many on our sleepy island.* I snort at my own humour. My sense of the funny has transformed under the influence of dry British humour. *And I bloody like it!*

I turn onto the coastal path. I don't want to run into Michael driving home.

At eleven, the sun is already high in the sky. It is another glorious summer day in Southbay. The coastal path is empty. Dog-walkers, for the most part, are early-risers, and it is already too hot for horse riding.

It suits me fine. I don't think I'm capable of even as much as a polite smile and a non-committal 'hiya'. I walk at a brisk pace along the grassy path, paying attention neither to the majestic cliffs nor the flowers that turn the sombre green into a colourful blanket.

Only when I reach the Lighthouse Keeper's Cottage do I catch myself thinking that I don't want to meet Jacqueline today. I don't feel like cuddling Winston either. If someone had told me yesterday that I'm capable of feeling this way, I'd have laughed into their face.

Murphy's law is probably the only one that works without failure, so of course Jacqueline walks out the door the moment I pass by the cottage. Winston squeezes between her and the door frame and runs to me, barking frantically.

"Good boy," I say, patting his silky head, immediately won over by his charm. "Aren't you the best boy ever?"

Winston licks my hands. His golden, fluffy tail rotates like a windmill. He would have gladly risen on his hind legs and put his front paws on my shoulders to lick my face.

"Hi, Margo!" Jacqueline walks over to me. "And I was going to call you. Now that I'm in good shape again, we can start planning our girls' outing." She smiles. This time, her smile reaches all the way to her eyes. But before I have time to bask in its warmth, it fades away. Jacqueline's lips press into a tight line. Something I haven't seen yet.

"Margo?" She doesn't have to say more so that I know that she sees through the Channel compact powder deception.

My gaze drops to the ground, and I can't make myself look up. A wave of deep shame washes over me. I feel completely unworthy of Jacqueline's attention. Women like her curl their lips in disgust when they hear about ugly things like a wife beaten by her husband. They think it's the wife's fault. *I would have never let anything like this happen to me.* I hear their posh-accented voices.

I shake my head. "I'm alright," I say weakly. "It's okay. It isn't how it looks…" Even when I speak these words, I feel that they sound fake. *It isn't how it looks.* It is the oldest line that all liars use.

"Has your husband done it? Has he hit you?" Jacqueline asks.

I wish she would let it go. Still, at the same time, I don't. I nod. "You see, I went to London yesterday. With my friends. New friends. They are from Latvia too, and they've just rented an office up in the business park..." my voice trails off. I am embarrassed by my mumbling. I can't say the truth. Michael was furious mostly because he expected his wife to be at the ready with a freshly cooked meal whenever he chose to return home. It doesn't sound like a justification of his actions – or of my passivity, for that matter.

"He doesn't want you to spend time with friends?"

I dare to raise my eyes, and Jacqueline looks almost like a different person. She isn't regally aloof like I'm used to seeing her. And the warmth that I haven't had enough time to enjoy has disappeared. She is collected and business-like, determined to get to the core of the problem.

"No... yes..." I mumble again, but I can't help it. "I didn't tell him I was going to London with them. It was a last-minute invitation, and..." I take a deep breath to collect myself. It does nothing to placate me. "His phone was off... I sent him a text, but he didn't get it. He was worried that something had happened to me..."

"If he was worried, why did he hit you when you showed up?"

"He has never done it before! It must have been stress, you know..."

"I know everything about stress and what it can cause." Jacqueline's eyes are sharp. I feel like she sees right through me, and it makes me want to melt into the ground. "When someone makes you worry about them, and it proves ungrounded, you can feel anger. But that anger usually is directed at something else. A person can break a vase or hurt themselves, hitting a wall with their hand. If the person who caused their worry becomes an object of their anger, it means that the reason isn't care or love. If someone says they hit you because they love you, it means they feel that they have lost control over you. And it drives them crazy."

My shoulders slump, and when I sigh, my breath comes out with almost a hiss. Winston, who has settled at my feet, stands up and begins licking my hand again. His soft side rubs against my leg, and for some reason, that is what makes me break down.

"I know I have to divorce him." I am surprised at how calm my voice sounds. "And I will. It's just it's not that simple. I have nowhere to go. I don't want to go back home to Latvia. I have to find a job first. And then, I have to wait until I save enough for the deposit so I can rent an apartment."

I know that Jacqueline won't help me. It's not something the locals do. In Latvia, people have smaller homes and lower wages. Maybe that is the reason why they share the little they have more easily. Back at home, I'd expect my friends to offer me to sleep on a sofa in their cramped living room for as long as I needed. Here, I am a stranger whom no one is obliged to help out in a time of need.

I am grateful for the sympathy, though; it's already more than I could have counted on. I expect her to tell me about shelters for abuse victims. I don't know anything about the social services system in England and what kind of help I could get should I seek any. *Maybe,* I think, *they'd just buy me a ticket back home. Who needs another mouth to feed for taxpayers' money?*

"Of course, it's not simple." Jacqueline's face softens, and she smiles. "Such situations never are. I know that for sure since I've seen more cases of domestic abuse than most people. My first job after graduation from law school was in a support services centre for domestic abuse victims. I could have chosen a law firm in London and dealt with cleaner issues like mergers and acquisitions. My parents would have wanted me to do exactly that." From the way she speaks about it, it doesn't feel like she's held a grudge against her parents. "I was a good girl who always listened to her parents, but in this case, I had to insist on my own way. In my early twenties, I was an idealist. I wanted to make a difference. Everyone is like this when they are twenty, I guess."

When I was twenty, I married a man thirty years my senior. I can't blame my youthful idealism for that. Only my childish folly. Thoughts rush through my head, but I decide not to voice them.

"I've seen women who've blamed themselves for what their husbands did to them. More often than you would think, they've returned to their abusive partners. And sometimes, it doesn't end well." Jacqueline pauses and looks at me with concern.

"Michael won't kill me!" I blurt out without thinking. Jacqueline keeps looking at me, and I feel uncomfortable under her gaze. I can't make a decision on the spot. Still, I can't bear it if she sees me as a pathetic coward.

"People who are capable of aggressive actions toward another person are unpredictable," she says calmly. "It is never the excess of caution that gets women into trouble. It is always the lack of it."

Winston whines as if he has understood Jacqueline's words.

I sigh. There's nothing I can say so I'd look good in this elegant and confident woman's eyes. "I can't do anything about it now," I say. "But I will. I will start doing something after we return from Cornwall."

She raises her brows. "Are you going on vacation?"

"No, Michael has an assignment there, and he needs to take both his car and the trailer."

"And he is using you as a driver."

I nod. Nothing can make me feel more miserable than I already do.

Jacqueline purses her lips, and lines appear on her smooth forehead. She doesn't say anything for a few moments. "Will you be safe there?" she muses, looking past me at the channel waters below the cliffs. "Please, keep your mobile on you at all times, alright? Call me at once if you feel that something is wrong. And do not hesitate to call the police. When you return, we'll meet and talk it through."

I nod again, afraid to burst into tears if I utter a word.

"I hope you don't consider me too intrusive." Jacqueline's blue eyes watch me warily. "You are a wonderful person, and I simply don't want anything bad to happen to you."

I can't fight the stinging in my eyes any longer. Tears spill, and I don't try to stop them. "Thank you, Jacqueline," I force myself to speak. "I don't think you're intrusive. I also think that you are wonderful. I'll call you when I'm back in Southbay. I…" My throat constricts, and I gulp for air. "I really need help to sort this mess."

"And I'm here to help you, Margo." Jacqueline touches my arm and gives it a light squeeze. "Everything will be okay. We will sort everything out together."

******

I still struggle to get my emotions under control when I arrive at the Groveland Bakery. Suzie understands what has happened at once, and with a stern expression on her face, fusses around me, settling me down at our usual table. She dismisses my feeble excuses about letting the choir ladies down. "That's not the most important thing at the moment," Suzie says before she rushes back to the counter.

"That bastard!" she exclaims, putting down a tray with tea and freshly baked scones in front of me with a clink. "Who does he think he is? Hitting a lovely girl like you. You've spoilt him with those muffins and everything. We shouldn't spoil men. The less we show them we care, the more they respect us."

Looking at Suzie's usually kind face burning with sincere indignation brightens my mood. Her dark eyes blaze on her tiny face. She would look like a rebellious teenager if only her short dark hair wasn't streaked with grey.

"You should divorce him as soon as you can. People don't change. If he's hit you once, he'll do it again." Suzie pours me a cup of Earl Grey. A spicy aroma of bergamot with a note of lemon touches my nostrils, and a calm determination descends upon me.

"I will ask him for a divorce," I say, taking a sip of hot liquid. It tastes divine. "I hope I'll find a job quickly. I won't be choosy. I'll take the first one that'll have me." I put a teaspoon of berry jam into my mouth. The sugar boosts my confidence even more. Besides, every time I talk about my plans, they start to seem more and more realistic. "It won't be easy to rent an apartment. I don't have money for a deposit. But I'll save. I've never had any spare money, but Michael has taught me new ways to economise." I giggle. Dry British humour makes you balance between a wish to laugh and an urge to cry. I have learned that in complicated situations, it can be immensely comforting.

"That's my girl!" Suzie generously smears soft butter over a scone and gives it to me. "I like your spirit. It's a pity I can't offer you a room. The house I rent is more like a cardboard box rather than a proper house, really. Besides, the owner uses the guest bedroom as a storage space for keeping his junk." Suzie shrugs. "I don't mind since I get to pay a reduced rent for letting him do that. I wouldn't mind being able to use the attic – he stores boxes with I-don't-know-what there too – but it can't be helped now. My husband left me peanuts when we divorced. And I haven't become richer since then." She laughs humourlessly, just like I did a moment ago. "I wish I could go back on our arrangement now." She gives me an apologetic look.

"It's okay, Suzie. It's already enough that I can talk to you about it. More than enough, to be honest. I've been feeling trapped, not having anyone to talk to about what's going on in my life."

"Oh, you poor mite." Suzie pours more tea into my only half-empty cup and takes another scone to smear it with butter. "At least I can feed you with comfort food. It isn't much, but…" She gives me the scone.

"But life is a bitch, and then you die." I take a bite from the pastry dripping with butter.

Crow's feet deepen around Suzie's eyes, now sparkling with laughter.

"That's my girl," she repeats her earlier phrase, with more emphasis this time.

We both giggle.

"Now I know I don't have to worry about you, Margo. With a spirit like yours, you'll be alright. And don't worry about Barbara. She knows that you are the best pianist we'll ever be able to lure into our old ladies' choir. She won't admit it, of course."

Comforted, I munch on the delicious scone when the morning encounter with Matilda Peckham jumps to my mind. I start feeling uneasy again.

"Suzie," I say, putting down the scone, "I met Mrs Peckham today, and she told me something strange."

Suzie's eyebrows go up. "Did she venture out of her house at last? That would be the first time in ten years, no less."

"No, no, she caught me on her doorstep."

"Were you spying on her?" Suzie clicks her tongue. "That'd be even better."

"No, I wasn't spying on her." I roll my eyes, but my mouth twists into a smile. Suzie makes me see the world in bright colours every time we meet. "I don't think I'd be rewarded with any sensation even if I did."

Suzie purses her lips and wags her finger. "You never know with these old decent ladies. They might surprise you."

"But not with the things that paparazzi hunt for. Anyway, she told me that on the day when Betty Burton died, she saw Mark King's car in her driveway."

You would think it wasn't possible, but at my words, Suzie's thin eyebrows shoot up even higher. "It was George's enfant terrible who killed our Betty?!"

"That's where it gets strange." Although my head is full of my own problems, the excitement of dipping a toe into the investigation starts tickling my nerves. I can't refrain from making a pause for a bigger effect. "She says it wasn't Mark in the car."

I certainly get the desired reaction. Suzie eyes grow wide as saucers. "Then who was it?" Her voice trembles with anticipation.

I sigh. "She didn't say."

"Well," Suzie slumps back in her chair and crosses her arms on her chest. "Why can't it ever be like in the crime movies?"

I shrug. The excitement dies out as quickly as it flared up. I remember that my husband – who hit me yesterday – probably waits for me at home, furious again at not finding me where, in his opinion, I belong. "If crime movies were like reality, people wouldn't want to watch them. And the guys in the TV and movies industry couldn't make millions."

"Did Matilda tell the police about the car?"

"No, and actually, that's why I remembered I had to tell you about this." I shake off unpleasant thoughts. Even if Michael hits me again, it won't change anything. I have made my decision, and I will stick to it. "I told her to go to the police and tell them everything. But I'm really not sure that she didn't forget about it right away."

Suzie chuckled. "I'm sure that she did. She might remember what dress she wore for the first date with her husband seventy years ago, but she most certainly doesn't remember what she had for breakfast today."

"That's what I thought. I know you are busy in the café, but could you still drop by Mrs Peckham and make sure she gets to talk to the police? I can't do it until after we return from Cornwall…"

Suzie's face turns stern again. "And why does that bastard need to drag you to the middle of nowhere? He could have asked one of his workers."

I look down at the half-eaten scone and the white film that has developed on the already cold tea. "Michael doesn't like to waste money on anything he can get for free." I still feel terrible saying such things about my husband. But I won't lie to make my husband look better in other people's eyes anymore.

"And you, love, should stop wasting your life on him."

I look up and nod. "You're right."

Suzie begins to cram cups, saucers, and cutlery back onto the tray. "Don't worry about a thing, Margo. I'll make sure Matilda talks to the police and tells them everything about the car and the guy she saw. I'll sit next to her when she makes that call if she hasn't done it already. And I'll drive her to the police station if they don't bother to come down to Southbay."

We both stand up. We both know I'd better get back home as soon as possible. The warm feeling envelops me when I look at my friend. In an unobtrusive, gentle way, Suzie has become my friend: the closest I have ever had.

"Call me the moment you are back." Suzie gives me a pointed stare before she takes the tray to the counter. I follow her.

"I will."

"Please, take care of yourself down there in Cornwall." Suzie packs cookies and pastry without cream filling into a paper box. "Here, love." She walks out from behind the counter and gives me the box. "Don't get yourself into any trouble. They say there are still pirate traps all over that coast."

We laugh, but we both know it's not the pirates she wants to warn me about.

"Thank you, Suzie. No pirates, I promise." I want to hug her. Maybe, one day, we'll progress to that stage too.

Hurrying down the coastal path on my way home, uneasiness churns in my stomach. Even though I've tried to persuade myself that I am brave, I don't want another confrontation with my husband. Still, after talking to Jacqueline and Suzie, I feel certain that eventually, everything will be alright.

CHAPTER 15

It is five o'clock in the evening, and Michael isn't home yet.

I have been busy since I returned from meeting Suzie. I did some chores and played the piano for two hours. Music has always been the best medicine for me.

I am not even angry at my husband for not thinking about warning me about the change of plans. I don't care anymore. I can't change him or the way he chooses to treat me. What I can change is the way I live my life, and that's what I intend to do.

I am reading a book when Michael finally returns. The story is so engrossing that the sound of the front door opening barely makes me stir.

My husband walks into the living room.

I reluctantly raise my head from the pages. "I've cooked the dinner," I say, skipping a greeting. "It's chicken in a sour cream sauce with garlic. I didn't know if we'd be eating at home today or not, but I can pack it for the freezer, or we can put it in a portable fridge and take it to Cornwall."

Michael doesn't say anything for a few moments, and I wonder what kind of thoughts are running through his head. To be honest, it has never occurred to me to ask my husband a simple question like: "What are you thinking about now?" The realisation catches me by surprise. *Maybe my inability to talk is the real root of our problems?*

"It's okay. We'll eat at home. We aren't going today. I had to go to Bournemouth to buy some tools. They didn't have them in Eastpoole or in Dorchester."

His tone is calm, and I'm not going to risk it by pointing out that he could have called or sent me a short text. I stand up, putting the book away. "I'll go heat our dinner then. Do you want some green salad to go with it? I need some time to chop everything for it."

I can't read the expression on Michael's face. He simply looks at me as if my words don't evoke any emotions in him. "No, don't bother with the salad. Some cherry tomatoes will be enough." He turns to go upstairs but stops before climbing the stairs. "And Margo?"

I halt midway out of the living room. "Yes?"

"Your chicken with garlic is always delicious. Don't hurry with the dinner. I need to take a shower."

Michael walks up, and I stand there, trying not to let my emotions spin out of control. This is the closest to an apology that I can get from my husband. For me, it's not enough. I don't expect him to show up carrying flowers and a jewellery box. Still, to say 'I'm sorry I hurt you. It won't happen again' seems like an easy task to me.

I march to the kitchen and get to work.

******

Later that day, we are in bed, and Michael wants to make love to me.

I don't have it in me to say no.

He is gentle, and I don't feel disgusted by his touch. He does all the things that he used to ignore back when sex was a part of our relationship. I feel warm and elated. I also feel loved, something that I haven't felt for a long time.

Afterwards, I lie in bed, and thoughts float lazily in my head. I don't want to concentrate on any of them. *Maybe*, I think, *I have overreacted. Marriage isn't supposed to be perfect. Ours isn't that bad after all. They say crises happen in every marriage. Maybe that's what we are going through now.*

It feels comforting to imagine that I can continue leading my quiet life on the beautiful island I now call home. It isn't ideal, but there are many things I have grown to enjoy. I could continue wandering along the coastal path and discover new places. People walking their dogs would say 'hiya' to me, and that warm feeling of belonging would spread warmly in my chest.

Until now, I hadn't realised how bleak and frightening being on my own would feel. Even though I had to learn to be independent and earn my own money rather early in life, I have never lived alone. I came to live with Michael straight from my mother's home. When I was sick, Mom took care of me. It would be so depressing to be ill and alone in a rented flat with no one to bring you a cup of tea.

Do I really have to make myself go through this ordeal?

Suddenly, it feels as though it's not the decision to marry Michael, but rather the one to divorce him, that is childish and rushed.

My husband's business is flourishing. His hard work over the last twelve months finally seems to pay off. Once he feels confident that he has succeeded, I'm sure Michael would want to start socialising with neighbours again. The Hammonds might start inviting us to dinner again. I might even gather enough courage to ask Mrs Hammond to let me ride one of her horses. I love horses…

A smile is playing over my lips when Michael comes out of the bathroom and breaks the daydreaming spell.

"I hope you realise it was your fault that I lost control yesterday," my husband says. "Don't do anything like that again." He climbs under the sheets and turns with his back to me.

The bubble bursts.

I toss and turn for hours before I drift into uneasy sleep. I dream about black glistening wrecks dangling about in the water, fully at the mercy of the ferocious waves crashing against the rocky shore.

******

We set off to Cornwall at eight in the morning. There is the promise of a beautiful day in the clear and already warm air. The green and the blue seem brighter, the sun having not yet reached the high seat it will climb to by noon.

The beauty of nature is the last thing on my mind, though, while I sit in Michael's jeep, nervously clutching the wheel. Since I've got my license, I have driven a car no more than a few times. Like all of my friends, I took a driving course right after I turned eighteen. It was the kind of thing everybody did, and it didn't occur to me to think ahead. Of course, I couldn't afford to buy a car, but at the time, it didn't seem relevant.

Now, gripping the worn leather wheel, with sweat tickling my back and a lump in my throat, I curse the herd instinct. If I hadn't followed it like a sheep follows a shepherd, I wouldn't have found myself in this situation.

I don't have time to contemplate my misfortunes for too long. Michael drives out into the road in the trailer, and I have to concentrate on keeping up behind him.

On the island, the traffic is light. By the time we join the dual carriageway that will take us to our destination, I feel comfortable enough not to clutch the wheel like a life ring. Still, it is not until after we've been on the road for more than an hour that my back relaxes, and I start appreciating the surrounding landscape.

We drive too fast to see anything in detail, but the overall impression is of a well-tended and carefully maintained countryside. We don't have to pass through any big cities, and we keep moving at a comfortable speed. Guide signs are dotted at what seems to be every few metres.

It gets a little rougher only when the road narrows to one lane each way. It makes me hopeful that we are close to our destination. We have been driving for more than four hours, and I need to use the bathroom. Michael hasn't pulled over or tried to call me to ask if I need to make a stop.

We drive through what I think is the centre of the village with a big parking lot full of cars and trailers. To the left is a café with 'takeaway' and 'the best fish and chips' signs above the windows, a Cornish pastry bakery, and a souvenir shop. About ten metres further, there is a local pub to the right.

We continue on the dirt road that winds between green fences. Cottages stand far from each other, and I can see the tops of swings, trampoline nets, and even bounce houses in the yards.

For a while, we drive along the track with only the grassy fields on both sides. Finally, we arrive at our destination.

The cottage is so picturesque that, at first, it is difficult to imagine that people can live there. It is white, with red bricks around its windows and front door. Rose bushes encompass its walls. The red only peeks tentatively from the tiny green buds, but it is already clear how magnificent the flowers will look when in full bloom.

A petite grey-haired woman walks out when we climb out of the vehicles. She is dressed in black trousers and a shirt with a floral print. She waits for us on the porch.

"Mr Birkett," she greets Michael in a reserved manner. "I hope your journey to Cornwall was nice."

"Hello," Michael walks over to the woman and shakes her hand. "Thank you. Yes, it was fine and without any delays."

The woman nods. "There is a space to park your trailer at the back. You can leave the jeep here, on the driveway."

"Thank you, Mrs Parry. I'll park it there right away."

Michael gets in the trailer and drives around the cottage.

Without saying a word, Mrs Parry walks into the house and closes the door behind her.

I stand in the driveway. I have no idea what to do. *Michael will be back in a minute,* I placate myself. To distract myself from a full bladder, I look around.

The scenery is breathtaking. It is similar to Southbay, with green rolling fields and dramatic cliffs. Still, this place has different vibes about it. Signs of people's activities are found all over our small island in Dorset. A wired stone fence runs along a significant segment of the coastal path, marking the borders of active quarries and the areas that are no longer operational. Walking along the coastal path, you can see cottages and the Groveland Business Park buildings. Here, it seems like you have reached the end of man's land. I haven't come close to the water yet, but I already feel intimidated by the power of the vast expanse. *Was it the shore that pirates in the old times used to frequent?* I think dreamily.

The pressure in the lower part of my stomach reminds me of the present.

I look at the cottage again. The door is closed. There is no sign of either Mrs Parry or my husband. I look at the rolling fields again. I seriously consider making a dash to the cluster of boulders if I don't have other options.

Then, I hear voices. They are muffled, and it takes me a few moments to figure out where they are coming from. Once I realise it's Michael and Mrs Parry talking behind the cottage, I go over to join them.

My arrival causes no reaction from either of them. They just keep discussing the scope of work Mrs Parry wants Michael to do. "We will be away for ten days," Mrs Parry speaks, not paying any attention to me. "As we have discussed previously, I hope it will be enough for you to finish the work."

"Your new conservatory will be ready for you to have your tea when you return from Spain." Michael smiles confidently, looking more like a salesman than a person who will actually perform the reconstruction works.

"Very well." Mrs Parry doesn't smile.

My lower stomach begins to ache, so I discard the

embarrassment and cough lightly before speaking up. "I'm sorry to interrupt you."

Michael gives me a look as if he is surprised to see me here. Mrs Parry turns her impassive eyes to me but says nothing.

"I need to go to the bathroom." The physical need is so pressing that decorum slides down the scale of my priorities.

Mrs Parry's face gives away both surprise and disgust. I feel like a mongrel, and not an especially cute one at that.

"The summer bathroom is to the left when you enter the back door," Mrs Parry speaks with reluctance. I strongly suspect she isn't happy about me setting foot into her fairy tale cottage. I can't place her accent, but I don't like it. Still, as things stand at the moment, I can't care less about anyone's opinion about me and my manners.

"Thank you," I say before rushing to the house.

The summer bathroom doesn't bear any resemblance to a fairy tale dwelling. It is tiny even by the measure of objectively cramped flats in the five-storey blocks back home in Latvia. I can barely turn with the door closed. A small sink hangs right above my knees when I sit on the toilet. White tiles above the sink are chipped in places, and there is no mirror.

I wonder if this was – or still is – a servants' bathroom. The cottage doesn't resemble a household with a doorman, maids, or kitchen staff. Even so, considering the way arrogant Mrs Parry has treated me, I wouldn't be surprised if it's the help that maintains the house's immaculate look.

I finish my business and wash my hands. There is only one faucet for cold water. The sink is so small that it splashes everywhere.

I don't see any towels, even paper ones, so I dry the floor with toilet paper as best I can.

When I return outside, neither Mrs Parry nor Michael is there. I walk over to the trailer. The door is open, and I see Michael rummaging in the cupboards.

He emerges before I manage to get in. "I need to buy

some materials," he says, walking past me. "I need to start the work tomorrow. I can't waste a whole day."

I follow him to the jeep parked in front of the cottage.

"You're staying here. I'm not going sightseeing," Michael informs me, putting out a bag with tools from the trunk. He walks back to the trailer, and I trail after him.

"Are we staying in the cottage while Mrs Parry is away?" I ask, trying to keep pace with my husband's stride.

He gives me a look as if I have lost my mind. "Of course not. What made you think that? We are staying in the trailer. Why do you think I had to drag it here, across half the country?"

"In the trailer?" I repeat. I always sound dumb when Michael acts like I am just that. "But there isn't a bathroom there. Or running water."

"So what?" Michael gets into the trailer, leaves the bag there, and climbs out. "It's only for a few days. There are showers in the public toilets down the coast there." He waves his hand, indicating the direction.

I dubiously look across the fields that sweep down to the cliffside. I don't see a single building or other sign that something else is there besides whispering grass, roaring waves, and rocks.

"And what will we eat? It's a long way to the pub and café in town."

Michael seems completely oblivious to my distress. "The trailer is packed with instant soups and crackers. You can boil water in the kettle."

My husband gets into the jeep. I grab the door before he shuts it.

"Don't overdramatise, Margo." Michael puts the key into the ignition. "You wanted to go on a vacation. Treat it like a camping trip. Let go of that door. I don't have time for this."

I do as he says and step back. I watch the jeep disappear around the bend. For a few moments, my head is empty. And then, all I want to do is scream.

CHAPTER 16

For about an hour, I sit in the trailer with the door shut. I don't even look out of the window. I simply stare at the wall lined with cupboards in front of me.

Anxiety pulls me out of my stupor. I don't want to repeat the awkward situation where I urgently need to use the bathroom again. Besides, I have no idea if Mrs Parry is at home and if I won't be banging at the door of an empty house.

I walk outside and stand there, checking the weather. Despite the breeze, it is already hot, so I decide against taking a cardigan.

I lock the trailer door and make my way to the cliffs.

The path is narrow but well-marked and rather even. It winds among the flat grassy fields, then dips down and runs between walls of thorny bushes with red blossoms. My mood lightens. It is beautiful here. Different from the more sombre beauty of Southbay. Here, the colours are more vivid, and the landscape more changeable. I feel the excitement of an explorer rising inside me. I will walk these paths as I do on our island in Dorset, and who knows what amazing things I will find.

The path turns right, and then it runs along the cliffside. Just like in Southbay, the stones with yellow letters announcing that you are on the coastal path mark the way.

The cliffs look more menacing here in Cornwall. Even with the sun generously blazing down its glistening light on the dark rocks, they remain grim. Also, stones are jutting out of the water further from the coast. Their sharp, rugged tops look like the teeth of some sea monster.

I walk for about twenty minutes when the landscape changes. Down below, there is a sandy beach. It doesn't run along the cliffside but shoots out into the water, forming a round-shaped cove.

The sight is so cinematic that I stop to admire it from the top.

The sun warms my skin, and the breeze gently cools it. It feels nice.

The narrow path leads down to the cove, and I follow it. At the foot of the cliffs, after crossing the sandy section that curves to the left, the path runs up again. Midway up the cliff, a few buildings are perched on the rocky slope. I am happy to find that one of these buildings houses showers and toilets. Everything looks new and clean. No unpleasant odours save for a faint smell of cleaning chemicals assault my nose when I enter.

Since no one is here, I inspect the showers, ensuring I can use them tomorrow. Basic cubicles with grey tiled walls have a bottle with shower gel attached to the wall. I am impressed. I also find a stack of toilet paper rolls in each toilet stall.

Having acquired the vital knowledge necessary to satisfy basic needs, I feel ready to move up Maslow's pyramid. I am excited to explore the beach of the cove. It looks like a perfect setting for a movie with rocks dotted around it.

Only a few people wander among the stone formations

that resemble a labyrinth. Familiar nods and smiles of greeting warm my heart. Mrs Parry made me feel like an annoying nuisance, so I welcome formal but sincere attention from these strangers.

I walk slowly in the narrow corridor between the rocks created by nature's fanciful hand. The light sand under my feet makes a striking contrast with the dark walls. Sunlight streams from above, driving away the shadows. I almost regret that I am not any good with paint and brushes. I could easily imagine being swept away by inspiration, engrossed in trying to transfer the surrounding beauty to paper.

On the farthest side of the beach, taller rocks stand as if guarding the cove from the vigour of the open sea. Today, the waves are tame. They roll gently onto the shore, leaving a lace of white froth on the water's edge.

I pause in the long passageway carved in the rock and raise my head to look at its arched ceiling. It seems like any minute, a cloud of bats will detach themselves from the walls high above and dash out, squeaking wildly. I just stand there in awe, listening to the waves whispering outside.

Walking out of the passageway, I stop again. In front of me, the water spreads as far as my eyes can see.

A man in long shorts with a backpack and poles in both hands is walking along the narrow sandy stretch. He nods and smiles, and I wave and smile back. When he disappears around the bend, I am alone with the rocks and the waves again.

I close my eyes and take a deep breath. The salty air is comforting.

I am strong, I say to myself and smile at the slogan's lameness. Still, the words make me feel better. "I am strong," I say aloud. There isn't any echo here, but I get the impression that the waves picked up my words. *They will take them to the vastness of the ocean.* The thought flashes through my mind like a tide.

"I am strong, and I will find a way to make everything alright," I say to the waves, and they reply with a soft, reassuring murmur.

******

Back at the trailer, I put the kettle on and make myself a cup of tea and some instant noodle soup in a bigger mug. I add some oregano crackers to go with it. After a long walk in the fresh air, it tastes heavenly.

Having finished eating, I go through the storage compartments. Since Michael hasn't ever taken me anywhere with him, I don't know what we have in the trailer. I find a lot of useful things, most of which obviously haven't even been used. There are stacks of towels and bed linen, as well as a set of folding chairs and a table.

I take one of the folding chairs outside. The idea that tomorrow I can have breakfast here cheers me up.

The sun is still high up in the sky. It has shifted from zenith only slightly, preparing for its descent beyond the horizon. With my back pressed against the side of the trailer for additional stability, I have almost fallen asleep, sitting in a flimsy chair.

I stir out of my slumber at the crunching sound of car tyres. The sound of the motor fades quickly.

"Mrs Parry has departed for her vacation. Spain, beware!" I giggle.

I stand up and stretch. As lovely as the warm sun feels on my face, a stiff back is the price to pay for the enjoyment if you don't have a proper chaise lounge.

I make myself another cup of tea and eat some sweet cookies. I take a short walk to the cliffs, and after I return, I read a book. The story pulls me in, and the uncomfortable chair doesn't bother me until the sun makes a swift plunge into the sea.

I am reluctant to get inside the trailer. I don't have claustrophobia, but it feels suffocating inside the cramped space. I pull out the bed from the wall and make it with fresh bed linen. Only when I am ready to go to sleep do I check my mobile phone. To my surprise, I find three unread messages.

Hi, Margo, the first one is from Jacqueline. *I hope you have arrived safely. Take care of yourself. Please remember that you can call me at any time. Jacqueline.*

I smile. I feel blessed my relationship with her seems to be developing into a friendship.

Hi love. Hope your husband behaves himself. He'd better since I have a contact in the police now. Take care and call me if you need me.

Suzie can make me feel like an Amazon warrior even when she is hundreds of miles away.

The last message is from Michael. *Back tomorrow morning.*

I put the phone on a narrow tabletop beside the bed.

My husband can do what he likes. I am not going to let the opportunity to explore Cornwall slip through my fingers.

******

The next morning, I wake up early but well-rested. It is barely after five, but the sun is already up. I love summers for turning the nights into fleeting moments, so different from the oppressive winter nights that last forever.

The way to the public bathrooms also seems quick and pleasant. I was worried a little that they might be closed so early in the morning. Luckily, when I arrive, I find them open. Besides, I am not the only one who prefers an early shower. I see an elderly couple coming down from the coastal path in the direction of the facilities.

Yesterday I hadn't noticed a campsite a little further down the coast from the picturesque cove. Dozens of trailers are parked there, along with tents. I am glad the area isn't as desolate as it looked at first glance.

After taking a long hot shower, washing my hair, and brushing my teeth, I feel revived and ready for a new day. With a towel hung over my shoulder, I stride along the coastal path back to the trailer. I've already made a plan for today. First, I'll go to the lighthouse I caught a glimpse of from the coastal path. Then, I'll walk to the village to check the shops and cafes there.

I am fully engrossed in happy thoughts when I stop

short at the sight before me.

A rider atop the magnificent black horse looks like a creature from a different reality. The horse's coat is shiny like exquisite silk. Its tail and mane are long and curly. They resemble the immaculate hairstyle of some diva from the Hollywood Golden Age.

When the horse draws nearer, I see that the rider is equally impressive in appearance. He is tall and tanned. His short black hair is wet, as is his bare chest. My eyes involuntarily slide down from his well-sculptured shoulders to a perfect six-pack on his abdomen. I bet that his hips are as toned as his torso. I can't see that, for the wetsuit he has pulled down from his upper body partly hides his legs. He carelessly holds the reins in one hand.

I stare at him like a fool.

My cheeks turn hot as I realise I know this rider.

"Margo!" Finley Hammond exclaims, pulling in the reins.

"Hi." I am too embarrassed to utter anything more coherent.

"What are you doing here?"

Before I can retort with '*I could ask you the same question*', he continues: "My parents have a cottage there, down by the lighthouse. Mom insists we spend some time here every summer. Before, we stayed here for at least a month. But with Dad's new job and my studies, we managed to reduce it to two weeks."

My wits return while he speaks. "It is beautiful here," I say. "I wouldn't mind spending here all summer."

"How long are you staying in Lizard?"

"Lizard?" I feel stupid. I haven't thought to ask Michael what this place is called.

"I know it's a funny name." Finley doesn't seem to notice my ignorance. "They say it comes from *Lys Ardh*, which means 'high court', but I think it's much simpler. Look at the map. The peninsula looks like a lizard stretching out into the sea."

"I guess it makes sense. They must have a lot of legends here," I say for the sake of saying something. As often happens when I am in Finley's company, all I can think about is how to get away from him. He is like a magnet toward which I gravitate by some will that I can't control. Getting too close is the last thing I need.

"Oh yes, this place is packed with legends. They say pirates' treasures are hidden all along the coast. It's just the cliffs here are too dangerous to try to look for them."

I don't know which way to look. Finley intimidates me. I want to talk to him, ask about his studies, and learn his opinions about everything from pirates' treasures to his favourite tea brand. Still, I know that for me, this path is more dangerous than the Lizard's cliffs. I don't want to suffer from a broken heart. The suffering brought by a broken marriage is already more than I can handle.

"Your horse is beautiful." I can't refrain from stating the obvious. The black horse is the most beautiful animal I have seen in my whole life.

"Alastor." Finley pats the horse's neck lovingly. I can't say who looks more attractive: Finley, with lean but strong muscles on his forearm rippling from the motion, or Alastor, with his long, curly mane scintillating in the sun. "He is Mom's favourite. He's got one hell of a temper, but with her, he never shows it."

It looks to me that Alastor extends his regards to his master's son, too. The magnificent black horse stands perfectly still while we talk. He doesn't even move his tail to demonstrate impatience.

"He is amazing," I say. "Look, I…" I don't lose hope of making a smooth escape.

"Do you want to ride him?" Finley robs me of my options. "Come on, jump on." He extends his tanned arm with an annoyingly rippling biceps. "Don't be afraid. It's fun, and I won't let you fall."

Tears spring to my eyes. I furiously blink, trying to force them back.

"I'm not afraid," I say too loudly. "Why do you think I can't ride a horse?"

"Can you? That's great! It'll be even more fun then. Hop on!"

My heart tightens at the lightness of his mood. For him, everything is so simple. Taking a girl for a ride with his beautiful horse. Breathtaking views. Laughing and joking. With a sudden pain that pierces me through, I feel how much I want it to be like this for me.

Usually, I don't allow myself to dwell on how different my life could have been if I hadn't married Michael. This time, I cannot resist. Colourful images flood my head. I could have enjoyed the easiness and carelessness of youth. I could have dated whomever I liked, breaking up with them when my heart desired. I could have gone to parties, visited exciting places, danced until morning, and woken up with a hangover. I could have the life of a young girl instead of the one of a hardened matron.

My enthusiasm dries out as unexpectedly as it has flared up.

If I hadn't married Michael, I would have still been in Latvia. I know many young people lead exciting lives there too, but I was never supposed to be one of them. I would have worked hard to make a decent career, to rent and then buy a small flat. I wouldn't have had time or energy to party all through the weekend.

"Hop on," Finley repeats with his hand still extended. "Next time, we can ask Mom to give us a second horse, so you can ride yourself."

"I have to go!" I snap and turn around. Traitorous tears spill, and I don't want Finley to see them.

"Wait, Margo." His tone changes to serious. He seems to sense that something is wrong.

Reluctantly, I turn back. "Look, Finley, it was nice to see you. I hope you are having a fantastic vacation. You probably don't see it since you've been here many times. But it's really great here. It's like stepping into a book or a movie.

It's just it's not a vacation for me, that's all. Please tell your parents I said hi."

"Did you go for a swim?" he asks, throwing me out of balance.

"What?"

"Your hair," he touches his head, "it's wet."

I touch my hair as if it has betrayed me. "I…"

He doesn't let me finish. "It's dangerous there in the coves!"

I squirm under the worried gaze of his green eyes.

"I'm not trying to be a jerk," he speaks hastily. "It's really dangerous there. Promise me you won't go swimming in the coves alone." Since I don't reply, he asks: "Margo?"

I sigh. "Sure. I won't go there alone. I wasn't swimming anyway. Look…"

Alastor shows signs of impatience for the first time. He snorts and delicately stomps his hoof.

"Easy, boy." Finley pulls in the reins firmly.

"No, no, it's okay. You go. Alastor knows he's been taken out for a ride and not for standing still." I stroke the black horse's cheek gently. Alastor snorts again and presses his wide, rough nose into my palm.

"Where are you staying?" Finley asks.

"In the trailer." I immediately regret my honesty.

"At the campsite?"

"No." I hesitate.

Alastor stomps his hooves more actively, determined to attract attention to his wishes.

"Easy, Alastor! Now of all times…"

I don't want Finley or his beautiful horse to feel uneasy. "Michael has an assignment here," I speak quickly. "He's renovating Mrs Parry's conservatory. We parked the trailer by her cottage."

"So, you're staying at Mrs Parry's?"

Alastor starts to walk, having exhausted his patience limits.

"Alastor! Stop!" Finley pulls in the reins again. But his

attempts to stop the mighty horse are futile. Now I see what he meant by 'one hell of a temper'.

"Sort of. You go now." I wave my hand. "I'll tell Michael that your family is down here in Cornwall. He'll call them."

Alastor keeps on trotting away. Finley turns in the saddle. "I will! I'll see you soon, Margo. And remember! not to swim in the coves."

I walk back to the trailer with my thoughts in disarray.

I want to go and see the Hammonds, but I know that Michael will not be ecstatic about the idea. I doubt that he doesn't know his friends own a house in Lizard. He has been avoiding them for a year, and the reason for that hasn't gone away.

Back at the trailer, I blow-dry my hair and put the kettle on. It is almost seven. Michael hasn't mentioned at what time in the morning he was planning to return, and I'm not going to sit and wait for him. If I've learned anything about my husband, it is his zero tolerance policy for wasting time. He wrote in his message that he'd be back in the morning. I think it's a safe guess that he plans to start working on Mrs Parry's conservatory today. And if this indeed is the case, he won't need me today.

I make myself a cup of tea and, before bringing it outside, take out a folding chair and a table.

I have just placed the mug on the table when I hear the sounds of the motor and then the brakes. A car door slams, and after a moment, someone knocks at the cottage's front door.

I cast a glance of regret at my cup of tea. Tendrils of smoke lazily swirl upward from the hot beverage.

Walking out to the porch from behind the house I see Melissa Hammond standing there. Dressed in white linen trousers and a white loose-fitting shirt, she is elegant as ever.

"Hi, Mrs Hammond," I greet her, coming over.

"Good morning, Margo." She is collected and a little aloof, but her eyes are uncharacteristically troubled.

"Michael isn't here, I'm afraid."

"Actually, I have come to see you. Finley told me he saw you earlier, and what he said made me worried."

I fight back the wish to fidget under her concerned gaze. "Has he managed to bring Alastor back home?" I try to change the subject. "It didn't look like he'd make it. You have a beautiful horse, Mrs Hammond, and he has a temper to match his beauty."

The troubled look leaves Melissa's face for a moment, and she smiles. Fine lines burst around her blue eyes, brushing away her aloofness. "Alastor is a precious boy. I am glad you like him."

"I don't think anyone can resist his charm. He is the most handsome horse I've ever seen."

"Thank you, Margo. You can come and ride him. His temper softens with women riders."

I smile dreamily. "I'd love to, Mrs Hammond. It is such a generous offer."

Worry clouds over her eyes again. "But, Margo, I have come to tell you that you can't live in a trailer."

If I were holding something in my hands, I'd surely drop it. "What? I..." I don't remember telling Finley about my current housing arrangements. I even congratulated myself on having succeeded in being cunningly elusive with my answers.

I can't lie to his mother now, though. I feel that her interest and concern are genuine, and she won't let go of this matter.

"Michael has an assignment here." I point at the cottage. "It's only for a few days. No longer than a week. I'm fine, really. Everything will be okay."

"You went to take a shower in a public bathroom, Margo. That's not okay."

I blush and lower my eyes under her stern look. I wonder if Finley ever gets his way with his mother when she wants him to do something.

"Margo, you don't have to live in such conditions," Melissa speaks in a softer voice. "We have a big house. We have enough space for guests to stay there with comfort. I wonder why Michael hasn't told us that he planned to come down to Cornwall…"

"He didn't know!" I feel so agitated that I interrupt her. "It was a last-minute assignment."

Melissa shakes her head. "This is probably my fault. I should have told Rowan to call Michael and tell him we were heading here for vacation."

I want to tell this wonderful woman that it is Michael's fault. If not for his thoughtlessness, I wouldn't be skulking about in search of a place to pee. I wouldn't be hiding from the people whom I want to see and get to know better. If not for my husband's hurt pride or midlife crisis or whatever it is that has turned him into a jerk, I wouldn't be spoiling the vacation of the family that I admire.

Instead, I mumble: "You don't have to worry about me." My incoherent words only strengthen Melissa's determination.

"I am going down to the village to do some shopping. I won't be long. On my way back, I'll pick you up. You are coming with me, Margo. I can't enjoy the vacation knowing that you are here without basic facilities."

My eyes start to prickle. "Thank you, Mrs Hammond. That is so very kind of you. I don't know what to say."

"You don't have to say anything, Margo. Just be ready when I drive back in about an hour."

"I hope Michael will be back by then…"

Melissa's gaze turns steely. "It doesn't matter if he returns or not. If he doesn't, Rowan will come down later to invite him over and tell him where you are." She turns and walks to her car. "Do you need anything in the village?" she asks before opening the door.

I shake my head.

"Good, we'll go there some other time anyway. You need a proper excursion." With these words, she waves goodbye and drives away in her silver Volvo.

I walk back to the trailer. I find my bag and put my

toiletries back in it. The small luggage bag with my clothes stands by the wall unpacked. I took only my pyjamas from there. Now I cram them back.

I am torn between relief and anxiety. The first feeling wins when I realise that, in the Hammonds' house, Michael will be forced to suppress his frustration and anger. I will be safe.

CHAPTER 17

The Hammonds' summer residence is lavish, almost royal. Two storeys high, with one three-storey section in front and two one-storey annexes, the brownish-grey brick house looks like the setting of a historical novel. Inside, it is similarly grand. With all the modern amenities, the furniture and décor maintain the impression of a dwelling from times long past.

I step over the threshold in awe of the surrounding grandeur, expecting a grey-haired butler to appear and take my luggage.

Instead, Rowan Hammond walks out from the depths of the intimidating mansion. He looks elegant and at ease, but I notice concern on his face. "Margo, welcome," he greets me. "Thank you for coming. We are very happy to have you and Michael as our guests. I've been trying to convince him to come over for years. But his life in London never released him from its clutches."

"Rowan," Melissa rolls her eyes but smiles good-naturedly.

"I know, darling," her husband replies with a mirroring smile. "I am just glad to have company. Usually, we spend our time here like hermits."

"And whose fault is that, darling?" Melissa's playful tone makes me feel like an intruder. It seems like, if I weren't there, the Hammonds would go straight to the bedroom the moment they saw each other. "You never make an effort at socialising with our neighbours."

Roman Hammond shrugs. "I prefer to socialise with familiar people."

"And what prevents you from getting to know our neighbours better?" Melissa dismisses her husband by turning to me and not waiting for his reply. "I'm sorry, Margo. You don't have to listen to the tales of old spouses. I will show you your room. We've prepared the guest annexe for you. We thought you'd appreciate more privacy."

I want to tell her that I like listening to any stories she feels like sharing with me. "Thank you." I manage to keep my fan-girl attitude in check. "You didn't need to go to so much trouble."

"Oh yes, we did." Melissa looks at me kindly. "I finally got you and your husband under my roof. I will do my best to make you want to visit us more often."

I don't know what to say. I don't understand her kindness and interest in my insignificant persona. Maybe their friendship with Michael means so much to them that they don't mind that I now come in a package with their old friend.

Melissa leads me through a passage running along the front of the house. Plush chairs are placed by the high bay windows. I can imagine myself there, spending hours with a book on a rainy day.

The guest annexe is a spacious room that not only boasts an en suite bathroom, but also has its very own conservatory. It is full of natural light, with a king-size bed dominating the space. I catch a glimpse of rattan furniture in the conservatory. I want to jump up and down; the joy inside me threatens to burst out with some childish display.

"This room is beautiful, Mrs Hammond," I say.

"Thank you, Margo. I'm glad you like it. My mother wouldn't agree with you. She wouldn't have allowed us to build this annexe in the first place. So, your words truly mean a lot. I'll leave you to get settled and unpack. I'll be making some tea later. Feel free to join us if you don't plan to go for a walk straight away."

Melissa leaves, and I look around properly. The room is indeed charming. With light streaming from windows on two walls as well as from the conservatory, it is pleasantly airy. I like the beige bedspread with a faint golden lustre and the white cushions with tiny flowers on the rattan chairs. Everything in this room speaks of an immaculate taste and attention to detail. If I ever have a house of my own, I'd like it to give the same impression.

I unpack my scanty belongings and hang the few items of clothing I have taken with me in a spacious wardrobe. In the bathroom, which is also comfortable and pretty, I place my toothbrush and toothpaste in a glass by the sink. I notice that there already are all the toiletries left for us by our hosts.

I can't stop myself from pressing my face to one of the fluffy lilac towels folded neatly on the rattan stand. The fabric is soft, and it smells of lilies-of-the-valley.

Still in the bathroom, I hear my mobile phone beep. I jerk involuntarily.

Where are you? The message from Michael says. My finger hovers over the *call* button. I press *Messages* instead.

I'm at the Hammonds. They invited us to stay with them. Couldn't refuse. Will you come over now or after you finish work? My hands tremble while I type.

The reply comes almost instantly. *Will be there in the evening.*

I am certain that the news has made my husband angry.

And I am glad that he has long hours of hard physical work ahead of him to cool off.

******

An hour later, I lie by the pool house.

By the time Melissa offers for me to take a swim in the pool, I can hardly be surprised by anything anymore. The house is not only luxurious, but it has everything you can think of to make you forget about the world outside its walls.

There is a garden behind the house. It would be more accurate to call it *grounds* since apart from flower beds and a gazebo, it also has a small coppice, and the winding paths seem endless.

Lying on a comfortable chaise lounge, I can feel the salty breeze on my face. I don't plan to sunbathe, for there is a risk that I'll fall asleep and end up with sunburns. Still, after the swim I have just taken in that pool, I can't resist the temptation to bask a little.

Despite my resolve to stay alert, I can't help drifting into slumber. I try not to keep my eyes closed for too long, but my eyelids grow heavier every time I force them to open.

"Margo, hi!"

A voice pulls me out of drowsiness. I open my eyes. My sight is unfocused, white circles preventing me from seeing who stands in front of me. I sit down straighter, shifting my legs from the chaise lounge. My vision returns to normal once my feet touch the ground.

"Hello, Finley." *At least, this time, he is fully dressed*, the embarrassing thought sneaks through my head.

"Look, Margo, I just wanted to tell you that I didn't want to set you up or anything." He thrusts his hands into the pockets of his long cargo shorts.

I have never seen a man with such perfectly proportioned calves. Whenever men put on shorts, the peculiarity of the male physique – thin legs – usually becomes painfully obvious.

What am I thinking about? I hope I haven't betrayed my

thoughts by staring.

"I have no idea what you are talking about." My voice sounds unnaturally husky. I clear my throat. "Sorry, I must've eaten too many of your mom's scones." I rub my eyes, mostly to distract myself rather than clear my vision.

"You mean her Welsh cakes." Finley smiles and relaxes.

"Welsh cakes?"

"Yes, Mom isn't a fan of scones. She never makes them. She says the mass production has turned them into fast food. And no one has any respect for fast food. Even those who eat it regularly."

"Thanks. I'm glad I didn't praise tasty *scones* then."

"Mom wouldn't take offence. Not from you anyway." Finley tenses again. "Does your husband know you are here?" He looks around as if expecting Michael to lurk somewhere in the garden.

"Michael? Yes, yes, of course. He texted this morning, and he'll be here by dinner time. I hope."

I stand up from the chaise lounge. Finley stares at me just like I was gaping at him a moment ago. With a delay, it dawns on me that I am rather underdressed. Almost completely undressed, really.

I am wearing a one-piece Speedo swimsuit that I used to wear when I went to the university pool back in Latvia. I was always conscious of my boyish figure, with wide shoulders and no waist. Now I'm grateful to my complexes. They have saved me from total embarrassment.

I grab a towel and clutch it to my chest. It doesn't help much since my legs are still exposed by high-cut swimwear.

"I… I'm…" I stammer. "I'm going to…" I point at the house. "I'll see you later."

I turn to leave. The realisation that Finley is also seeing my half-naked buttocks colours my face deep red.

"Wait! Margo…"

At least, he is jabbering too.

"Are you an early riser?"

I am so surprised by his question that I turn back. "Yes,

why?"

"Mom told me you are a better rider for Alastor. I thought we could go for a morning ride together. Tomorrow."

I'm holding on to the towel, which is too short anyway for a proper body covering, like it's a life ring. Finley's offer is too tempting to discard because of panic. I haven't ridden a horse for years. I am not entirely sure that it works the same as riding a bicycle, and that I won't fall down the moment after I climb atop magnificent Alastor. Still, I can't refuse.

"At what time in the morning?" I ask.

Finley beams. "It's better to go early. At six." His face clouds over again. "We can go later. I mean, if your husband doesn't like the idea of you sneaking out of bed so early…"

I lower my hand with the towel. This is ridiculous. People parade on the beach dressed more scantily, and no one pays attention.

The thing is, Finley definitely pays attention. I can see that in his eyes. Those green eyes that hypnotise me.

"My husband," I speak in a steadier voice, "is here to complete a project. He is up with the roosters, and where I go is the last thing on his mind."

A glance Finley gives me is too serious for my comfort. "Okay, great. Then I'll meet you at the stables at six tomorrow?"

So, they have stables here. Fantastic. I almost utter the inappropriate comment aloud.

"Great. I'll see you then."

He hesitates. "That is… I mean… that's if you don't want me to show you around today…"

Yes! Let's go! My inner voice shouts excitedly. Butterflies tremble in my stomach at the thought of spending time with him. "I don't think that's a good idea," I say instead. "I'll see you later. Thank you for the invitation."

"Sure." He puts his hands deeper into his cargo shorts pockets. "And don't bother with breakfast. We'll have a picnic on the beach."

As if I could eat even a bite before my date with Finley. *Date?* I shrug, naively trying to shake off the trembling and the butterflies.

"That sounds lovely." I cringe at how prudish I sound. Just like Barbara Southwell.

Back in the annexe, I strip off the swimsuit and go straight to the shower. I stand under the steaming hot water for a long time. An idea about a cold shower enters my mind, but I shudder at the thought.

The water helps without turning a pleasant procedure into torture. I feel calmed down, refreshed, and ready to face whatever challenges are there in store for me.

******

Michael arrives after seven. I don't feel comfortable, worrying about him being late for dinner. The Hammonds, though, don't show any signs of impatience. I like their laid-back attitude, which contrasts with Michael's pedantism.

My husband greets me with a curt 'hi' and doesn't bother even with a quick peck on the cheek. It is enough for me that he doesn't make a scene in front of the Hammonds, scolding me like a misbehaved child.

"Mike, my old friend." Rowan Hammond looks so sincerely glad to see Michael that I wonder if my husband has really changed so much after he married me and if this dramatic change is my fault.

Michael winces at Mr Hammond's greeting but smiles: "Do you want me to call you Ro as if we're back at school in year 6?"

"Sorry, pal, I couldn't resist seeing your face. You always hated it." Rowan pats Michael on the back. "Will you find your way to the dining room? I'll go tell Melissa that we are ready for dinner."

Mr Hammond walks over to the kitchen, and the uncomfortable feeling returns once I am left alone with my husband. I trail behind him on the way to the dining room.

Michael sits down on a chair with his back to a

panoramic window, and I'm forced to sit facing the open doorway too. I hear birds chirping outside. I'd like to watch what those little ones are doing.

"How is it going with Mrs Parry's conservatory?" I ask when the silence becomes too pressing.

Michael makes me regret opening my mouth. "The old bat wants to have everything and pay nothing for it." His lips curve unpleasantly when he speaks. "If it wasn't Hughes who'd asked me to help her, I wouldn't have agreed to this."

I have no idea who Hughes is. Before I have time to weigh the pros and cons of asking, Michael continues: "Hughes, the guy I worked for in Bournemouth, knows everybody in the southwest. Parry is his relation, so I couldn't say no. But now he owes me, so he'll send all his rich landowners to me."

I almost blurt out my impression that he envies them, those rich guys who own beautiful homes along the coast. I bite back a sharp response on time.

"That's great," I say flatly. "You'll have plenty of work."

Michael sits back and crosses his arms on his chest. He looks out of place in this elegant but homely room. He has changed out of his work clothes, of course, yet, there is an aura about him that he doesn't belong. In this house, everything is about love and care: about each other, domestic comfort, and aesthetic beauty. While Michael's thoughts are stuck at some point in the future when his plan is supposed to come to fruition. It seems that everything that fills his life now frustrates him. I think it is because he believes that it distracts him from that distant goal.

I choke off a sigh.

The Hammonds unwittingly rescue me, arriving with plates filled with food.

"I hope you're hungry," Rowan announces joyfully. "We have enough food to feed an army."

"Cornish air facilitates healthy appetite." Melissa smiles as she takes the plates out of a dish cabinet that looks antique. "I haven't asked if you have some special preferences, Margo." She looks at me, placing the plates on the table.

"You don't have to worry about me," I say hastily. "I could eat a horse right now. It must be the local air."

From the corner of my eye, I notice Michael pursing his lips at my comment.

"I am glad." Melissa smiles. "I like it when people have healthy appetites."

I smile back.

"I'm sorry I'm late." Finley walks into the room and sits down by his father, who has taken a seat across from Michael and I.

"You haven't missed anything yet." Rowan chuckles good-naturedly. "But I'm not sure you'd find a lot left on the table if you'd shown up twenty minutes later."

"Rowan." Melissa gives her husband a look of mild reproach.

"I am just trying to teach our son some discipline, darling." Mr Hammond stares back at his wife with wide-open eyes full of innocence. "You know what they say nowadays about stricter methods. I'm trying to be creative."

Melissa rolls her eyes.

"Hello, Mom, Dad. I'm here, in case you forgot." Finley waves his hand theatrically. "Good evening, Mr Birkett. I'm sorry I stormed in without a greeting. My parents – they can be so distracting." He rolls his eyes, imitating his mother. Both of them look adorable.

"Hello, Finley." At least, with the Hammonds, Michael doesn't sound annoyed. "That's parents for you. To their kids, they always seem frustrating."

"Thank you. I'm glad you understand. They," he points at his parents with a nod, "seem to believe they are totally different from everybody else."

"But we are different." Melissa brings over a glass decanter with lime water that stood on the dish cabinet. "We didn't push you to go to university, did we?" She sits down and hands a bowl of boiled potatoes to her husband. "If not for Margo, you would have still been frittering your time away hanging around with Mark."

Silence falls over the table for a few minutes.

My cheeks burn, and I don't know if I should say something or maybe apologise for my unasked advice.

"You are right, Mom. And I'm grateful." Finley looks me in the eyes. "Thank you, Margo. I was acting like a fool."

"You are welcome," I mumble. "But I didn't really mean to…" I stop, searching for the right words.

"Let's eat!" Rowan Hammond announces. His happy manners are contagious. "All's well that ends well."

Today, I cannot agree more with this expression. The dinner is splendid. Still, I feel as if a huge weight has been lifted from my shoulders when it ends.

CHAPTER 18

A day is at its most beautiful at dawn.

I can't help halting on the doorstep to admire the mesmerising charm of the early hour. The grass covered with diamonds of glistering dew invites you to run barefoot across the lawn. The birds are chirping gaily as if they're announcing the arrival of a new day. The sky is undisturbedly blue, with only seagulls and no clouds.

I take a deep breath, and sweet aromas of summer blooms hit my nostrils. A whirlpool of wild joy rises in my chest, putting me at risk of bursting out laughing. I inhale the fragrant summer air and smile.

It is going to be the most amazing day.

I rush across the lawn to a small coppice, behind which stand the stables. As embarrassed as I was yesterday at dinner, I'd still managed to pull myself together and ask Melissa where the stables were.

The birdsong is even louder among the trees. I make an

effort not to stop and listen to them.

When I arrive, the massive stable door is already open with neighing coming from inside.

I enter the long, dim space. Finley stands by an open door to one of the boxes and brushes an elegant bay. From the horse's appreciative sounds, it is apparent the two are good friends. I walk over and clear my throat. Finley turns. His face lights up when he sees me.

"Hi! You're here. I was afraid you wouldn't wake up this early. Come, meet Admiral."

I feel more at ease once I realise that Finley is as nervous as I am. I walk to the open box and pat the horse's silky cheek. "Nice to meet you, Admiral." It feels confusing that I want to touch Finley too. The animal rubs his nose on my palm. I'm grateful I can focus my attention on the horse. "Sorry, big boy, I haven't brought any treats. It's bad manners to feed someone else's horses, you know. What if you are on a diet?" Admiral moves his ears as if he understands what I am saying. "Next time, I'll ask before coming to visit you, okay?" Admiral raises his head from my hand and presses his nose to my cheek.

"Alright, that's enough," Finley laughs and puts the brush into a special compartment on the wall. "If you continue charming the horses, Mom won't let me ride any of them."

I put up my palms mockingly. "I'm sorry. I won't touch any of your horses except Alastor." I hear neighing from the box across the aisle. I raise my eyebrows. "See, even the horse doesn't like your attitude."

Finley only laughs, walking over to the box where Alastor's noble head with that incredible black mane already hangs over the low door. He unlocks the box and leads Alastor out. The horse is already saddled.

"Here is your horse, madam." He gives me a mocking bow. "Alastor definitely doesn't like my attitude or anything else about me. I am glad you two have found each other."

"Thank you very much. Something tells me you won't

be sad if you see me fall from him." I feel light-hearted, and I don't want this fleeting easiness to go away.

"It's Admiral who won't be sad. He'll be happy to carry you back." Finley gives me the reins and goes back to Admiral. "Traitors. All of you," he says to Alastor and Admiral, and then rolls his eyes. They are twinkling with mischief.

We walk the horses out of the stables. The door is like a sun portal filled with light. To be honest, I do feel like I am in some kind of fantastical movie.

Finley stops and turns to me. "Will you be okay climbing on him?" He points at Alastor. "We used to have a special bench for those who aren't comfortable with getting in the saddle from the ground. But it got lost. Maybe we burnt it when we were here for Christmas, and it turned out that Dad forgot to buy logs for the fireplace."

"No, no, I'll be fine," I say hastily. "I haven't done it for a while, but I think I'll manage."

"It's okay, let me help you." Finley releases the reins.

"No, I'll be fine!" It's already embarrassing enough that I have to stop myself from touching him. If he touches me, I am not sure I'll be able to resist.

"Okay, okay, I only wanted to help." Finley turns away and takes the reins again.

I drop the reins I've been clutching and grab the front of the saddle. I pray with all my heart that I don't fail miserably. If I do, the risk is high that I'll end up kissing Finley, who will come to my rescue, unsuspecting of the consequences.

I put a foot into the stirrup and push my body up. My first attempt is a failure. Luckily, Finley is busy with getting on the horseback. He doesn't notice my helpless fumbling about Alastor, who stands majestic and unperturbed like a king's horse. My second try is more successful. That is, if you can say successful about an awkward scrambling up, with my belly plastered all over the horse's body before I can straighten up and adopt a more dignified position.

"Ready?" Finley asks, unaware of my struggle.

"Sure. Lead the way," I manage to utter without panting.

"Great. Let's go."

Admiral walks at a relaxed pace, and Alastor follows. I use this calm time to reacquaint myself with being on horseback. Seven years are enough to forget how to boil an egg, let alone manoeuvre a massive animal. Still, I am surprised how quickly I settle into Alastor's rhythm. My body synchronises with his flowing movements as if it has been waiting to be given a chance to do it again. The familiar feeling of exhilaration fills me, and soon, I want to move faster. I want to feel the speed and the wind whooshing in my ears.

"Would it be okay if we go a little faster?" Finley asks.

"I'll try not to fall." I don't know what made me reply with this sarcastic remark.

He turns his head slightly. "I believe in you."

"Thanks." I take a better hold of the reins, hoping that my body remembers the scarce skill I used to have with horse riding.

Finley puts Admiral into a trot. The bay horse has a beautiful gait. His step is solid and even, so different from the erratic jumping of lower-bred horses I used to ride. I watch the rider and the horse admiringly for a while until a few hits right between my legs make me concentrate on the riding technique. No one ever taught me how to do it properly, but I have learned the basics by watching others. I slightly raise myself and sit back, trying to keep up with the horse's rhythm. It doesn't go smoothly; once in a while, I lower into the saddle too quickly and get bounced back up. I don't care about the pain. Even if I walk like a cavalryman tomorrow, it will still be worth it.

We trot across the grassy area, Admiral and Alastor agile and fast like the wind. I feel the sun on my face. The breeze cools down my burning cheeks. The rugged coastline stands out cinematically against the backdrop of the bright blue sky and the channel waters that are just a few shades darker. On the gently climbing slope to the right of the path, a few long-haired cows stand, chewing and watching the horizon.

Finley raises his hand, and I understand that this is a signal to slow down. I pull in the reins, and Alastor changes into walking. We draw level with Admiral and walk side by side.

"The path is too rocky here for trotting," Finley explains the change of pace.

"Okay." I feel content simply sitting on horseback. I think I'd feel happy even if Alastor stood and watched the horizon like the cows we have just passed.

"So, I know it makes me look like an ignorant jerk…" Finley gives me a sideway glance, checking my reaction.

I roll my eyes but smile.

"Yes, I know, no matter what I do or say, it won't change how you see me," he continued. "So, since no bigger damage can be done by asking, I'll ask. Where did you learn to ride a horse?"

"Didn't you know?" I raise my eyebrows and purse my lips. "Every Latvian kid learns to ride a horse at the same time as we learn to ride a bike."

"Really?"

His handsome face is so serious that I can't contain myself and laugh. "No, of course not. Sorry, it's just you are so funny sometimes."

"Not funny, pathetic. Pathetically ignorant, I'd say." He fumbles with the reins in his hands, and Admiral neighs in protest. "Sorry, pal." Finley pats the horse on his neck. I watch his tanned hand making gentle stroking moves and feel the longing in my chest.

"Your knowledge is enough to live a good life," I say quickly. "And that's what matters. We have a lot of smart people in Latvia. It doesn't help them earn decent money so they can have a good life."

"Is it why you decided to move here?"

"I moved here because I was stupid." I regret voicing the first answer that came to my mind. "I like it here. It's beautiful," I hastily correct myself. "But I have to find my place here. I didn't think about it before I came here."

"You will. I believe in you. You are one of those smart Latvian people who *will* have a good life."

I look down at my hands and align the reins so they are the same length. I am confused by Finley's sincere tone.

"Ah, well, we'll see." I bend forward to caress Alastor's shiny black mane. "The horses. You asked how it is that I can ride." I am glad I have an excuse to change the topic. "I didn't go to a riding school or anything. My grandmother lived in the countryside, and I used to spend my summers with her. She had a neighbour who had horses. He didn't breed them or anything. He was a…hmm…" We didn't know that for sure, but we thought that our neighbour was a retired criminal. He bought a huge land plot with fields, a forest, and even a small river. Only bandits and foreigners had the money for such investments. I'm not ready to share this with Finley. It would require a further explanation. Instead, I choose a safer option. "He wanted to feel like he was an English lord, I guess," I say. "You know, owning the land with no neighbours for miles around. He even brought deer there so he could go hunting with his friends."

"Did he allow you to ride his horses?"

I nod. "Yes. He probably thought it looked cool that someone was riding horses on his lawn. He didn't have saddles – any equipment, really. Horses were for the countryside lifestyle image. We rode without saddles at first. But then, my friends brought old saddles, bridles, and everything that lay in their grandparents' barns, gathering dust. We had no idea what we were doing. We shared what we read or saw on TV and immediately put it into practice. Looking back now, I can't believe none of us got any serious injuries. It was reckless."

Finley smiles without looking at me. "Childhood is about being reckless."

I shrug at his remark. "I guess. Anyway, I wouldn't do anything like this now. I was afraid to drive a car after a break. I would've never climbed on the horse if I hadn't done it before."

"I'm glad that you've done it before." Finley still doesn't turn.

I know that my cheeks are now the colour of beetroot, so I don't mind him not seeing it.

We ride in silence for a while. Because it is so early, not even seven, the air is still pleasantly cool. At the same time, it is warm enough to be comfortable wearing short sleeves.

"Now you'll see the best part. This way." Finley pulls the reins to the right, and Admiral obediently turns and starts climbing down the slope. I don't have to do anything to make Alastor follow him. Both horses obviously are familiar with the route.

We go down the gentle slope. The breeze and the salty smell are a little stronger here. And then, there opens a kind of corridor in the rocks. It is wide enough for one horse to walk without touching the walls.

We move slowly in single file. The stone tunnel descends smoothly, and the horses don't show any signs of agitation. The rocky walls grow higher, and without the sun rays from above, it becomes darker. The path snakes down in wide semicircles. It is not possible to see what lies ahead or what we've already left behind. The feeling of being lost in time tickles my nerves. I can't get rid of the illusion that all of this isn't happening to me. It resembles a dream from which I can wake up any minute.

Finally, after yet another bend, the path stops descending, and the horses walk more briskly. The rocky tunnel ends, and we walk onto the wide sandy beach.

"It is so beautiful," I exclaim, instinctively pulling in the reins.

The view is indeed not something you see every day, even if you live among the stunning Dorset landscapes. A crescent-shaped beach stretches under the walls of towering cliffs. Caramel-coloured sand looks lighter against the dark grey rocks. The waves roll onto the shore with a gentle hissing sound, leaving a thin white lace in their wake.

We are the only people on this hidden beach.

"I was hoping you'd react this way." Finley makes Admiral turn around and walk back to where Alastor and I stand. "I wanted to see your face when you saw this view for the first time."

"Thank you," I answer without looking at him. "It is amazing." I want to be alone here, among the majestic nature, with its rough edges and soft colours. I could find balance within myself while watching nature doing the same. Alastor moves beneath me, and the urge to feel like I am flying overwhelms me.

"Can we gallop here?" I ask. My voice sounds husky, but for once, I don't care.

"That's what we've come here for," Finley chuckles. "Are you sure you are ready for it?"

It doesn't matter, I want to say. "If I start feeling like I'm falling, I'll shout."

"It'll be too late." Finley shakes his head, looking doubtful. "You haven't sat in the saddle for a while. Maybe it's better to start with a fast trot? We'll come here again every day if you wish…"

"No!" I am surprised at how loud it came out. "Sorry. I'll be alright. I used to gallop without a saddle, remember? With all this sophisticated gear, I'll definitely be fine. Besides," I make a sweeping gesture with my hand, "there's sand everywhere. I won't break anything if I fall."

Finley still looks unconvinced. "Falls from a horse are very dangerous."

"Are you afraid your mom will scold you? Or maybe even flog you? I've heard they still do that in posh schools over here?" I raise my eyebrows, challenging him.

Finley doesn't take offence. Instead, he throws his head back and laughs. "Yes, making Mom unhappy is something to be afraid of. It's just you haven't seen her wrath yet. And I doubt you'll even get a chance to see it. She loves you."

I blush with pleasure. "Your mom is amazing. You are

very lucky."

His face turns serious. "I hope I'll meet yours when she comes over next time."

I look down at my hands and finger the reins. Alastor neighs and takes a step forward. "So? Let's try, okay? If I fall, I'll tell Melissa that it was my fault."

"I'm not worried about Mom. I don't want you to get hurt." Finley sighs but makes Admiral turn. "If you feel that something is wrong, shout, okay?"

"I will. They'll hear me across the channel in France, I promise."

"Great."

We start with a trot. Horses' hooves make almost no sound on the wet sand. The salty air invades my nostrils like a harbinger of great adventures.

"Ready?" Finley asks, not turning back.

My heart makes a leap. "Yes."

And in the next moment, I am flying.

Alastor follows Admiral, keeping a comfortable distance from the leader. Alastor's stride is long and steady. My head starts spinning, and my heart rate accelerates, but it lasts only for a few moments. The rhythm of the moving horse makes my muscles tense and then relax. Once I settle into the galloping pattern, I don't feel like the horse carries me. I feel like the horse and I have become one, and we move together in perfect unison.

The sun generously spills the light everywhere. The water and the sand glisten with all the rainbow colours. Even the dark rocks don't look menacing. Whirls of sparks shoot out from the black anthracite surface whenever a sun ray caresses the grim, stony wall.

I feel like I am in a fairy tale or in a parallel reality. Everything shines like diamonds here, the air is always warm and fragrant, and the exhilarating ride never ends.

I feel happy and loved – not by a person, but by the world itself.

We reach the place where, from a distance, it looked like

the beach ended with the cliffs stretching out right into the water. Now that we're here, I can see that the thin line of sand curves around the protruding rock. Finley raises his hand. I am not sure if it is a common gesture accepted among riders, but I guess it is a signal to stop.

Admiral slows to a trot, and Alastor follows suit.

Finley stops his horse before the bulging rock that shoots out onto the beach.

"There is another cove behind." He points at the towering stone wall. "It's smaller, and it's flooded most of the time. It's only possible to walk there in the summer."

"Another hidden gem," I say.

"That's Cornwall for you."

We smile at each other.

"Ready?" He presses his feet into Admiral's sides. The horse starts walking.

"For a new adventure? Always." I don't have to do anything to make Alastor move. He follows Admiral.

"A perfect adventure buddy." Finley chuckles, leading his horse down the narrow sandy path around the bend.

"That's me."

"Don't fret if Alastor steps into the water. The pass is too narrow, and the horses don't like to scratch their sides on the rock. Just let him walk on."

We follow the curving path, and I have to gasp in admiration again. The little cove is another perfect filming location. The sand is lighter here than on the bigger beach from where we came. The cliffs don't stand like vertical monoliths but cascade down from the topmost point. They resemble sandcastles built by children, so erratic and illogical these formations look. Some pinnacles stuck out like spears, while others hide below, giving the false impression that there are empty spaces between the rocks.

Finley crosses the short distance until the further end of the cove and jumps down the horse. "It's the best place for a picnic, here by the rocks. It's never windy."

I slide down Alastor, hoping not to embarrass myself

with my lack of skill.

Finley takes a blanket out of the bag attached to the saddle. "Have a rest. Your legs need it. Every time I ride after a break, I feel like I've been put through some medieval torture."

"Thanks." I am so happy after the ride that I don't feel like arguing. Besides, he is right. My thighs do ache and even tremble a little.

I sit down on the blanket and look at the water. It is almost windless, and the waves aren't crowned with white caps. Only when they roll onto the shore do they leave a thin, frothy line before retreating. The sun has risen higher, and a few innocent-looking clouds dot the blue sky.

"Thank you for showing me this place," I say when Finley returns with a wicker basket. "I wouldn't have found it myself."

"I'm glad you like it. Most girls don't care about things like this. A trendy bar in London is what interests them." He opens the basket lid and starts taking out plastic containers, plates, and utensils.

I am not a girl, I want to say. "I don't care about bars. But I really liked London."

"I haven't seen much of it, only the museums during school excursions. But you know how it is, at that age, you are more interested in chatting with your friends than in cultural heritage."

Finley opens the containers and empties them into the plates. There is a selection of ham and cheeses, as well as strawberries and grapes. He gives me an empty plate and a plastic fork. "I didn't know what you like, so I took everything that was transportable."

"Thanks." I hadn't thought about food until this moment. Now, I feel ravenous.

"I could show you a few hidden gems in Southbay, too. And I'd like to explore more of London with you."

My appetite vanishes. I can't make myself look at him. I know what I'll see. And Finley's piercing green eyes aren't something that would help me calm down.

"I am married, Finley," I speak, not raising my eyes.

He puts the plate down with more force than necessary, and a few grapes fall down on the blanket.

"Your husband doesn't love you." He turns away in frustration, clenching his fists.

Startled by his outburst, I don't reply. All the joy I have been feeling evaporates, and the dull uneasiness takes its place. I look at the sparkling water and don't find any comfort in its shimmering glitter that seemed magical to me a moment before.

"How can you know that?" I almost whisper.

I hear him sigh. "I'm sorry, Margo." I know that he has turned back to me, but I can't face him yet. "I'm really sorry. I shouldn't have said that. I don't know what I'm talking about."

I cast a quick glance at him from the corner of my eye. I want to fling myself into his arms.

"It's just I…" he continues, "it's just I like you. I mean, I really like you. You aren't like any girl I know."

As if of their own will, my eyes search his face. "I'm not a girl from your class at the university," I speak slowly. "I am a married woman. And my husband is your father's friend."

I would give anything for these words to be untrue – to somehow be made untrue.

As he looks at me intently, he doesn't speak. I don't have it in me to tear my eyes away. I like him too. I like him too much to keep ignoring it.

Finally, Finley shrugs. "Even if you were my best friend's wife, it wouldn't make me not like you."

"If your best friend was someone like Mark, he wouldn't mind." I pull my knees up and hug them. Anger is a welcome distraction.

"Why?" Finley straightens his back and shoots me an alert look.

"Ask him. But he probably won't remember a thing. He

was so drunk."

"What has he done?"

Worry in his voice awakens the butterflies in my stomach. "He hasn't done anything, thank goodness. But not because he came to his senses and changed his mind."

"Margo? Tell me what happened?"

I look at his handsome, tanned face with these green eyes that never fail to hypnotise me and tell him everything. I feel like the weight has lifted from my shoulders. Keeping everything to myself was a burden I wasn't aware I was carrying.

"Did you tell anyone about this?" Finley asks when I finish my story. "Have you been to the police?"

I laugh. "Why? What would I tell them? Nothing has happened."

"Margo, this is serious." I thought he would be angry, but his face is grave. "He can't just get away with something like this. You should at least tell his father."

I laugh again. "I don't think that George King would bother with giving his son a lecture on the good and evil. It seems to me that the only thing he cares about is his business. He'd blame me anyway."

"You don't have to think, just do it. Mark can't get away with assaulting you. This is wrong."

I shrug. "Many things in life are wrong. Nothing can be done about it."

"But this isn't one of those things."

"Look, I just want to forget about it, okay? It's not like he'll be chasing me around the island. He was drunk. It was a one-time thing. It won't happen again."

Even as I say it, I know it's wrong. Mark King lives with the conviction that everything in the world is there for his taking. If no one shows him that this isn't true, someone could get hurt. Still, I am not ready to step into the limelight.

Finley turns away and, for a while, doesn't say anything. Then he looks at me. "Thank you for telling me. Mark is a jerk. Nobody can change that. Let's eat. It was supposed to be a nice morning ride with a picnic. I don't know about you, but I'm so hungry I could eat a horse." He casts a quick glance at Admiral and Alastor, who are standing by the rock and looking absolutely serene. "Sorry," he winks at me, "it wasn't the best choice of expression, I guess." And he laughs.

I giggle too. "No, it wasn't. These horses are very smart. I even think they might understand our speech."

"Admiral, Alastor, you are the best guys ever!" Finley raises his voice on purpose. "I mean it!"

Both horses react to the sound of his voice by giving him a fleeting look before returning to swishing their magnificent tails.

"See, no harm done." Finley pulls out a bottle of lemon water with slices of fruit on its bottom. He gives the bottle a good shake. "I didn't think wine would be a good choice for our outing, so I took this." He fills two plastic glasses and hands one to me. "It seems I have an issue with choices. It needs to be addressed."

"Maybe you should talk to a shrink."

"Maybe. But first, I have to find one." He raises his glass. "To solving all our issues."

"Yes, to that." I take a sip, and then another one. The lemon water is surprisingly delicious.

For the rest of our picnic and also on the ride back, we don't talk about serious topics. Finley tells me about his studies at Bournemouth University and his student life. He explains that technically, the campus is located in Poole, but it is closer to the beaches of Bournemouth than to Poole's. I tell him about my own time at the university back in Latvia. We don't discuss the future, and I like that we are simply having a friendly chat.

Upon our return, we meet Melissa in the stables. "I've just finished cleaning the boxes," she informs us. I can't help wondering if they don't have people who do the hard and dirty work. A man in his sixties dressed in overalls comes from behind the stables building. He has a pitchfork in his hands, and I guess I've gotten an answer. Melissa simply enjoys working in the stables. I admire that, as I admire Finley's mother in general.

"I'll take a ride, and then we could go on that shopping and excursion trip to the village. Would you like that, Margo?" Mrs Hammond asks while walking another beautiful horse out of the stable. I instinctively know that the dark, almost black, bay with a narrow white stripe on the forehead is a mare.

"That sounds fantastic," I reply.

"Then I'll see you in an hour and a half." Melissa gets on the horseback. She does it as elegantly and easily as she does everything else.

"Don't jump over the neighbours' fences too much, Mom."

Finley's parting words make his mother turn and smile at him. "I will certainly try, Finley. But I won't make any promises."

"Sometimes I wonder how Dad puts up with her." Finley shakes his head.

"She is amazing," I say before entering the house. "Your mom is amazing. You are very lucky."

"I know." He smiles, and his eyes twinkle, making him look younger. "I'll see you...?"

I almost run away from the question on his handsome face.

"At lunch, I guess. Thank you. The secret beach was great," I blurt out in one breath and walk into the house.

"I'll see you then," I hear him say. It takes all my willpower not to run back to him and tell him that I want to spend the whole day with him, never leaving his side.

CHAPTER 19

It turns out to be a wonderful day, and I don't want it to end.

Melissa drove us to the village, and in every shop, she chatted with the staff or the owner. From the questions she asked, it was clear that she knows them well and, what is more important, she genuinely cares. She introduced me to everyone, and when she did, she said: "Please meet Margo, our guest from Southbay." My accent inevitably led to inquiries about where I am from originally and then to questions about Latvia.

We had lunch at the Cornish pastry café. Melissa treated me to a traditional pie called a Cornish pasty, with a history dating back many centuries. It resembles the kind of meat pies that are popular in Latvia. Melissa explained the difference between a pie and a pasty, and I filed this information away to avoid embarrassing situations with locals.

When we return, Rowan and Finley join us, and we have a proper lunch together in a gazebo in the backyard. We talk easily about the things of no real importance, but which are so exciting to discuss among friends. We get carried away, relaxed after a tasty meal and the outdoor activities we all indulged in in the morning, and sit there chatting for a few hours.

When it is time to start making dinner, I offer to help. Melissa at first refuses, saying that I would better take a walk or lie down. But I insist, and she finally agrees. I don't want to spend any more time than it is absolutely necessary with my husband, and I am afraid he might return soon. I think that Melissa sees me through, and it lets me hope that she also understands that this isn't the only reason behind my willingness to help her.

We keep on chatting while preparing the meat and vegetables. Today, we are going to have a leg of lamb for dinner. I make a suggestion about the sauce, and Melissa agrees to try it. We put the lamb into the oven and set the vegetable casserole aside. It will go into the oven later since the meat needs more time to cook.

Then, Melissa makes us tea, and we sip it companionably, nibbling at Welsh cakes.

"I'll have to go on a diet soon." I put down the piece of pastry on the saucer. "But everything is so tasty, I can't stop eating."

"You have a healthy appetite of the young." Melissa smiles at me kindly. "Besides, here, in Cornwall, nobody ever needs to worry about dieting. It's impossible to stay still here, so you automatically burn all the calories."

"That's true." I nod, taking up the Welsh cake I haven't finished again. "I walk a lot at home in Southbay. But here, my physical activity seems to increase even more."

Melissa takes a sip of her tea. I like the way she holds a cup. Truth to be told, I like everything about her. She reminds me of Jacqueline. Something in her manners and in the way she talks makes me think that the two women are from the same circle. And I am way down below their level.

"Do you like it in Southbay, Margo?" Melissa asks.

"Yes, very much. I love it. It's so beautiful there. And

everyone is so friendly."

"It is very different from your home country, I assume."

"Yes, it is." I take a moment to put my jumbled thoughts into words. "Latvia is beautiful. Different, of course. We don't have cliffs or high mountains, nothing like that. But still, there are many nice places there. And the Old Town of Riga is beautiful. And the seaside. But I didn't live in those beautiful places. I lived in a small town with nothing to do and nothing to see."

"I understand." Melissa nods. "It might seem insignificant to have everything at your doorstep, but it is, in fact, very important. I have known people who've never been to London despite it being less than an hour away from Virginia Water. That's the town where I grew up."

Something about the town's name sounds familiar.

"Do you know Jacqueline Fisher?" I ask when puzzle pieces click into place. It is incredible that I remember the name of the town I heard only once. I admire Jacqueline, and it doesn't cease to amaze me that she has become my friend.

Melissa looks surprised. "Jacqueline? Yes, actually, I do. She also used to live in Virginia Water."

"It's just I remembered that she told me she is from there too. It is a pretty name for a town."

"Indeed, it is." Melissa smiles. She doesn't seem annoyed by my bluntness. "And it is a pretty town. Many would say that it is the prettiest town in England. But if you ask me, I believe that Southbay is prettier." She pours us more tea. "That is what I told Jacqueline when she said that she was planning to leave London. She didn't want to move back to Virginia Water and was looking for other options in the countryside. We weren't close friends, but I am the only one from our school who moved to Dorset. Our classmates either stayed in Virginia Water or moved to London."

"I think she is glad that she has taken your advice. The Lighthouse Keeper's cottage is wonderful, and she has a dog. Winston is amazing. He and Berlin would run together for hours."

I haven't seen much of the Hammonds' huge and lovable Leonberger's dog since my arrival. Berlin seems to be comfortable on his own here, wandering around the vast estate but not venturing outside its borders.

Melissa raises her eyebrows. "It sounds like Jacqueline has settled down in Southbay. I am glad to hear it. Thank you for telling me about her, Margo. I get distracted by so many things these days that I forget about what is really important. I'll call her once we return to Southbay. Maybe we can all have lunch together sometime."

"That would be wonderful. I'd really like that." Although it doesn't look like Jacqueline has moved to Southbay to seek the company of the people from her past, I believe she wouldn't mind if Melissa offered to renew their acquaintance.

The timer on the oven beeps, and Melissa puts in the vegetable casserole. We then go and lay the table outside in the gazebo. It has already become my favourite spot. I imagine how nice it would be to spend a few hours here reading a book during the hottest part of the day.

Michael returns around seven. He seems calm and content, so I take it as a good sign. His schedule for Mrs Perry's conservatory renovation is tight, and that suits me fine. It means he will be away from the early morning and until dinner time.

The conversation at the dinner table isn't as easy and light-hearted as the one we had during lunch. Still, thanks to Rowan Hammond's outgoing personality and smooth temper, the atmosphere is relaxed enough for everyone to enjoy the evening.

Long before the sunset, the sun begins its gradual descent into the channel waters. Gentle and warming, the golden light leaves the lawn and moves to the coastal path to caress the dark cliffs before saying goodbye until dawn hour.

After the early start and almost the whole day spent

outside, I am ready to go to bed. I help Finley clear the table and load the dishes into the dishwasher. I don't know if Michael plans to stay to talk some more with Rowan, and I don't want to ask.

I go to the annexe and take a long shower. The hot water feels like a luxurious reward after a long day.

Already in my pyjamas, I remember that I'd thought about bringing a glass of water to keep it on the bedside table. Sometimes, I wake up feeling thirsty in the middle of the night. I don't want to rouse everyone, creeping around the house in the darkness and breaking something fragile on my way.

I put on a cardigan so as not to parade through the Hammonds' household in just my pyjamas, and head to the kitchen. I pour myself a glass of water, and I am ready to go back when I hear the muffled sounds of voices.

Overcoming my reluctance to talk to Michael, I still decide it's a good idea to say goodnight to our hosts.

I walk into the living room and find it empty. I look around and see that the glass doors leading to the outside terrace are partly open. Although the sun has set, it isn't completely dark outside. Still, the lights on the porch obscure rather than illuminate those who are sitting there, reflecting from the glass.

I reach out for the door handle but stop when I hear the words: "Why did you marry her then?"

I recognise Rowan Hammond's voice.

A glass clinks, something having been put on the glass table.

"I don't know. It seemed like a good idea then." My husband's voice sounds unfamiliar.

"Margo is a nice girl," Rowan continues. "Haven't you thought that she deserves better?"

"And what does she deserve? I've brought her here, and it's already better than what she would have in Latvia. Have you been there? The country still looks like it hasn't left the Soviet bloc."

My throat tightens and I swallow, trying to get rid of the painful lump.

"I haven't been there, so I can't comment on that or argue with you. But I don't see how your wife can benefit from all our country has to offer if she doesn't work or study."

"Who do you think I am, Rowan? A charity organisation? She has already benefitted enough from our marriage. I am sure that she'd gladly get a proper diploma for my money. And then what? She'll run away with some young upstart from college. I've had enough of being fooled by women."

The glass clinks again. I can't see from the tears clouding my vision. I guess Rowan has refilled their glasses.

"Cecilia didn't fool you. She fell in love. It happens."

I hold my breath upon hearing Michael's ex-wife's name.

"Right. She fell in love with a man who now lives comfortably spending my money."

"He is an artist. Creative people often have a powerful charisma."

"That's fantastic. But the bills must be paid. And he doesn't pay them with money he's earned from selling his art."

"He might become famous. You never know."

"Do you think he'll share his fortune with me if he does?"

Rowan laughs. I don't think he can stay grim for a long time. "I guess not. Life is unfair, my friend. There is nothing we can do about it."

"Exactly. Keeping that in mind, I don't feel like making it even more unfair."

Michael's voice is cold, without a trace of humour in it.

"For you. It is perfectly understandable that you don't want to make it more unfair for you. But what about Margo?"

If I could, right now, I would hug Rowan Hammond.

"And what about her? Rowan, I'm not exploiting child

labour, for God's sake. That's how you're making it sound. Margo has everything she needs. She has a good life. A much better one than she would have if I hadn't married her."

"There is always room for improvement."

I imagine Michael rolling his eyes and pursing his lips at these words.

"She can improve her bookkeeping skills by helping me with the company's accounts. You do know what pain in the neck these financial issues are."

"Oh, yes. Don't remind me about it." Rowan sighs. This is clearly something that burdens him. "I think I told you that Clarence and I decided to do the accounts ourselves to reduce business running costs. I didn't know what I was getting myself into." The clinking of glass indicates the extent of his frustration. "I suffer every time I sit down to fill in those tables. It's a complete nightmare. All those figures look like a maze to me. And they never match! I sit for hours looking for mistakes, and I seldom find them myself. Melissa isn't a mathematician either, but at least she is able to figure out where the problem is."

"You hit the jackpot with your marriage."

"I know. Who would have thought that someone like her would so much as look at someone like me twice." Rowan chuckles softly.

"You haven't done badly for yourself. So, she must know that she made the right decision, giving you a chance."

"I hope she does."

In the silence that follows, birds' cries sound loud like emergency sirens.

"I can't believe I fell into the middle-age trap." Michael's voice pierces the calm. My stomach starts to churn with a premonition of something unpleasant. "She was young and eager. It was a new experience. I thought I deserved it. Especially after what Cecilia had done. But you know…"

My throat burns, and my eyes sting. I want to run away but can't move from the spot.

"…sex with a young girl in a foreign city is a great way to unwind after tough negotiations. But it has simply worn off. The excitement, the drive. I shouldn't have married her."

I step back, unable to continue listening. Fleeing from the room as if it is on fire, I slam into something. Luckily, it is something soft, and I grab hold of the back of the couch to steady myself.

I stand, panting and trying to fight back tears, when a sudden noise startles me. I blink to clear off the blur.

"You knew!" I choke out when I see Finley struggling with returning a chair he has overthrown back into its place under the table. "You knew and didn't tell me. Let me talk and make a fool of myself. Men! You are worse than old women sitting on the benches nosing into other people's business."

"I don't understand…"

The confusion on Finley's face only angers me more. "Of course you don't! Who cares about what happens in places like Latvia? Everyone must know about the queen, the fog, and the Sunday roast, but not about old women in the yards of five-storey high-rises…"

I turn around. Embarrassed that I've lost my temper in such an ugly way, I am still fuming. I've known all along that Finley and I have nothing in common. We are from different worlds. Even if – *when*, I correct myself – I divorce Michael, the Hammonds aren't likely to be ecstatic if their son starts dating someone like me.

"Margo…"

Finley calls after me, but I march on, anxious to hide from everyone.

Alas, I can't hide from my own thoughts. I crawl into bed, desperate to fall asleep before Michael comes back, and fail to even calm down, let alone drift into unconsciousness. My body is rigid, and I toss and turn, unable to settle into a comfortable position. It feels like all my nerves are uncovered and shaking, sending tiny shock waves through my limbs.

I'll go home, jumbled thoughts seethe in my head. *I'll go home tomorrow. I'll call Mom and ask her to transfer some money to my account. I'll buy a ticket and go home. I can't take it anymore.*

I jump out of bed and open the window. Michael hates sleeping with windows open, but right now, I couldn't care less about his whims.

I get back under the blanket and fall into uneasy sleep.

CHAPTER 20

In the morning, I wake up in an empty bed. Michael has already left. I take it as a bit of luck that I really need.

I take a long shower and wash my hair. Then I sit in the room for an hour. I try to read, but all I can do is just skim through pages, not grasping the meaning of the words and sentences.

At ten, when I am sure everyone is busy, I venture out of the annexe. I grab an apple and a few cookies from the counter in the kitchen and hasten out.

Hurrying down the front path, I almost bump into Rowan Hammond. "I'm sorry!" I exclaim louder than I intended. "I wasn't looking where I was going."

"Good morning, Margo." Mr Hammond smiles at me, and I wish that his laid-back attitude would rub off me. "It's okay. Nothing is broken." He chuckles at his own joke.

"What are your plans for today? If you want to see more of the surrounding area, we could drive to Penzance or St. Ives. I'm sure Melissa and Finley would love that, too. Actually, we should do that more often. Maybe then our vacation in Cornwall will seem more exciting to everyone."

"Thank you, Mr Hammond. It sounds wonderful. But I haven't seen Lizard properly yet, so it's already very exciting for me to wander around here." I don't let it slip where I plan to go today.

"Of course. We are so used to the beauty of this place that we need a reminder from time to time."

We can get used to anything, I think, walking down the path that winds between rocks and thorny bushes. *But I'm going to break the vicious circle.* The last phrase, which I have read in the novel about a painful divorce, stuck with me. That is what my life has been like for the last year: a vicious circle I can't step out of.

I choose a rocky path that runs along the shore closer to the cliffs than the main coastal path. It isn't dangerous, but walking here requires more concentration, and it's not suitable for riding. I doubt anyone would look for me here, and that is what I want. I need time to be alone with my thoughts, even if it hurts to think about what has happened to me and what I have to do to make things right.

I wander for hours, making stops to stare at the waves. There isn't much here besides the waves and the rocks. I would even call this part of the picturesque peninsula dreary. Today, the subdued colours and loneliness suit me. I sit down on the ledge with the view over the lighthouse.

I know what I have to do. In fact, I have known for a while now. I simply didn't have the courage to take the final step. It still scares me to be left to my own devices, but at the same time, the thought of being independent is exciting.

Seagulls shriek, chasing one another and diving into the waves for the fish. I wonder if they feel as utterly free as they look.

As I make my way back, I don't feel free from my

worries. Still, I am calm enough to face Michael and the Hammonds without making a nuisance of myself.

At dinner, I chat with Mr Hammond about possible day trips to Penzance and St. Ives. I avoid looking at Finley and pretend that my husband isn't sitting next to me. I am tired of staying attuned to other people's expectations. For the first time in quite a while, I focus on my own.

"You could take a day off and come with us to Penzance, Michael." Rowan Hammond seems oblivious to his friend's lack of interest in sightseeing. "I bet you haven't been there. And there should be advantages to being your own boss. Mrs Parry's conservatory won't go anywhere."

Michael barely raises his eyes from the plate to answer. "The work isn't going to do itself," he says. "Besides, I'm not interested in these tourist traps along the coast. There is nothing to see there except for what they make a huge buzz about in the media. No one would care about seeing these places if they weren't told they are must-sees."

Mr Hammond chuckles good-naturedly. "You never were the adventurous type. Even at school. Do you even know where the headmaster's office was?"

Michael doesn't smile. "I didn't have time for silly things. I still don't."

Is this what I am to you, I want to ask, *just another silly thing?*

After dinner, I go for a walk. I don't want to go far since my legs still throb after a more challenging hike earlier today. Having settled on the grassy ledge, I watch the sun colouring the sky and the water in the hues of orange and gold. Birds fly above, piercing the air with their screams. I see them land on the ledges below.

After the sun sets, it gets dark quickly, so I hasten back.

I am so engrossed in my thoughts that hearing someone calling my name startles me.

"I am sorry if I scared you, Margo." I am relieved to recognise Melissa's voice. "Would you like to join me for a glass of wine after your walk?"

I enter the gazebo. Melissa sits on the bench that runs

along the inner perimeter with her legs stretched comfortably. The padded bench is strewn with additional cushions.

"It's okay. I got carried away. Too much fresh air."

There isn't any other light in the gazebo save for a few tea candles flickering on the table.

"I can relate to that." Melissa's white teeth flash in the semi-darkness when she smiles. She puts her feet down on the floor and walks to the table. "I have some red frizzante and also some of the white left," she says, inspecting the bottle. "Both aren't as cold as they should be. I hope it's all right. Which one?" She looks at me, lightly touching the bottles.

"I don't know." I shrug. "I'm not an expert on wines. What will you have?"

Melissa smiles again. "Okay, then, let's finish the frizzante. It isn't as bad when it's warm like Chardonnay."

She pours the wine and gives one glass to me. "Let's sit there if you don't mind." She nods at the bench.

I sit back, pressing comfortably into the cushions. "It's so quiet." I take a sip of the sparkling wine. Tiny bubbles gently sting the inside of my mouth. It feels nice.

Melissa casts a glance around. "Yes, I love sitting here in the evening. Even when there is a storm during the day, it almost always quietens down before the night."

Strings of small bulbs adorn the ceiling of the gazebo. Reflecting the trembling light from the candles on the table, they twinkle like fireflies. It is cosy and magical.

We don't talk for a while. I let the atmosphere of a warm summer evening envelop me. My head buzzes lightly from the wine. My thoughts are as light as feathers; they swirl lazily, not causing any pain or discomfort.

"So, Margo, would I be much mistaken if I say that you like Finley?"

I almost jump out of my seat. "I… I don't… I would never…" I don't finish.

Melissa waves the hand in which she doesn't hold the

glass. "I asked because I want it very much to be true." She looks at me inquisitively.

I put my glass on the wide top rail of the gazebo, for my hands are shaking. "How can you say that?" My voice trembles. "I am married."

She stands, and putting her glass on the table, walks over to me. Then, she sits down next to me. "But you aren't happy in your marriage. It isn't a crime. It happens to millions of people. I don't think that people shouldn't be given a second chance if they made a mistake."

"But if I made one mistake, don't you think I will make more?" I desperately want her to reassure me.

"Most certainly. You will make tons of mistakes in your life, Margo. I have made plenty of them. And sadly, some of them can't be fixed." She smiles, but her eyes remain sad. "But it isn't like this in your case. You are young. You have all your life ahead of you. I would hate to see you ruin it because of one mistake. Besides, it isn't only your fault that your marriage hasn't worked out the way you hoped. With marriages and relationships, it is always about two people. And sometimes, more than two."

I want to hide my face in my hands and cry. But I don't do it. It has been enough tears.

"I do like Finley," I say, not looking at Melissa. On the table, candle lights dance, and their reflections flutter on the sides of the glasses and bottles. "But I don't want to make new promises. I don't know if I can keep them."

"Lucky for us, we can't predict the future. We can only take the chances that get thrown our way and check if they work. Sometimes they do, even if it seems impossible at first. But sometimes they don't. It's not a tragedy. It only becomes tragic when you force yourself to stay in the situation you want to escape from."

"It's not right to run away the moment it becomes tough." I try not to slip into reflections about what I possibly have done wrong in my failed marriage.

"No, it's not. And still, if the tough moment doesn't pass

but turns into tough times, to leave may be the only right decision." Melissa takes my hand, and I almost forget about the promise not to cry I made to myself. "The right decision for both of you," she says softly.

It is painfully embarrassing to realise that Melissa knows how Michael feels about his decision to marry me. She and her husband don't have secrets from each other.

"It still feels bad. It feels like a failure."

"Of course it does, sweetheart." She rubs my shoulder soothingly. "We invest so much into relationships. And the emotional pain can be worse than physical. Physical pain passes, while emotional wounds heal much longer."

"Some of them never heal," I say, thinking about Mom and how she never got over whatever happened between her and my father.

"It is enough not to make them deeper."

Melissa squeezes my shoulder and rises. "Well, I think it's about time we have more wine. Or," she turns, "if you prefer tea, I could go and make us some. And also, some cake. It seems that no one had a particular appetite today. Did you like the apple crumble?"

I stand up too. "I'll help you. I'd love tea and the cake. Everything was so tasty that it simply didn't fit in."

"Alas, everything in life comes with limited capacity. Except for human folly, maybe."

I smile at her dry humour and follow her into the house.

In the kitchen, we find Rowan Hammond peering at a laptop with an expression of extreme puzzlement on his face. His eyebrows, usually slightly raised in a permanent state of happy wonder, are knitted together on his grim face.

"Hello, darling." Melissa walks around the kitchen island, touching her husband's shoulder. "I thought you hadn't even brought the computer with you. You said our time in Cornwall was supposed to be time for complete relaxation."

Rowan groans. "Accounts! They are pure evil. But unavoidable like death and taxes." He runs his hand through his short hair. "I know I promised not to bring work here. And I don't reply to Mr Wilberforce's emails, do I? His bladder is old enough to endure two weeks without medical examination... Margo, I apologise." Rowan looks at me, ruffling his hair again. "This financial maze makes me as grumpy as Mr Wilberforce, if not grumpier." His pleasant face looks almost comical, wearing the expression of a boy who has stumbled upon an unsolvable task during a class.

"Maybe I could help?" I offer. For me, numbers, tables, and calculations don't seem half as complicated as relationship and emotion issues. "If it's not confidential, I can have a look."

"You can sell it on the black market if you want. I don't care if the whole world knows how much I earn as long as the reports are submitted to HMRC." Mr Hammond pushes the laptop to me when I sit down on a bar stool beside him. "Be my guest. If you make these numbers match, you'll be my hero."

"I would gladly help you, darling," Melissa speaks, not turning to us, busy with cutting the cake and putting tea things on a tray. "But unfortunately, I'm as bad at it as you are. I'd be looking at these Excel sheets for hours before I could find where the mistake was."

I quickly scan the open spreadsheet dotted with angry octothorpes indicating errors. *Don't start by looking for big issues. Always begin with checking the small things. Correct them, and if the problem persists, it will inevitably be easier to find.* I always hear these words from one of my university teachers before I begin searching for the problem in calculations. Small things are easy to overlook. You don't see them simply because you see what you intended to enter rather than what your fingers eventually typed.

Having removed unfortunate errors that the logic of a human mind wouldn't consider as such, I am left with two cells that need manual correcting. "Do you have physical or electronic copies of these two invoices?" I ask Rowan, pointing at the two titles of suppliers.

"Of course, of course, give me a minute." Mr Hammond, who has been watching what I was doing as if I was mixing a magic potion, jumps down from his chair and starts rummaging in a black laptop bag. Papers spill out of it, and Rowan carelessly puts them back, not caring if they become crumpled in the process. "Here they are!" he exclaims, triumphantly producing a batch of dog-eared documents. "I knew I had them somewhere." He gives me the papers, shaking his head. "We've already used almost everything we bought here," he points at the invoices, "but the financial reporting burden doesn't let anything disappear without a trace."

I hear Melissa laugh behind my back. "You are supposed to be fond of exact sciences," she teases her husband.

"Reporting to HMRC isn't a science," Rowan retorts, "it's a nightmare."

I compare the amounts in the invoices with what Mr Hammond had put into his Excel spreadsheet. Just as I suspect, they don't match. The discrepancy is only a few pennies, but for the software, it doesn't make any difference. I put in the right numbers and press *Save*: one more habit I have acquired during my studies.

"Here you go." I move the computer toward Rowan. "Now it should be fine. I'm not an expert, but Mr Billings – Michael's accountant – has taught me the basics. Even if there are some mistakes, the revenue service will send you a letter asking you to correct them. And this is usually quite easy to do."

Rowan stares at the screen in amazement. "I can't believe it," he says after a moment. "Margo, you have saved me. What a pity that I am not a fairy godmother, and I can't grant you a dozen wishes – one or even three simply aren't enough."

"You've already done more than enough for me, Mr Hammond. I'm glad I could help. Why don't you hire a specialist to do it for you?" I switch the topic from praising me to a practical issue.

Rowan Hammond sighs, but I can see that he is back to his easy-going and cheerful self. "It was a silly idea. When we planned our private practice, Clarence – Clarence Potter, my colleague and a good friend – offered that we do the accounting ourselves. He insisted that we put equal shares into the enterprise, and since his share ate up all his savings, he wanted to be sure that he would be able to cover all running costs. So, since we couldn't really cut down other expenses, we agreed to at least save on accounting services. A huge mistake!"

"I understand. You couldn't have known that it would be difficult. The information on those official websites always makes it look so easy." Mr Hammond nods, and I am glad to see the twinkle in his eyes again. "But I think it'll really be easy for you soon. You filled in everything, and that's the main thing."

Rowan shakes his head. "It will never be easy. Math has never been my strong side. Isn't it ironic that I had absolutely no trouble learning the names of more than two hundred bones in the human body in Latin, while formulas, equations, and those nightmarish integrals always seemed like mumbo-jumbo." He presses a few buttons and closes the laptop with a satisfied *phew*.

"I'd never learn even one-tenth of those bones. Even in my native language." I shake my head. "Don't worry. I can help you get those reports right for submission until you learn how to do it."

"I have a better idea." Having put the computer in the bag, he looks as if a huge burden has been lifted from his shoulders. "You could just do those reports for me. I will pay you, of course. I won't tell Clarence about it…"

"Okay, that's enough talk about work." Melissa comes over with a tray laden with tea things. "Margo has other issues to think about right now rather than your problems with strategic business planning."

Instead of retorting, Rowan smiles at his wife. "I am sorry, Margo," he says to me. "I got carried away. Finding out that there is hope to get rid of this punishment – self-inflicted, of course," he casts a quick glance at Melissa, and she nods, "was more exciting than discovering that my parents were going to give me a bicycle for my tenth birthday."

Melissa rolls her eyes. "Shall we go, Margo? Would you like to have tea with us, darling?"

Rowan stands up and takes the tray from her. "Let me help you with this. I'd rather watch something you don't usually let me watch. So, you can have your girls' talk without reservations."

"Thank you, darling." Melissa and I follow Rowan outside. "It was a polite way to tell us that our talks are incredibly boring," she tells me in a conspiratorial whisper.

Soon we are settled back in the gazebo with cups of steaming tea and the apple pie that, after cooling down, now tastes even better. I can't resist asking: "Don't you think it would be better for Finley to date a different girl?"

Melissa takes a sip of her tea before replying. "Do you mean a British girl?"

"That too. But I meant a girl without so many problems." I tuck into the apple crumble to replace the bitterness of the words with sweetness.

"Everyone has problems. For example, Finley's problem is his nosey mother." Melissa's smile glistens in the semi-darkness.

"You aren't nosey. You are... progressive."

Melissa laughs. "You know, I've heard it somewhere that by the age that a woman can become a grandmother, she turns into a copy of her mother. If someone had told me that when I was twenty, I'd have been enraged. At that time, I thought my mother and I were different species. And look at me now!"

"Did she give you advice about your personal life?"

"I would put it slightly differently, but yes, you can say that she knew what was best for me. I didn't believe she knew me at all. But now, after decades, I admit that she knew me better than I did myself."

We keep silent, drinking tea. There is something about tea that makes things right. No matter how frustrated you are when taking the first sip, you always feel better after you finish the cup.

"It is difficult to imagine a mother who wouldn't like Mr Hammond," I break the silence first.

"Do you know where Rowan and I first met?" Melissa's voice sounds as if she is trying to suppress laughter. "I was in that rebellious phase of someone who has never lacked anything in their lives, but who found that having everything isn't enough. A friend of mine invited me to a meeting of anti-royalists. I didn't understand it then, but she was more interested in meeting boys than abolishing the monarchy." Melissa giggles. "In that respect, she was right. We were the only girls at that meeting. It's funny, but while I found the heated discussions about the royal family spending huge sums of taxpayers' hard-earned money on luxury and foreign trips extremely exciting, I was the one of the two of us who found a boyfriend that day."

"It's a usual thing for a man to have strong political views."

Melissa gives me a half-smile that hides a meaning I cannot read. "Indeed, it is. It is only that my family was strict on what kind of strong political views a person was allowed to have."

While I try to think of an appropriate comment to this highly confusing statement, she continues: "You see, my family attended Royal Ascot every year. The Royal Enclosure membership was something my mother valued more than many other privileges in her highly privileged life. What would she say if she knew that I haven't attended Royal Ascot in the past two years?"

Melissa falls silent, clearly contemplating the things I have no idea about. I feel inadequate and don't say anything. She probably senses my discomfort, because she pours more tea into the cup that I have abandoned and puts a piece of pie on my plate.

"I understand that for you, it all must sound like a complete mystery. Why should anyone but us here know something about the races in Ascot and the old-fashioned hierarchy of their attendants?" Melissa's voice is kind. "You see, that is what makes you special, Margo."

"I think that it makes me ignorant."

"We all are ignorant about the things we haven't grown up being taught about."

"Anyway, I want to learn more. If I want to stay in this country, I have to learn more about its traditions."

"And do you want to stay here in England?"

"Yes, I've decided to try to make a life for myself here." For once, I am not happy that the darkness partly obscures the expression of my face. I want Melissa to see it in my eyes that my words are sincere. "After the divorce."

"I am truly glad to hear it. There are many opportunities for you here. I'm not saying you wouldn't have them in your home country. I simply don't know much about Latvia. But I know that your talents and hard work will get rewarded."

After a pause, I ask: "Did your mom try to stop you from marrying Mr Hammond?"

Melissa laughs. "Oh no, quite the contrary. Mother was the one who persuaded Rowan to make an honest woman of me."

Reacting to my silence, she explains: "Mother wasn't ecstatic about my relationship with Rowan. At first, she ignored it. She pretended that I didn't have a boyfriend. She kept inviting suitable young men to dinners at our house and made sure all of them were good-looking and not only from a good family. She wasn't as subtle as you would expect from someone who believed that the Regency era shouldn't have ever ended. But I have to give Mother her due: she wasn't blunt in her matchmaking endeavours either."

"Why did she change her mind?" Melissa's life story was more fascinating than any movie that I'd seen.

"Ironically, I think that her reverence for the same old Regency times' rules did the trick. More than having a daughter married to an anti-royalist and someone whose family never set foot on the Ascot racecourse, she was afraid to have an unmarried daughter. You will probably find it hard to believe, but every girl over twenty-one from the families my parents were friends with was married."

I did find it hard to believe, but for reasons different from what Melissa must have thought to be true.

"I got married at twenty-one," I tell her. "But among my friends, I was the only one who did."

"I am sorry, it was so tactless of me."

"No, it's okay. I understand what you wanted to say. Who marries at twenty-one nowadays? A... hmm... a few years back, I guess it was more common."

"A few decades ago, it definitely was. But I didn't want to be like everybody else. You see, I wanted my life to be as different from the one of my parents as it was possible."

I don't know what to say. From what I have seen so far, the Hammonds enjoyed not a less privileged lifestyle than Melissa's parents. "Do you think you haven't succeeded in that?" I finally ask.

Despite the dark, I see her shake her head. "Luckily, I have. But now I see how childish my ideas about what is important were. Back then, I didn't realise that I was fixated on the principles rather than the essence of things. And in that, I was just like my mother. It's a pity I understood that too late to tell her. We wouldn't have had a hearty laugh about it, that's for sure. She wasn't prone to displaying her emotions. But it would mean so much to me if she had known."

I feel a pang in my heart. I miss my mom. At times, I forget how much. "I'm sure that she knew. You said yourself that she knew you well."

"I really hope so. But still, it would be such an enormous consolation if I had been open with her. At least, at the very end, before she died."

That wouldn't happen to me, a sudden thought startles me. *The next time I call Mom, I will tell her everything about Michael.*

"I think it's our biggest problem. We can't find the right words just when it's the best time to say them."

"I think now is the right time to have more wine." Melissa smiles, standing up.

We move from the table to the comfortable bench. After tea and the apple crumble, the fizzy wine tastes better.

"So, my mother wasn't happy about her daughter living in sin," Melissa continues the story she had started before.

"With an anti-royalist," I add, feeling more relaxed in her company.

She giggles. "I guess it was what made the sin even worse in her eyes. Well, in fact, we weren't living together. I still lived in a flat my parents and the parents of the two girls who entered college with me paid for. My roommates got married and moved out, so I lived there alone. But Rowan lived in dormitories. He refused to live in a place he couldn't afford to pay for. He stayed the night from time to time, of course. I didn't share the details with my mother, but she knew. She suspected, that is. And I think it was something that stopped her from sleeping at night."

"Why did you refuse to get married?"

"I didn't have a chance to accept. Rowan didn't make a proposal. And before you say anything," Melissa raises the hand, "I thought it was perfectly justified. At that time, I firmly believed that the marriage concept was outdated."

"What made you change your mind?"

"Getting married." Melissa takes a sip of her wine. "I know I make it sound awfully confusing. So, here's the whole story. Mother disapproved – putting it mildly – of the fact that we had been dating for more than a year, and she still didn't have a wedding date to mark in her calendar. She wasn't what you'd call subtle in letting me know her opinion on the matter. But I was adamant. Marriage didn't matter, I used to retort whenever she raised the subject. Two people who love each other don't need approval from the government institution to keep loving each other and stay faithful." Melissa takes another sip and sighs. "I knew it would make her drop the topic. And I knew that my words hurt her. Once, when I was upset about something else, I even told her that I was surprised she pushed marriage on me while her own brought her so many bitter disappointments." She paused and then continued: "It was a low blow, but at the time, I thought I was right, hurting her like this."

"But you said your mom valued the privileged life she had. I thought it meant she was happy in her marriage."

Melissa shakes her head. "I guess she was happy in her own way. She valued what she had and closed her eyes to anything that marred the perfect image she worked hard to maintain. She didn't marry beneath her. My father's family equalled hers both in status and wealth. It was important to her. I am not sure she would have married a man who didn't tick all the boxes even if she had fallen madly in love with him. She would have rather spent her life alone but still admitted to all the best houses, with her reputation unscathed. Anyway, she married my father, and their marriage was what she expected it to be. Father was unfaithful to her, but so were most of Mother's friends' husbands. She told me that herself when I crossed the line and offended her by hinting at Father's affairs."

She falls silent, and I also feel that I need a moment to process what she has told me. "Cheating is wrong," I finally say, "but I don't know what is worse: to work at three jobs trying to make ends meet after you proudly dumped your cheating husband or live in comfort with a man who spends time with other women from time to time and still takes you to royal races."

I hope I didn't cross the line with my honesty. I am glad to see Melissa's smile glisten in the semi-darkness of the gazebo. "I would have never thought of looking at it from such a perspective. Thank you, Margo. I hope you will give my son a chance, so I can regularly talk to you."

I blush. It is flattering to be praised by someone like Melissa Hammond. But I feel that being honest with her is the least I can do for all the kindness she has shown me since our first meeting. "I like talking to you too." I take a deep breath. "I'm not sure I'm ready for a new relationship. I don't know when I'll be ready. I think I need to live on my own for a while. I need to understand how it is and if I can." I look down at my knees, unable to meet Melissa's gaze.

"I feel awful."

I raise my eyes.

"I don't want you to think that I have any expectations," Melissa continues. "This is so embarrassing. I behave just like my mother. If a while ago someone told me this would happen, I'd never believed them."

"So, how did your mother make Mr Hammond agree to marry you?"

Melissa giggles. "First, she didn't leave him a choice. And second, she staged everything in the way that he believed it was his own idea." She drains her glass where only a few drops of wine are left. "Mother was a perfect strategist. I will never reach her level of perfection. She invited Rowan to a family dinner. She couldn't wait until Christmas or some official occasion. So, she presented it as an informal dinner for the closest circle. Besides Rowan, she invited some distant relatives whom we met only at weddings and funerals. The only reason she chose that particular family was that their son wasn't married, but everybody knew that he was in a long-term relationship. I don't know why he didn't marry that girl. To be honest, I was too absorbed in my own life to be interested in the lives of others. Anyway, I imagine it took Mother some effort to locate perfect companions for that dinner. But when she thought that something was really important, she was unstoppable in achieving it. And here goes the best part." Melissa stands to pour us more wine. "Over dessert – as I said, a perfect strategist – Mother mentioned a garden party she planned for the following summer. A twenty-third wedding anniversary was something worth celebrating, she said. And she went on sharing her thoughts about the importance of marriage." Melissa giggles again. I can't resist laughing, too. The scene, as if from a historical movie, plays in front of my eyes while she tells her story. "After she finished lecturing us on propriety rules, she focused her regal stare, that could make a person confess to anything, on Rowan. I can tell you, Margo, that even now, after a quarter of a century has passed, I still feel the shiver running down my spine at that moment. I didn't even open my mouth to try to prevent the disaster I believed was about to happen. I was frozen."

"And what did she say?" I exclaim, putting the glass on the balustrade. I can't concentrate on anything save for Melissa's words.

"She praised Rowan. She said that it was so rare, but because of that, even more praise-worthy for *a young man from a new generation*," she mimicked her mother's cutglass accent, "to respect traditions. She said that long-lived traditions haven't endured centuries to be flung aside lightly. Then she added that she always believed late spring weddings were a quintessence of good taste."

"I'm surprised Mr Hammond didn't run away." The wine untied my tongue.

"I was surprised that he took it calmly, too. Only years, if not decades, later, did I realise that my mother understood Rowan better than I did. She knew that his decency wouldn't let him unmask her or leave me. Rowan told me after dinner that he was thinking about proposing himself, but he was afraid of putting me off. He said that he loved me for my progressive views, but he thought that views shouldn't turn into obstacles. We got married in May, and our wedding day was the most beautiful day of my life." A dreamy look appears on her face. "But the most important thing is I have never regretted that decision. And it doesn't matter that it might seem that it wasn't entirely my own."

We sip the wine in silence. I want to tell Melissa so many

things. I want to share my thoughts and dreams with her. I feel that she would understand, maybe even better than I do, what has led me to make wrong decisions and what can be done not to repeat the same mistakes. "What makes you think that Finley and I have a future?" I ask. "You could choose any girl for him."

Melissa smiles kindly. "I didn't choose you for him. He has chosen you himself. As a mother, I simply noticed it. And as a mother, I want my child to be happy."

I shake my head. "I don't understand." I feel so vulnerable. I don't think I'll ever trust my own judgement on things like love, marriage, and relationships again. Still, I want so badly to trust Melissa's judgement right now.

"He has listened to you. It doesn't happen often. People in general are prone to stick to their opinions. And it is especially true for young people. With the spirit of rebellion hot in their blood, they rarely admit they have been wrong. Finley believed that education wasn't important. All his friends and the girls he dated agreed with him. They thought it was cool. But when you told him that he was a fool to rob himself of the opportunity…"

"It was tactless of me. And Finley would have plenty of opportunities even if he hadn't finished school."

"Exactly. That's exactly what the girls he dated told him."

She didn't have to say more.

"They didn't want to put him off," I say. *And lose a chance to get all his family's privileges,* I add to myself.

"But you didn't care what the spoilt rich boy would think."

If I were sober and less tired, I'd feel totally embarrassed by this accusation that hit home. As it is, I burst with laughter, almost spilling the wine. "I don't know why I thought I knew better." I rub my nose, which has started to prickle after bubbles from the wine got into my nostrils. "I guess it simply seemed unfair that someone who could have everything he wanted didn't grab it and wasn't even grateful."

"And you were right. You told him what we were afraid to tell him. I felt so helpless. I knew that he was going to regret it later, but my hands were bound. He wouldn't have listened to me. I didn't know what to do. Mother would have found the right words. I often remembered her skilful scheming in domestic matters. And then you came, and the problem I thought was unsolvable miraculously got solved."

"I think Finley would have figured it out by himself what's best for him."

"I hope so. But with your help, he did it early."

We exchange smiles. And then, I yawn.

"I think we'd better go to bed." Melissa rises from the bench, stretching her hands behind her. "I'm glad we have talked, Margo."

I help her put the glasses and what is left on the table onto the tray. "I'm glad too. Thank you. For everything." I want to tell her that she has changed my life, but even in my current dizzy state, I know that it would be too much.

Before we go back to the house, I ask: "Can I take Alastor for a ride in the morning? I won't trouble anyone."

"Of course you can. You don't have to ask me. And don't worry about tacking him up. Stanley is usually up and somewhere around the stables at six. Just find him and ask him to help you."

We hug before saying goodnight.

As I walk to the room I share with Michael, I don't think about the difficult conversation I will soon have with my husband. I only see a beautiful black horse running at the edge of the waves and hear the wind whooshing in my ears.

CHAPTER 21

Another marvellous summer day in Cornwall begins with Alastor carrying me across the field to the coastal path. The grass is covered with sparkling dew, and the air is fragrant with a cacophony of aromas.

I want to go to the secret cove, which Finley had shown me, but I am not sure I can find the trail that goes down there. "Take me to that place where you can run freely," I say to the horse. Maybe for him, these words mean nothing. Still, whenever I talk to him, he turns his head slightly and watches me with his big dark eye.

The horse's rhythmic movements feel like the gentle swaying of a cradle. I have almost forgotten how incredible it is to ride a horse. I resist the urge to bend forward and press my head to Alastor's neck.

I am not surprised when Alastor turns right from the path and walks down the slope. We enter the shadowy coolness of the rocky path, and inside me, something shifts. *I am free.* The thought is familiar rather than shocking, as if it has already settled in my subconscious a while ago but didn't surface in my mind until now.

We walk out onto the beach. I am not a skilful rider, and I am not sure if I can start Alastor into a trot and then gallop. I squeeze my legs and press the back of my feet into his sides. "Let's run a bit, beautiful boy. Trot!"

Elated that he has actually understood and obeyed, I enjoy the active trotting pace for the length of the cove. We gallop back to the path opening, and then back to the protruding rock that hides the entrance to the smaller cove.

I pull in the reins, and Alastor carefully makes his way around the ledge.

Once we are in the cove, I jump down and lead the horse to where we last had the picnic with Finley.

I sit down on the sand. I don't have a plan; it is more like an expectation of what might happen. There is no logic behind this evasive feeling that tickles my heart, and it makes me tremble with anticipation. This time, it is the anticipation of something good. Something that could change my life. I have never felt like this before. I have always prided myself on my practical approach to life. Now, I wonder if this pragmatism has led me to the situation when I have to leave the past behind and start over.

I sit, watching the waves. The morning light sparkles off the water.

Inside me, the anticipation of joy grows.

I am waiting for Finley. If he comes, there is a chance for us to be together. He can find me here only if he knows me. And in my heart, I know that he does.

I don't hear the sound of the hooves. My eyes catch the silhouette of a rider on the horseback first. For a few brief moments, the sun turns it into a black pencil drawing. Soon, the illusion dissipates. I rise and walk toward Finley, who has climbed down Admiral and now approaches me, walking fast.

We meet in the middle of the picturesque cove hidden

among the dark cliffs of Cornwall.

We hug, and standing there, locked in Finley's arms, seems the most natural thing in the world.

The last piece of iron armour I have put around myself falls away, and I can finally breathe. I can breathe freely and do what makes my heart blossom with anticipation of happiness.

"Hi," Finley speaks after the first overwhelming moments have passed.

"Hi," I reply, breath caught up in my throat.

"You've made up your mind," he says softly. "I'm glad."

I keep my face pressed to his chest. "I'm not making any promises."

"That was supposed to be my line."

I look up and see that he is smiling.

"It's your chance to reconsider what you are getting yourself into." I tease him, feeling ridiculously confident that nothing I say can make him change his mind about us.

"What will stop me from doing it later?"

"Your mother's wrath."

He laughs, then hugs me tighter and kisses my hair.

We walk back to the rock where I left Alastor. The black horse neighs, greeting Admiral.

"You know, your horses are amazing," I tell Finley. "I've always thought that horses are unique creatures. But yours really are like from a book or a movie."

"I'm glad you like them."

He spreads the blanket he has brought like he did the last time, and we sit down.

"So, what now?"

I turn away from his intense stare and look at the glistering water. I don't want to think about serious things right now. I want to lie wrapped up in Finley's arms and listen to the waves.

"You go back to your university in Bournemouth, and I go back to Southbay," I finally say.

"And then?"

"I can't tell you yet. But I will after I get the divorce."

"Will you go back to Latvia?"

"I hope not."

"You could live with us. With my parents. I'm sure Mom would agree."

I shake my head and turn back to look him in the eyes. "No, I don't want to do that again. To rely on others to organise my life for me. I want to try to be independent. Even if only for a little while. Who knows, maybe I'll hate living alone. But I must try to see what it's like. It's something I haven't done yet, and I think it's important for everyone to test themselves."

Finley nods slowly. "I understand. It made me look at things differently when I went to live in Bournemouth. It felt strange at first. I realised how helpless I really was with the most basic things. I hadn't realised before how many simple things parents did for me, and I took it for granted."

"I'm glad you understand." I bend to brush off the sand from the blanket. "Look, I don't know if it will work. Between us, I mean. It feels strange to discuss it. But I… I like you and want to try. As I said, I'm not ready to make any promises. Maybe I won't find a job or a flat, or I won't earn enough money to pay all the bills. I can't know any of that beforehand. I know it's my fault that I haven't bothered to find out more about these simple things. But I can't change that. I can only do things differently in the future."

Finley digs his foot into the sand. "It would be too easy if you just moved in with me in Bournemouth while I finish my studies."

"You don't have to do that. I'm sure any girl you choose would be more than happy to move in with you and enjoy the carefree student life."

He pierces me with his green eyes, which an ordinary person and not a movie star shouldn't be allowed to have. "I don't want any girl. And I have already chosen."

I sigh, not out of exasperation but because I feel overwhelmed. I still can't fully believe this is happening.

"There is nothing special about me. You shouldn't put your life on hold for me."

"To me, you are special." He still watches me intently. "I've been thinking about you all year since I left for Bournemouth. Student life is full of distractions. So, if it weren't a real thing…" he doesn't finish, turning away.

I pull my knees to my chest and hug them. I want to say many things. All of them rush through my head, tumbling upon each other. Finally, I can say what I want to be true. "I know that it's a real thing. I just don't want to get hurt again."

Finley moves closer to me and puts his hands on my shoulders. "I will never hurt you, Margo. I would rather let you hurt me."

I untangle my hands and clasp them around his neck. We look at each other, searching for something we can't put into words. The longer I gaze at his face, more handsome than ever with that serious look in his eyes, the more confident I become about our future together. I want this. I want to give the future with Finley Hammond a chance. I don't know if I have deserved it or if it was meant to be. I don't think about the things beyond this moment. That is what seems to matter the most: every single moment we will spend together from now on.

"I will do my best not to ever hurt you." As I speak, my head starts to spin. I want to press my lips to his. Still, when Finley lowers his head so that I feel his breath on my cheek, I turn away and press my face to his shirt. "I know it's stupid, but I want to do everything the right way this time."

He doesn't release me from his arms, stroking my hair. "It isn't stupid. You are right. It is easy to make mistakes. To do the right thing is always harder. We'll do as you wish."

We don't speak or move for a while. The feeling of his warm body so close to mine is exquisite. I never want it to end. I feel safe and calm.

My stomach churns. I haven't eaten breakfast today, too impatient was I to get to the secret beach and start waiting for Finley.

"I wish you'd taken a basket with all those tasty things you brought the last time." My cheeks turn red as I try to mask the embarrassment of breaking our romantic moment with humour.

"My fault." Finley hits his forehead with his palm. "I should have known that I ought to feed you before talking about love."

I giggle. "You still have time to learn."

"That I will do. You can be sure of that." His gaze turns serious for a brief moment, and then we both burst out laughing.

CHAPTER 22

On the drive back to Southbay from Cornwall, I don't clutch the wheel as if my life is hanging on a thread. I am still nervous about driving the busy roads, but the panic is gone.

Besides, this time, I am not going to allow Michael to make a four-hour-long drive without a single stop. I haven't had a chance to tell him to stop somewhere midway so I could stretch my legs and use the bathroom. He was brisk when we said our goodbyes with the Hammonds and didn't talk to me before getting into the trailer. It doesn't matter. I honk when I feel I need a break and keep honking until my husband takes notice.

I know it infuriates him when I don't behave according to his proper behaviour standards. Countless times, the fear of causing his displeasure stopped me from ensuring my own comfort. I will not suffer for the sake of pleasing Michael anymore. It hasn't brought any results anyway.

I follow the trailer to a car park of the roadside cafeteria. Once we both park, I climb out and walk past my husband, telling him on the go that I need to use the bathroom.

Inside the small, clean space, it smells of flowers. I wonder what brand of air freshener they use.

When I wash my hands, my phone beeps in my bag.

They have found Betty's killer, I read a message from Suzie. *Will tell you more when you get back.*

My eyes widen, and I resist the urge to call back right away.

I'll be home today, I type. *But I'm not sure what time. I could pop into the bakery?*

The reply arrives promptly. *Come over when you can. I'll be baking until late. You won't believe it when I tell you.*

On my way out, I peek at the café's counter. I am not hungry, but I wouldn't mind having a cup of coffee. My newly acquired self-confidence doesn't extend as far as forcing Michael to make more stops until we reach Southbay. So, I take a deep breath, letting the delicious aromas of freshly brewed coffee and pastry tease my senses, and rush back to the car.

Michael is sitting behind the wheel of the trailer when I return. Without acknowledging me in any way, he waits until I get into the jeep and drives out of the car park.

Back at the cottage in Southbay, we barely exchange a few phrases before he stalks upstairs.

This time, I haven't asked Michael what he wants for dinner. I've informed him that a casserole with fish is the easiest option and that it will be ready in an hour and a half. I did contemplate offering for him to go out and have a hassle-free meal after a long journey. Again, my boldness hasn't yet grown beyond certain limits.

I wash my hands at the sink in the kitchen and take out fish from the freezer. After putting it into the oven to defrost, I go upstairs to change.

Cooking calms me, and before the oven beeps to let me know the casserole is ready, I'm already humming a tune that played a few times on the radio during the drive from Cornwall. I lay out the table and call for Michael. I imagine him cringing at the loud sound of my voice. He always demands that I go upstairs to invite him to meals rather than raise my voice, calling him from the kitchen. *He'll have to deal with it,* I say to myself.

After we have eaten, I serve coffee with a selection of treats I always keep for situations when there isn't time for baking.

We haven't talked during the meal, save for a few necessary phrases.

"Suzie sent me a text when we were driving. I'm going to the Groveland Bakery to find out what happened. Do you want me to bring anything special from there for you?" I ask, cleaning away the dishes.

My husband gives me a look as if I offered to invite a third person to our bed.

"No," he says curtly, and not adding anything else, leaves the dining room.

******

On my way to the Groveland Bakery, the fatigue after a long drive creeps up on me. Walking along the coastal path, I feel lightheaded and slightly disoriented. I try to breathe slowly, hoping that fresh, salty air will revive me.

When I arrive, the Groveland Business Park corridors are empty. It isn't even five o'clock, but normal business hours here are until four. I still can't get used to it, for back home in Latvia, a usual office day lasts from nine to six.

The sound of my steps is so loud that it is unsettling.

I briefly contemplate popping into Laura's office to check if she keeps British or Latvian business hours. But, almost simultaneously, I discard the idea.

Suzie's bakery door is closed, which is an unofficial indication that today, the cafeteria has stopped serving customers. When I enter, I see a few customers having their tea with pastry. Suzie always allows clients to finish their meals without hurry.

I can't see her behind the counter, but the door to the kitchen is open. Suzie also doesn't change her schedule if some customers haven't bothered to leave on time. If she's planned to start baking at four-thirty, she would retreat to the kitchen at that time, not waiting for the last clients to depart.

After sitting down at my usual table between the window and the counter, I don't have to wait long. Suzie emerges from the kitchen, flushed but smiling. Her smile widens when she notices me. "Margo! I'm so glad you've made it back."

I smile back, amused that my friend makes it sound as if I've just returned from a dangerous mission. "I'm happy to be back. Cornwall is fantastic, but nothing can compare to our little island."

Suzie wipes her hands on her apron and sits down beside me. "I've just put a new batch into the oven. I have thirty minutes to tell you the news." She casts a quick glance across the room at the two tables, each occupied by a middle-aged man. Neither pay any attention to us. "It was the guy who works for George King. Marek *Kow... Kol...* anyway, I can't remember these foreign names for the life of me. He is *Polish*." She pronounces 'Polish' as if it is something more like 'from the future'.

I need a few moments to put two and two together. As much as I like Suzie's easy and inartificial manner, sometimes it is challenging to follow her erratic train of thought.

"George King's worker is that mysterious Betty Burton's visitor?"

Suzie nods vigorously. "I'm sorry for spilling it out on you like this. I just couldn't wait to tell you. Yes, it was the man who works for George King. Who could have imagined?"

"And what did he want from Betty?"

Suzie widens her eyes and moves closer to me. "His boss told him to make Betty agree to sell her cottage and the land.

He wanted to build more houses on that plot and sell them for millions."

"And Betty refused." I can see Mrs Burton's kind face turning stern once she realises what the unwelcome guest wants from her. I swallow the lump in my throat.

"You bet she did." Suzie's eyes fill with tears. "I'm sure she told him to get out of her property. And added a few words that he'd never have the courage to repeat to pass over to his boss. But it was too much for her. Poor Betty." Tears leave two paths of moisture on Suzie's face. "Such cruelty. So thoughtless of that… bastard. To threaten an elderly woman, a kind, beautiful soul as she was. And for what? Doesn't he have enough money? Doesn't he own half of the island and more already?" She wipes off tears with her apron. Now, there are speckles of flour on her cheeks.

I take her hand and squeeze it. "It's unbelievable. People are greedy. Some simply can't get enough."

She pats my hand. "That's life. I guess it's because I haven't learned how to earn money that I don't understand the obsession people have with it."

Before I open my mouth to reassure her, the door opens, and two men walk in.

Instead of telling them the café is closed, Suzie frantically starts dabbing at her face and smoothing her hair. When the men reach us, she greets them in a high-pitched voice and almost giggles. "Detectives, what a pleasant surprise! You are always welcome. What can I get you? Coffee? I remember that was your preference last time, am I correct? I have freshly baked chocolate muffins, right out of the stove. Would you like some?" Suzie stands up abruptly, almost overturning the chair.

"Please do not trouble yourself. We know we've arrived outside business hours." The taller man in a pale blue short-sleeved suit shirt and brown trousers speaks in a calm voice. His manner is so soothing that my mouth, which was at risk of hanging open because of Suzie's unusual behaviour, stays firmly shut. "I thought we'd pop in to see if you were still here since we've already driven to Southbay on another assignment." The man blushes slightly, and his gaze drops to the floor for a moment. His companion's lips twitch in a similarly unassuming manner, as if he is hiding a smile.

I do my best not to let my lips stretch into a ridiculously wide smile that would make my facial muscles hurt. I am not as good at suppressing natural urges as the policemen.

"I'm glad you thought about popping in! You are always very welcome at the Groveland Bakery. Please, come anytime." Suzie's cheeks are a sweet shade of pink now. If this isn't the most uplifting scene I have witnessed since I was a child, I don't know what is.

"Thank you." The tall detective fails at not staring at the bakery's owner. "I will take you at your word. This place serves the best coffee and muffins across Dorset."

Suzie and the detective continue looking at each other as if they are two teenagers in a school cafeteria. I find it incredibly touching and wouldn't mind for this lovely scene to continue. Alas, the other policeman, obviously more used to such displays, clears his throat. "I told Penny I'll be back for dinner today," he says, "and my car is at the station in Eastpoole."

"Sorry, mate." The tall detective tears his eyes from Suzie with difficulty. "We'll be getting back in a minute." He looks at Suzie again, and another layer of charming pink covers her already-flushed cheeks. "I was wondering if you have any information on when the Birketts plan to get back from Cornwall. The duty officer has been given the task to call them regularly, but you know..."

"Mrs Birkett is here!" Suzie exclaims in that girlish tone she seems to have adopted when the detective is around. "I'm sorry. I haven't introduced you. This is Margo Birkett. She is the one who helped you find poor Betty's killer! Margo, this is Peter... that is, Detective Fletcher. And this is Detective Mills."

Suzie and Detective Fletcher exchange the cutest smiles.

"Mrs Birkett. It is a pleasure to meet you. I am Detective

Chief Inspector Fletcher, and this is my colleague Detective Sergeant Mills."

With a balding hairline and watery blue eyes, Chief Inspector Peter Fletcher isn't a handsome man. His eyelashes and eyebrows are so light that they are almost non-existent, and his skin is covered with liver spots. Still, it isn't these unattractive things that I notice about him. It is the kindness of his face and the soft, humorous twinkling of his eyes.

"Nice to meet you, detectives." I shake hands with both policemen. "Thank you for finding who upset Mrs Burton. She was such a wonderful lady."

Detective Fletcher inclines his head. "I understand that it was a hard blow for the local community."

Suzie nods a little too vigorously, dabbing at the corners of her eyes. "She will be missed."

Detective Fletcher smiles at her and addresses me again: "You did a great job persuading Mrs Peckham to come to the police and share what she remembered later. When our colleagues talked to her the first time, she didn't seem to remember anything we could use to solve the case."

I feel my cheeks turning crimson. Peter Fletcher is such a nice man. He reminds me of Raymond Billings, the accountant. I hope everything will work out between him and Suzie. "Thank you, Mr… uhm… I mean, Detective. I didn't know if she would follow my advice. And I'm sorry I didn't come to you straight away to report what she told me. My husband, you see… he got that urgent assignment in Cornwall…"

"Do not worry about it, Mrs Birkett. It isn't a crime to have a busy life. That's our job to catch bad guys."

I see Detective Fletcher's colleague raise his eyebrow in his unassuming manner to express his emotions. I guess it isn't the senior officer's style to use such clichéd phrases.

"Still, we need you to come over to the station and fill in the forms and write an official statement at some point," Fletcher continues.

"No worries, I'll bring her over when it's convenient for you!"

The three of us look at Suzie, Detective Sergeant Mills and I are unable to suppress our smiles.

"I mean, I've been to the station in Eastpoole already, and for Margo... that is for Mrs Birkett, it can be stressful to go to the police alone...and you are so busy..." The redness also covers Suzie's neck now, but I haven't seen her so radiant since I met her.

"Of course." As much as I enjoy watching a fiercely independent Suzie Fortuneswell – who likes to stress that she'd never get involved in 'lovey-dovey nonsense' again – behaving like a sixteen-year-old in love for the first time, I choose to save her from further embarrassment. "I'll come and sign everything. Tomorrow? Is it okay if I come tomorrow?"

"Absolutely. If you can make it there until noon, it will be perfect." Detective Fletcher's kind smile has probably soothed many a victim during what I imagine has been a long career.

"I'll close down the café, and we'll be at the station before noon." Suzie doesn't want to be saved.

"Then we'll come in the morning," I say. "Will you be there at nine? Suzie's customers won't appreciate being left without their lunch."

Fletcher nods and smiles at me. "Indeed. It won't take long. I'll ask someone to give you a lift back to Groveland."

"That's very generous." The adoration clearly written all over Suzie's face is precious to witness.

"Ms Fortuneswell, Mrs Birkett," Detective Sergeant Mills says pointedly, declaring the end of the visit.

"I will..." I would swear that Peter Fletcher wants to say *I will call you*. He checks himself in time and says instead: "I will see you tomorrow at the station. The coffee is terrible, but the duty officer has brought some homemade cookies today."

"I'll bring the muffins." A smile spreads over Suzie's

delicate face, turning her crow's feet into rays of joy. "With white chocolate. Your favourites."

Before Detective Sergeant Mills turns away, I see a real smile finally making an appearance on his serious face.

When the door after the detectives closes, I turn to Suzie and can't refrain from winking at her. "Detective Fletcher is definitely a catch! Only you could make something as huge as the news about the police having found a killer pale in comparison to your own news. You two are in love!"

Suzie's gaze darts to the corner where the two late customers sat. The tables are empty. The men obviously left when we were talking to the detectives.

"It's too early to say that," she says, the deep blush turning her eyes into sparkling gemstones. "It's too early for anything. Besides, I'm not sure I want to start all this hassle with a relationship again…"

"Nobody asks you. Life doesn't ask you." While I try to find the right words, another couple whose dynamic hit me the moment I saw them comes to my mind. Laura and Max. I don't even know if they are together or if they are indeed only colleagues, but something about them makes me believe that true love exists. I have caught the same vibe watching Suzie and Detective Fletcher together. "Does he make you feel happy? We are taught to listen to our minds, while it's our heart that always tells the truth."

Suzie looks at me earnestly, her small face still glowing. "You are right. You are a wise woman, Margo. Wiser than I was at your age."

I shake my head. "Life has taught me to be wise the hard way. If only I had been that wise before I messed up everything."

A beep comes from the kitchen. "Muffins are ready. I have to take them out."

"I have to be going anyway." I don't want to return home to Michael. A walk along the coastal path seems like a far better idea.

"Have you made any decisions yet? Have you both

talked?"

"No. That is, yes. I've decided to ask him for a divorce. But I haven't told him yet."

The oven beeps again. "You know what?" Suzie speaks quickly. "We have to have a girls' night out. Then we'll talk everything through, and not only poor Betty's murder. With that, I've forgotten to ask you how things are for you. That Miss Marple thing has gotten the best of me. Let's go out, sit somewhere in a nice café, on the terrace, like people do."

The mobile phone vibrates in my pocket. I snatch it out, afraid that it's Michael looking for me. To my relief, it is a text message from Jacqueline. *Will you be back home soon? I was wondering if you fancy a lunch out upon your return. Jacqueline.*

"It's a great idea," I say to Suzie. "But would you mind if we make an addition to our company? I became friendly with Jacqueline Fisher lately, and we could have that girls' outing together."

"Sounds perfect. I thought she didn't talk to any of us islanders. It would be interesting to get to know her at last."

"She is wonderful. You'll see. And I think you'll get along as soon as you know each other better."

"I am intrigued. I'll meet you at the Business Park bus stop at eight-thirty tomorrow?"

"Sure. I hope the bus arrives on time. I don't want to make Detective Fletcher wait." I can't refrain from raising my eyebrows while giving my friend a meaningful smile.

"Detective Fletcher is a patient man," Suzie says, already on her way to the kitchen.

"I'm sure that he is. But I hope you won't test his patience for too long."

Suzie laughs, and I leave the café – which is filled with heavenly smells of freshly baked pastry – with an easy heart.

CHAPTER 23

Jacqueline, Suzie, and I sit on a terrace outside the South Rock B&B's restaurant.

The spacious decking is a new addition to Maureen Easton's flourishing business. She has gone to great lengths to make it as perfect as possible. Both the flooring and the balustrade are painted pristine white. Flower planters – also white – adorn the balustrade. Overflowing with blue and white blooms, they make the place look posh.

Six tables for four stand at a decent distance from one another, so B&B's visitors can enjoy some privacy along with excellent service and food. We occupy the table closer to the balustrade. It offers an unobscured view over the channel.

"It's pretty, of course, but matching flowers *everywhere*...." Suzie points at the delicate glass vase with blue and white flowers in the centre of the table. "You can call it attention to detail, but I call it obsession."

My friend has been frowning, a deep vertical line taking

a permanent position on her forehead, from the moment we entered Mrs Easton's establishment. I immediately regretted offering it as an alternative to some place in Eastpoole. It isn't that I have a special preference for Maureen Easton's B&B. But this time, I thought it was wise to choose the lesser of two evils. Michael wasn't happy when, yesterday at dinner, I announced that I had an early appointment at the Eastpoole police station. He didn't comment because, as I suspect, it wasn't something I could cancel. Having lunch with girlfriends, on the other hand, was. So, when I told him about it, he muttered through clenched teeth that he didn't know that while he was working hard to build a business, I spent my time befriending old matrons. I knew better than to argue. I simply said that we weren't going anywhere far, and if he needed me, he could always find me at South Rock B&B.

Now, I feel that it would have been better if we'd chosen another place for our girls' outing. With my own rollercoaster of events in the last few weeks, I had totally forgotten about Suzie's struggles in the entrepreneurship department. An outside sitting area for customers has been her long-standing dream, but bureaucratic obstacles and a lack of money kept preventing her from making it come true.

I became worried about how my two friends would get along only after I invited Jacqueline to join Suzie and me for lunch. It didn't soothe my fears when I saw them together. The two women couldn't be more different. Both were attractive and friendly, and still, in just seeing them side by side, I realised the abyss that divided them. Jacqueline was all elegance, refinement, and self-composure. In contrast, Suzie was sharp-tongued and fussy.

To my infinite surprise, the two hit it off the moment I introduced them to each other.

And now, after Suzie makes her bitter comment about the flowers, Jacqueline laughs rather than lets it slip as inappropriate. "This place does have a Stepford Wives vibe.

Striving for perfection can take on a form of neurosis. I think it's a safe guess that they will charge me if I break this vase." She picks up the glass vase to take a closer look and then puts it back. "But these are pretty indeed."

"The Stepford Wives were supposed to be pleasing to the eye too." Suzie shakes her head and settles against the back of her chair, studying the one-sheet menu.

I also focus my attention on the menu. There is nothing I can do to change Suzie's life in an instant. I might as well enjoy the food Mrs Easton takes pride in.

"Miss Fisher, what a pleasant surprise to meet you here."

I raise my eyes, and my appetite vanishes at the sight of Barbara Southwell looming over our table.

"Good afternoon. It is such a beautiful day today. It would be a crime not to spend it outside." Jacqueline speaks with such calm that I can't say if she really doesn't know the name of the most prominent member of the local community or makes the point by showing that she doesn't. "And this is the best choice of where to spend it."

Barbara Southwell handles the situation with a matching aplomb. She simply nods, not bothering to offer a topic to continue the conversation.

"Hello, Mrs Southwell." The tension makes me uncomfortable, so I intervene almost against my will. "I wanted to say that I'm sorry for skipping the last two rehearsals. I know the choir needs me. I hope it won't happen often."

Barbara slowly turns her head to look at me. She is a tall woman, and sitting while she stands makes me feel small. "I hope you had a pleasant vacation in Cornwall, Mrs Birkett. We certainly count on your presence since we still haven't found anyone who could replace Betty."

It hurts that she speaks as if I am only a temporary fill-in.

"It's a regular thing during summer. People travel more often. You will go to visit your daughter in Newquay in August as you always do, don't you, Barbara?"

As usual, Suzie saves me from Mrs Southwell's intimidating attitude.

"Thank you, Cornwall is amazing. We were staying with the Hammonds. They are such wonderful hosts."

I cannot deny that it is a tad rewarding to see astonishment on a formidable woman's face. "I see." She recovers disappointingly quickly.

"Ladies, welcome!" The plump, smiling face of Maureen Easton appears from behind Mrs Southwell's stout form. "I hope you are comfortable out here on the terrace. It tends to get windy, especially in the mornings. But the fresh air makes up for it, don't you think?"

"Thank you, it's lovely." The three of us chorus almost in unison.

"What can I get you? The kitchen is a bit slow today. The B&B is full, you know, and people are coming over from as far as Eastpoole to have dinner here." Maureen spreads her hands to demonstrate her helplessness in the matter while beaming with self-contentment.

I take a quick look at the menu, but with the nervousness clouding my eyes, I can't read a single line. "Everything looks lovely, Mrs Easton," I blurt out the first thing that comes to mind. "But sometimes I'd like to taste something new. Rabbit stew, for example. I don't think I've ever seen it on the menu."

Maureen and Barbara stare at me with identical looks of sheer terror on their faces. Mrs Easton's mouth even falls slightly open. Until this moment, I have only read about people's skin changing colour from white to red and back to white. Now, I watch the phenomenon with my own eyes.

I hastily turn back to check if someone has fallen from the cliffs into the water. But the view is as tranquil and breathtaking as ever.

Barbara recovers first. "I do understand there might be certain difficulties you must be facing while adapting to life in a foreign country, but demonstrating such disrespect...." Her lips tremble when she speaks. "It is unacceptable."

I am horrified. I have no idea what I have said to trigger such a reaction. I can't even utter the words of apology, for I don't know what I am supposed to apologise for.

"Oh, for God's sake!" Suzie comes to my rescue again. "You two behave like... two little kids. I bet you know by now that Santa Claus doesn't exist. I don't believe you are seriously sticking to these old ridiculous superstitions!"

"You should be ashamed of yourself, Susan Fortuneswell!" Barbara fumes. I wouldn't be surprised if smoke came out of her ears at this very moment. "You were born on this island. You must respect its traditions!"

"Fearing words as if they cause plague isn't a tradition!" Suzie spits back. "It's a silly superstition no one outside Southbay knows about! Ask anyone in London or Manchester if the word *'rabbit'* makes them cringe in horror, and they'll laugh in your face. And you expect Margo to know about these silly tales?"

"*Margarita* is a new member of our community... It is her duty to learn about our traditions...." Maureen, still pale as a sheet, stammers in a choking voice.

"It is *your* duty, Maureen, to treat your *clients* with respect," Suzie snaps at Mrs Easton. "All your clients. And not only those you consider your equals. It's not that your assessment always matches the reality. You should learn to mind your own business."

"I could say the same about you!" the B&B's owner's plump face turns an alarming shade of purple. "It is you who has never cared to mind your own business! You always had to poke your nose into other people's lives!" Maureen swings to face Barbara, almost knocking her down. "You know it as good as I do, Barbara. She tried to steal your husband too! Say something!"

Even in complete shock, a tiny part of me remains that can appreciate the embarrassment and confusion on Barbara Southwell's face.

"Okay, ladies, perhaps we shouldn't overstay our welcome at this friendly establishment." Jacqueline gracefully rises from the white chair. "We shall not disturb your clients with our loud behaviour, Maureen. Besides, it threatens to spoil our experience of spending time together if Margo cannot find what suits her fancy on the menu. And I do not wish that. I wish that my friend is happy."

Jacqueline speaks with a pronounced what I imagine is a 'posh English' accent. I have never heard her speak like that. I am not even sure I understand correctly that this accent marks a person out and above the general crowd – and Mrs Easton's usual clientele. From the look of terrified awe on B&B's owner's face, now void of any colour whatsoever, I realise that my guess is right.

"You can't… you don't… I assure you, Miss Fisher… ladies… that you aren't disturbing anyone."

As if to contradict her last statement, an elderly couple, who have been giving us only fleeting looks of curiosity before, now stare at us. Jacqueline casts a quick apologetic glance in their direction. I swear that next, she will wave a hand in a royal greeting gesture just like the queen when driving in her cortege along the streets of London.

Of course she doesn't. Instead, she continues: "Thank you for your hospitality, Maureen. It indeed outmatches the best places in London." She turns to Suzie and me. "Please forgive my unpardonable forgetfulness. I get like this these days. I guess it is the lack of City life stress that does this to me. Ever since I came to Southbay, the owner of Southbay Heights Hotel has invited me to the hotel's restaurant whenever I feel like visiting. The food is said to be superb there. Mr Prescott reminded me of his open invitation when we met this year in Ascot. Do you think now would be a good time to accept it?"

Dressed in a simple white shirt and beige slacks, Jacqueline still looks regal.

I am torn between giggling hysterically, crying, and hugging my amazing friend.

"I think now is definitely the best time to use Mr Prescott's hospitality." Suzie nods with a serious expression on her face.

"Yes, yes, that's a great idea. I've never been to the Heights Hotel. I imagine the views from their restaurant are amazing." I am finally able to follow my friends' suit.

"Lovely." Jacqueline slings her miniature brown leather bag over her shoulder. "I cannot promise they serve *rabbit* there, but I am certain that they will be happy to accommodate the requests of *my* friends."

The three of us barely make it out of the B&B when we burst out with laughter. I honestly can't remember when the last time was that I laughed like this. My face hurts, and my stomach is in knots, and still, I can't stop giggling. I know I'll start hiccupping soon. Suzie has already hiccupped a few times, which sent us all into a new fit of laughter.

"Barbara's face was something. Did you see it, Margo?" Suzie smears the tears all over her face, trying to regain composure. She is lucky she isn't wearing any make-up. "It was a sight to remember. Thank you, Jacqueline. Even if you never go out with us again after this, you've already done something I've never thought I'd have the pleasure to experience."

Jacqueline dabs delicately under her eyes. She is wearing mascara, but the laughing hasn't gotten it smeared. "I'll most definitely go out with you two again, you can count on that. Of course, if you'll have me. I haven't had so much fun in years. It's a pity I haven't met you earlier, Suzie. It is my fault, of course. I've lived here like a hermit for almost two years."

Both Suzie and I look at Jacqueline, who is so totally the opposite of the hermit concept, and burst out with laughter again. She joins us.

"Right." Suzie recovers first. "It has to stop. Otherwise, my ulcer will open up, and you don't want to get to know the woman that monster turns me into. We have to decide what we'll do now. There is no way we are going to this dusty crypt of a hotel, let alone eat there."

"I wasn't going to drag you there." Jacqueline shrugs. "It

was the first thing that came to my mind when I saw I needed to put a damper on those two ladies."

It takes a considerable effort not to start laughing again.

"So, if you don't mind," she continues, "I'd like to invite you to my place. I know cooking wasn't on our agenda, but I can fix up a seafood pasta rather quickly. And I have champagne. I think today is as good a day as any to finally open a bottle. Or two."

"If champagne is on the agenda, you can lure me in with beans on toast, sweetheart," Suzie declares. "I have tart shells in the freezer, so if you have cream and some berries, I'll make us a grand dessert to go with the bubbly."

"Sounds good to me. More than good, actually. I haven't tasted homemade tarts with filling in decades. What about you, Margo? Do you approve of the plan?"

I nod enthusiastically.

The three of us walk up to the Groveland Business Park. After fetching the tarts and a whole bunch of other sweets from Suzie's bakery, we make our way to the Lighthouse Keeper's Cottage.

Winston greets us with his usual over-the-top joy and refuses to leave the kitchen while we cook our meal.

With a bowl of steaming seafood pasta and an impromptu salad, we settle in the spacious and modern conservatory. Jacqueline keeps the transferable wall removed in the summer, so we enjoy the salty breeze without getting sunstroke.

After Suzie had defrosted them in the oven, we leave the tarts to cool down on a rack.

"I cannot wait until we have consumed enough champagne to make it easier for you. Suzie, you simply must tell us everything about your career as a husband stealer."

I look between the two women, half-expecting Suzie to throw a plate with pasta on the floor and storm out. To my relief, Jacqueline's comment only makes her throw her head back and laugh. "There isn't much to tell, really. And I must say it's a pity. After living all my life side by side with

Maureen and Barbara, I almost wish they had a reason to be so poisonous and bitter."

"But there must be *something*. Something that has triggered their vindictive behaviour worth the feud between *Montecchi* and *Capuleti*."

Suzie rolls her eyes, putting a generous portion of pasta into her mouth. "I don't have the slightest interest in dwelling on the triggers of those two. But I can assure you that I am not a Juliet, and neither of their husbands are anything resembling Romeo."

"And still…?" Jacqueline pins a shrimp on her fork and, before eating it, gives Suzie a mischievous look.

Suzie snorts. "And still, these two old trouts believe that I've almost robbed them of their marital bliss. As if they can boast of having any."

Jacqueline raises her eyebrows, urging her to continue.

Suzie sighs. "Okay, okay, you aren't any better than them and won't let me eat in peace."

Jacqueline and I shake our heads in unison.

"As I said, there isn't much to tell. William Southwell and I dated in high school."

"You were Barbara Southwell's husband's girlfriend?!" I almost spit the pasta.

"Was it before or after he became Barbara's boyfriend?"

"You two are absolutely unbearable." Suzie starts eating with an exaggerated concentration on the food. "I won't tell you a thing until I'm full and happy."

"Sorry," I mumble.

"You caught us unprepared, Suzie. Maybe we should open the champagne without waiting for dessert?" Jacqueline's tone is apologetic, but I see the twinkle in her eyes.

"Oh don't worry. We'll drink your champagne in due time, you can be sure about that." Suzie points at our host with the fork. "I was sixteen. He was eighteen. We thought we were grown-ups, while in truth, we were kids. We knew nothing about life or love. William wasn't a bad fellow. He was handsome. He still is." Suzie's eyes cloud over. "And he was funny. Oh my, how he made me laugh. We had some great moments together. But we were young, and little depended on us."

"What happened?" I ask.

"The usual thing." Suzie shrugs. "His family was rich. My family was poor. We came from two different worlds. Let's say, for the Southwells, food rationing was a phrase from a newspaper headline. For us, it was a reality. It's not surprising that they didn't want a black sheep like me in their family. I don't blame William. They told him he was free to do whatever he wanted, but he shouldn't count on their support if he married me. I guess the thought about competing for a college scholarship and then struggling to get a mortgage terrified him."

"If he gave up on you so easily, it means he doesn't deserve you." I blush when two older women look at me kindly, saying nothing. I sound like a naïve little girl.

"He didn't love me enough. That was what I told myself. And if he didn't, he wasn't worth crying over." Suzie puts down her fork and leans back in the rattan chair. "But, of course, I cried. You would think that such bitter wailing would have melted even the cruellest of hearts. Alas, it only hardened my mother's. One night, after I'd been sobbing myself to sleep for three days in a row, she came to my room with a belt and said that if she or Father heard a sound from me again, I wouldn't be able to sit for a month."

"That's awful, Suzie," Jacqueline says.

"Such were the times. Mother also said that it made absolutely no difference which lad gets between your legs every night. The outcome is the same."

My hand involuntarily flies to my mouth. "That's terrible."

"In a way, she was right. Life isn't an even road covered in rose petals. But she was also wrong. It does matter whom you choose to walk that road with. William must congratulate himself on making the right choice every day of his life. He lives in the house his and Barbara's parents helped them buy, and over three decades, its value has tripled. If he had chosen to stay with me, he would have probably been practically homeless, spending all his money on food and rent."

We keep silent for a few moments. I feel dumbstruck by the realisation that my troubles with Michael aren't unique.

To ease the pressure, we turn to our plates and finish the pasta.

"Before you tell us your story with Maureen's husband, I insist on getting the champagne." Jacqueline stands and collects the plates.

"I'll make those tarts." Suzie joins her. "Just show me where the mixer is."

"How can I help?" I jump from my seat.

"Keep Winston company, please. The poor thing has been craving for attention since morning." Jacqueline pats the golden retriever's silky head. Winston had trodden out of the house once he heard we were collecting cutlery and dishes.

"Of course. With pleasure."

I settle on the rattan sofa and cuddle the friendly dog. Winston sits on his haunches with his head on my lap. Once in a while, his tongue rolls out to lick my hands, but his fluffy tail twitches, indicating that he is overwhelmed by emotions.

When Jacqueline and Suzie return and I join them at the table, Winston jumps onto the sofa and places his chin on the white throw blanket. Jacqueline gives him a pointed stare and shakes her head. The dog closes his eyes.

"I haven't done that in a while," Jacqueline says, removing the foil and the wire cage from the champagne bottle. On the label, it says *Louis Roederer*. "I hope I won't have to replace the roof. It's new." After unwinding the wire loop, she puts the wire cage away and holds the bottle by its neck. "The moment of truth." Holding the cork with one hand, Jacqueline gently twists the bottle. The cork pops from the bottle's neck.

"Hurray!" Suzie clasps her hands. "If we can open a bottle of champagne, what do we need men for?"

Jacqueline fills the three glasses with bubbly liquid. "Let's drink to that!"

We clink glasses.

I take a sip. Bubbles scratch my throat. I can't say I love champagne, but the process of drinking it puts me in a celebratory mood. I take a strawberry from the tart. The sweet and sour tastes mix in my mouth. Champagne and strawberries do go perfectly together.

"So, the story with Martin Easton is even less romantic." Suzie takes a sip of champagne. "Maureen simply wants to have *the story* to make her life look less plain than it is. After the divorce, I needed a distraction. You know, to take my thoughts off the vicious 'it's all my fault' circle. I had to move back in with my parents. They weren't supportive, as you can probably imagine, and staying with them didn't help me get back on track. So, when I saw an advertisement about a group walk along the coastal path, I knew it was what I needed. Our coast hadn't yet been included in the World Heritage list back then. The walking tour was organised by an enthusiastic couple who wanted to test it so they could later offer it to tourists. The participation fee was symbolic. I knew that the money I had wouldn't have lasted for long anyway. It was a wonderful trip. We slept in tents. Every day, we watched the most glorious sunsets and dawns. I'd never seen such vibrant colours covering the sky, not before that trip nor after. We stopped to watch birds that I had no idea existed. We had picnics on the rocks. I was still young and didn't suffer from eating mainly apples and digestives for a week. Besides, everyone shared their supplies with the group." She pauses, then shakes her head. "I can't believe I never thought to repeat the walk. Nowadays, it's a huge thing, with infrastructure in place to enjoy a longer tour."

"It sounds amazing. We should do this walking tour

together someday soon," says Jacqueline.

"I'd love that." Suzie and Jacqueline exchange smiles.

"Was Mr Easton on that coastal walk, too?" I can't believe I am so blunt.

"Actually, he was." Suzie nods. "Martin and I were the only ones travelling alone. The other eight people in the group were couples. Moreover, we were the only ones in our thirties. Others were in their twenties. Eager to enter the big world. Enthusiastic about everything, at the same time trying to look cool and mature. Lovely kids they were."

"And what made Mr Easton run away from his Maureen?" Jacqueline asks. "She doesn't look like a woman who appreciates being disobeyed."

Suzie laughs. "He said he needed a break. He said his life was perfect. He loved Maureen and their two kids. But they got married when they both were nineteen. They had kids one after another almost right away. He said he needed to have at least a few days without the chaos of family life."

"So much for the family bliss," I mutter.

"It isn't for everyone, that's for sure. I think my life would have turned out differently if my marriage hadn't failed. I would have appreciated the companionship and the feeling of safety a decent, loving man could have brought into my life. But to be honest, and I know it sounds awful, I've never regretted not having children." Suzie takes another sip of champagne. "Do you have children, Jacqueline?"

Jacqueline shakes her head. "No, and I don't regret it either."

"We talked a lot during that walking tour. Martin and I," Suzie continues. "We discussed books we'd read and political events that shook the world at that time. He told me about Maureen's determination to make their newly opened B&B the best accommodation in the whole of Dorset. She wasn't interested in books or politics. She said that if you don't concentrate on your business, you cannot succeed. Martin repeated that he admired his wife. But I saw that he'd have wanted her to pay more attention to his interests." Suzie stops talking. She puts the flute on the table and gently rubs its slim stem. The glass catches the sun's rays, spilling a tiny rainbow. "Martin Easton is a good man. Nothing happened between us on that walking tour, I swear. In the eighties, we weren't yet so emancipated as to even think about treating a broken heart with a meaningless shag. Pardon my language, loves. But Maureen has always been one nasty woman. I guess she measures everyone by her own standards. She put it into her head that I slept with her husband on that trip. And although she never gave even the slightest hint that she wanted a divorce, she did go to certain lengths not to let Martin forget his *mistake*." She makes quotation marks with her fingers.

"Did Maureen share the details of the conversations she had with her husband with you?" Jacqueline asks. "What a cunning woman indeed."

Suzie grabs her champagne glass and downs it. "Well...," she stammers. "Maureen hadn't spoken with me for months after that trip. Martin himself told me about their conversations. We... uhm... we met once in a while. We took walks together and discussed books."

Jacqueline raises to refill our glasses. "To friendship," she announces. "Sometimes we don't choose our friends, but we should always appreciate them."

"Amen." Suzie raises her glass. Before she manages to put it to her lips, her phone beeps in her bag. She nervously fumbles in it and, having finally located it, presses it to her ear. "Peter, hi," she chirps, her cheeks turning pink. "What a wonderful idea. Of course," she nods. "Do you know the Lighthouse Keeper's Cottage? I'm visiting a friend here." She pauses, listening. "Yes, you can pick me up. See you soon." She hangs up and gives us a flushed look. "Sorry, loves. I hate to leave you, but... Thank you for today. We'll repeat it, won't we? It'll be your turn to share your dark secrets."

We walk out of the house and wait on the porch for

Detective Fletcher. He arrives in his battered, rusty red Vauxhall, climbs out to shake hands with Jacqueline and me, and takes Suzie away to what I hope will soon turn into a metaphorical sunset: the most beautiful in their lives.

"We still have champagne and those heavenly delicious strawberry tarts," Jacqueline says. "Are you in a hurry?"

"Absolutely not," I reply. "I haven't even tasted the tarts yet."

Jacqueline smiles and gestures at the cottage. "Well that will never do. After you."

******

A few champagne glasses later, I feel tipsy and light-headed. We have moved from the table to a more comfortable set of rattan armchairs. A platter with the remaining strawberry tarts and an almost empty bottle sits on the low glass table in front of us.

"So, what about those rabbits?" I slur the words a little, but I know Jacqueline won't judge me. "With all that hysterical laughing and scandalous revelations, I forgot to ask about it."

Jacqueline giggles. "Oh, that. It's a local superstition. I haven't heard about it until I moved here. Quarry workers used to blame the poor creatures for landslides. They claimed they'd seen furry balls leaving their burrows every time right before a rock fall, and the bad omen label stuck. I don't understand why islanders still maintain the superstition. It seems to me that the rabbits reacted to the underground stirring before a landslide. Just like rats jump into the sea when a ship's hold begins to fill with water. No magic here, only the pure instinct of survival."

"And what am I supposed to call rabbits if I need to refer to them?" I try to force my brain to start working, but for the life of me, I can't remember the other name for wild rabbits.

"You can choose between 'underground mutton', 'long-eared furry things' or 'bunnies'," Jacqueline replies with such a serious face that we both burst out laughing.

"I mean, I've heard a lot of strange things since I came to England," I say after I have calmed down. "No offence, you'd probably find just as many, if not more things you'd consider strange in Latvia. But this… the word 'rabbit' a taboo…," I raise my eyebrows to accentuate my words, "This is by far the weirdest thing I've heard."

"Everyone has a skeleton or two in their closet." Jacqueline shrugs and fills our glasses. "Have you talked to your husband about divorce? I am sorry I didn't ask you earlier."

I take a big gulp of champagne. "No, I haven't. But I've made a decision, and I'll stick to it."

"How can I help?"

"It's already enough that I can talk about it. Thank you, Jacqueline. I still need to find a job and start saving for renting an apartment."

"I think I can help you with that." Jacqueline puts her glass on the table. "I am contemplating changes in my life too. Leaving my job in London was the right decision at the time. But now I feel that I am ready for new challenges."

My heart sinks. "Are you going back to London?"

"No, of course not." She smiles sadly. "That chapter of my life is definitely over. My former colleague – my boss, actually – has been trying to persuade me to return since the day I left. But I knew it wasn't a vacation that I needed. I needed a complete lifestyle change."

"Were you really working for the BBC?"

"Is that what they say about me here?" A slightly amused expression makes Jacqueline look younger.

I nod.

"Well, that's true. I did spend thirteen years working there in the Legal Department. While others were doing exciting things, bringing legendary stories to life on screen, I was covering up for creative people's mistakes. So that these mistakes didn't influence the company's profits."

"It doesn't sound like you enjoyed this job."

"I didn't. My husband made me believe this was what I

needed. Don't get me wrong, it was rather exciting at times. And I didn't have so much as one boring day at that job, or any repetitive, monotonous ones. Winning a case after case was exhilarating. It was like a drug. We worked eighteen hours a day and often on weekends, too. But after a particularly difficult case, we would take a three-week long vacation in a place like Bali or the Bahamas to balance the pressure and stress. We were a good team."

"Did you decide to divorce because your husband didn't like it when you quit?"

"Our divorce hasn't been finalised yet." Jacqueline sighs. "But no, I left John because he cheated on me."

"I'm so sorry that happened to you."

We don't speak for a while. I try to imagine why any man would ever think about cheating on someone like Jacqueline. To me, she is the most amazing woman I have ever met.

"Anyway, we weren't talking about me," Jacqueline speaks first. "My divorce is a done deal. Formalities don't matter. Whereas you are only at the beginning of this process. And as I said earlier, I want to help. I think I have a solution to your job search issue. Not so long ago, my former boss left the BBC, too. He started a private law practice in London, and business is going so well that this month, he is opening an office in Southampton. He wanted me to lead it. I refused. This kind of responsibility isn't what I need. However, I accepted a case-by-case advisor role. It suits my... well, it suits me better. And I think an Assistant Accountant position in the firm would be perfect for you. It is a small office with a team of ten. It won't be as overwhelming as joining a big corporation. What do you think?"

I am speechless. I open and close my mouth a few times before I can utter something coherent. "I don't know what to say. You shouldn't have... I mean, I'm thankful that you've thought about me. But..." I stop and take a deep breath. "I'm really thankful that you think I'm capable of doing this job. You don't know me. I mean, you don't know if I am any good. It means so much. Thank you."

"I've worked with people for twenty years. I am pretty confident I've learned to make an unbiased judgement. But I have to warn you that this job isn't a walk in the park. Besides, you have a long commute to consider. Do you think you are up to spending three hours on a train every day?"

I don't hesitate a moment before answering. "It won't be a problem. I used to travel by train a lot back in Latvia. I'll have to learn a lot for this job. I'll read and make notes on the journey."

Jacqueline nods. "Besides, it won't be forever. I'm sure you will find a better job once you learn everything there is to learn for a successful career somewhere in *the big four*."

"I won't... I wouldn't..."

She smiles at me kindly. "I want to help you, not to trap you, Margo."

"Thank you. Thank you so much." For the first time in a long time, I don't want to cry at the expression of kindness toward me. I want to dance from joy.

"And one more thing." Jacqueline's face turns serious. "While you are looking for an apartment, you can stay here. Before you start protesting, let me assure you that you won't be bothering me in the slightest. On the contrary, I would appreciate some company. Since I bought this place, I've been considering transforming the small annexe at the back into a unit that I could probably rent out. If you agree, I could start doing it right away. I have already talked to a construction company, and they've said it won't take longer than a month to make it ready for living in. It will have a separate entrance and a kitchen. I hope you will say yes."

This time, it takes me longer to react. I even take a sip of champagne before answering. To say I am touched by Jacqueline's kindness is an understatement. I am completely overwhelmed.

"Or do you think you'll be looking for an apartment in

Southampton to be closer to work?"

The look of sincere concern on Jacqueline's face pulls me out of my stupor. "I won't!" I exclaim too loudly. "I don't want to leave Southbay. I love it here. I mean, I know I'll be away from here a lot, but still, I'll have the weekends and bank holidays."

"And an annual vacation."

"Yes, that too." In Latvia, employers often prefer to comfortably forget about the Labour Law provisions regarding an annual four-week vacation.

"Then, we have a plan. I am glad. All that is left for you to do…" She smiles at me sympathetically.

"… is to tell Michael I want to divorce him."

"And Margo?"

"Yes?"

"I truly believe it would be beneficial for you not to put this talk on the shelf."

Her words don't make me cringe. I know she is right. I've been putting off the most important decision of my life for too long already. It won't be easy to tell my husband that I am leaving him. Still, there is no use in waiting for the right moment, simply because the right moments for such conversations don't exist.

"I'll talk to him tomorrow." I am too drunk, and it is too late to do it today anyway.

"And remember that it hurts the most at the beginning. It gets better, I promise."

I want to ask her if it has already gotten better for her. But my head is spinning from all the champagne I consumed. The jumbled thoughts about the conversation I'll have to live through tomorrow buzz like bees, not letting me concentrate on anything else.

Jacqueline walks me to the door and makes me promise to call her tomorrow after I've talked to Michael.

CHAPTER 24

"You deceitful... scheming... little bitch."

With my mouth agape and my hands trembling, I stand in the living room doorway.

Michael advances on me as if in slow motion.

My eyes are fixed on the blood covering his right hand and dripping to the floor.

A moment ago, he had smashed a cup in his palm. The howl he had emitted when the hot liquid burnt his skin was bone-chilling.

I think about having to dress his wound, but my husband seems to notice neither pain nor blood.

"I knew you would do something like this. I knew I couldn't trust you."

I can't move. My legs are like two tree trunks firmly rooted in the ground.

"Let me bandage your hand," I say, hoping he would pause.

To my infinite relief, he does.

Michael stops and looks at his blood-covered palm.

I take a deep breath and then take a small step back.

My husband's head snaps back up. "Where do you think you're going? If you step outside this door, don't you dare come back. I'm done with your tricks. Running around, talking bullshit about me. Bitch!"

"I've never... I... You have to calm down."

My heart beats so fast that it makes it difficult to speak.

"Don't tell me what I should do!" Michael roars. "I have given you everything! *Everything*! A new life in a decent country! And you waltz in and tell me you want a divorce. It's me who should want to get rid of you as soon as possible! Who do you think you are? Shameless slut!"

I take another tentative step back.

"You don't love me, Michael." I hate that my words sound like whining. "It will be better this way. For both of us."

"Love? What does it have to do with love? You stupid little... You'll pay for this. You won't stay here. I'll make sure that you get sent back to your shithole of a country. And you'll be cleaning piss and vomit in some shitty place for the rest of your days. You deserve nothing better. You aren't *worth* anything better."

I cannot cry. A painful lump forming in my throat won't let me breathe. My chest is so tight that it feels like I won't even be able to gulp for air when I need it.

"Michael, please, it doesn't need to be this way."

He stops moving. The man I'm married to looks at me as if I am the most disgusting thing in the world. It feels like a punch to my stomach.

"You wanted it to be this way. Did you think I'll smile and give my blessing so you could live happily with some fool who's fallen into your trap like I did?"

"I don't... I haven't..."

"You won't see a penny from me! Did you hear? I'll send you back to Latvia penniless just as you arrived here." He clenches his fists and winces at the pain. His face turns red.

"I've never wanted anything from you. I helped you…."

Michael's left eye twitches. "It is your *job* to help me. Did you think I'm some kind of sugar daddy? Of course you did. All of you do!"

Tears finally cloud my eyes. I turn around, take a few more steps to reach the front door, jerk it open, and run outside.

I don't see much on my way to the coastal path. Cars beep when passing me by. I probably look like someone to be avoided rather than in need of help.

Only when I turn from the road to cross the field leading to the coastal path do I notice that a low cloud covers everything in a milky film. I thought it was my tears that made my vision blurry. I know it is dangerous to wander close to the cliffs when the visibility is low. Even so, I continue walking. I need time to collect myself. My thoughts are in disarray, and I can't put them together to understand what I should do next. At the moment, I am certain of only one thing: I cannot return to the place I haven't learned to call home, to Michael.

As I walk, the white fluffy patches fly around me. I haven't gone to the coastal path in this kind of weather before. If I weren't in such a state of shock, I would find the experience intriguing. It feels like I've stepped into a parallel reality, with all familiar things having disappeared.

I replay this morning in my head. It started as usual. I cooked and served breakfast in the dining room. I did everything how Michael likes it. I figured he would be in a better mood if we talked after a good meal. I was wrong.

The story of my life.

I have made so many mistakes and misjudged so many situations that I am not sure I'll ever understand how life works.

Every time I've made a choice, it's led to a disaster.

I shake my head as if it will help dissipate the gloom.

I stop just in time to prevent myself from stumbling over

the 'coast path' stone sign.

Turning right at the sign, I walk a little and then step down from the path. Wide grassy ledges start here, gradually descending before giving way to an abrupt fall. I go down the ledge, stepping carefully not to trip over a stone. I am pretty sure I keep a safe distance from the cliffs. When I see the silhouette of a cluster of rocks, I know I must go around it to continue the descent.

I stop, unsure how far I am from the precipice.

If I had been closer to it, I might have fallen when a hand grabs my shoulder.

I scream.

"Get back home, Margo."

Michael's voice does nothing to calm me.

"What were you thinking wandering to the cliffs when it's a peasouper out there?"

Did I overreact by running away?

My foot slips on the rock, and I am caught up in a time loop for a moment. In reality, I struggle to regain my balance and not fall over the cliff. At the same time, I see my whole life rush past my eyes like changing pictures in a kaleidoscope. I see my mother frowning in concentration. I see my granny's kind face. I see the friends I left in Latvia. And then, I see Suzie, Jacqueline, Melissa – and Finley.

Michael tightens his grip over my shoulder. His hand slides lower, and he grasps my arm.

A gust of wind cuts through the fog.

Now, I can see that I'm standing right on the edge of the precipice. Down below, waves crash against the stone wall. The power they can't resist pulls them back into the sea, dragging them across the rocky bottom.

Michael's fingers curl around my upper arm. He steps closer and pushes me to the edge.

Something hot explodes in my chest. I yank my arm to free it from my husband's grasp.

"Let me go!" I cry.

He keeps clutching the sleeve of my T-shirt. I notice

blood stains on the white fabric.

I slap his loosely bandaged hand with as much force as I can muster.

Michael howls and loosens his grip.

I run.

I run through the fog, not caring if I have chosen the right direction. The only thing hammering in my mind is to get far away from Michael Birkett. The man who tried to push me off the Southbay cliffs.

******

I am out of breath with no idea where I am. I stop and bend over, pressing my palms into my knees.

My heart beats like a thousand little hummers. I hear it clearly in my ears.

I try not to panic. *Michael isn't following me.* I repeat it like a mantra. It doesn't help. He did follow me earlier. And he found me. And he tried to kill me.

I shudder at the recent memory.

The milky film covering the island seems to get more transparent. I hope I'm not imagining it.

I walk carefully, trying to peer through the white veil that has transformed the familiar surroundings.

The grassy field seems endless.

I cling to the thought that it must be the South Rock plateau. At least it is warm. The air is still, with all its summer fragrances dampened by the fog.

I glimpse two rows of thick bushes, and my heart makes a leap. I know where I am.

I turn right and run up the path between the thorny bushes.

******

"Jacqueline." I almost fall into the house when Jacqueline opens the door. "I can't believe it. Michael tried to kill me."

I stumble into the hall with my friend's hand supporting me gently around the waist.

"Here," Jacqueline seats me down on a chair. "You need

to catch your breath. Have you been running? From him? Did he chase you?"

I close my eyes and lower my head to my knees. Someone once told me it helps against nausea. I need help in that department at the moment.

"Are you alright? Margo? Please say something."

"A moment," I mumble, not moving from my position. "I'll be alright in a moment."

"I'll go and get you something that I think will help. Don't panic. I'll be right back."

I nod into my knees and raise one hand.

I hear a clinking sound coming from the kitchen. When Jacqueline returns, I am in better shape.

"Here, drink this." She hands me a small glass with burgundy liquid. "It has always helped women in my family to get over men's stupidity or worse."

I take the glass and down it with one gulp. It tastes sweet and burns right through my throat to settle in my stomach, spreading pleasant warmth. It reminds me of the red currant bounce my grandmother used to make. Once in a while, she'd let me take a small sip, ever since I was thirteen.

"Does it work?" I ask, closing my eyes to keep the nice sensation for longer.

"Of course. It can't change the way men are. But it soothes our nerves so that we don't care about trying to change them."

I open my eyes and smile. "I like that concept. It makes everything look easier."

"So, what happened? You told your husband about the divorce, and he attacked you?"

I sigh. "Pretty much. He started shouting at me after I told him. He accused me of... horrible things. He threatened me. And when I ran away, he chased me and tried to push me down the cliff."

Jacqueline covers her mouth with her hand. "That's terrible! Margo, I am so sorry you've had to go through something like this."

"At least, now I'm one hundred percent sure that the decision to divorce Michael is the right one."

Jacqueline walks over to the curved-legged table placed by the window. A vase filled with white fragrant roses occupies its surface. She opens the drawer and takes out a small packet.

"Here, eat a couple of these." She hands the packet to me.

"Mint candies?"

"They mask the smell of alcohol well. But don't get too close to your husband anyway. Keep behind me."

"What are you going to do?"

"I'm going to make that brute you had the misfortune to marry regret the day he decided he could get away with hurting you. And I'm going to negotiate the most beneficial divorce settlement for you, of course."

CHAPTER 25

By the time we arrive at the cottage, I feel as if I haven't just gone through a deeply traumatic experience. I feel calm, detached even. I simply follow Jacqueline, who obviously knows better how to set things right.

Jacqueline presses the bell button and steps down from the narrow porch. She crosses her arms on her chest. "Don't say anything, Margo," she instructs me. "Trust me, I know how to deal with people who are used to always getting their way. I've grown up among them."

The door opens, and Michael appears. Nothing about him gives away that he tried to commit a crime against another human being a short while ago. A fresh, neat bandage covers his palm. A man who is good with his hands has hurt himself while making yet another improvement meant to make his family's life better, that's all.

"Margo, where have you been? Get in the house right now." He doesn't seem to consider that I might have come back with any other purpose than to beg for his forgiveness.

"Good morning, Mr Birkett," Jacqueline speaks in a business-like tone, with an inscrutable expression on her face. "I am Jacqueline Fisher. And I will be representing Margarita Birkett in the divorce process. Here are my contact details. For any communication with Mrs Birkett, please don't hesitate to call me or send any relevant correspondence through regular or electronic mail. Mrs Birkett has expressed a wish not to be contacted by you during the divorce proceedings."

She gives him a card, which he takes automatically. Jacqueline's words don't register with him, though. "What? What's going on, Margo? I've had enough of your circus. Get in the house and we'll talk like grown-ups."

"As I said, no direct contact with my client. Effective today. I shall send you the divorce settlement documentation next week. What is required from you now…"

Michael doesn't let her finish. "Who are you? Don't tell me what to do. Margo is my wife. We can settle everything between ourselves, without nosy neighbours. Margo." He steps down from the porch. A vein bulges on his forehead. Read blotches appear on his neck. "What is this performance about? Get in the house and we'll talk."

Jacqueline also takes a few steps back to keep her distance from my husband. She gently pushes me to stand behind her.

"My name is Jacqueline Fisher," she repeats what she has already said. "I am a solicitor. Margarita has informed you of her wish to dissolve your marriage. I shall see that her interests in the process are being observed."

"Stop talking bullshit!" A piece of saliva flies out of Michael's mouth. "No one has mentioned divorce! If you think you can earn handsomely by ripping me off, think again."

"You wanted to push me off the cliff!" I shriek from behind the protection of Jacqueline's back. "So much easier than divorcing me, hah?"

"Margo." Not looking at me, Jacqueline puts a hand on my arm in a warning gesture. "Please. Let me deal with it. Mr Birkett," she addresses Michael, who looks like he is ready to charge at us. "I would strongly advise you to cooperate. I have evidence at my disposal that domestic abuse has taken place in your marriage. Photographic images of the bodily harm you inflicted on your wife, Margarita Birkett, with the date and time fixated. You would be right in suggesting that it cannot be proved that you were the one who caused those injuries. Still, I would recommend you not to pursue that path. Over the short period of time she has been residing in Southbay, Margarita has become a respected member of the local community. Quite a few people – whose good opinion the authorities, I assure you, will take into consideration – will testify that your wife has been exposed to continuous psychological abuse from you during the course of your marriage. Two episodes of physical abuse, whether proved to be performed by you or not, will not work in your favour, do you agree?"

"You... bitch...." Michael's face is red, with a thick vein pulsating on his forehead. He moves on us and we retreat, standing almost on the sidewalk now. "I know the likes of you. Born with a silver spoon in your mouth. You think you're better than everyone else. That you *know* better than anyone. You've never lifted a finger to get anything you wanted. Get off my property and let me talk with my wife!"

Keeping a hand on my arm, Jacqueline patiently listens to Michael's outburst. I can only see part of her profile, but I know that her face is a mask of confidence and reserve.

"I shall permit myself to repeat the advice you gave me earlier. Do not tell me – or Margarita – what to do. I would also appreciate it greatly if you stopped musing about my personal struggles. Under the present circumstances, they are irrelevant." There is steel in her voice. The kind of authority that even Michael can't resist. "Mr Birkett, let me point out a few things that I believe are crucial for us to come to a mutual understanding. As far as I understand, you are the owner of a new but already flourishing business. A business that Margarita has made a tremendous input in. The success of your enterprise depends on your reputation among your potential clients. I am familiar with everyone who owns an estate of any significant worth all along the coast from Norfolk and down to Cornwall. My parents have always been friendly with the Duke of Norfolk. I could ruin your reputation with one call."

She pauses. My husband looks deflated. All his aggression is gone.

"So, if we have cleared up this important issue, we can move on to practical aspects," Jacqueline continues calmly. "I believe it will be beneficial for both parties not to relive the unpleasant experiences that have led to the dissolution of the marriage. I strongly advise you, Mr Birkett, to accept the provisions of the divorce settlement, which I will send you next week. To avoid the typical misunderstandings that tend to prolong the proceedings, I'd like to inform you that it will contain a certain amount of financial means, which you will undertake by paying Margarita until she marries again. I am sure you are familiar with this commonly accepted practice. Next, although I have yet to discuss it with my client," she squeezes my arm gently, "I will encourage Margarita to abstain from including any provisions regarding communication between you in the future. But to do that, I expect to receive verbal confirmation from you that you will never seek contact with her. Would that be possible, do you think?"

Michael nods. He touches his bandaged palm with the other hand.

"Good. That's everything I wanted to cover with you during this pre-settlement meeting." Jacqueline turns to me and, rubbing my arm soothingly, asks: "Do you need anything from the house, Margo? It is okay if you don't feel ready. I'll provide you with anything you need."

"I'm fine, thank you. I'll go get my stuff." I am surprised at how confident I sound. And feel.

I walk quickly to the house. When Michael turns to follow me, Jacqueline stops him. "I must insist that you wait outside while my client is gathering her belongings."

Once in the cottage, I find the luggage bag I arrived in England with. The rather battered but sturdy grey trunk used to belong to my grandmother. I pack as much as I can, making sure I don't leave any of my books behind.

"I'm ready," I say to Jacqueline, walking outside. I avoid looking at Michael.

"Perfect." My friend smiles at me. "I am glad we have come to an understanding, Mr Birkett. I believe it will be beneficial for everyone. Expect to receive the paperwork shortly."

Michael nods, turns, and trudges off. With his shoulders slumped and bent head, he looks twenty years older.

******

"You are amazing," I say as we walk back to the Lighthouse Keeper's Cottage.

My equilibrium is restored, so I don't need Jacqueline to support me. It is almost impossible to believe I was a wreck less than an hour ago. I feel strong and enthusiastic about the future.

Jacqueline waves her hand, dismissing my praise. "At my ex-job, I used to put arrogant men like your soon-to-be-ex husband in their proper place every day."

"Thank you. I couldn't have left him without you."

Jacqueline smiles.

We are interrupted by a tow truck passing by. I wouldn't have paid any attention to it if the car it carried hadn't stirred painful memories.

"That's Mark King's car," I note, watching the dark blue BMW being taken away by the old tow truck. "I wonder what happened. It couldn't have broken down so badly that it had to be taken away. It is practically new."

Jacqueline doesn't manage to answer when two more vehicles pass us by. One is a huge movers' lorry with a '*we deliver happy endings*' slogan on its side. It is followed by George King's flashy cream Mercedes with a cream leather interior.

I automatically raise my hand and wave, but neither George behind the wheel nor Mark in the passenger seat seem to see me.

"Where are those two going?" I muse. "I thought George King was plotting to take over Southbay."

"Circumstances change." Jacqueline shrugs. "Investors and developers run out of money and new sources to get it from all the time."

With the road empty again, I notice that we've stopped right across from Matilda Peckham's house. I am not surprised that the curtains in the window twitch slightly.

"Would you mind if we pop in to see the old lady?" I ask. "It'll be quick, I promise."

Jacqueline smiles and makes a sweeping gesture with her hand. "After you."

We cross the street, and I knock at the door. It opens almost simultaneously with the last tap.

Mrs Peckham is wearing a soft yellow dressing gown and a crocheted night cap in a matching colour. For myself, I have classified her choice of attire as a uniform designed to lure innocent neighbours into believing that the old lady has drifted from reality. I haven't yet made up my mind on what the purpose of this display is.

"Good morning," Matilda greets us, tucking white strands of fluffy hair behind her ears. "It is going to be a lovely day today, isn't it?"

"Good morning, Mrs Peckham. I'm moving to live… uhm… elsewhere. And I wanted to drop by to tell you to call me if you need anything." I am certain she gets all the necessary assistance from social services. Still, it feels right to let her know she is not alone. To be honest, I have no idea if she has any relatives. I've never seen anyone visiting the old lady. But it's not that I've been sitting and watching my neighbours day and night.

"Thank you, love. That's such a sweet thing to say." Mrs Peckham speaks in her chirping voice.

"I'll give you my number…" I stop and look at Jacqueline. Of course, I haven't got a pen and paper on me.

Jacqueline takes a card from her pocket and hands it to Matilda. "Here. Margo will be residing with me for a while, so you can reach her at my number."

Mrs Peckham takes the card and puts it into the pocket of her dressing gown without giving it a look.

"That's good. I'm glad. Truly glad. It's good that you young girls support each other. That's the way it should be." She nods as if talking to herself. "Back when I was young, all of us were helpless, dependent on our parents or husbands." She shakes her head. "Yes, such were the times. Men got away with many things… awful things… I'm glad they don't get away with them nowadays. I'm sorry for George's boy, though. George was such a sweet little fellow back in the day…"

"Did something happen to Mark?"

Mrs Peckham's face is vacant.

"Mark King, George King's son. You said you're sorry for him."

The old lady's eyes twinkle with suppressed excitement. "Oh yes, Mark. Poor boy. So young. The police caught him driving drunk. Someone *called* them," she lowers her voice to a conspiratorial whisper. "I do not support *informing* on people, but George's boy could have killed someone or himself."

"Who would do such a thing?" Shocked by what I've heard, I don't consider how Matilda Peckham has obtained such sensitive information.

The old lady shrugs. "I wish I knew. The police don't share their secrets."

"Is that why the Kings are leaving Southbay?"

Matilda cocks her head to the side, which makes her look

like a bird. Her pale blue eyes shine mischievously. "George is a big boy now, and he has enough secrets of his own. Haven't you heard? It's because of him that Betty died." Looking a bit disappointed when I nod, Mrs Peckham continues: "The committee for construction or something – I can never remember these long important titles – stripped him of his licence. One would think he has his quarries to live on, but apparently, his money was coming from building those ugly boxes they call modern family dwellings all over the island."

Jacqueline and I exchange glances.

"Sometimes, it is justice, not money, that prevails." Having finished, Matilda Peckham stares into the distance.

"Sometimes it does. This time, it's you who helped to make sure justice was served."

Mrs Peckham's watery eyes return to rest on me. In them, there is absolutely no recognition of what I am talking about.

"You did the right thing telling the police about Mark King's car…"

Matilda coquettishly pats her yellow nightcap, moving it back so a few white fluffy strands fall on her forehead. "Nonsense, love. If I had talked to a police officer, I would have forgotten my own name." She giggles.

"But Mrs Peckham…"

Jacqueline lightly touches my arm. "I think Mrs Peckham needs to rest. It is lunchtime soon."

"Oh yes, lunch." Mrs Peckham's face lights up. "I have some leftovers of the delicious chicken pasta which that lovely young man brought me yesterday. The portions they bring are always *so* huge. As if I could ever eat so much food in one go." She puckers her lips as if offended by such a preposterous assumption.

"Sounds great, Mrs Peckham. Enjoy your lunch."

We say our goodbyes and turn to leave when Mrs Peckham calls after me: "I'm glad that you've left that beating bastard husband of yours, love. I wish I could've done that when I was your age. Luckily, he died the day before he hit forty. They call it *korma* these days. I've always called it simply justice."

******

On the way back to Jacqueline's cottage, I suppress the urge to laugh. Not unlike justice, which sometimes prevails over scheming and cheating, humour takes the upper hand when you are torn between laughing and crying.

When we close the door behind us, Jacqueline and I simultaneously start chuckling.

"*Korma*… God gracious… That's probably the best slip up I've heard in years." Jacqueline's shoulders shake while she tries to put off her shoes.

"I wonder if it wasn't some secret ingredient in Mr Peckham's chicken *korma* that made him meet his *karma* one fine evening before his fortieth birthday." I too struggle with the laces of my footwear. "I've always thought it a silly superstition when men refused to celebrate their fortieth birthday. I think I need to update my opinion."

"I've never heard about it. Why can't men celebrate it?"

I shrug, dabbing at my wet cheeks. "To be honest, I have no idea. It's considered bad luck, I guess."

"Well, don't tell any superstitious people about the *kormic* death of Mr Peckham then. It might get them overexcited. And overexcited superstitious people are…"

"… not a good thing."

"Not a good thing at all."

We look at each other and shriek with laughter again.

"Poor Mrs Peckham," I say, following Jacqueline into the kitchen. "It is so sad when a person fades away, every day losing who she was bit by bit."

Jacqueline presses her palms onto the counter and, not looking at me, says: "Yes, it is very sad. But at least she doesn't seem to realise it. It is much worse when your body fades away faster than your mind."

I stop short, staring at my friend. I have said something that's upset her. But I am at a loss as to which of my words has caused her distress.

"Jacqueline, I'm so sorry… Sometimes I speak before thinking…"

She raises her head. I panic, seeing her noble, beautiful face so full of hurt.

"It's not your fault, Margo. I wanted to talk to you about something for some time already. Now is as good time as any. I'll make us tea and we'll talk, okay?"

I nod.

She puts on the kettle and takes out the cups from a cupboard.

While the water boils, I'm afraid to break the silence. Something tells me that Jacqueline Fisher wouldn't offer a warning if what she was going to say wasn't huge.

She pours Earl Grey into our cups, and when she speaks, I wish with all my heart that my intuition has yet again proved to be sleeping and blind.

"Last year, I was diagnosed with multiple sclerosis," she begins.

I clutch at the cup, risking breaking it, to prevent my hand from flying to my mouth.

"It was January. We had just celebrated New Year. John – my husband," her lips curve into a flat line, "my ex loved celebrating New Year's Eve on a grand scale. Most people preferred spending Christmas with their families, but he found a way to gather everyone at a time when even heartless business sharks let the façade slip and wish that magic really existed. So, he threw a party on December 31, inviting everyone whom he considered useful. I must give it to him, he knew how to make people feel special. He was never greedy. He urged me to spend on clothes, jewellery, and exotic travels, not caring about draining the bank account of his annual bonus. He knew that we'd never be short of money." She took a sip of her tea. "When my mother died, a special clause in her will made him sure of that. He earned a lot and spent a lot. He'd been successful before he met me. But marrying into a family like ours opened even more doors for him. What made me think he was different from other successful men is beyond me. He cheated on me. I found out about it so easily that it should have made me think. It didn't. I was furious. I was hurt. But I believed the most ancient lie men tell their women."

She pauses, and I barely dare to breathe. I have never seen Jacqueline so vulnerable.

She takes a deep breath before continuing. I see that the memories she shares still hurt. "I told you that I divorced John because he was unfaithful. I lied." She drops her gaze and stares into her cup. "I left him because I knew John wasn't a man who would push his wife's wheelchair with a smile on his face. I knew he would cheat on me again, and I'd feel miserable for the rest of my life." Jacqueline sighs, still not looking at me. "I didn't want you to see how weak and pathetic I really am."

"I would never... You aren't..." I protest.

She smiles at me weakly. "I know that you are too good to judge me, Margo."

"You are strong. You are the strongest, the most amazing woman I know."

"Thank you. I consider it a blessing that our paths have crossed."

I feel deeply moved and honoured. "I don't know what would have happened to me if I hadn't met you."

"I'm glad I could help you a little. And I hope I'll be able to help more."

We drink our tea in silence.

Jacqueline sighs as if preparing to share something she doesn't want to share. "I hadn't been feeling well since summer. It wasn't anything specific, just an overall feeling that something wasn't right. I was always tired. I couldn't get enough sleep, no matter how long I slept. I thought it was because of the long hours and stress at work. By then, I'd been working sixty or even eighty hours per week for years. But I wouldn't have gone to see a doctor if I hadn't dropped right on the street one day. It was the most bizarre sensation. I felt as if I didn't have a leg anymore. The shock made me stumble, and I fell. They put me in for an MRI right away. My heart was beating so loudly that I didn't hear all the banging and clicking inside the machine. I didn't have to wait for answers. That's the privilege you get in private medical institutions." She chuckled humourlessly. "Not that I appreciated that privilege back then. I was numb. The doctor told me I'd been sick for years. He kept asking me if I hadn't noticed any symptoms, anything unusual. He was professional and attentive, but to me, he seemed pushy and rude. He stopped asking questions when I screamed. He didn't resume our consultation until I'd stopped crying my eyes out. Then he told me that multiple sclerosis wasn't the verdict people usually consider it to be. He said it wasn't curable, but that there were treatments and medicines that could slow it down. And a lot of his patients enjoy decades of active life after they learn about their diagnosis."

"You look healthy to me. If you hadn't told me…"

"I know. The doctor was right. The medicine I have to inject three times a week helps. For the last eighteen months, I haven't felt that my health is worsening. On the contrary, since the beginning of summer, I've even started feeling stronger."

"I'm so glad. Jacqueline, I want to help you. You know that I'd do anything to help you, right? Just tell me what I can do, and I'll do it."

She smiles. "That's why I shared my sad tale with you. You can help me. In fact, we can help each other."

"I'll do anything to help you."

"I've already invited you to make use of my spacious accommodations." She makes a theatrical gesture as if outlining the contours of the room. "But we have yet to discuss the terms of your stay."

"I'll pay whatever price you'll ask."

"Good. That won't be a problem then." Her eyes twinkle when she speaks. "I refuse to take any money from you. I consider your company, and an occasional walk with

Winston when I don't feel like venturing outside, a reasonable payment to cover your rent."

I am speechless. I know I have to say something to talk some sense into this incredible woman, but the right words escape me.

Jacqueline takes advantage of my shocked state and goes on, laying out her plan: "I realise that you are young and won't want to live here with me forever like two spinsters from the nineteenth century. You will fall in love and get married. And this time, your marriage will be blissfully happy. Don't argue with an old, sick woman," she raises a hand in warning when her last sentence makes me produce a protesting sound, "it isn't polite. And I don't want you to entertain some silly notion that you'll have to repay me. I know it might sound rather shocking, but I have enough money not to ever think about it for as long as I live. I do hope, though, that I won't live too long to test this theory." She winks at me. "So, live here as long as you want and need, build your career, and when you are rich and famous, married to a prince or a duke, I'll sit here, watching a beautiful Southbay sunset, and think that I've at least done one right thing in my life."

To that, I can only reply with two words: "Thank you."

The words are short and simple, but they come from the bottom of my heart.

******

I wake up to the touch of warmth on my face and someone stroking my hair.

I shut my eyes right after the source of the warmth proves to be the setting sun. The brief moment is enough to recognise who is the source of the other pleasant sensation.

"You turned in Mark to the police." My voice is hoarse from sleep. "Why would you do that to a friend?"

I hear Finley laugh. I am not ready to open my eyes yet.

"I was only being a responsible citizen. Isn't that something you've always tried to teach me?"

"I thought we were just chatting. Like friends. It wasn't my intention to teach you anything."

He laughs again. "Pardon me, madam, for my unpardonable mistakes."

At this, I crack one eye open.

"At the risk of falling deeper into your disgrace, I must admit I'm not sorry."

I sit up. Now, my back is to the blazing sunset, and I can open my eyes properly.

I am on the rattan sofa in Jacqueline's conservatory. I must have fallen asleep at some point after we came to sit here to talk more about our plans for the future.

"I forgive you," I speak softly.

Finley hesitates before taking my hand.

I smile and entwine my fingers with his.

We look into each other's eyes.

"Thank you," I say.

"For what?"

"For… everything."

We sit without speaking for what feels like a long time. The warmth that doesn't come from the glorious Dorset sun wraps me into a cocoon. I want to stay in this cocoon forever.

I know that this is a life-changing moment for me, and this time, it is for real. When I met Michael, I didn't think about choices or decisions. I was simply following what seemed a natural path, which was leading me into the exciting but unfamiliar unknown.

Now, everything feels different.

I have not acquired the power to envisage what lies ahead. Still, this time, I am certain that I have made my choice with my eyes wide open.

"I told you you'd wake her up." Jacqueline walks into the conservatory with a tray laden with a cup of tea, a sugar bowl, and a plate with cookies. Her tone is accusing, but the contents of the tray betray her care for our guest's comfort.

"I don't mind," I say. "My grandmother always told me

that it's a bad idea to sleep through the sunset. It makes you groggy, and you won't feel rested anyway."

Both Jacqueline and Finley smile.

"Now we know where your wisdom comes from." Jacqueline puts a tray on the table. "I guess I'll have to go back and make more tea."

She walks back to the kitchen but stops in the doorway. "And then, we will have champagne. I think the occasion calls for it."

When she leaves, I move closer to Finley and put my hands around his neck. He hugs me tightly and kisses my hair.

There are so many things I want to tell him.

We have all the time in the world to find out if, among them, words of love are the most important ones.

EPILOGUE

Five years later
London, Sloane Street
June 2010

I study my reflection in a full-length mirror. I am happy with what I see, and it makes me blush.

Wearing a lemon yellow bodycon dress with a thin red leather belt, I look like someone you'd expect to see on the streets of London among the fashionable crowd. The dress isn't so tight as to make me feel uncomfortable. Still, it shows off my tall, slim body in a subtle but natural way.

I arrange my hair in a casual knot. I've learned to do it so it doesn't look like a messy bun. My hair is longer now. Before the annual cut, it reaches a few inches below my shoulder blades. I don't wear it loose most days, but I love it long like this.

Have I dressed up to soften the blow I am about to deliver to the man I love?

I shake my head, my eyes fixed on my reflection.

I often dress like this. It is more appropriate to wear dresses and skirts in London. In Southbay, whenever I went, I'd be asked if it was a special day for me.

I don't want to hurt Finley, but I have to think about what I need first.

I sigh. I know I am not being fair. Since the day we celebrated my official divorce four years ago, Finley Hammond has been nothing but attentive to my needs and wishes. No matter how inconsequent they sometimes were.

As they say these days, we do not owe anything to anyone. Still, I feel that Finley deserves honesty from me.

My gaze shifts from my reflection, and I take in the full-length mirror. It was one of my many whims Finley agreed to easily. We don't need a mirror like that in the London apartment. Even less so in our attic bedroom, which I insisted on converting into such. But Finley knew it was important to me to get this mirror. It stirred up emotions in me that helped me overcome the drama I had to go through with Michael.

Finley knows that little things like that matter. They make a difference.

It's one of the million reasons I can't postpone telling him the truth any longer.

I walk downstairs and pick up my bag. I check if the key, my phone, and other essentials are there.

I cast a glance around the living space. We don't have a door between the living room and the kitchen. It adds space. It's not that we need any. The three-bedroom flat on Sloane Street is more spacious than the two of us need. In the two years we have been living here, I've grown to love it. I will feel sad leaving it, even though I know that it's the right decision to move on.

I walk out into the street. The June sun is generous. I put on sunglasses. It isn't a long walk to St. James's Park, but twenty-five minutes should be enough to gather my thoughts and prepare for an earnest talk I need to have with Finley.

I walk down familiar streets, not thinking about the turns I have to take. Instead, I scroll through memories and dear faces in my head.

Last summer turned into a delightful wedding season. Every time I remember the two dreamy celebrations, each lasting for more than a day, my heart fills with warmth. What a wonderful time we had!

Suzie and Detective Fletcher got married last June.

My wonderful friend would want everyone to think that it took Peter a while to break through her defence of the strong, independent woman who doesn't need a man in her life. But we all know that it is not true. The couple had their struggles in sorting out their living arrangements and professional issues before they could take the next step in their relationship, which they both desperately wanted to take.

Suzie finally got to add a terrace to her bakery in Groveland Business Park. Jacqueline Fisher helped make her dream come true. Her connections, knowledge, and experience didn't make the process faster or smoother, but she did make it happen. I have learned that it is what truly matters.

Suzie got her floor-to-ceiling panoramic windows as well. She and Jacqueline confessed – with sighs of exhausted contentment – that it was these windows that prolonged the approval time of the remodelling project. I agree with Suzie that it was totally worth it. When I sit at my usual table close to the counter in the cosy Groveland Bakery on sunny days, I can see all the way across grassy fields to the cliffs rising from the waters of the English Channel.

My mom got married in July.

Sir Romuald Granville has earned my eternal respect for making my mother happy. And for being the kindest and most patient man I have ever met.

My mom met Sir Granville when she came to visit me in October of 2005. When I told her I'd left Michael, she pleaded for me to return to Latvia. She then wanted to fly to England, but the wedding season was in full swing, and with her work, she couldn't leave. Listening to me talking to Mom on the phone, Jacqueline offered for her to come and stay with us for as long as she wished once the wedding fever was over. Mom came – and almost stayed. She met Sir Granville at the Hammonds' summer garden party, and a week later, he professed his love for her.

My mother wasn't easy to conquer. A noble English gentleman or not, Romuald Granville had to go to great lengths to make her agree that love and marriage would make her life better rather than complicate it. First, Mom insisted on learning English. It was the first sign that Sir Granville had a chance. Mother hadn't shown any inclination to bother learning it when her only daughter had married an Englishman and moved to England. Another sign that, to me at least, spoke volumes of Mom truly being in love was that she let Romuald pay for these lessons.

When Mom came for a visit the following year in May, she spent half of the time with Sir Granville in his estate in Devon. It was clear that the pair had more in common than the ability to speak the same language. Still, I wasn't surprised that she made him wait – and I suspect, suffer – for three more years. She claimed that getting married at their age was nonsense. He insisted and repeated his proposal every time they met, making it harder for her to refuse. Once, he took her on a boat trip along the Jurassic coast cliffs, and, steering into a cove, dropped to one knee right when a beam of sun struck through the rocky ceiling of a secluded space with water surface reflecting the gold. He made another failed attempt in his garden decorated with fairy lights and candles in such a lavish way that would put the creators of famous fantasy movies to shame.

It didn't discourage him that Mom kept saying no. She was the woman he wanted, and he was determined to not let her miss a chance to be loved, for he knew that she wanted him too.

When they finally got married last July, Mom was fifty

and Romuald was almost sixty. Never in my life have I seen a bride and groom so happy and so deeply in love with each other.

For the three years after I left Michael, I stayed in Southbay. I loved living at the Lighthouse Keeper's Cottage with Jacqueline. As she promised, she arranged for the annexe to be renovated and turned into a one-bedroom flat. It was a miracle that the builders finished the renovation within the agreed time. Even so, while they were working, neither Jacqueline nor I minded that I stayed in the spare bedroom.

Two years ago, Finley got his diploma and was offered a job in the BBC's offices in London. During the time of his studies, we had a kind of long-distance relationship, which, in truth, was proper dating. Finley came to Southbay every weekend. And since I was busy during the week anyway, it felt like we were together all the time.

Once I announced to the universe that I was open to work, I had more offers than I could handle. I accepted all of them, of course.

Finley's father had persuaded his business partner, Mr Potter, that they needed help with accounts. It suited their small practice perfectly that I worked from home, so my services were cheaper than if they had hired an accounting firm.

Raymond Billings offered me a position as his assistant to deal with the technical part of the job. He had taught me to deal with more sophisticated issues too, and working with a professional like him has been a blessing.

In September 2005, Laura told me that she and Max had decided to return to Latvia and get married. She said that Southbay was wonderful, but she loved the medieval streets of Riga Old Town and the endless sandy beaches of Jurmala more. She explained that their recruitment company still had a few ongoing projects and offered for me to monitor the fulfilment of their contractual obligations. I was paid decent wages for overseeing the contracts' implementation for the next five months, and after they all finished, Mr Billings helped me with wrapping up the company's activities. He also shared the amount Laura's employer paid for his services.

Over the next years, more and more people from Latvia came to England to work. Rumours travel fast, for they seldom encounter obstacles, so I began getting calls and emails from companies around Dorset to perform small translation tasks to and from Latvian.

When Finley finished his education, the decision to move with him to London came easily. I had a stable income from various sources, and neither of my employers required my physical presence in Southbay. Besides, it had been my dream to taste what living in the legendary British capital was like.

Life in London turned out to be a whirlwind of impressions. The two years that I spent living with Finley in the beautiful apartment on Sloane Street were an experience of a lifetime. The Hammonds had insisted we make proper use of this exclusive property for as long as we wished.

Walking through Green Park and crossing the Mall into James's Park, I feel a pang of regret. I have grown to love walking the streets and paths the people who made world history have trod. I know that I will miss London.

I notice Finley sitting on our favourite bench. He is feeding the slices of apple to a squirrel. I cannot be sure that every time it is the same squirrel we feed sitting in this spot, but I choose to treat the animal as a friend.

"Hey you!" I greet Finley. "Spoiling the wildlife, as usual? The poor thing will get fat and drop from its tree one day."

Finley's face lights up when he sees me. He stands to give me a hug. He is tanned from his frequent travels, and his green eyes make him drop-dead gorgeous.

I put my arms around his neck and kiss him on the cheek. This man still makes my head spin every time I touch him.

We sit down on the bench and feed the squirrel for a while. The tiny thing looks agile and fit despite the outrageous amount of food it is capable of consuming.

"I have to tell you something," we say simultaneously.

We look at each other and laugh.

"I'll go first," I say despite my reluctance to break the news.

Finley makes a gallant gesture. "Be my guest."

I take a deep breath. I don't want to disappoint this amazing man. The man who has made me feel loved. The man who has made me believe in love again.

People like to say that those who have gone through traumatic experiences require special treatment and care. While all they want is for the victims to pretend that nothing has happened, so the ones around them don't have to adjust.

Finley isn't like that. He took great care to ensure that my transition period between feeling down and heartbroken was as stress-free for me as possible.

"I know we'd planned to do it together. And not right now. In a few years. But I've found us a perfect home in Southbay." I rattle off and hold my breath. I look down at my nervously clasped hands.

Finley doesn't reply. Instead, he resumes feeding the squirrel that looks like it doesn't plan to leave the impromptu restaurant anytime soon.

"Jacqueline told me she found the cottage, which is as close to what I keep describing as my dream home as possible. I couldn't resist. I went to view it last weekend when you were in Morrocco." I have to keep talking to prevent myself from panicking.

The BBC likes filming their ads and show trailers in exotic locations, so Finley gets to travel around the world. Sometimes he goes on business trips twice a month.

"How have the three of them settled into the communal living?" Finley asks, giving the greedy squirrel a piece of carrot. The animal sniffs a new treat suspiciously. Then snatches it away and starts eating.

"They don't live *together*. The annexe has its separate entrance."

Suzie and Detective Fletcher accepted Jacqueline's offer to rent the annexe I had vacated when I moved to London. She had set the rent lower than the market, making it impossible for them to refuse. They did want to decline her invitation, both too decent to jump at the opportunity that could potentially put everyone into a somewhat awkward situation. I was glad Jacqueline didn't let them do it.

"Suzie and Peter are happy to have their own place where they don't have to sacrifice their comfort because of financial limitations." Like Suzie, Peter Fletcher was in the position of a tenant who had to agree to discriminating conditions set by the landlord. After the divorce, his income became insufficient to cover both his financial obligations toward his ex-wife and everyday bills.

"I am really glad that everything has worked out for them. They both are fantastic people."

I dig my nails into my palm. "So, what do you think? Will you hate it if we buy the house now and not wait a few years? I understand that it's impossible to commute from Southbay to London every day and that we'll see each other only on weekends, but…"

"… but we are busy with our jobs anyway. And it's not that we spend every evening in front of the TV like a proper couple, too fed up with each other and life to even speak to each other." Finley's lips twitch while he finishes my sentence. He has incredibly sensuous lips. The way they curve when he speaks or smiles…

I shake my head so as not to get too distracted. Besides, I am not finished with showering the man I love with blows that can harm our relationship. "And one more thing." My tone is firm, I even raise my chin to show that I won't be wavered. Inside, I am shaking with fear it might be too much even for Finley. "I will pay my half for the cottage. I've been saving the money Michael was paying me according to the divorce settlement, and I want to use it to pay for my first home. Our home. It is important to me to know that I contributed my share."

I hold my breath.

Jacqueline had negotiated a hefty monthly payment from Michael that would have allowed me not to think about earning a living until I got married again. For me, though, it wasn't an option to put myself at risk of being fully dependent on someone again. My marriage taught me a bitter lesson, but maybe because of how hard it hit me, I learned it well.

I know that Finley's parents would gladly buy us any house we wanted. They had already let us use their upscale property in London: one that I wouldn't have been able to pay my half of the rent for. It isn't that I'm not capable of accepting what I can't afford. I know how lucky I am that the Hammonds have taken me under their wing. Still, there are lines I am not prepared to cross. As terrified as I am at the perspective that Finley gets offended by the idea of buying our first home using my first husband's money, I have to try. If he lets me do this, it will give me the sort of closure and confidence that I have contributed something tangible to our relationship.

Finley gives me a look full of kindness before he replies. "If it makes you happy, that's what we'll do."

My heart makes a leap. "Are you saying…?" I lick my lips. I want to hug and kiss the man I love now that we are done talking about serious things.

Finley smiles and speaks in a light tone: "I'm saying that I'll gladly take a look at that cottage that has bewitched you. Not to offer my opinion about it, but to sign the papers and get the boring stuff over with. Is it furnished? Do we have to make any improvements before we move in?"

I feel like smiling and bursting into tears at the same time. Finley is the most amazing man I have ever met. I'd never dared to dream I would be with someone like him, or that a man like him would love me unconditionally.

An image of the two of us covered in paint, sitting on the floor and going through a batch of DIY magazines flashes in front of my eyes. A traitorous tear escapes, sliding down my cheek and plopping on my lemon-yellow dress. When Finley took me to London to show the apartment we were going to live in, I demanded the attic be converted into a bedroom and painted white. I had seen a photo of a white attic bedroom in *Red,* and it stuck with me as an epitome of a carefree living. When I saw that picture, I visualised a confident young woman who knew better than to let anyone hurt her.

"Did I say something wrong?"

Finley's voice, full of concern, makes me want to immediately start reassuring him.

I smile. "On the contrary, love," I speak, refusing to let my emotions prevent me from telling him what is really important. "It's because you always say what's right. It is even unnatural." I pretend to glare at him. He laughs. "And I love you for it. So deeply."

Finley takes my hand and presses it to his cheek. His skin is so hot that I turn my palm and cup his face, worried that I have unnecessarily upset him.

He releases my hand and pulls something out of his pocket. Then he drops to one knee. He does it swiftly, so I don't have time to protest.

"Margo," he looks up at me. His eyes twinkle with a mix of emotions so deep that it takes my breath away. "You are the most... stubborn, fierce, caring, overly serious..." At this, I arch an eyebrow, but I have to blink furiously to fight back tears. He kisses my hand and continues: "Yes, you *are* serious, and I love that about you. You've made me change my life, and for that, I'll be forever grateful."

I can't restrain the tears anymore.

Finley opens a little black box he is holding. The sun catches in the facets of a heart-shaped diamond and dances off the tiny emeralds surrounding it.

"Margo, you are the most incredible woman that I've

met. And since I seriously don't believe there exists anyone even remotely resembling you...." He makes a dramatic pause. It does have a desired effect: people hurrying through the park stop and look at us.

"Will you do me the honour and allow me to show you my love and gratitude every day of our lives until death shall us part?"

I press my palm to my mouth, so I don't embarrass myself in front of strangers by screaming. My heart beats frantically in my chest. I exhale, the heat of my skin burning my nose. I take a deep breath and, rising to my feet from the bench despite my shaky legs, pull Finley up with me.

"I will, Finley," I say. "I can't promise it'll be easy to spend as long as the rest of your life with me. But one thing I can promise you..." Caught up in the elation his public performance has stirred in me, I too pause to add weight to what I will say next.

People around us go quiet. The squirrel on the back of the bench freezes, having stopped fidgeting and asking for more food for a moment. Even the ever-present cacophony of birdsong seems to have ceased.

"I promise you, Finley Hammond, that I will do everything I can to make sure that you stick to the promises you've made me today."

The crowd erupts with applause and laughter.

We kiss, not to let the kind people's expectations down. I know too well how uplifting and inspiring witnessing the happiness of others can be.

"I'll do everything I can to make you as happy as you've made me," I tell my future husband quietly so only he can hear.

In the heart of the city that, over the centuries, has witnessed historical events of global significance, the moment of clarity overwhelms me.

My happiness matters. It gives me the privilege to share happiness with the people I love.

THE END

ACKNOWLEDGEMENTS

First and foremost, I'd like to thank my husband, without whose support and encouragement I wouldn't have embarked on the most exciting journey of my life. He was the one who said that my stories deserve to be let out into the world. The fact that he keeps repeating it even after having gone through a few years of living with a wife, who had turned into a classical crazy creative, says a lot.

I'm grateful for my mother, whose strength, vivacity, phenomenal energy, and love have set an example for me of a life worth to have been lived. Like legendary Scarlett O'Hara my mom was unstoppable when it came to protecting her loved ones. The most valuable lesson I've learnt from her is that no matter how dramatically the world around you changes, no matter how crushing the blows are, there's always hope to live through these times. And if you manage to live through them, you are a winner.

I'll never be able to find words, which would be powerful enough, to express my deepest gratitude to my aunt, who'd raised me not simply like her own child, but also like the most precious gift life can bestow on someone.

I'd also like to thank my father, from whom I've inherited a spark of creativity. He had discovered he had a talent late in life and didn't have enough time to leave more than a dozen poems. But they are the dearer to me since I know that there won't be more.

I'd like to thank every reader of my books. It means a lot to me; more than anyone can probably imagine. Nothing warms the author's heart like a review from a reader who enjoyed their story and connected with the characters.

Last but not the least, my sincerest gratitude goes to the absolutely amazing Writing Community on Twitter, as well as the community of authors on Instagram.

ABOUT THE AUTHOR

I've been in love with books for as long as I remember myself. The typewriter my first attempts at writing had been made at still sits proudly on its shelf in the basement, and when I go down there, I always have an urge to save it from its exile.

I've always been writing something. Diaries, letters, poems, short stories. I'd even attempted to write a novel a couple of times when I was about thirteen. Still, there was always something more important than my writing. There was always "real life" reminding me of its undeniable claims. "You have to study, you have to work, there is no place for fruitless dreaming," it whispered. And I moved forward as if running on rails I couldn't step down from.

I'd spent fifteen years, trying to fit into the office work pattern. Do you remember Kevin Kline in the "In & Out" movie – "men do not dance"? Well, that used to be my philosophy – real people don't write books. They work, they build careers, they travel through the corporate jungle. And despite I was feeling miserable and out of place every day of that climbing the ladder process, I managed to build a relatively successful career after an ambitious shift from the private to the public sector. The job I had wasn't boring. It was actually pretty exciting. I worked with internationally funded projects and met people from all over the world every day. But it failed to ignite a spark in my heart.

After my son was born, I had a unique chance to stop and rethink not only what I'd achieved so far, but what I really want from life. I made a decision to leave my old life behind, and I've never regretted it. Changes in the daily routine led naturally to changes in my way of thinking. I finally allowed myself to be who I really was.

Since then, I have published six books.

The Neglected Merge fantasy romance/drama trilogy:
- Book 1 "Neglected Merge"
- Book 2 "Tangle of Choices"
- Book 3 "Shifting Directions"

Books set in Latvia:
- "Finding Your Way"
- "The Accidental Cop"

Women's fiction:
- "Broken Chances"

I'd love to connect with my readers and hear your thoughts about my books.

Please visit my website:
www.evekoguce.com

You can also find me on social media:
X/Twitter: @EveKoguce
Instagram: @eve_koguce_books
Facebook: Eve Koguce Books

For authors, reviews are more precious than gold. So, if you enjoyed reading any of my books, please, take a few moments and share your thoughts on any of these platforms:

Amazon: www.amazon.com/author/evekoguce
Goodreads: www.goodreads.com/eve_koguce
BookBub: www.bookbub.com/authors/eve-koguce

Reviews don't have to be long and detailed. Just a few sentences describing what you liked and how you felt about the characters is enough and deeply appreciated.

Made in United States
Orlando, FL
26 July 2024